FAR MEMORY

BOOKS BY JOAN GRANT

Far Memory Books:
Winged Pharaoh
Eyes of Horus
Lord of the Horizon
So Moses Was Born
Life as Carola
Return to Elysium
Scarlet Feather

———

Far Memory

———

The Scarlet Fish and Other Stories
Redskin Morning

———

The Laird and the Lady
Vague Vacation
A Lot To Remember
Many Lifetimes *(with Denys Kelsey)*

FAR MEMORY

by Joan Grant

ARIEL PRESS
Columbus, Ohio

First published in 1956 in Great Britain by Arthur Barker Ltd.
as *Time Out of Mind*
First Ariel Press edition 1985

Second Printing

This book is made possible by a gift
to the Publications Fund of Light
by Mike and Linda Lane

FAR MEMORY

ISBN 0-89804-141-4

FOR

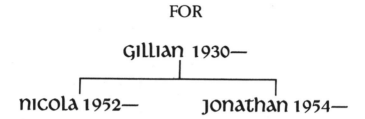

GILLIAN 1930—

NICOLA 1952—   JONATHAN 1954—

table of contents

PART I

PART II

PART III

PART IV

PART V

FAR MEMORY

PART ONE

CHAPTER ONE

travelling incog

I was conceived in the Blue Grotto at Capri in June 1906. Two months before this event, so exceedingly commonplace except for its locale, Jack and Blanche Marshall had embarked on a motor tour abroad, for in the previous autumn they had taken Margery and Iris, Blanche's daughters by her first marriage, from Cherbourg to Boulogne. Neither of the children, packed into the back of the car which was open like a dogcart, with Kate Saunders, the lady's maid, and all the luggage, had enjoyed the trip. Iris, who was then seven, remembers praying for punctures so that she could collect windfalls from roadside apple trees, which were the only bit of France she could see from her seat hinged to the door. Margery, aged thirteen, quarrelled with Kate, who was car sick. So everyone was relieved when it was decided that they should not come in the new 24-h.p. Renault, but instead go to seaside lodgings at Aberdovey.

This trip, to extend far beyond the convenient escape routes of the Channel Ports, was planned with the care worthy of a safari into Darkest Africa. Petrol in cans, spare parts, and tyres, had to be sent ahead to establish supply-dumps along the route, and, knowing Blanche's idea of the amount of luggage required even for a week-end, there must have been times when Jack regretted the lack of a string of porters.

The law which required that a horseless carriage be preceded by a man with a red flag had recently been repealed, but children and livestock had not yet learned even the rudiments of self-preservation from motors; so Blanche, swathed in

3

dustcoat and veils, armed herself with a bugle on which she tootled to give warning of their approach. The most careful forethought could not always overcome the mechanical frailties of the Renault, and often they were night-bound in remote villages where fleas abounded and the primitive sanitation appalled Blanche's sensibilities. She sprinkled Keatings' with a lavish hand, and with the optimism of a female Hercules faced with the Augean Stables, decided it was her duty to make at least a dent in the indifference to hygiene shown by the Latin races. No one except Blanche, and she claims to have forgotten, knows why she decided that her first task was to educate the children to blow their noses. To this end she purchased quantities of cheap cotton handkerchiefs and flung them graciously to the populace who probably thought her fanfares heralded the arrival of a circus. Disappointed that most of these tributes to Hygeia fell neglected in the dust or were carried away on the wind, she wrapped each one carefully round a pebble so as to achieve a more accurate aim. It was a time when the English were still a fruitful source of largesse, and the delighted cheers of her audience soon turned to angry mutterings when instead of receiving sweets or coins they imagined themselves to be the victims of an obscure practical joke. But Blanche does not easily relinquish an idea, and in spite of her husband's anguished protests she continued to replenish her stock, until on at least one occasion Jack only just managed to keep the car a short head in front of a field of foreigners, enraged and armed with pitchforks.

The pace became more gentle in Italy; although there were minor crises such as when Jack refused to stop to pick up Blanche's favourite picture hat which had blown off when they were bowling along after a frustrating series of punctures. In Florence they had arranged to meet Sybil Westmoreland, who was touring in a Delauney-Belleville with her maid and chauffeur; and they proceeded in convoy with her until they came to Sorrento. Here the three of them were most favourably impressed by the excellent service in the hotel. Before they had been in their rooms an hour, an abundance of flowers arrived with the compliments of the management. The food was superb, and the staff almost embarrassingly obsequious. None of them was particularly surprised by this solicitude, and had they been, it is unlikely that they would have thought of questioning Sybil's chauffeur. This excellent man, well aware that his status in the staff dining-room depended upon the rank of his employer, and doubtful if his personal conviction that an English Countess outranked even the most grandiose of foreign title was accepted abroad, had secured his comfort by a tactful interchange with the hall porter. When asked what rank was indicated by the coronet on the door of the Delauney-Belleville he had replied, with a conspiratorial wink, 'Sorry, cock, can't tell you. We're travelling incog.'

The following morning, Sybil—who in due course would become my godmother—decided to spend a lazy day recovering from the fatigues of the journey. Perhaps Blanche would have liked to do so too, but her husband was an indefatigable sightseer. Together they took the boat to Capri. She is an exceedingly bad sailor, but fortunately it was a calm, blue day; for otherwise I doubt if he could have persuaded her to board the little steamer. On disembarking they found the quay lined with militia in full dress, complete with band. Jack, not wishing to miss an attraction which had been omitted from Baedeker, approached the officer in charge of these gleaming ranks on the pretext of asking for a light for his cigar. The officer was not only obliging but effusive, so Jack enquired in stilted Italian which must unwittingly have indicated annoyance, 'What is the reason for this display?'

Instantly the captain's confidence, which until then had been as glossy as the cock's feathers in his hat, began to droop. A voluble Italian tide bore on its flood a flotsam of words that Jack could comprehend. Improbable as it seemed, there was no doubt that the man was imploring his forgiveness for an excess of zeal which had caused a flagrant dis-

5

regard of their desire to remain incognito. It was a devilish awkward situation. Ought he to carry it off? But if he did, and the august persons for whom they had been mistaken arrived on the next boat?

The Italian's limpid eyes seemed about to brim over in a freshet of tears. To an Englishman anything, even the risk of being incarcerated in a foreign gaol on a charge of false pretences, was better than being involved in a public display of lachrymose emotion. 'The incident shall be forgotten,' said Jack hastily, and as this did not seem enough to restore calm, added, 'Forgotten except as yet another example of the courtesy shown to us by the loyal people of Italy.'

As a further boon he proffered a cigar, which the now radiant captain stowed carefully away in a pocket of his splendid uniform, saying that it would be a relic treasured by his children and his children's children. There was no holding him now. What could he do to show his gratitude? Mules were waiting to convey them to a villa of Tiberius, but would they prefer horses—his own charger for instance, an animal of spirit?

Jack knew that Blanche would refuse to mount even the most placid donkey. He had meant to leave her for a siesta in a hotel and go alone to the Roman villas, but he dared not risk her unwittingly giving them away. He must keep her under his eye until they could escape from the island. But how and where? He thought rapidly, came to a tactful and, for me, momentous conclusion.

'We wish to go to the Blue Grotto—alone. You will understand that we sometimes grow weary of being stared at.' He made his voice a shade peremptory. 'The ordinary er—tourists can visit the Grotto some other day.'

At a flick of the captain's fingers two N.C.O.s leapt from the ranks, seized the picnic hamper, the cushions, the rug, and marched briskly off with them towards the landing-steps. 'I shall myself be your courier,' exclaimed the officer delightedly. 'Sentries I shall post to see that you are not

6

disturbed—the cream of your guard of honour.'

Blanche, who had not understood a word of the conversation, had been about to suggest that the man should be invited to eat with them. A searching glance from her magnificent brown eyes had assured her that his fingernails were clean. It might amuse Jack, and there was plenty of food. Jack realised her intention just in time to prevent her creating fresh opportunities for ravelling this already tangled skein. Trying to sound regretful that the gilded birds must keep their gilded cage, he said firmly, 'I fear that it might cause undue interest if you came with us, so let the usual boatman row us to the Grotto. A second boat must be provided to take him away while we picnic in privacy. I may even decide to bathe. He will return only in time for us to embark on the afternoon steamer.'

Sorrowfully the captain accepted the royal command. 'It shall be as you wish,' he said with a wistful smile. 'I cannot come with you, so I send with you my prayers that you take back to England only happy memories of our beautiful Capri.'

But when they returned that evening to Sorrento my parents took more than memories with them: they took me.

CHAPTER TWO

ᕭaRBy anᕭ joan

I was born on the 12th of April 1907, the day before Iris's ninth birthday. She had been promised a brother or sister as a birthday present, and, having been told that babies are found under gooseberry bushes, had dug a lot of holes in the kitchen garden before I arrived. I did not enjoy being a baby in spite of the care that was lavished on me. Everyone else was too big and I was too small. The louder I yelled the less they understood what I was trying to say; and if I cried because of a frightening dream they thought it was wind.

My grandfather had died in February after a hunting accident, so when I was six weeks old we went to live with my grandmother, Jennie Marshall, at No. 2 Primrose Hill Road, a house within lion-roar of the London Zoo. Life became more interesting as soon as I was old enough to sit up in my pram, which was often left outside a public house in Kentish Town while my nanny sat inside and sipped whisky. 'She was such a nice woman,' Iris told me later, 'that I used to buy her peppermints, and spring onions off barrows, with my pocket money, so that my Mother wouldn't smell whisky on her breath. She was sacked before you were old enough to remember her, because she drank at home too and hid the empty bottles in a spare-bedroom chimney. They were found when a fire was lit and it smoked.'

I can remember the next nanny quite clearly because she was in love with one of the keepers of the Monkey House at the Zoo. Instead of dull pram-rides in Regent's Park I spent my mornings with the chimpanzees, drinking my glass of milk with two entirely congenial companions who sometimes allowed me a bite of their bananas or popped into my mouth a sawdusty grape.

My favourite person was Jennie, although I was only taken to see her for an hour after tea. Then the hour with Grandmother became shorter and shorter until I was only allowed to kiss my hand to her round the half-open door. I was eighteen months old when, without any warning, or perhaps I was warned when I wasn't listening, the landau took nanny and me to a railway station, and a train took us to Hayling Island, where Father had bought a cottage for me. After a few days nanny went back to London because she wanted to be nearer the Zoo, and Nanny Walpole came to look after me. It was Nanny Walpole who told me that my grandmother was dead.

8

The resentment I felt in finding myself trapped in the body of a baby flared up again soon afterwards. Perhaps the long, flat beach, the sand dunes with their harsh, bleached grasses, the restless sound of the sea, stirred latent memories in me. I was not always Joan, but sometimes a Greek boy, training to be a runner on a hotter, brighter shore. I knew the feel of his muscles, and the ache in them when he had run too hard; the smooth oval of the pebble clenched in each hand as he crouched with his toes on a mark at the start of a race. When the lovely swiftness of a young athlete's body was particularly strong I used to shout, 'Watch me! I can run fast— faster than anyone!' And then weep because I could only drive Joan's little girl body ridiculously slowly across the Hayling sands.

I was happier when the rest of the family came to live at Hayling. My cottage only had two bedrooms, so they took a furnished house near it while Father built a house large enough for us all. At first it was only ditches in the six-acre field adjoining the cottage. Then there were walls low enough to walk along, which soon became taller and could only be climbed by ladders, which I was not allowed to do. When the roof was put on there was a party for all the workmen, with a very great deal of food on trestle tables, and barrels of beer.

The house started by being quite an ordinary size, with a dining-room, a morning room, and a drawing-room facing the sea; and bedrooms, dressing-rooms and nurseries above them for Mother and Father, Nanny Walpole, and me. Stretching out behind were more bedrooms and bathrooms for Margery and Iris and visitors, over the servants' part of the house. At the end of what was going to be the garden Father had built a real tennis court and a billiard room. One morning I was in the tennis court with Father watching the walls being covered with a special kind of cement. Thirty men were working up ladders and the man who had invented the cement, who was called Mr. Bickley, was there too. Suddenly

Mother rushed in and shouted, 'Out, all of you! The roof is going to fall in!'

Everyone stared at her and then looked up at the roof—a glass roof with iron girders that had been put in by a firm which roofed railway stations. It looked perfectly solid, but Mother became so angry at not being obeyed that Father ordered the men to stop work; so they climbed down the ladders and filed out of the building. For about five minutes they stood about, trying not to show that they thought Mother was being ridiculous. Mr. Bickley was saying to Father that if the walls cracked because the work had been interrupted he could not be held responsible. Mother was holding me by the arm in case I tried to run back into the court, which I had no intention of doing. Suddenly there was a grinding noise and an enormous crash. Clouds of dust belched out of the openings where the side-gallery windows were going to be. 'My God, it *has* fallen!' said Father. Mr. Bickley looked as though he was going to be sick. Some of the workmen swore under their breath, and I saw three of them take off their caps and cross themselves. The only person quite unmoved was Mother, who said calmly, 'What did I tell you, Jack? You must admit there are advantages in being married to a witch.'

When the court was mended there was a party for the opening match and a special train to bring spectators from London. Soon afterwards Father caught a cold while he was walking back through the garden to the house on his way to have a bath after playing tennis. So he decided to build a lot more house to join the two bits of Seacourt together. It was not nearly so easy as it sounds, and took a lot of planning with scale models made out of cigar boxes on the billiard-table.

'You can't pull down the servants' hall,' said Mother firmly.

'Well, we shall have to move the stoke-hole,' said Father.

'Nonsense, Jack! I will *not* do without baths or adequate heating while you reshuffle the plumbing.'

'But there is no other way of joining the house to the court.' He paused for thought. 'I had not intended to build more than a simple addition to the ground floor, but if I were to add an extra coal-cellar, a storeroom or two, I could use them to support an *upstairs* passage....'

When he began, the upstairs passage ended with the back staircase, one flight leading down to the kitchen quarters, the other up to the attics and the servants' bedrooms. By the time he had finished there were five more spare bedrooms and about fifty yards more passage, with four right-angle turns in it. This led to a door into a gallery, with stairs leading down into a music-room—which had an alcove overlooking the rose garden that was large enough to contain Jennie's concert-grand piano. From the music-room a door led into the side-gallery of the tennis court. Everyone else was very pleased with the new room, for I was the only one who noticed that it was haunted.

While the house was still being built, the field was turning into a garden. There were five gardeners, and Patrick the Irish garden-boy, who gave me my first puppy. When I first saw the puppy I thought he was a grown-up dog because he was already much larger than Mother's Blenheim spaniels or Iris's fox terrier. 'He is only three months old, Miss Joan,' said Patrick proudly. 'Won't he be growing into a wonderful great dog, and he given the chance? Would you take him for a present now?'

The puppy was licking my face and I wanted him more than I had ever wanted anything. 'But he's your puppy, Patrick. You mustn't give him to me.'

'And you don't have him, he'll be killed surely, so he will. Wouldn't he have been drowned in a sack before his eyes were open if I hadn't bought him for five shillings? Vexed me mother was at the sight of him, and now she's taken against the poor dog though he does no more harm than track a bit of dirt into the kitchen and fluster her chickens.'

I had to do a lot of persuading before I was allowed to have him, but Nanny Walpole, who had once looked after a child who had been badly bitten by a Pekinese, persuaded Mother that the bigger the dog the more reliable it would be with children. Father named him Darby because I was called Joan. He grew and he grew, which was not surprising as his mother was a Mastiff and his father a Great Dane—until at last he was too big to sleep in the nursery, so a kennel was built for him near the greenhouses.

He never went to his kennel except at night until Nanny Walpole had to go away for two months because her sister was ill. A horrible 'temporary' came, called Nurse Vincent, who disliked dogs almost more than she disliked children. The only person who got on with her was Lambal, the head gardener, whom I hated because he was always complaining to Mother that Darby's enormous footprints ruined his seed beds. Nurse Vincent was so bossy that I avoided her as much as possible, and the easiest way of doing so was to hide with Darby in his kennel and refuse to come out. One day she lost her temper and told Lambal to drag me out of it. He pinched my arm and I yelled. So Darby, who was being a lion defending its cub, bit him in the arm. It was not at all a bad bite. Darby wagged his tail to show me it was only a warning, but it tore Lambal's shirt and he was furious.

The red-faced, angry woman dragged me back to the house and shut me in my room for the rest of the day—being shut in my room without picture-books or toys was the only punishment which was officially allowed. I knew Patrick would remember to take Darby his dinner so I was not really worried, only bored at wasting an afternoon indoors; until Mother brought my supper and sat cosily on the bed. This was unusual when I was in disgrace, and I began to be suspicious when, after vague generalisations about the importance of little girls learning to be unselfish, she told me that Darby had gone to look after a poor child who loved him even more than I did. The child was a cripple who had no legs.

12

Darby was going to pull her about in a little cart with red wheels so that she could go to the beach. 'Some little girls are not lucky enough to have a goat-cart like yours,' she added persuasively.

'She can have the goat-cart *and* the goat,' I said quickly, and dived under the bedclothes. Mother sighed and left me. I lay huddled in the dark cave of blankets trying to think of a way Darby could be rescued. He must be shut up somewhere before being sent away. Patrick and I would find him, probably chained up without food or water in some horrible shed. We would call and call until he heard us and barked. We would break down the door and Patrick would cut the chain with a hacksaw. Darby would be hungry, so I must remember to steal a joint from the larder on my way out. There was bound to be a tap somewhere and he was clever at drinking from my cupped hands. We would find somewhere safe from grown-ups, and if any of them came to find us we would tell Darby to bite them until they ran away....I would explain to him that they needed biting, and hard.

I escaped from the house before breakfast, with a sirloin of beef which I could hardly carry and my pockets stuffed with provisions for the journey. I had decided we would go to Ireland, where Patrick said people were very kind to dogs, the larger the better. I found him in the stoke hole cleaning a spade, a red-eyed Patrick who told me the dreadful truth. Darby had been shot and Patrick had buried him.

Almost as terrible as Darby being dead was thinking that Father had given the order for his murder. The only comfort I had in that awful, endless day was the discovery that Father had only fallen into the trap of believing a grown-up. Lambal had seen an opportunity for revenge on Darby and me, and taken it. He had said that my dog had suddenly turned savage and would have gone for me if he had not come to my rescue. As soon as I told Father what had really happened he nearly cried he was so sorry, and let me listen while he sacked Lambal.

13

I used to visit Darby's grave in the shrubbery and talk to him, not because I thought the real him was still there, but because there must be something like a telephone connecting dead bodies with the people who used to live in them. This must be true, for otherwise why did my favourite housemaid go to visit her sister's grave on her day out? She took flowers and used to say, 'Poor love, she was ever so fond of peonies'—or sweet peas, or whatever the flowers happened to be. Darby had never been fond of flowers, but so that he would not feel in any way neglected I put some on his grave every day. To be sure he heard me I lay flat on my face and talked right into the ground. My mouth sometimes got so gritty that I had to rinse it out in the water-butt.

Then I heard people talking about something which was soon to happen, something to do with flying. 'It's coming right over the house,' they said. As though it was important. I was only mildly interested until I heard someone say, 'It's the Flying Derby.' Then I knew why they were excited— but no one was nearly so excited as me! Darby was coming to fetch me: a Darby larger and more beautiful even than before, a Darby with wings, on whom I could ride to the real country where we both belonged. Horses sometimes grew wings, for I had seen one called Pegasus in a book, and dogs were much wiser than horses.

The days passed so slowly that every hour of them might have been the long, slow hour of 'afternoon rest'. But at last Darby's Day came. Trembling with excitement I stood with lots of other people on the flat roof of Seacourt. 'There it is!' someone shouted. Had I remembered everything? Yes, my magic china mouse was in my pocket and I had said good-bye to my rabbits.

There was a black speck dazzling in the eye of the sun. The sun made my eyes water....Or did I already know it was not Darby? I felt tears running down my face—people would see. I must run, run until I found somewhere to hide, before they stopped looking at the flying machine.

As I stumbled down the steep wooden stairs which led to the attics I heard someone say, 'What a difficult child—too much excitement. She must be over-tired.'

CHAPTER THREE

WORÒS anÒ music

The fact that someone as kind and clever as Father could be deceived by Lambal convinced me that I must never believe anything until I had proved it for myself. Nurse Vincent was excellent material on which to practice being disobedient, but unfortunately she sometimes gave me orders which it would have been far more comfortable to obey. Unless she had forbidden me to go out in the garden at night it would never have occurred to me to do so, for I was afraid of the dark. Things were there, as she said, Things which lurked in the shrubbery waiting to punish little girls who annoyed their nurses? Could the Things creep in through the windows and attack me when I was too fast asleep to run away? Would They squeeze between the brass rails at the foot of my bed or slither over them? I thought about the Things so much that I had to make myself go out at night and see if they were really there. So I got out of the music-room window and made myself walk along the darkest, bushiest paths; but the bushes only rustled and never turned into hands that clutched at me—which was a great comfort and a reward for being disobedient.

An Irish housemaid said, 'The fairies will get you if the moon shines on your face while you are asleep.' It was a cosy idea until she enlarged upon the habits of cluricauns and pookas—I knew I would hate living underground, and pookas sounded far too large and formless for comfort. So only a strong sense of duty to disobedience drove me to keep myself awake at the full moon and then draw back the curtains and lie, wrapped in an eiderdown, on a moonlit patch of floor, trying to go to sleep before the moon's beam moved on, and wondering in what strange company I might wake.

'Little girls who tell lies are struck by lightning,' said Nurse Vincent, who had been eavesdropping when I had been telling Patrick that I used to be a Red Indian. This was a splendid opportunity to prove my truth, so when the next storm broke I escaped naked into the rain and stood with my arms upstretched to the vivid sky, free and exultant. She got soaked when she had to fetch me in, and the silly woman was terrified of thunderstorms. If I said 'Damn' as Father quite often did, she told me that 'children who used wicked swearwords frequently annoy God so much that He strikes them dead'. Blast, Dash, and Damn were my repertoire, but Patrick, when pressed, supplied Bloody, with the warning that it was not only 'a bad word' but blasphemy. Patrick's God seemed to be very unreasonable, for why should He mind anyone saying Bloody, which Patrick said meant, 'by Our Lady', when the Lady was His mother and very kind? He tried to explain when I asked him, but I still didn't understand and he said worriedly, 'It just *is* Miss Joan, but I'd have to be a priest and you a Catholic before we'd know *why*.

It would be very uncomfortable to believe in a God who was so fussy about swearing, but it might be risky to prove that He didn't exist. If Patrick's God *did* exist and struck me dead, how would He do it? Not by lightning, for that was reserved for liars, but to be on the safe side I had better choose a night of friendly stars and clear weather. Would He use a swift blow on the back of the neck with the side of His hand, like Patrick used to kill a sick rabbit? 'A clean, quick death, so it is,' he had said.

It rained for several days, and I was relieved because I was not really looking forward to having to make sure God didn't mind about swearing. It would have to be a night without clouds so that He could see me. Then one came, so I couldn't put it off any longer. It is surprisingly easy to leave a sleeping house even when you don't bother to be especially quiet. I wore my dressing-gown and slippers until I got down to the beach. Then I took them off because I felt it would be impolite to ask questions of God while I was hidden in clothes.

The sea was uncovering the sands, gently drawing back smooth sheets of dark water. 'Bloody!' I whispered, 'Bloody!' There was no answer except the soft sough of the sea. It was cold and my teeth were beginning to chatter, but I managed to say Bloody quite clearly and loudly. Still nothing happened. I looked up at the sky. The stars were so bright that God could certainly see me. 'Bloody!' I shouted. 'Bloody, and Blast and Damn!' Suddenly I felt beautifully happy. I knew that I need not believe what other people told me about God.

Nanny Walpole came back a few days later, which was very lucky, as it would have been far worse if Nurse Vincent had still been with me when I broke my leg. It happened when I was on my way to Diana Beddard's seventh birthday party, so it was the 23rd September 1911. The back gate which we always used because the other three were kept bolted, had a lock that could be opened with a key from either side and was of four-inch iron-studded oak. Running on ahead with the key, I saw that a plank was leaning against the door and covered the keyhole. So I pulled it away, and the door fell on me.

The next thing I heard was Patrick's voice shouting for people to help him lift it off me; and him cursing the workmen who had been repairing the door and left it propped only by a plank while they went off to fetch new hinges. I was lying face-downward with only my head free from the weight that was crushing me into the gravel. The door was so heavy that it took four men to lift it. Nanny Walpole was trembling so much I thought she would fall over when she picked me up. 'Mother of God, look at her leg!' exclaimed Patrick. Nanny

Walpole, trying to prove to herself that I was not really hurt, stood me on my legs to see if they were broken. One of them was. There was a sickening feeling like going down much too fast in a lift, and a crunching noise. Then I fainted.

Iris, who was in the dedans, which was full of people watching Father playing an important match, remembers a maid rushing in and shrieking, 'Miss Joan is dead! Her back is broke: she's dead!' My back was not broken, although a vertebra between my shoulders had been badly damaged. While they thought I was unconscious I heard people saying I might be paralysed.

If I cried when my broken leg got cramp it made Father unhappy, so I tried to remember being somebody who was clever at hiding her tears. This was not very successful until in a dream I met a woman whom I used to be fond of long ago. She was a Roman, and lived in a white house with a fountain and cypress trees in the garden. Her pain was much worse than mine, and when she could not help crying she collected her tears in a very beautifully shaped bottle, thin blue glass flecked with gold, and sent them to the temple as an offering to a goddess. I collected my tears in a little round medicine bottle, but when it was full I did not know where to send it, so I kept it on the mantlepiece.

The plaster cast was too tight, and when Dr. May took it off he saw my leg was crooked; so a surgeon came down from London to put it straight again. He brought an X-ray machine with him, which crackled and sent blue sparks across the pitch-dark room. Father held my hand while my leg was being put in the right position, so I felt quite brave even though it hurt far more than when the gate broke it.

There was a nice man staying in the house called Mr. Pizey. He had a flying-machine, which looked like a Bath chair with canvas wings tied on with wires, and as soon as I was well enough for my bed to be pushed to the balcony he used to fly past above the sands at low tide to amuse me. Iris read aloud, and told me fairy tales, but I began to worry in

18

case I would have to spend years and years in my boring bed. Then I stopped worrying, for Jennie came to see me and promised that I would soon be well. I recognised her the moment she stood beside my bed although I had not seen her since she died. I asked her whether I should tell Father she was here, but she said it would be better if her visits were our private secret. She never came except when I was alone, so I had to pretend that I could not settle down to sleep while anyone else was in the room.

Sometimes she played the piano for me. I knew her music, although I had only heard tinny echoes of it from the wax cylinders she had made for a kind of gramophone before I was born. It seemed quite natural that I could not see the piano though I could see her hands, which were very like Jack's and mine, weaving the music from the invisible keys. I always thought of Father as Jack and Mother as Blanche while Jennie was with me—I suppose because relationship to her was no longer important.

Nanny Walpole went to look after someone's new baby as soon as I no longer had to wear irons—the irons were because my good leg went bandy from putting too much weight on it while I was on crutches. I missed her very much: but I still had Jennie.

CHAPTER FOUR

SERGEANT'S MESS

After Nanny Walpole left, I had a series of nursery governesses, none of whom I liked. Mother cannot have liked them either, for none of them stayed more than a few weeks. They must have been lonely at Seacourt, for I now had lunch and tea with my parents, so they ate every meal alone, except breakfast, and inhabited an uneasy no-man's-land between the dining-room and the servants' hall. I suppose I ought to have been better company for them, but I infinitely preferred the more fertile pastures beyond the green baize door.

Until the 1914 war the kitchen was ruled by a chef. The first of these was an Alsatian who suffered from an illness which made him see large blue porpoises glaring at him out of the kitchen wall. None of the family knew about this until, in the middle of a dinner party, he entered the room in hot pursuit of his kitchen-boy whom he was trying to kill with a cleaver. The guests went to ground under the table, until on the third lap Mother spoke so sharply to him that he fled, to lock himself in the store-room, from which he was removed by three ambulance men and taken to hospital.

He was followed by Rene, a Parisian, to whom I rapidly became devoted. It was beneath the dignity of his High Bonnet to cook for the nursery or the servants' hall, but by the time I was six I had learned to rejoice at the subtlety of a sauce, to tremble with indignation when a *souffle* passed the peak of perfection because of some delay in the dining-room. One night he let me come close to his heart when, on my nocturnal prowlings, I found him weeping in front of one of his *chef-d'oeuvres*. It was a sculpture in sugar, an enormous cake in the likeness of a tennis court, complete to the net and the chase lines, the *tambour* and the *grille*.

'She is so beautiful,' he whispered over and over again. 'She is my child, and to-morrow they will stick a knife into her heart and she will be cake only.'

It was a solemn thought and I began to tremble. These were his toys, dearer to him than any teddy bear, for he had made them. The giant salmon, its spine a garden of pimento and tarragon flowers, which I had seen sleeping on its private iceberg in the larder; the capons, dressed in smooth white satin sauce; the stained-glass-window jellies; these too would die. What could I do? I could think of nothing helpful and began to cry, wiping the tears furtively on the sleeve of my red flannel dressing-gown. It was he who consoled me. 'We must have courage, my little one. We must remember that beauty lives for ever in the fond memories of the stomach.'

Not only the raw materials of his craft but people also responded to his Gallic genius. Mother, much as she appreciated his food, often got angry with him....I thought her utterly unreasonable at the time, though now I understand that it was tiresome for her to have to keep on finding new recruits to fill the gaps in the ranks of his minions, whom he despised and bullied until they gave notice. When she descended upon him in wrath he would rush out of the house, not routed but to pick her a bouquet of flowers as a peace-offering. It tried her high, for these were always specimen blooms, preferably those being jealously guarded for a flower show. If Worsfold, the kind head gardener who replaced loathsome Lambal, tried to protest, Rene would fly into a tantrum shouting, 'Only the best is good enough for Madame. You do not dare deny it!' If she rejected the flowers he would sink on his knees and recite her a poem, which unnerved her as, being little more of a linguist than I am, she could understand only one word in ten and so felt at a severe disadvantage.

One day I was assisting him to prepare a *julienne* of vegetables—so kind a man he was that he never let me guess how much I hindered. I stretched out my hand too far across the chopping-board, too fast for him to withhold the flashing knife. The top joint of my finger hung by a sinew. I screamed, and the Chef fainted.

Luckily Dr. Beddard was staying in the house, and did such an excellent repair that I have only a thin white scar on my fourth finger. Rene took the accident far more hardly than I did, who thoroughly enjoyed suddenly being the centre of attention. Every night, when my nursery governess had gone down to her solitary supper, he brought offerings to me: chocolate rabbits stuffed with cream, marzipan birds perched on spun-sugar nests, *pates* of crab, rich morsels of duck *mousse*, banquets in miniature on which I thrived.

Some clash of temperament at last sent him away, a clash too loud to be muted by poetry or flowers. I remember only the ache of his absence, and Mother saying that 'Rene left in disgrace.' But he came back to visit us during the Kaiser's war: 'the only man of his regiment to be left alive', having lost a leg and gained a Croix de Guerre.

As no one believed me when I told them about the interesting people I had been before I was Joan, I considered it quite permissible to tell lies when they were necessary to protect my freedom; until my conscience became annoyingly active after a conversation with Worsfold. It was strictly forbidden to ride my tricycle past the cucumber frames, but one day I did so and cornering too fast, fell through the largest one. I was not hurt, nor was the tricycle; so I hastily buried the broken glass and more obviously damaged leaves in the rubbish heap, and congratulated myself on having efficiently covered my tracks...being unaware that in the soft earth I had overlooked one unmistakable footprint. Challenged by Worsfold I stoutly lied. Truth was far too expensive a luxury when the cost would have been to have my tricycle taken away. He led me to the frame and in silence lifted a leaf, making me take off my shoe and fit it into the incriminating evidence. He then took me to the potting shed and solemnly described the rot which would spread through the entire household because Miss Joan told lies. Patrick would say he had stoked the boilers when he had not done so, and all the melons would get frosted. Tizzard would only pretend to water the lettuces and they too would die. Carpenter would find it easier to lie than to give sugar to the bees....Why not, if Miss Joan did? And the bees would starve to death instead of making honey. I was so moved that I even offered to own up to Mother, but to my relief he said this was not necessary as I had already owned up to him.

Duncan Duncan Wilson, our tennis professional, came into my life when I was four. He had been christened Duncan Duncan because he had a paternal and a maternal uncle with the same name, and his parents wanted to make sure that neither of them was offended. Long before he started teaching me to play the game, which was not until I was seven, I used to watch him stringing rackets or re-covering tennis balls, nine dozen to each basket of them, in his room at the end of the court while he talked about tennis. He told me there were grossly ignorant people who confused it with lawn tennis, a very inferior game played outdoors which should be referred to by the well instructed as pat-ball or lawners. It was, of course, our tennis that was the Game of Kings. Henry V might not have beaten the French so thoroughly at Agincourt, after the Dauphin had started the war by sending him a basket of tennis balls as an insult, unless he had been determined to prove that he could win as easily on the battlefield as he could in the court. Anne Boleyn might have kept her head if she had taken the trouble to appreciate the game. 'She probably annoyed the king by clapping when he lost a chase, or by forgetting to clap when he put a nice shot into the winning gallery,' said Wilson.

'Perhaps she talked at the wrong moment and put him off his stroke,' I said feelingly, for long before I could read I had learned that the notices in the dedans meant, 'Silence is Requested when the Ball is in Play.'

'She did not watch from the dedans. There was a lot of betting and ribald language among the spectators in those days, so it was not considered suitable for ladies. The king made a window into her apartments for her to watch him from. It is high in the end wall above the *grille* in the court he built at Hampton Court Palace.'

'Is his tennis court still there?'

'It is, Miss Joan, and has been played in every year since Henry the Eighth was Champion of England.'

The sequence of over four hundred years remains unbroken, for during the war, although the court was closed,

Father and Wilson played a match there each year.

Whenever I felt in the mood for a gossip, I only had to go to the laundry, where Mrs. Pink inhabited an echoing cavern of ironing and steam. She was immensely fat, and her welcoming smile displayed gums as smooth and rosy as the best York Ham, until one day—although taught that it was rude for children to make personal remarks, I exclaimed, 'You've got *teeth*, Mrs. Pink!'

She blushed, and whipping the dentures from her mouth, hid them in the pocket of her starched apron. 'Tell me, Miss Joan, did I do wrong to take them?' And before I could think of anything to say she hurried on with her tale, while I perched on the edge of the ironing-table.

'It was this way, dearie, if you see what I mean. In me spare time I do laying-out...which is to wash and tidy up a corpse to make the poor dear thing look nice to meet its Maker...the same kind of thing, only different, as Miss Saunders does to make your mother pretty for a grand party.'

Kate wouldn't even touch a dead mouse, so I doubted if she would be much use with a dead person, but I was far too interested to argue the point.

'I was doing this yesterday for a lady,' continued Mrs. Pink earnestly, 'real lovely she looked, and suddenly, when I came to tie up her jaw...tie up their jaws you must while they're still warm and put pennies on their eyes...the thought jumped right into my mind, ''She'll not be wanting those teeth where she's going, and a bit of cotton wool to plump out her cheeks will do her just as well in her coffin.'''

She stared down at her clasped hands in silence for a minute, large kind hands, the skin soft and wrinkled with long years of suds, the knuckles gnarled with the weight of wet linen. Then she looked into my eyes. 'I whipped them out of her mouth and into mine—and they fitted a treat. Is it a sign that I did her not wrong, Miss Joan, that they fitted so well?'

How could I reassure her? I stared at the ceiling as though

searching for inspiration, which I was. 'She is very glad, the lady who gave you her teeth,' I said firmly.

'But are you sure, Miss Joan, that it wasn't stealing? Theft is wicked, and a double weight of sin if one dares to steal from the dead.'

There were tears in her eyes. It was essential to speak with authority. 'The lady who *gave* you her teeth has just been talking to God. ''God,'' she said, friendly as anything, ''here am I safe in Heaven, crunching apples as loudly as a horse. And never an apple could I more than mumble unless my dear Mrs. Pink had relieved me of my teeth and left my jaws free for your new ones to grow in.'''

Then there was Sergeant-Major Spencer, who gave me boxing lessons. He had been a P.T. Instructor in the Brigade of Guards, and, clad in a white singlet which displayed his still magnificent torso, he roared at me as though I were a genuine recruit. I found the P.T. boring, though I would never have admitted it; but then came the glorious moment when he marked out a 'ring' with a piece of chalk on the music-room floor, and with perfect solemnity would manoeuvre on his knees, so that I had a chance of landing a straight left to his jaw. He acted as well as he boxed, and I almost believed him when at the end of our six rounds he would talk out of the side of his mouth, saying that his missus would have to give him mince again for supper as I had knocked all his teeth loose. He would twirl the needle-sharp points of his waxed moustache and say pontifically, 'Miss Joan, don't you ever fight dirty: no putting a penny between your knuckles so as to break the bridge of the other fellow's nose, no hitting below the belt, mind, no rabbit-punches.' Then, with a broad wink he would add, 'Never fight dirty— unless it comes in the line of duty to teach someone a lesson.'

While we shared elevenses—it was quite easy to imagine that my glass of milk was a second tankard of beer—he recounted magnificent adventures. Sometimes he went blow by blow through triumphs in the ring, and, best of all, acted the rout of a score of Dutchmen he had taken prisoner in the Boer War, when they attacked him after realising he was out of ammunition. 'Wonderful what you can do with a broken bottle if you're put to it,' he would say with relish, and then, being rather inclined to point a moral, would add, 'always provided you've paid proper attention as a nipper to your Indian clubs.' I thought swinging Indian clubs was rather hard work, but to please him I swung them higher and wider while he bellowed orders at me until the points of his moustache quivered and I trembled with effort, and at his praise glowed with pride.

I was strictly forbidden to fight with visiting children unless both parties wore boxing gloves, but the taunt, 'You're only a girl!' sometimes spurred me into action. Even my near neighbour and exact contemporary, John Mallet, was not exempt from an occasional bout; at six we were engaged, and I felt it only fair to convince him that he would have no need to be ashamed of any feminine weakness in his future bride. We were sparring amicably when I knocked out one of his front teeth. In the horror of seeing it lying on the grass I entirely forgot that children shed their first set of teeth and grow a new lot. I had done something appalling to my darling John! John would have to wear false teeth. I couldn't possibly marry anyone with false teeth! My terror of dentures was ingrained, for a malevolent nurse, who came while Nanny Walpole was on holiday, used to put her 'uppers and lowers' in a glass beside my bed, arrange a night-light so that they appeared to have a hellish phosphorescence of their own, and say in sepulchral tones, 'If you so much as stir finger or toe while I'm down at my supper they'll scold you proper—you see if they don't!'

Remembered fear and present guilt drove me to hide in tears in the potting shed. There John discovered me, not, as I expected and would have considered fair, to gloat over the punishments I might expect, but to comfort me. 'It was loose anyway,' he said, offering a slightly bloodstained handkerchief. 'Father told me to tie it to the doorknob and then slam the door, but I kept moving faster than the door so it didn't work.'

He displayed the trophy, tied in a corner of the handkerchief on which I had just blown. 'I'll put it under my pillow to-night and Mother says a fairy will turn it into a shilling by morning. It's all rot about the fairy, of course.' He eyed me, but I was too subdued to argue the point, which made him feel sufficiently senior to offer advice. 'When your teeth come out you might get as much as half a crown: they know you believe in fairies.' He gave me his tooth-shilling the next morning, and I accepted it gratefully as I needed it to bribe one of the gardeners not to tell Mother that he had caught me climbing a tree. But gratitude gnawed: would a boy have accepted the money or gone out and won it for himself? First thoughts suggested that as girls often had to suffer starched drawers and frilly petticoats the least that boys could do was to offer the resources of their money-boxes. I think I would have let it go at that if the current nursery governess had not the curious foible of reading aloud to herself from the Bible during breakfast. I thought she was slightly dotty, but more mature judgment suggests that she did it in the hope that fragments of scripture would be digested with my porridge and so shrive her for working in a heathen household where she had been strictly forbidden to give her pupil any religious instruction.

That particular morning 'an eye for an eye and a tooth for a tooth' suddenly broke through the haze of cold bacon fat at which I was staring. This seemed so apposite that it startled me. Was it a hint from God that I owed John a tooth, or could I repay him as soon as possible with a shilling? The reader-aloud must have been encouraged because I suddenly paid attention, for she repeated even more sombrely, ''a tooth for a tooth''—Do you understand, Joan?'

God had given me more than a hint: it was an order. I prodded my front teeth with a tentative tongue and one woggled a little. It was an unexpectedly sickening feeling, but fortunately quite definite. Patient tongue-work during the day improved the situation. I tried the string-and-doorknob technique but it was quite ineffective; for, like John, I could move faster than the door. I banged the tooth, not very hard, with the handle of a hairbrush. I stared at myself in a mirror and imagined, so well that it made me red with indignation, that a gang of hostile boys was chanting, 'Cowardy, cowardy custard!' at me. But even this did not kindle a spark hot enough to fire a neglected powder-keg of courage.

Mother, no doubt driven frantic by two successive luncheons at which I slowly but determinedly chewed only on my front teeth, offered to pull it out for me. I refused, although reluctantly, for much as I wished to get it over I did not feel sufficiently confident to face a drawn-out performance in her bathroom, while sterilised linen was dipped in antiseptic and mouth-wash prepared, which I had to endure when she dealt with gumboils. In case her offer was repeated I sought aid from Patrick, who performed the operation with a pair of pliers in the stoke-hole.

In the jeweller's box which had housed my Christmas brooch, wrapped in tissue paper and tied with my best hair ribbon, I presented my tooth to John. Twenty years later we met at a cocktail party. He was then an attache at the British Embassy in Rome and I had just written *Winged Pharaoh*. He showed me a small object attached to his watch-chain: it was my tooth, mounted in gold.

CHAPTER FIVE

nineteen-fourteen

Through the golden summer of 1914 there blew the chill
of an era's evening, but in the small circle which my memory
lights I remember only one anxiety. Could God be absent-
minded as a grown-up, or worse, was He deaf? I wanted a
pony but only God could get me one. Mother, who had
always been a martyr to 'what might happen', put me off
with, 'One day, perhaps, darling; when you're bigger.'
Father was even less responsive. Years later he told me that
he had always loathed horses but had ridden to please his
father, and was determined that I must never be allowed to
make a similar sacrifice to filial piety. I had discovered that it
was tactless to nag grown-ups. A seed firmly planted in their
minds, and occasionally watered with a wistful smile, produced far better fruit. But apparently it was necessary to nag
God, or why did my current governess make me say the same
prayers every night—words which had become so smooth by
repetition that the pattern in them had been worn away.
'Our Father Whichartin Heaven,' I gabbled, and then, when
I was private, went on to the serious matter of praying for a
pony. 'Please God, I want a pony for my seventh birthday,
which is on the twelfth of April,' I said loudly and clearly. 'A
brown pony with a black mane and tail; small enough for me
to get on without anyone helping, and large enough for me
still to be able to ride when I am taller. I want a riding-on and
not a pulling-a-cart pony, and I will call it Ruby if it hasn't
got a name already; but if it has a name it does not matter at
all.' What request could be more clear and concise?

I gave Him six whole weeks to make His arrangements;
surely that was long enough for Him to inform my parents of
what needed to be done. One morning I saw bricks and a
barrow-load of mortar outside the row of outhouses where

tools and fertilisers and fruit were kept. One of them was being turned into a stable for Ruby! I was so sure of this that I knew exactly what the manger, and the rack for her hay, would be like; and I carefully avoided going near the place so as not to spoil the glorious moment when I first saw her in it. I kept on praying, in case God did not realise that grown-ups are terribly apt to be forgetful or change their minds; although this did not seem really necessary after Mother told me that I was to have a wonderful, and very expensive, present for my birthday, that was too large to be put with the others in the pillow-case at the foot of my bed.

Hardly pausing to tear the paper off my other parcels I ran downstairs. Father was in the hall. 'Where is it?' I said, hugging him. I was so excited that I nearly said, 'Where is Ruby?' which might have spoilt his pleasure in thinking it was a surprise. 'It's in the dining-room,' he said. 'We'll take it down to the beach directly after breakfast.' A pony allowed indoors? Oh, how lovely of Father! And the sands would be perfect for me to learn to ride.

But it was not a pony. It was a scale-model of a Cunarder, which cost 50 pounds and went by real steam. The grown-ups enjoyed playing with it when the sea was warm enough for them to bathe; but I never liked it.

Soon after this Father went to Paris to play in the amateur tennis championship of France...Frenchmen called the game *jeu de paume*. He took Mother of course, and Margery and Iris, Wilson and Kate; which made it all the more disappointing that he did not take me. 'We shall only be away about ten days, and you are a bit too young for Paris,' he said consolingly, and gave me a complete works of Jules Verne as a parting present, four volumes bound in brown leather.

I always disliked being told I was too young for something I thought I would enjoy doing, so Father's kindly remark stung a bit. Had the French girl I sometimes dreamt about ever been to Paris, and if so, how old was she? I had seen her in a green velvet riding-habit when she must have been a little older than Iris; but she was not in a city then, she was on a black horse galloping through a forest. There were several other riders with her, and some hounds which were chasing a stag. Usually when I saw her she was younger than this, about ten or eleven. She lived in a house with a steep grey roof and faded green shutters in which most of the rooms were shut up. It was built on three sides of a courtyard which had grass growing between the cobblestone. There were no other children, but she was quite happy and had a little carriage drawn by a pair of piebald ponies which were not much larger than her enormous dog. She was allowed to drive them herself so long as she did not go near the village. There were certain people who had recently come to the village who must never find out that she still lived in the chateau.

The night before my family came home I had a long and complicated dream about her, of which I remembered enough to know that she *had* been to Paris, when she was nineteen. She was only there for a few weeks, and spent them in a dungeon where she was so lonely that she tamed a rat for company. Even in the middle of the day there was only a greenish twilight, and the only time she saw the sun again was on her way to have her head cut off by the guillotine.

It might have been a terrifying dream, but oddly enough it was rather comforting; because now I knew that beheading does not hurt at all. There was only a loud thud and a feeling of falling head over heels. The next minute she was jumping over a stream to join two men who were waiting for her on the other side of it...two men whom she very much loved.

Father lost the French championship by a stroke—quite literally, as if he had missed the ball which was losing a hazard chase he would have won the point and the match. It was a great pity, as otherwise he would have been champion of both countries; for two months later he won the Gold Racket at Lord's. Soon after they got home, Billy Grenfell came to stay at Seacourt, with two friends who had also been 'rusticated' from Oxford. Rusticated was not so bad as being

31

'sent down', which was the same as expelled, for it was only being sent away for the rest of the term. They had been to a fancy-dress ball as Ancient Britons, in leopard skins and woad, which, for some incomprehensible reason, was considered indecent.

I knew Billy already and he had promised to marry me, which was very nice of him because he looked like a Greek god, with curly yellow hair. I loved him devotedly and put flowers on his pillow, which were secret messages that I looked up in Margery's book called *The Language of Flowers*, which came in useful when I had to remind him that he had forgotten to come to say good night to me.

The other two were Willy Williams and Cyril Asquith. They had a tutor called Mr. Lindsay, a diffident young man who later became the Master of Balliol. Billy used to make bets with Willy, giving him such long odds, ten pounds to a shilling, that they were always taken on. The first I remember is when they took me to buy sweets and I saw a huge bunch of bananas outside Mr. Jones's shop. Could Willy Williams eat them all in twenty-four hours? There were two hundred and fifty, and although Mother insisted that his stomach would be so distended that it would press on his heart and kill him, he managed to swallow the last one with ten minutes in hand—in the dedans, after playing three sets with Wilson to shake down his banana breakfast.

After dinner Father sometimes played the banjo, while Herbert Rubens, who with his brother Paul wrote muscial comedies, *Miss Hook of Holland* and *The Country Girl*, accompanied him on the piano and the others sang. Father played the banjo beautifully, and had a band of forty banjos when he was at King's, and took them to play at Oxford, and even in a concert-hall in London. Sometimes I was allowed to come down to listen, but when not allowed I could hear very comfortably lying on the floor of the music-room gallery.

The next bet was Willy Williams running four times to the Ferry and back in two hours. The total distance was sixteen miles, but he was good at marathon running and was pretty sure he could do it. I followed with Father in the new car, an open two-seater Phoenix with very shiny brass headlamps, which perched so high on its wheels that I had a splendid view of the heads of other spectators. Mother set up a first-aid station at the gate of Seacourt, which was both the starting and the finishing post, with rolls of sticking-plaster and boracic lint for blisters, and bottles of liniment to rub on his legs.

Iris came with us in the car, clutching a thermos of beef-tea. The only time she got him to take any it was so hot that he spat it out on the road, which I thought very robust of him, and a jar of chicken jelly which melted and slopped on to the red leather seat until, Father, who had a horror of anything sticky, noticed it and made her throw it into a hedge.

Billy, who always wanted to lose his bets because Willy Williams was hard up and it was the only way of making him accept money, ran with him part of the way, and Asquith and Lindsay coached him through megaphones from bicycles. By the third lap there were a lot of people watching, not only people who had heard about it through us, but holiday visitors who had drifted up from the beach. Willy Williams was beginning to look rather pale and sweaty, but he was still going strong until he came to the home stretch, when suddenly he got cramp in the legs and fell down in front of the Post Office. Father jumped off the car and gave him brandy from a silver flask, waving aside Iris's offer of restorative soup. He held his stop-watch in front of Willy William's eyes and kept telling him that he had only another quarter of a mile to go and had still got seven minutes.

'Get up, old boy. Get up! You'll do it easily!' urged Billy.

'On, on!' shouted Mr. Lindsay.

'Oh, please get up—please,' pleaded Iris, now almost in tears. She had turquoise blue eyes and cried easily without them getting red. Willy Williams tottered to his feet, raised a gallant hand to acknowledge the cheering crowd, stumbled a few yards and fell flat on his face.

Someone shouted, 'Shame!' Other voices took up the cry. 'Shame! Leave the poor perisher alone can't yer? Shame! Leave 'im alone!'

I suddenly realised they were really angry, the anger which makes you suddenly twice as tall and very much stronger. Billy ignored them but I was frightened, for I knew the tingle that was pricking down their arms into their fists, and the hot feeling in their spines. I felt quite wobbly with relief when Billy said at last, 'Too bad, old chap,' and helped Father lift the groaning man into the car.

They were going to stay with us until the end of the Long Vacation, but on August the fourth the newspapers had huge headlines screaming WAR! Everyone said it would be over by Christmas, and talked as though killing Germans would be more fun than a day's hunting.

Billy came to see me when I was in bed that night before he went away. He stared out of the window at the roses—that summer there were so many roses in the garden—and said without looking at me, 'This really is good-bye, Joan.' Then he kissed me. He knew he was going to be killed, and so did I. His death was even quicker than by guillotine: he was blown to bits.

His mother sent me some lines from a poem his brother Julian wrote the night before he too was killed:

> The blackbird sings to him, 'Brother, brother,
> If this be the last song you shall sing,
> Sing well, for you may not sing another;
> Brother, sing.'

CHAPTER SIX

new worlds

While Father was in Paris he had arranged to go to America in September to play tennis with Jay Gould. The war would be won by our Army and Navy so he saw no reason to change his plans and we sailed from Liverpool in the *Lusitania*. I enjoyed the voyage very much, for, like Father, I was a good sailor. Mother and Margery and Iris stayed in their state-rooms, and Kate was kept busy looking after them. On the second day we ran into a storm and a boy called George helped me to invent a splendid game. The carpet had been rolled back in the largest saloon in case anyone wanted to dance. No one did as it was too rough, so we slid backwards and forwards on door-mats as the ship rolled, going even faster when I had the bright idea of sprinkling Margery's talcum powder on the polished floor.

Father took me up to the boat deck to watch us coming in to New York Harbour. It was very beautiful, with sky-scrapers shining in the pink light of sunset and mist rising from the Hudson River as though we were approaching a city built on clouds. We were a long time in the Customs shed and when we got to our hotel I was too tired to notice much except that the porters and the bell-hops were nearly all Negroes.

As soon as I saw them I knew I should like America. Emilie Grigsby, who often came to Seacourt and is still one of my very favourite people, had a maid called Mary Dabney, who used to be her black mammy when Emilie was a child in Kentucky. I loved Mary, for she understood about haunts and nightmares, and used to sing to me in her soft black-velvet voice while she rocked me on her lap when I was far too old to be cuddled by anyone else.

I woke early and as neither Margery nor Iris would get out

of bed, and only mumbled when I prodded them, I decided to go out and explore New York. Father had given me a five-dollar gold piece, so I wandered round several shops and bought presents for the family and an ice-cream soda for me. There were ice-creams for sale even in chemists' shops, with names like Knickerbocker Glory and Sunrise Banana Split. I walked a long way between ices—I had fourteen including 'sodas' before the end of the day, and when the lights went on I realised I had forgotten how to find my way back to the hotel and had no money left. There were far too many people on the pavements now, and I began to be frightened. I think I might have panicked if a small black hand had not slipped into mine and a warm, soft voice said, 'Missie come home now?'

George Washington Jones was a bell-hop from our hotel and had been following me all day in case I got lost. No one knew he was with me, so poor Mother had been worried....I felt very guilty at not leaving a note to say I was only going out for a private explore. She and Father had been telephoning policemen and offering rewards, which got larger the more certain they became that I had been kidnapped. I had always been secretly afraid of being carried off by gipsies, but I never thought about them that day as I saw no caravans in New York. It was a happy day, and ended happily too, for everyone was so relieved to see me that there was hardly any row, and George Washington Jones got the reward, large enough by this time for him to go home to his family in Alabama and not to have to be a bell-hop any more.

Americans chatted to strangers, even foreigners and children, without waiting to be introduced; and nearly every room in our hotel apartment, which was on Fifth Avenue overlooking Central Park, had a door into the outside corridor, so it was easy to find plenty of people to talk to. Americans moved fast, like children; even grandmothers were sprightly. Rice pudding had ice-cream on top of it. When Kate found me reading in bed and unscrewed the bulb from the bedside lamp I could see perfectly well by the light of somebody's huge illuminated sign of a kitten endlessly unwinding a ball of wool.

Central Park had rocks to climb and Margery let me talk to the other children and tried to make Mother let me have roller skates like they did; but Mother said I would be sure to break my leg again. I had never been in an omnibus or on the underground railway until one day it was raining so hard that Mother had to get on a trolley-car as there was no taxicab in sight. She waited for someone to help her up the steps, but the trolley-car driver only grinned and said, 'Step lively, lady!' And she had to hop in quickly before he sent it swaying and clanging down the street.

I had a lovely lot of Father to myself: meals and museums and the aquarium, and sliding on the ice at an outdoor skating rink. He also took me to billiards matches—nice because there were no other children, but a bit too long without even whispering.

The day he took me up the Statue of Liberty was important. We climbed an openwork iron staircase that spiralled round a pillar which was the lady's spine. Suddenly a woman three places in front of us began to shriek and cling to the rail. She thought she was going to fall over and squash on the floor far too far below us. I would have liked to turn back, but this was impossible because we were part of a long snake of people. 'Are you feeling all right?' said Father anxiously. I knew he was feeling dizzy too, so I said I was not in the least frightened. A man tied a scarf over the hysterical woman's eyes and took her by the elbows and made her go on walking up the stairs. When we got to the top she was lying on the floor with a nurse looking after her. We went up to the Torch and there was a wonderful view, but I did not enjoy it as much as I might have done because I kept on thinking of having to climb down the stairs again.

We had lunch in a restaurant, and then Father, who knew I had not enjoyed the morning much, said I could choose what we would do for the rest of the afternoon. 'Anything?' I wanted to be quite sure this was not a choice only between things considered suitable-for-children. 'Anything,' he said stoutly. 'You earned it this morning. You looked so green, my Gingerbread Rabbit, that I though you were going to throw up.'

'We will go on the Elevated Railway...I'll gargle as soon as I get home if you like and catch any fleas that get on to me before they bite Margery.'

He agreed at once, and we spent a very interesting two hours rattling above the streets and seeing into other people's windows when they put the lights on without drawing the curtains. It seemed a pity not to make use of the opportunity to go in the underground railway, too, which would be an important adventure to put in my letter to Diana, so I said, 'Now we will go back by subway.'

'Sure you wouldn't rather do that another day? It will be very crowded now when the offices and the shops are just closing,' he suggested hopefully. But I was firm, and he laughed and said I was a glutton for punishment.

Almost as soon as we had clicked our way through the turn-stiles I began to have doubts, and the roar of too many people in a hurry sounded so much like an underground river that was carrying my canoe into a whirlpool that I tried to become an Indian Brave who would not be frightened even in such a dangerous situation. This didn't work properly, because I had only started after Joan got so wrapped up in her feelings that she was too heavy to shift. I was rather feebly pretending to be leading my war-canoes against an enemy tribe who had invaded our hunting-grounds when someone shouted, 'Keep back, keep back!'

But we were swept towards the voice as though we were logs in a beaver dam breaking under ice-floes—until we jarred against another dam, men with their arms linked to hold back the surge of humans. I was squashed against one of the men, but under his arm I saw a small pool on the platform. Someone has spilt a pot of red paint on it, and I was surprised that people made so much fuss at the thought of getting paint on their shoes.

Father tried to pick me up, but there was no room for him to bend down, so I steadied myself by holding on to his legs. 'Don't look!' he said urgently. I tried to keep my eyes shut but my eyelids refused to obey. It was worse than not being able to hold them open against a nightmare. It was not red paint and an old mackintosh on the platform. It was blood, and there was a dead body under the mackintosh. It was dead or they wouldn't have covered its face. Someone sobbed, 'He jumped right in front of the train. I *saw* him!'

Then I saw the boots, large black boots with leather laces and tags sticking up at the back. The boots were standing neatly side by side next to the rest of the man's body, as though he had taken them off before getting into bed. But the train had taken them off for him. I cannot remember exactly what happened next, except that Father said, 'Help me get this child out of here, damn you!' And I was lifted over the top of hundreds of heads which felt like flying in a dream, the kind when you are far too heavy to do it safely.

Then Father and I were in the street and my beaver muff was damp and smelt sour, so I knew I had been sick down myself and someone had wiped it off while I was not noticing. 'You feeling all right, old thing?' he asked. When I said I was, he patted me and said, 'Well, I'm not.' And we went into a hotel and he had brandy and I had ginger ale.

'I don't think we'll tell your mother,' he said tentatively. 'Or would you rather we did?'

'She'd only fuss,' I agreed quickly. 'I'll find the loo-lady and get her to wash my coat for me or Mother will think it was too many ice-creams.'

'You are a very competent child,' said Father, and gave me a dollar for the loo-lady, who said the English were tough babies when I told her about the boots. It helped to tell somebody.

Father must have guessed that I wasn't looking forward to

39

going to sleep, for he telephoned Mother and said he was taking me out to dinner and a muscial comedy; and then he put the receiver down quickly, before she could say that I had already had too long a day. I was bustled off to bed as soon as we got back to our hotel, and went to sleep so quickly that I expected to have a nonsense dream about the things I had been thinking deliberately...the dinner with Father and the singing girls dancing in rows with men in very shiny top hats.

But I found myself standing alone on the platform, alone except for the boots and the man whose feet were still inside them. He was lying on his side, his hands clutching his leg stumps. Then he saw me, and at the same moment I saw myself. Instead of being only a child I was grown-up, about eighteen I should think. 'Agnes,' he pleaded, 'Agnes, help me.' He loved Agnes, who had been his daughter, more than anyone else, which is why I looked like her to him. I stood quite still, absorbing into me the love between them so that I could use it to help him. As Agnes I knelt down and put my hand on his forehead. 'Shut your eyes, Pa,' I said soothingly, 'and I'll soon get you fixed up. You've been at the whisky again and you're seeing things.'

He closed his eyes obediently, but he was still very frightened. His fear made it difficult for me to keep hold of his affection for Agnes, and at the same time act as the real part of me without becoming clouded by little Joan's terror. My fingers fumbled with the laces of the boots, for the blood on them was black and hard. But at last I peeled off the stiff leather and sat crosslegged with the severed feet in my lap. The toes were misshapen, with broken, dirty nails. So I began to straighten them very gently between my fingers, breathing on the worn skin of the insteps as though I was cleaning the earth from a windfall apple. When he was ready I turned him on his back. He appeared to be sleeping, and after I had made his clothes disappear I washed him all over very carefully, with water from a jar that someone had set beside him for me to use. His flesh was old and tired even when it was clean again. But when I fitted the bones of his severed feet to the stumps of his legs they began to grow together; and the new life in his feet began to flow up into him, and the skin and the muscles of his body gradually became young again.

He had been a nice-looking young man, clean shaven instead of a grey stubble of beard, and with strong fair hair instead of a few sodden, tattered wisps. I put him into a blue shirt and flannel trousers as he was not yet used to being naked. The platform had changed while he was changing, and now he was lying on spring grass under a willow tree. Between the long leaves I could see tall buildings beyond a lake, buildings which seemed incongruous until I recognised them from a different context. We were in Central Park, and I thought I had not been loving enough to bring him safely into Heaven. Then he yawned and opened his eyes, stretching his arms luxuriously in the warm, clear light. A girl in a pink dress came running along the path beside the bright water. He scrambled to his feet, laughing with joy, and ran towards her calling, 'Agnes! Agnes, I'm here! I'm here!'

And I was Joan again, a child who was not allowed to roller-skate in Central Park.

CHAPTER SEVEN

soothsayers

We spent Christmas in a house on Riverside Drive with a lot of very old people, and soon afterwards I began to look forward to going back to England as none of Mother's American friends seemed to have any children. When people came to tea I usually curled up inconspicuously in an arm-chair so that I could read instead of displaying 'intelligent interest.'

One of our visitors I liked was Hereward Carrington. He wrote books about ghosts, but only seemed to see bits of them swaddled in ectoplasm; which Father told me privately was probably cheese-cloth smuggled into the seance by the medium. So I was prepared to like another visitor who was said to be 'psychic'; but the moment I saw Aleister Crowley I thought of him as a kind of human toad.

Only Mother and Margery were in when he came. Father was playing tennis at the Racquet Club and Iris was out shopping with Kate. The Toad sat on a sofa beside Margery and paid her fulsome compliments while she kept edging away. He said she reminded him of a beautiful golden gazelle—which must have been a change from being told she was like the women in pictures by Dante Gabriel Rossetti. Her beaux used to give her Rossetti reproductions which she hung in her bedroom until there was no more space on the walls for any more.

After tea had been cleared away Mother gave several hints to the Toad that it was time for him to go, but he stayed on and on until at last she gave an even broader hint by saying she had to go and write some urgent letters. The moment she had left the room the Toad took his black pearl tie-pin from his purple satin cravat and stuck it into Margery's arm. He pretended it was an accident and blotted the bead of blood with his handkerchief—a white silk handkerchief with a purple edge. Margery was too terrified to shriek, but when he tweaked out a strand of her hair she squeaked, 'Mother!' She was so frightened that she sounded like a mouse.

I was just about to do something, and trying to become the kind of person who would know how to do it, when I saw Mother standing in the doorway. The Toad had not noticed her yet. He was gloating at Margery and saying, 'Now you are in my power, for I have your blood and your hair. I need a nail-paring too, but I am so great a magician that I can manage without it.'

Then Mother was really splendid. She looked at least

twice as tall as usual and her eyes seemed fiery and enormous. 'My white magic is stronger than your black magic,' she declaimed. 'Down on your knees, you grubby little sorcerer!' Her voice went through him like a sword and I almost expected him to ooze over the cushions. He tried to out-stare her and then half tumbled, half slid off the sofa and shambled across the room. He pawed at the door handle, and then I heard him stumbling away down the corridor.

When Mother was sure he had gone she sat down abruptly in a chair and I knew her legs were shaking, as they always do when you come back into yourself too suddenly. 'What a very disagreeable man,' she said, as though he had been an ordinary person who was a little drunk. She looked sharply at Margery. 'You are looking quite green, child. Go and give yourself some sal volatile.'

Then she saw me, and for a moment looked worried. But she realised how proud of her I was feeling and I knew she was very close to tears. She blew her nose and said briskly, 'Always remember I am an efficient tiger when it comes to defending my cubs.'

The stateroom tickets and the Not Wanted on Voyage labels were on the sitting-room mantelpiece although we were not sailing for another three weeks, when Mother suddenly stared at them and said, 'The *Lusitania* is going to sink on that voyage. Jack, change the reservations!' Then she noticed I was in the room and told me to run along to bed. Father began to argue with her even before I had shut the door, which was rather surprising, as he must have remembered her taking us out of the tennis court before the roof fell in, and after that there was her foreseeing of the *Titanic*.

That had happened two days before my fifth birthday, so it was on the 10th of April 1912. We were all on the roof of the Seacourt watching the *Titanic* go down the Solent past the Isle of Wight on her maiden voyage. Mother, who until then had been as cheerful as everyone else, clutched Father's arm as though she were dizzy and cried out, 'That ship is going to

43

sink before she reaches America!' He tried to soothe her but she only became more agitated. By now everyone was listening. The scullery-maid exploded into nervous giggles and the other servants looked embarrassed and hastily withdrew to the far end of the roof. People gathered round Mother and tried to convince her that the *Titanic* had been built in a new way which made it impossible for anything to sink her. All this did was to make her angry. 'Don't stand there staring at me! Do something! You fools, I can see hundreds of people struggling in the icy water! Are you all so blind that you are going to let them drown!'

I whispered to Iris, 'Is the ship really going to sink?' But she did not answer until we had slipped away and were out of earshot. 'I don't expect so,' she said consolingly. 'Mother has always been afraid of shipwreck because her best friend and the best friend's daughter were on a ship called the *Waratah* which vanished without trace.'

During the next five days everyone was careful not to mention the *Titanic*, but Mother was nervy and Father looked harassed. It must have been almost a relief for her when everyone knew that the *Titanic* had struck an iceberg; not nearly so lonely as waiting until it happened.

I remembered all this so clearly while I was having my bath that when they came up from dinner I crept out of bed and listened at the sitting-room door. 'Well, it's the best I can do,' Father was saying resignedly. 'I spoke to nearly everyone in the Cunard office, but the only alternative accommodation they could offer was for a sailing the day after to-morrow...on the same ship.'

'Oh, that's all right,' said Mother calmly, 'the *Lusitania* is not going to sink until the voyage we were going on. I suppose she will be torpedoed as it is too warm for icebergs. Poor things, I feel so sorry for them! However, there is nothing we can do about it in wartime, so I had better go and tell Kate to start packing.

Mother was so relieved at the change of plans that she was

not even put out when he gloomily told her that we should all have to travel in very inferior cabins. Margery grumbled a bit at having to share with Iris and Kate and me, but I thought it far more fun to climb a little to a bunk than to sleep in a stateroom in an ordinary bed. The parents had a two-berth cabin next door. There was so much luggage in it that Father had to climb over a wardrobe trunk to get to his bunk—which must have been tiresome for him as he had to keep climbing out again to hand nux vomica pills to Mother from a blue morocco medicine-case with dozens of little bottles in it. Mother had recently become a very ardent homeopath.

It was not nearly so enjoyable as the outward journey. The ship did a lot of zigzagging when we were chased by submarines; and Father told Mother—which was rather tactless of him—that he had overheard one of the ship's officers say to another that they would probably sink. Jules Verne—luckily I had bought the volume which contained *Twenty Thousand Leagues Under the Sea*—was a great solace when the others were too busy being sick for me to keep comfortably asleep. When I could not avoid thinking about submarines I imagined myself having dinner with Captain Nemo in the *Nautilus;* with Father sitting on the other side of him, smoking a seaweed cigar.

There were no other children on board, and as Father spent most of his time with other men having grown-up conversations about the war, I made friends with Hal the lift-boy. He drew very well, especially caricatures, and let me run the lift so that he could get on with his drawing. He was doing a particularly funny one of an old man who was asleep with his mouth open on a sofa opposite the lift, when the old man woke up and caught him at it. Instead of being angry he was amused, and said he was an editor from New York and would give Hal a very good job on his newspaper. Hal accepted eagerly—he had always wanted to be an artist, but said he had another two voyages to do to finish his contract. The editor praised him for being so conscientious and bought the caricature for twenty dollars. I did everything I could to make Hal promise to stay in America as soon as he got back there. But it was no use. He said it would look as though he was afraid of being torpedoed, and that he would send me a post-card to prove I was only fussing.

I never received the postcard. A little later Mother met an old lady plodding up the stairs in a hotel and asked her why she did not use the lift. 'I never go in lifts,' said the old lady. 'I was on the *Lusitania* when she was torpedoed. The ex-plosion made the lift-gates jam and all the people in them were drowned like rats in a trap.' Hal must have been one of the poor dear rats who would not leave the ship that was going to sink.

CHAPTER EIGHT

hell on earth

By the summer of 1915 Father was working for the Muni-tions Inventions Department of the War Office and only came down to Seacourt for week-ends. So I thought it might be amusing to go to boarding school, having recently read several school stories by Angela Brazil. These had been rather a nice change after a more solid diet of H.G. Wells and Conan Doyle, and ploughing through ten volumes of Captain Marryat, which had been rather hard going—except for *Mr. Midshipman Easy*. I only persevered with Marryat because Father thought I was going to enjoy them, and then he put me on to W.W. Jacobs, sea stories about 'old salts' who were always chewing quids of tobacco. I experimented with the insides of four Turkish cigarettes, but the tobacco in them must have been the wrong kind for chewing, as I was very sick and had such a splitting headache that I was kept in bed for a week. Dr. May thought it was sunstroke until he realised it was only nicotine poisoning; but the sunstroke theory stuck in Mother's mind, and after that she was always insisting on hats.

The school I went to in the autumn term was near Great Missenden in Berkshire. When I knew I was going there I was happy and excited, for now that John had gone to prep-school there was no one near my own age to play with except during the holidays. If I had been foresighted, like Mother about the *Lusitania*, I would have known that I was deliberately allowing myself to be sent to hell.

The demons were disguised as ordinary girls, in white flannel blouses and gym tunics which matched their bloomers of navy blue serge. They had secret societies and private jokes and their own incomprehensible code, and instantly recognized that I had been brought up in a different way and must be given no opportunity of joining their herd. At first the mistresses were nice to me because I was good at lessons, but soon they went sour too.

There were dozens of silly little rules. Everyone was supposed to sneak on themselves and put a black mark beside their names in the 'Confession Book' if they had talked after Lights Out or touched the new wallpaper when they went up or down stairs. If there were more than ten black marks it meant a hundred lines at the end of the week. I wrote so many lines that my handwriting has been difficult ever since. I was scrupulously careful to give myself black marks as I thought it was like being put on my word of honour, so my conscience was clear when the headmistress addressed the whole school after morning prayers. She announced quite blatantly that God was very disappointed because some of her pupils had not been owning up to their sins, and that He had sent a little bird to whisper in her ear and tell her the names of the naughty ones. There was a heavy chandelier hanging from the ceiling above her head, but I had learned by this time that God was unlikely to send it crashing down to punish her, and the dove He used was too peaceful a bird to bite her ear off, even though she had publicly accused it of being a sneak. She was deliberately teaching children to hate God: so she must be working for the Devil! Something must be done, and quickly. I prayed that God would choose some other champion to fight for Him, but there was not a flicker of indignation from the pudding-faced rows, not a twitter of protest. Quaking with terror I managed to get to my feet. 'You are a wicked old woman!' I shouted. 'God never sent His dove to sneak to you—for such a black lie. He ought to strike you dead!'

After that my only friends were six worms—they had been three worms before a particularly horrid child had chopped them in half, which I kept in a tin under a stone in the rockery; and two stick-insects which had been given to me by the Botany Mistress. The stick-insects made little black pellets in their box which I thought were eggs, so I made a cotton-wool nest for them and stuck it to my chest with sticking-plaster, hoping the warmth would help them to hatch. After about a week, one of the prefects found it and roared with laughter: the little black pellets were only stick-insect dirts.

The days were cold, grey misery, but the nights were even more lonely, for I had to sleep in a dormitory with six other girls, so Jennie never came to see me. Before half-term I decided to run away. This needed careful planning, as I could not escape to the town and take a taxi because the three pound notes Father had given me had been 'locked safely away' as soon as I arrived, and I could not travel far on sixpence a week pocket-money. I found out from a friendly van-driver that the last train to London went at three minutes past midnight. If I stowed away on it there would be no train until the morning for a mistress to follow me. It ought not to be too difficult, for boys in books were often stowaways in ships, and trains should be even easier.

No one heard me climb down from the balcony. Fortunately there was curly ironwork to which I tied a rope-ladder made from skipping ropes stolen from the gym. I ran silently along the grass verge of the avenue—this was the worst bit as it was supposed to be haunted—and made good time to the station. There was no one about and the platform lights were very dim, so I hid until the train came in and slipped into the luggage van and crouched behind some milk cans.

The van was not even opened at the next two stations. I was cold, but tremendously excited at the thought of how pleased Father would be to see me when I arrived in time to have breakfast with him at the Royal Automobile Club. I had no anxieties about getting there, for at Paddington I would take a taxi and tell the hall porter to pay for it.

Then I heard voices. The doors of the van slid back and a man came in carrying a lantern. I was well hidden but he found me. On the platform was a policeman. I had not allowed for the appalling ingenuity of schoolmistresses. They had found the rope and guessed that I was making for London; while the roads near the school were being searched in cars they had also warned police stations up the line.

'Cowardy, cowardy custard! Poor baby can't bear being away from its Mummy!' the demons chanted. At least they could not add the taunt of 'cry-baby', for my nose often bled so I kept a handkerchief daubed with red ink in my pocket so that I could clap it to my face and rush out of the room when I felt that horrible tight feeling in the chest which means you are so full of tears that nothing can stop them brimming over. In an attempt to prove that I was not cowardly I challenged the largest available bully to six rounds without gloves on—in any case there were no boxing gloves in the gym. Rather to my surprise she readily accepted, and agreed to fight me in the dormitory at midnight. When I said I would fetch my sweets from the cupboard in the dining-hall to provide refreshments for the ringside spectators, quite a number of girls said they would risk coming to watch. It was Strictly Forbidden to take your own sweets, or anyone else's and however lavish the box only three sweets were doled out after lunch each day by a mistress, and the rest left to go stale. I got my three boxes of chocolates, and a plum cake in a tin that Mother had sent the day before, without any difficulty because I had had plenty of experience of moving quietly through a darkened house.

About thirty girls, whispering and giggling, were in the dormitory when I got back, and helped me to move the furniture and mark out a ring on the linoleum with tooth-paste. My opponent was gloating, being four years older than me and two stones heavier, but I had behind me the incalculable weight of Sergeant-Major Spencer. I told her the Marquess of Queensberry's rules, or as much of them as I could remember, and she agreed to abide by them. If I had known her better I would have started with a penny in my fist, for she cheated abominably, scratched, kicked, bit, and even pulled my hair. Eventually I lost my temper and split my knuckles on the bridge of her nose. Her silly nose was not even broken though it streamed with blood. Instead of grinning when I tried to shake hands, she screeched, and one of the little beasts ran and fetched the headmistress. The headmistress dragged me by the hair to a bathroom and said I would spend the night there, locked in, and on my knees begging God to forgive me for my sins. Luckily there was a cupboard of clean bath towels; so I made myself a comfortable bed in the bath and enjoyed the first private and peaceful night since I came to school. I was feeling so virtuous that I knew God would be pleased, but I was not sure whether to thank Him or Sergeant-Major Spencer for my victory, so I thanked both.

A rumour that I had attacked the prefect unprovoked and while she was asleep soon spread through the school, and I was more unpopular than ever. I wrote anguished letters home, imploring them to take me away, but, though the possibility never occurred to me, the letters were destroyed by the mistress who censored them before stamping. Mother sent me a book called *Misunderstood*, about a boy to whom

50

everyone was horrid until he died, when they all felt dreadfully sorry.

As neither Father nor Mother even mentioned my misery in their letters, I should have to give them a sharp lesson, and this I could do by dying. Clearly in my mind's eye I saw myself lying in a coffin, while my hard-hearted parents knelt sobbing beside my bier, which was wreathed in luxurious white flowers. After their hearts were properly melted I would appear to them, an angelic and beautiful ghost, and smile my forgiveness before floating gracefully away to some happier realm where I would be fully appreciated. I was considering methods of putting this plan into operation—I disliked the sight of blood too much to open a vein in the bath like a Roman, and was too frightened of heights to relish throwing myself from the balcony—when a mistress provided the solution by saying that if I ran about without a dressing-gown I should catch my death of cold. I waited until the other girls were asleep and then went on to the balcony in my nightdress and poured a ewer of water over myself. It was freezing hard and I made myself stay outside until the nightdress froze enough to crackle. I was determined to make a really good job of getting pneumonia and not be left even more miserable with a streaming cold.

Except that having pneumonia rather badly is uncomfortable, the plan worked admirably. Mother fetched me away in an ambulance, and even though I was slightly delirious I knew she was giving the headmistress and the matron a good rich slice of the hell I had suffered in their boarding school.

CHAPTER NINE

night ∂uty

During most of the rest of the war years I was either at Sea-court, where I attended the Misses Baker's day-school, 'A Seminary for the Daughters of Gentlemen,' as it was des-cribed on a brass plate on the door; or an equally innocuous establishment at Brighton; where we briefly had a furnished house so that Father could come down from London every night. I was a model pupil to the point of smugness, winning good conduct prizes for punctuality and neatness. At Hayling I even joined in net-ball, which I considered such a ridiculous game that I was always thinking of something else when I was supposed to be running after the ball. English govern-nesses were unobtainable, at least by us, for they all much preferred war work, so I had Mademoiselles who were refu-gees. One of them was a kleptomaniac and another had worms.... 'Everybodee 'as worms,' she cried indignantly when challenged by Mother. 'Zee long ones, zee short ones, and zee little round ones—I 'ave them all.' She was sent off to a nursing-home to get rid of them, and her successor almost succeeded in getting Mother to banish Vodka, my bull terrier, from my bedroom. Vodka very naturally took a dislike to her, and so did Joey and Freddy, Mother's marmosets, who used to sit happily munching mealy worms on the picture-rail until she came through the door, and then take a flying leap on to her head. If she kept still I could disentangle them quite easily from her elaborate hair, but if she shrieked they were frightened and made messes, which put an end to French lessons for the rest of the evening as she took ages shampoo-ing it.

School and Mademoiselles were only the outer rind of my life at this period; what was happening to another part of my-self was far more difficult to tackle. In the ordinary way the war made little difference to me, for I had no close relations at the front. There had always been lots of visitors: now they wore uniform, for upwards of a dozen officers were billeted at Seacourt after a school of musketry was established on the island. Mother liked looking after sick people, so there was nothing unusual in having invalids and hospital nurses in the house, although now the patients had been wounded. But I began to have war dreams, which became increasingly detailed and vivid no matter how hard I tried to shut them out.

I used to find myself on a battlefield, grown-up and usually in the uniform of a Red Cross nurse, although occasionally I was a stretcher-bearer. I knew I had reported for duty and received specific orders; either to explain to a man who had just been killed that he was safely dead, or to encourage him to return to a body that was not due to die yet although it had been severely wounded.

At first the memory of the dreams was no more pleasant than it had been to remember going to the man whose feet had been cut off by a subway train, and I tried to remember them more clearly. Very soon I prayed not to remember them at all, but it was too late. I had to get so close to the person I was trying to help that I became part of him; feeling, seeing, fearing as he did, until I could slowly, so very slowly, instil my own faith into him and so free us both from the slough of pain and terror. I remember crawling through a sea of mud with blood trickling out of my mouth and ears. I remember lying in a shell-hole on top of a putrefying corpse with my arm blown off at the elbow. I remember hanging on rusty barbed-wire and trying to cram the slimy purple snakes of my guts into a hole in my belly.

If I tried to tell anyone about my dreams, it worried or even frightened them. I was an 'imaginative child'. The war must not be mentioned in my presence. I was forbidden to read newspapers....As though I wanted to read about the war! Iris tried to comfort me by saying that soldiers who were killed in battle went straight to heaven, and I tried to share her comfortable theory that the casualty lists were made up from people who had been shot neatly through the forehead or blown to bits like Billy.

I might have been able to convince myself that ordinary Joan was not exaggerating the horrors she saw if I had not seen the photographs taken by Glory Hancock. She was married to Father's first cousin, Mortimer, and was another of my favourite people. Since the very beginning of the war she had been a Red Cross nurse, working so close to the front line that she had won decorations for bravery that were usually awarded only to men.*

Early in August 1916 she came to Seacourt for a couple of nights to leave Westray, her son, with us for the summer holidays. He was two years older than I was, and had been a staunch ally since, at the age of six, he had thrown one of his football boots at a nanny who was deliberately pulling my hair. It hit her on the head and knocked her out. 'Glory is going to America on leave,' said Westray. 'Officially she is visiting Grandpa Battle in North Carolina, but why she is really going is to prod the Americans into helping us finish off the war.'

'How is she going to prod them?'

'With photographs—photographs she has taken in casualty clearing stations and hospitals. She doesn't know I've seen them but I have, and they are jolly ghastly.'

'Can I see them?'

'No, they would give you nightmares.'

'Nightmares!' I said scornfully. 'What do you know about nightmares?'

'These aren't nightmares. These are real wounded soldiers, soldiers whom Glory helped to operate on, and nursed, and some of them she had to sew up in blankets

* Chevalier Ordre Couronne with the title Comtesse Hellancourt, Croix Civique, Croix de Guerre Belge, Croix de Guerre Francaise avec Palme, Ordre d'Elizabeth.

to be buried when in spite of her they died.'

'I don't believe photographs can be nearly as awful as dreams. I dare you to show them to me.'

So he did. They were locked in Glory's suitcase but he knew where she kept the key.

When I was my real self in dreams I was sometimes very afraid, but I could face the fear and fight against it. When I woke up I was only Joan, a child not yet eleven, defenceless against the memory of sights, and fears, and smells. The smells were sometimes so persistent that I had to rush to the lavatory and be sick. To keep awake I used to pull down my pyjama trousers and sit on the cold strip of parquet in the doorway between the bedroom and the passage carpets, shifting to another cold patch when the first one grew warmer. I tweaked hairs out of my scalp. I pushed matches under my finger-nails. I held my eyelids open until the skin became so stretched that at the age of ten they were as creased as an old woman's. It took me a long time to learn that even when sleep appears to be an enemy it is useless to try to escape from it.

Trying to cut off my dream-life, I behaved as a smug little schoolgirl; for I longed to be safe and ordinary, a unit in a crocodile, a number in a class, a name cut with a penknife in an ink-stained desk. But the longing did not stop me dreaming. One morning I came down late to breakfast. There was a young man still at the table and no one else in the room. He was just another man in khaki, but the loneliness of keeping my dreams secret was so acute that I said, 'Somehow I know you will not laugh at me. Last night I was with a man called McAndrew when he was killed. I can describe the regimental badge although I cannot remember the name of the regiment, except that it was not an English one. And I can tell you the slang name of his trench.'

The young man did not laugh. Instead, he identified the regiment by my description. It was Canadian. Soon afterwards he wrote to Father, 'For heaven's sake don't

55

laugh at the child. I cannot attempt an explanation, but I have checked what she said. A battalion of that regiment went over the top on a night attack a few hours before she told me it at breakfast. A private called McAndrew was among the killed. She was even correct about the local name of the front-line trench.'

Father did not tell me about the letter until years later. I doubt if it would have helped much if he had. It became easier not to remember my dreams too vividly after Diana came to live with us because of the Zeppelin raids on London. She had been my best friend since before I broke my leg on my way to her birthday party. The summer holidays, when the Beddards took a furnished house at Hayling and I saw Diana and her brother Michael every day, were the best parts of the years; but it was even better having her staying at Seacourt.

When she was younger she wore frilly pinafores, which never got torn or dirty even though she climbed trees better than I did. Florence, her nurserymaid, brushed her long hair round a box-wood stick into ringlets glossy as barley sugar. Now she wore a velvet snood like Alice in Wonderland, but her blue eyes had the same guileless expression which had always come in so handy in defending us from grown-ups. After her first day at the Misses Baker's, she decided it would be a waste of time to continue to go to school. 'But how can we get out of it?' I said dubiously. 'I have only just got rid of the last Mademoiselle, and she was quite awful. Mother is letting your Florence look after me, but if she gets a governess for us...'

'Leave it to me,' said Diana briskly. 'Within forty-eight hours I shall be expelled. Then we can have a daily governess like I have in London. They leave directly after lessons and are practically no trouble.'

I doubted whether she would manage it, for I had never achieved such a simple solution in spite of all my efforts at boarding school. I underrated Diana. Next morning after Prayers she laid herself neatly down on a mat in the entrance hall of the school and began to scream. She screamed when mistresses gathered to ask what was the matter. She screamed when children flocked from the classroom to stare. She screamed when the parents of a prospective pupil came to the front door and then hurried away without even waiting to interview either of the Misses Baker. The only time she stopped screaming was during the lunch hour. The moment the gong went she walked calmly downstairs, washed her face and hands, and ate every morsel on her plate; so that the mistresses could not comfort themselves by thinking she had a stomach-ache.

The second day she followed the same routine. Miss Baker gave me a note to Mother. It implored her to remove the 'difficult child who is staying with dear little Joan, as we fear she is not having a good influence on the other girls'. Mother was so offended at this gratuitous insult to the angelic daughter of dear Maud that never again did either of us pass through the portals of the Seminary for the Daughters of Gentlemen.

Our daily governess came from Portsmouth every day by the ferry and was a kind old thing, so we were very nice to her. It was a blow when the raids stopped—or else people got so used to them that they were ignored—and Diana went back to London. Father had been in Birmingham helping 'Skipper' Wilson to invent the Tanks, but now he was back in London, so in September 1918 we all went to a furnished maisonette in Baker Street. There was no room for a resident governess, and Mother decided to send me as a day-girl to a convent in Cavendish Square. I had been baptised twice, once as a Roman Catholic by a fervent one who happened to be staying in the house when I was a baby, and whisked me round to her church to save my soul when she discovered that Father had no intention of having me christened; and a second time C. of E., as he thought that the two ceremonies, both of which he considered barbarous, would cancel each other out.

The only nun I knew was Sister Arsene, who was the

theatre-sister in the French Hospital in London. One of the consulting physicians there, Dr. Septimus Sunderland, who had been Mother's doctor when I was born, used to send her to us when she needed a rest. The first time she came cannot have been very restful, as it was to nurse me during the first month after I broke my leg. I loved her, for she was very sympathetic about nightmares and gave me a picture of an angel which she said would protect me when I was asleep by standing at the head of my bed, and a medal of Sister Therese of Liseaux who was called The Little Flower because she sent down roses from heaven which turned into miracles. So I expected to be happy in a convent.

But I was not happy. I was terrified. The nuns with their black rosaries jangling in the folds of their black habits, the echoing underground tunnel which joined the two houses in Cavendish Square, the shapeless black overalls we had to wear, formed the background of a terror which was all the more dreadful because it was illogical. Why was I so frightened? The nuns were kind. The other girls did not bully me. The lessons were easy. Why did I feel that something horrible was going to happen to me there?

I did not find out that the thing I feared belonged not to the future but to the sixteenth century until I was writing *Life as Carola* nearly twenty years later. All I could then do was to pray frantically to escape the daily purgatory of the walk down Wigmore Street, the horror of the doors closing behind me. On the eleventh day my prayers were answered, by my catching Spanish Influenza.

We all got it except Mother, who looked after us all as so many people in London had it that we could not get a nurse. The maid died and her body turned black before the undertaker could come to take it away. Iris nearly died too, of double pneumonia.

By the beginning of November we had all more or less recovered, and on the eleventh of the month I was walking down Baker Street with Margery when suddenly I heard maroons going off. I felt tears trickling down my face. 'The war is over!' said Margery, and I saw that she was crying too.

Through streets which were filled with cheering people we all went that night to the Criterion Restaurant and had a table in the window overlooking Piccadilly Circus. With us was Dickie Pettle, whom Margery had been in love with since he came to Seacourt to be nursed after being very badly wounded. He had not asked her to marry him, and I knew this had made her unhappy. Quite suddenly in the middle of dinner he raised his glass of champagne and said in front of everybody, 'Margery, please will you marry me? I couldn't ask you while the war was still on as I was afraid of being wounded again and landing you with a cripple.'

She said, 'Oh, yes, Dickie!' And the rest of us tactfully went out on to the balcony and left them together. It seemed that everyone in London was in Piccadilly Circus that night, kissing, singing, cheering, dancing, climbing lamp-posts, clinging to Eros. But some of the bravely dancing people were crying: for them the end of the war must have come too late.

PART TWO

CHAPTER ONE

Intimations of mortality

Iris had been unofficially engaged to Ronald Kershaw since she was eighteen, but, as he was in the R.A.F., Mother did not consider him 'a good match', and so she had to wait to marry him until she was twenty-one. I enjoyed being her bridesmaid—the wedding was from Emilie Grigsby's house in Brook Street—but now she had gone I should have been more lonely than usual if the Workman family had not come to live in Hayling. I was very fond of them all, although Kirsteen, who was three years older than me, and Tommy who was my contemporary, were my special allies.

Kirsteen was at a boarding school in Scotland and seemed to like it there, but I had no intention of going to one again so I jumped at the suggestion that I should have lessons with Mr. Lewis. He was a crammer, and until Mother bullied him into taking me, his pupils were all boys. She did it, I think, to give herself a breather from Mademoiselles and governesses.

There were eight boys of thirteen or fourteen, being forcibly fed with information after having failed to get into Public Schools through the front door, and four older ones who were trying to pass into Sandhurst. At first the younger ones bullied and the older ignored me, so after about a fortnight I decided to do something about it.

Dividers fixed to the forearm with two strong elastic bands, leaving the spikes protruding half an inch beyond the point of the elbow, were a stroke of genius. The spikes were concealed by my jersey, but a sharp nudge brought a startled yelp from an offending neighbour. It would not have been fair to let them suffer more than a cold glance or biting sarcasm from Mr. Lewis, so when danger from that quarter threatened I would stare wide-eyed at my victim and say, 'I think poor Derek—or Cecil—or Valentine—has been stung by a wasp,' and produce in evidence a dead one which I had tucked under the leg elastic of my bloomers.

I tried different tactics on the older boys, and managed to make two of them believe that I had been cruelly bullied by the other, and so enticed them into fighting a duel; at least it was a duel in my imagination, though it was only a fist-fight behind the shrubbery, which ended in one of them getting a black eye and the other a nose-bleed.

For two happy days my rival champions vied with each other to do my prep for me, but on the third morning I found they had been caddish enough to compare notes and were bent on revenge. 'We shall catch you on your way home and give you a thrashing, you little beast', they hissed at me during elevenses. Probably they only intended to give me the fright I deserved, but I believed I was in danger of something close to murder. It might even *be* murder! If so, as I glumly decided during that interminable afternoon's lessons, it would be little satisfaction to know that they would hang— even if I were waiting at the bottom of the drop.

I achieved a fifty yard start by climbing out of the cloakroom window and over the garden wall, but they were lurking by the gate and saw me before I turned the corner. Terror gave me a turn of speed, but I knew I would never keep it up until I reached the haven of the back gate into Seacourt. So I dodged into a nursery garden and hid in a cucumber frame. Luckily there were plenty of leaves on the plants and the glass was whitewashed, so they never found me; although I heard them prowling around and muttering dire threats, like Mr. McGregor after Peter Rabbit. For the next week I had to pretend to have a strained ankle so that Wilson could drive me back and forth to school. Then the other two big boys took pity on me and provided a bicycle escort.

Mr. Lewis, who for a long time had been crippled by arthritis, gave up taking pupils at the end of the year. So once again I had a series of governesses—tired old women who had forgotten how to teach, but 'were no trouble in the house and looked after the linen.'

Then, in January 1921, Father went to Pau to play tennis and took Mother and me with him. He only intended to stay a fortnight, but developed a virulent type of local 'flu and so eventually we stayed there nearly three months. The Mademoiselle hired to take me for walks was sad and spotty, but the days were enlivened by playing Jeu de Paume with a young Basque pro on whom I secretly doted, and being flattered by elderly Frenchmen, who, never having seen a female play the game, used to make congratulatory noises from the dedans and give me bunches of carnations.

Mother suddenly remembered that when, four years earlier, Iris had nearly died from blood-poisoning after pricking her thumb on a rose bush, she had recovered—after three operations—when Sister Arsene sent her a bottle of holy water from the Grotto at Lourdes. It now seemed clear to Mother that Father's illness was due to she and Iris having failed to make a pilgrimage of gratitude to Lourdes; to her it did not seem at all illogical that God would vent His annoyance with them on Father. So Iris was sent for, and came reluctantly because she had to leave poor Ronald all alone at Calshot.

I was eager to go to Lourdes for I believed then, as I do now even more strongly, in miracles and hoped to see one happen. But Lourdes was a bitter disappointment. It poured with rain and Iris's shoes were so wet that Mother insisted on stopping on the way to the church to buy her a dry pair, which were a size too small and of very ugly patent leather. Father, who was always acutely embarrassed in any religious building, peered dutifully at the votive offerings on the walls and tried to pretend he was only in a museum. The Grotto itself was even more depressing. Two very grimy old women were washing their ulcerated sores in the pool and from it another was filling a medicine bottle. The hanging crutches clattered in the cheerless wind—so few crutches for all the thousands upon thousands of faithful who had been there. 'I hope people have the sense to boil the water before they drink it,' muttered Father fretfully, 'or it really will be a miracle if they don't catch each other's diseases.'

'Some have been cured here,' I whispered back, 'or there wouldn't be any crutches.'

'God, if he exists at all, which I very much doubt—as must any sane man who considers the appalling cruelty and misery which exists in the world—must be ubiquitous,' said Father.

'He is. But people don't believe it. They have to have labels for everything before it is real to them....They want everything real to be solid, and it never is.'

My voice trailed away into the silence, broken only by a party of monks with sad, pinched faces, rattling the beads of their rosaries. It was a very lonely day.

On the way back to England we spent a fortnight in Paris, where Mother had laryngitis and Father nearly walked me off my feet round museums. The evenings were much gayer as he felt that after the bread and butter of culture I had earned the cake of the Folies Bergeres or the Moulin Rouge instead of finishing the day at the Opera or the Comedie Francaise. Trying to make myself look less like a schoolgirl, I bought myself a lipstick and used it lavishly; which Father let me do so long as I wiped it off before we went back to the hotel. The lipstick proved to be an error, for I put it on when Mother reluctantly let me go alone to look at shop windows in the Rue St. Honore and the Rue de Rivoli when Father was busy.

'Frenchmen have such nice natures,' I said cheerfully at luncheon. 'It really pleases them when someone else looks happy.'

'How do you know?' enquired Mother suspiciously.

'Because when I smile at them they smile back, and six times this morning I have been called *une jolie petite fille de joie.* ''A daughter of joy,'' isn't that a nice way of saying ''so glad you are happy!'''

Mother pursed her lips and frowned at Father who went red with suppressed laughter. 'It is not at all funny, Jack,' she said severely.

'What's the joke?' I asked anxiously. But they did not tell me, and it was a long time before I ceased to resent the parental decision that I was not to go out alone again in Paris.

Father had treated me as an equal even when I was a small child, but now he did me the honour of keeping me with him when the women went to the drawing-room after dinner. If there were no visitors we played chess, to be praised if I managed to win one game in five, to be called a Boiled Owl if I missed an obvious move. He was delighted when I could visualise the game well enough to play it without looking at the board.

A lot of conversation to which I listened while the men drank their port was over my head, but as I had a photographic memory for dialogue, fragments of many objects gradually fitted together and formed a wide if somewhat chaotic pattern. The square root of minus one, the prospects of splitting the atom, sociology, developments in physics, in medical technique, to all these I listened absorbedly, for as they were of interest to Father they were of enormous importance to me, a source of knowledge which, if I could only acquire it, would make him as proud of me as though I had been his son. Sir Richard Gregory, F.R.S., the editor of *Nature*, a lifelong friend of H.G. Wells; Sir Theodore Cook, editor of *The Field*, with one blind eye and a rich fund of good stories; C.G. Lamb, Professor of Engineering at Cambridge, whom I loved more than all the others; Tommy Horder, later to become Lord Horder, the Royal Physician, who said to me, 'Never believe blindly in doctors, Joan, but use your critical faculty. I am the greatest diagnostician in England, and hundreds of my diagnoses are wrong.' To them all, and to many others among my father's friends I shall always be grateful that they talked, and let me listen, and never seemed to mind my being there.

The only one with whom I did not have to pretend to be a boy or an embryo scientist was Mr. Lamb. He had never seen a ghost, but Psychical Research was a hobby nearly as dear to him as collecting rare beetles. He had been a friend of Jennie's and told me that if my grandfather had let her become a concert pianist she would have been world-famous.

'Jennie gives me music lessons,' I said, suddenly no longer shy to talk about it. 'Father knows I would never be a first-class pianist so there is no point in my having lessons, but Jennie knows I need music and she teaches me. Sometimes she plays the piano with me—music that is quite different to the ordinary tunes I have learned.'

As I was speaking I knew that Jennie was in the room with us, so I went to her piano. Music, strong, passionate music, flowed out of my hands. With the last crashing chord she left me. Mr. Lamb looked pale and mopped his forehead. 'Extraordinary,' he said. 'Quite extraordinary but completely evidential. Do you know...No, of course you don't, how could you? That what you have just played was often played to me by your grandmother...I have not heard it since she died.'

'Perhaps I heard it at one of Mrs. Workman's concerts. She often has pianists staying at Gothic Lodge.'

'That you most certainly did not do. Only one copy of that music ever existed. It was given in manuscript to the Czar of Russia, who sent it to your grandmother. I have a very accurate ear, although I play the piano not as a musician but as a mathematician operating a pianola.'

'Then I must have heard Jennie play it when I was a baby, and remembered it. Babies remember far more than grownups give them credit for.'

He took out his tobacco pouch and carefully rolled a cigarette before answering. His hands were shaking and he spilled shreds of tobacco on his black alpaca jacket.

'Infantile memory would be the logical explanation, if in this instance it were possible to take refuge in logic. However, I happen to know that the manuscript of that music, together with several other manuscripts of similar value, was burned two years before you were born. I did my best to dissuade your grandmother from taking such drastic action, but she said, ''My dear Mr. Lamb, no one else shall play my music now that I know that I shall never be able to play the piano again.''' There were tears in his eyes and he blew his nose loudly to hide his emotion. 'Until after you were born I was the only person except her doctor who knew she was suffering inoperable cancer...it had already spread from her breast to her right arm. Jennie Marshall was not only a great musician, she was a very heroic woman. Thank you for convincing me that she is still alive.'

CHAPTER TWO

planchette

'Joan shall be the first woman undergraduate to get a First in the Mechanical Science Tripos,' decided Father and Mr. Lamb. And I was so eager to make them proud of me that I accepted the assignment, as I would have done if they had wanted me to try to become a trapeze artiste or ride a bicycle on the high wire.

'But I must have a governess who at least knows enough to get me through Little Go,' I reminded them. For they were already happily visualising their entry romping home in the Scholastic Stakes because Mr. Lamb, who both set and judged the course, would have trained their filly by coaching it in the evenings, so handicapping all the other starters.

I was prepared to put up with a grim, uncongenial blue-stocking, probably with steel-rimmed spectacles and a strong moustache. But instead, Miss Griffiths came. She was beautiful in a black-haired Celtic way, and so small that she only reached to my shoulder. She bubbled with vitality, and I loved her; for she made the dull alloy of text-books shine like steel. For nearly a month we kept strictly to our roles of Governess and Pupil. Then one evening I found her running headlong down the passage from the music-room; and I knew she was more frightened of the haunt than I was myself. 'So you feel it too, Griffy!' I exclaimed. I had never presumed to call her anything less formal than Miss Griffiths before.

She rolled up her right sleeve. I had noticed that she always wore long sleeves even in the evening, but thought this was only because she had not expected to be living in an overheated house. A hairy birthmark, as large and as black as a bat, enfolded her right elbow. 'I was born in a Welsh village, with the blood of the Princes of Cymry in my veins,' she said in her lilting, musical voice. 'The midwife told my mother that this mark on me is the sign of a witch. Almost the first thing I can remember is being taught to hide it even from other children....It is, of course, only superstition—but it is lonely being feared as a witch, so I became a mathematician.'

'Oh darling Griffy,' I said, hugging her. 'We ought to be better witches because we can do trigonometry; and neither of us need be shy about it now there are two of us having to be much cleverer than we want to be.'

We tried to tackle the haunt in a scientific manner. Griffy, who had read a lot of books on psychical research, bought a planchette, a little triangular board with a wheel at two of its angles and a pencil stuck through a hole at the third. We took turns at resting our fingers on it very lightly and waiting for it to do 'automatic writing'. For me it never moved. For her it wrote with increasing vehemence, at first in such large, sprawling letters that it rushed off the edge of its foolscap and skidded on the polished table, or dug its pencil into the cloth. Then we gave it double sheets of drawer paper, until it learned to write neatly in three quite different kinds of hand-writing. The third of these went from right to left and when it first started we thought it must be from someone who had been Chinese, until we found it was only Latin written upside down.

The most interesting of the three writers, and the one who came the most often, was a girl who had been drowned for witchcraft at the end of the seventeenth century, when she was twenty-three. Looking back, I think it must have been an earlier version of Griffy herself, but oddly enough this did not occur to either of us at the time. She too had a birthmark, which caused people to come to her in search of the old wisdom. She made love potions, which worked because no one would have dared to consult a witch in those days unless they wanted love enough to make it come true. She very seldom cast spells, and then only greyish ones, such as putting warts on a woman who was cruel to cats.

It was after the bit about warts that it occurred to us that if warts could be put on by witches they could be taken off by the same means. This was relevant as Iris had four on the sole of her foot which had been burned out or cut out, and were still as painful as ever after a year. There was an old cowman on Hayling Island—he was over seventy and had never been to the mainland, who was said to have wart magic. So I persuaded Mother to let him try to cure Iris. All he did was to rub her foot gently with some green leaves and mutter an incantation under his breath. He refused to accept any money and seemed offended at it being offered. Within three days the warts fell out and she never had any trouble with them again.

The efficiency of the wart-magic encouraged us to try to de-haunt the music-room. Planchette was rather vague about the procedure and was apt to ramble off into Latin, which was tiresome as some of the words it used were not in our diction-ary. We decided to make our attempt on Midsummer Eve, when there was a full moon, and the parents were away in London. We made a pentacle with white tape secured to the

floor by new brass drawing-pins. At each point of the pentacle there had to be protective herbs, but as we could not
obtain all the ones the Latin-writer wanted we had to make
do with the nearest botanical equivalent, and use spring
onions instead of garlic. The seven silver candlesticks were
easy as I knew where Mother kept the key of the silver chest.
At first we could not understand why seven were needed
when there are only five points to a pentacle, but planchette
pointed out rather crossly that the other two were to be held
by us, 'within the protection.' The candles should have been
of 'pure wax,' which Griffy said meant bees-wax as opposed
to tallow dips, which, being of animal fat, were impure.
Making candles from bees-wax turned out to be too difficult.
It took ages even to make thin ones, and the wicks would not
burn properly, so we had to use 'Price's self-fitting: sixes'.

We spring-cleaned the music-room and put a lot of flowers
in it. Luckily we had chosen the day of the local fete, so we
let all the maids go to it and told them they could stay as late
as they liked at the dance afterwards. We cleaned the candlesticks, first with Goddard's plate-powder and then, following instructions, I gave them a final polish, 'on the white
thighs of a virgin'. Then we washed our hair, cut our nails
short, and had specially long hot baths with a lot of scent in
the water: 'The devil hateth sweet smells.' I even gave
Vodka a bath just to be on the safe side. She hated the music-
room, so I shut her in my bedroom in case she got worried
about me and came scratching at the door to interrupt us at a
crucial moment. If I had been more experienced I should have
kept her with me, for dogs are quick to pick up warnings of
danger, like canaries in submarines.

Supper was only green vegetables as we were fasting.
Griffy said fasting would be an added protection. By eleven-
thirty I was longing for the maids to come back so we could
use them as an excuse not to go on with it. The moon was
shining on the rose-garden when we drew the heavy red curtains across the seven windows. 'Are you sure we couldn't

leave even one window!' I said. But Griffy was adamant. 'All the books say ghosts materialise much more easily in a closed room.'

I was thankful that the rite required candles, for it would have been unbearable to have stayed there in the dark. For nearly an hour the candles burned clearly, and I had begun to feel confident that nothing was going to happen. Then, quite suddenly my heart began to thud and I could feel cold sweat trickling down my body. Griffy was shuddering so I knew she felt it too. In a trembling voice she began to recite the Lord's Prayer. Terror was like a black wall around us, shutting us into a prison—no, worse, into a grave. The candles streamed in an icy draught and guttered out. I heard myself scream, 'Run, Griffy! Run!' Blindly in the thick darkness we ran, knocking over a candlestick, stumbling up the stairs to the gallery, clawing at the door into the passage until at last we found the handle.

We both spent the rest of the night in my room, with Vodka on the bed between us and all the lights on. And for the first time we heard the ghost grumbling and hating along the passage, pacing slowly and heavily as far as my bedroom door. An hour after dawn we collected enough courage to go and tidy up the music-room. In the cold daylight the pentacle only looked rather silly.

When I heard that Sir Oliver Lodge and his wife were coming to stay, Griffy and I were very relieved. Although to Father he was the famous physicist we had read his book *Raymond*, about how he was often in contact with the son who had been killed in the war, and we thought he would be able to cure the haunt. I hardly liked to mention it to him for several days as he seemed not to notice anything odd in the room; but eventually I did, after making him promise not to say anything to the parents. I told him an expurgated version, as I was afraid that he might think Griffy was an unsuitable governess if he knew she had encouraged me to tackle spooks.

'Do you see anything there?' he asked with his kindly smile.

'I don't often *see* it, thank goodness—only a few times. He is a monk with cold blue eyes. They seem to glitter in the shadow of his cowl, which is always drawn forward over his forehead. But I often feel him—and so do other people, and hear footsteps. The footsteps are sometimes worse than anything else. I know it sounds silly, having a monk in such a modern house.'

'Not at all,' he said consolingly. 'The uneasy spirit has no knowledge of any building subsequent to his own time. I could quote dozens of examples.' He did, and I found it most reassuring for a great scientist to talk so naturally about things which I had learned to keep private except with Griffy.

'But you promise not to tell my parents? It worries them when I see things that other people don't see; and life will be much easier when they think I've grown out of it.'

'Certainly I will promise. I think the best thing I can do is to suggest to your Mother that she has some seances with a medium I have recently been investigating, a Mrs. Johnstone. She will almost certainly get in touch with your ghost, and once he has been able to tell his story he will, no doubt, cease troubling you all.'

Mrs. Johnstone came, and stayed for a fortnight. But in spite of all her props...a trumpet which was put under running water from the bath tap to 'refresh the control's voice', a red shaded night-light, hymns on the gramophone, the only 'manifestation' she produced was her own voice varied by rather clever ventriloquy. There were usually about a dozen 'sitters'. All of them, except Griffy and I, who sensed there was nothing less solid than Mrs. Johnstone and her trumpet behind the 'phenomena', and Father, whose critical faculty was far too keen to be blunted by mumbo jumbo, in all sincerity signed papers for forwarding to the Society for Psychical Research, attesting that the medium was genuine because they had heard her voice and her control's speaking simultaneously.

A year later, after quarrelling with Sir Oliver, Mrs. Johnston boasted to him of the fact that she was a fraud who had been vastly amused at the gullibility of himself and his fellow investigators.

Other mediums, amateur and professional, came to Seacourt in the next few months. Spiritualism was fashionable at the time, and in the most ordinary households 'table turning' was an after-dinner game as an alternative to bridge or Mah Jong. But those who were not bogus only had a small talent which was fast disintegrating under the necessity of trying to keep appointments with the disembodied, as though genuine intuition were as immediately available as a rabbit placidly nibbling lettuce in a conjuror's hat. Then Mr. Meade, a stevedore from Portsmouth Dockyard, was brought to Seacourt by someone who was only too accurately convinced of his supernormal powers. Poor little man, he became so easily possessed by the uneasy dead that it was painful to see his body jerk and writhe as they used his tongue to pour forth a stream of Arabic, or Hindustani, or Ancient Greek, with a fluency which convinced the most hardened and erudite sceptics.

To everyone except Griffy and me this was proof of the immortality they craved. To us, who could sense the quality of the source, it was a demonstration by demons. We prayed desperately to be given the power to protect his body and sustain his soul against invaders; but we were not strong enough. All I could do during his last seance, held in full daylight with thirty people present in the music-room, was to leap to my feet and make the sign of the cross, which brought him, gasping and twitching, out of his trance. I implored him to listen to me, to promise never again to let his body be possessed. 'The gates are now locked against the demons unless you of your own free will reopen them to the enemy,' I declared passionately.

I was given a sharp lecture by Mother for speaking of subjects of which I knew nothing, and Father told me not to make an ass of myself in public. But for three months Mr. Meade did not give any more seances. Then, I suppose he could no longer resist the sense of importance they brought into his drab little life, or the three guineas he charged for hiring his body to the ungodly, for he wrote to Mother saying that he had once again resumed his bookings for 'trance sittings.' The same day he wrote the letter he went into a trance while walking along a girder in the dockyard. He fell forty feet, not to die, but to linger for years in a hopelessly crippled body with a mind insane from a skull fracture.

After Mr. Meade, the ghost became more tangible even to stalwart non-believers. The maids would not enter the music-room to draw the curtains, unless two of them went with the lights full on. A hearty Rugger International, who cheerfully accepted my 5 pound wager that he would not sleep there all night, fled from the room at 2 a.m., although a proper bed had been taken there for him so that he could not pretend he got cramp sleeping on the sofa. A visiting coleopterist hastily left after what he swore must have been a ton weight crashed to the floor within three feet of him—'And nothing fell although I heard it!' he muttered to me as with trembling hands he packed his precious beetles into a specimen-case.

Griffy was so afraid that she only dared to sleep with a large ebony cross clasped to her chest. We burned the planchette, and everything it had written, in the schoolroom fire. And I decided to try to become a safe, competent, scientific materialist.

CHAPTER THREE
Incompetence of witches

Mother, who easily became tired of people, now took a dislike to Griffy; so I worked even harder so that there could be no excuse for her being sacked. So long as Mr. Lamb continued to write glowing letters to Father about the results of the papers he set me every two or three months, Griffy would be safe. Even when I had taken Little Go, at sixteen, she would still have to stay for another year until I was old enough to go to Girton; for I was to work at a programme arranged by Mr. Lamb which would give me a twelve months' start on the other first-year undergratuates who were taking the same Tripos.

It was January, and I was still only fifteen, when Iris came back alone from Malta, where Ronald had been stationed for two years, to have her first baby at Seacourt. For a few days she resisted being treated as a half-witted invalid. Then she submitted to fussing, footstools, and having her bulge disguised with chiffon scarves. Women who until then had seemed perfectly ordinary human beings, now revealed themselves as ghouls. Symptoms they had suffered, the more squalid the better, seemed to confer on them the right to scare poor Iris; and I did my best to defend her by staying within earshot whenever they came to call and trying to shut them up by asking direct and intimate personal questions. With one pious lady, who told Iris that it was 'Our Dear Lord's Will' that she should suffer torments, I lost my temper, which led to me having a considerable row from Mother.

Iris knew very little more than I did about what actually happens when a baby is born. Even the doctor would only say, with false jollity, 'You leave it all to me—you'll know all about it soon enough.'

'Don't let's think about it,' said Iris pathetically. 'But I

74

do so wish Ronald was here so that he could make me believe that having a baby is perfectly natural. '

Griffy was a broken reed, for being unmarried and forty-two, babies were a subject which she steadfastly put out of her mind. Fragments of information casually dropped by Mother were equally unsatisfactory. The baby ought to emerge head first, but even this was uncertain as there was something dire called a 'breech' which could occur only too easily if the expectant mother failed to Take Care, or even ran too quickly upstairs. It was useless to consult Father, for about childbirth he was neither knowledgeable nor even interested; so I searched the library until I found a text-book on gynecology. After two long sessions with it I put it back on the shelf, and decided that Iris would be far better off without any of the information I had gleaned from its terrifying and almost incomprehensible case-histories.

I began to regret the absence of the planchette, until I remembered that the poor little witch had died a virgin—she often mentioned this fact as though it were very meritorious—and the other two writers had been elderly men. I tried to remember if I had had a baby in an earlier life, but the Greek runner and the young woman who had been guillotined, the Red-Indian girl and the Roman one who had taught me how to collect my tears in a medicine bottle, were as barren of the required information as Joan herself.

Iris prayed, and so did Griffy and I, that Ronald would be home before the baby was born. But Mother wanted the field to herself, without a son-in-law claiming even a corner of it: and her prayers were the more effective. The day he was due to leave Malta the word flashed round the house that the Pains had started. Griffy and I were banished to our sitting-room. The doctor arrived. Father locked himself in his study. The maids huddled on the back stairs listening, except when they heard Mother coming along the passage.

Hours passed. I took charge of the commissariat, sending up trays at intervals for the nurse and doctor, and taking others to leave discreetly outside Father's study door. More hours passed. Griffy tried to send me to bed but was glad of company when I told her not to be silly.

I was lurking at the far end of the passage when I heard the doctor's voice speaking sharply to Mother. She came out of the room and hurried past me with tears in her eyes. Had something terrible happened? Was Iris or the baby dead? No, if they were dead she would have gone to Father instead of shutting herself in her dressing-room. Perhaps there was something I could do to help....Anyway, if the doctor told me to clear off it would be better than lurking in doorways and suspense. The doctor seemed quite pleased to see me. He was busy and so was the nurse, who was dripping chloroform from a bottle on to a gauze pad she was holding over Iris's face. Iris was snoring and moaning at the same time. Then the doctor held the baby up by its heels and it began to cry. He fiddled with its middle and then wrapped it in a towel and handed it to me. 'Take it to your mother and tell her she has got a granddaughter. And tell her I will let her know when she can come back in here.'

I took the baby into the nursery next door, put it in the middle of the nurse's bed as I was frightened of dropping it, and sent a maid to fetch Mother. Mother was very pleased with the baby, especially as it was a girl, which she had predicted. Iris and Ronald both wanted a boy. Then I remembered Griffy, and found her huddling miserably by the fire. When I told her it was a girl she burst into tears. 'Oh, poor Mrs. Kershaw, she wanted a boy so much! Why wasn't the doctor quick enough, or did he deliberately refuse to do it because your mother wanted a girl?'

'Do what?'

She blushed, and then resolutely blew her nose. 'Refuse to turn it inside-out.'

'Turn *what* inside-out?'

'Dear child, why must you always insist on being so explicit? I suppose I ought to really not tell you, but as you have already seen so much...'

'Griffy, darling. Please don't hedge!'

She put on her 'imparting information' voice. 'Baby boys and girls, like men and women, have different reproductive organs: but these are the same thing in reverse, inside-out in the case of boys, outside-in in the case of girls. If a doctor is competent he can turn them in or out—so long as he does so immediately the baby is born—before the organ has time to set, which it does, like jelly, soon after it comes into contact with the air.'

I felt guilty for not having read the gynecology book more carefully. If I had not funked studying the text that went with the pictures I should have been able to see that everything was done properly: by now I would have converted a niece into a nephew.

'Griffy, are you quite sure? What about people who keep on trying to have heirs for earldoms. They would have clever doctors...'

'Some people are too superstitious to allow this simple operation to be performed. Roman Catholics, and Masons too, I believe, are quite adamant against it. But it never occurred to me that your mother would be so prejudiced. I thought she prided herself on her medical knowledge, otherwise I should have warned your poor dear sister to make sure that her doctor was enlightened and competent.' She hugged me. 'You have behaved splendidly, darling, and I am very proud of you. There is nothing so important in the training of character as a thorough grounding in scientific method.'

'Witches seem to know even less than scientists about having babies,' I said forlornly. 'Oh damn! What is the use of remembering bits of who you were before if you don't remember anything really useful?' If I had known what needless additional misery I was to suffer, less than four years later, through ignorance of natural processes, I should have felt even more forlorn.

A fortnight later the war between Mother and Griffy flared

up into such a blazing row that it burned up my education in a single day. Mother sacked her and I went to Father and announced that if she went I would never do lessons of any kind again.

He was appalled. 'You are going to Cambridge. You must go to Cambridge. Everything is arranged.'

'Then tell Mother that Miss Griffiths is to stay at least until I have passed Little Go.'

'There are other governesses,' he protested. 'You had dozens before you took a fancy to this Welsh woman.'

I had never felt quite so angry or so determined before. 'Father, you can choose between my education or giving in to Mother. You cannot have both.'

'My dear child, you cannot, must not, force such a choice on me. It is your mother's business, not mine, whom she considers suitable as your governess. She has never got on with Miss Griffiths...'

'But I have! For her, and for you, I have worked my guts out. I have done three years' work in fifteen months...'

'Your work has been excellent. Lamb thinks you may be a mathematical genius.'

'Then let Miss Griffiths stay. If she goes, I give you my word of honour that I will never open another text-book, never go to Cambridge, never even sit for an exam.'

'And, my God, you mean it!' he said despairingly, and walked off to Mother's room. They argued for hours; and Mother won. Griffy left in tears next morning, a fortnight before my sixteenth birthday. And that was the end of my scholastic eduation.

CHAPTER FOUR

mino unoer matter

I made it quite clear that for Mother to engage another governess would be a waste of the booking fee and the return fare, so, as my refusal to go to Cambridge had revived her hope of sending me, like Margery, to a finishing school in Paris, she got me a French maid. At first, recollecting my battles against Mademoiselles, I was a little wary of Marie; but in spite of her pride in the frilliest of caps and aprons and her unfailing efforts to make me take trouble about my clothes, we soon got on very well together and chatted happily, each in her own language. She took her 'maiding' seriously, always insisted on running my bath and then washing my back before holding out the bath towel in which she patted me dry. The other maids, whom she despised for their lack of chic, were rather unkind to her, and so, to cheer her up, I let her manicure my nails and polish my toe-nails, and as she was 'an excellent needlewoman' she made embroidered nightgowns for Mother and taught me to sew.

She stayed with me for two years and then went to Glory Hancock. Mortimer's regiment was stationed at Aldershot, whence she wrote me a vivid description of her *grand succes* at a dance in the Sergeants' Mess. 'Certainly, my dearest Mademoiselle, I shall find myself a husband who is a military man.' But her plans for the future were drastically revised by appendicitis, the onset of which was so swift that she had to be taken to the Military Hospital in the middle of the night. Soldiers' wives were admitted in cases of emergency, but when Glory went to the women's ward the following morning Marie was not there. Nor was she in any of the private wards. Glory, now thoroughly alarmed, was about to investigate the mortuary when a nurse recognised her. 'If you are looking for the emergency you brought in last night,

Mrs. Hancock, he is in C Ward. I have got screens round him, but Matron thinks it might be better to put him in a private room.'

'Him! What are you talking about?'

The surgeon was summoned, and explained that during the operation a kind of tuck had come undone which demonstrated beyond doubt that Marie was a man.

Marie, now Marius, stayed with Glory until he was used to wearing the suits and shirts, the socks and ties, with which she outfitted him for his new role. She helped him to write a letter breaking the news to his elderly parents. Fortunately they were delighted to hear that God, who in spite of their prayers for an heir had provided them with eight daughters, had suddenly relented and supplied a grown-up son. After he returned to France, Marius sent me photographs of his wedding. He made a very handsome bridegroom, and a year later his wife presented him with twins. I did not show the photographs to Mother, although they amused Father enormously, because she was still rather touchy when any of her friends mentioned 'Joan's French valet.'

Marie was still Marie when Father suddenly decided that as he was taking a tennis side to play against Cambridge during May Week I should go with them.

'But not to the dances,' said Mother firmly. 'She isn't Out yet. Sixteen is far too young.'

It was his turn to put his foot down and he did so with unusual success. 'It is not my fault that she has decided to curtail her scholastic education. Therefore she had better put up her hair and stop pretending to be a schoolgirl.'

As he had only given Mother three days' notice she was displeased, and so, instead of taking me to London to buy clothes, my dress for the Trinity Ball was run up by Miss Seely, the family sewing-maid. Miss Seely was a friend of mine, and read me the most remarkable stories from the *News of the World*, which turned even an escorted journey to London into an imaginary adventure. Behind every bookstall, under every railway carriage seat, lurked White Slavers intent on carrying off nice young girls like me to Buenos Aires. The White Slavers were sometimes disguised as hospital nurses who lured you into an ambulance, in which you were chloroformed on the way to the docks; or as dear old ladies who proffered bags of acid drops so heavily doped that you never woke until you reached the nameless horrors in store in South America. She was not explicit about the horrors, but shuddered when she thought of them until her orange wig trembled like a rook's nest in a gale. 'Do not ask me to enlarge, Miss Joan, dear, but promise me, if it should ever happen, that you will throw yourself from the window and die bravely, impaled upon the area railings, rather than suffer a fate far worse than death.'

Dear Miss Seely—she was at least seventy. And if her stories had any first-hand knowledge behind them, certainly she had never been in an establishment where the girls were taught to sew. Slash went her scissors through the remnants which Mother could never resist buying at sales. Remnants were Mother's only economy, and a more false one can seldom have existed. Odd lengths, improbable materials, shrill colours, all went further to encumber the shelves of an enormous cupboard in the sewing-room. Miss Seely's repertoire was limited—the Magyar sleeve for day, and for evening wear the picture frock: two tubes, a small one for the bodice, the other, for the skirt, as large as the material would permit and cobbled together at the waist. My first ball dress was the harsh pink of cheap sweets, garnished with a berthe of old lace, 'Much too good to cut, so it must be gathered.' In it I felt less like a human being than an upholstered dressing table.

I comforted myself with the hope that, although I was bound to be an appalling flop at the dances, I could at least show to advantage in the Cambridge tennis court. But even this solace was taken from me, as Father changed his mind and said that the undergraduate opposing me would be chagrined to be beaten by a girl....And of course Father would have been even more chagrined had his daughter been defeated by an undergraduate.

To make matters worse my nose bled ferociously at the most awkward moments during that ghastly May Week, so, at the Trinity Ball the final touch of horror was added to my appearance by an enormous Dorothy Bag containing six of Father's largest handkerchiefs, a quantity of cotton wool, and a bottle of adrenalin.

Kirsteen, in a Lanvin frock, was a tremendous success, and took a passing fancy to a young man called Leslie Grant, who was at Trinity and played third string against Seacourt. Her brother Tommy was my official partner. I was fond of Tommy, but dancing made his feet hurt. Mine hurt too, for my slippers were soaking from walking on the wet grass of the Backs, and so would not slide quickly enough on the floor of the marquee for me to get them out of the way before he trod on them.

I had only two dances with Leslie, and spent them walking round Great Court, telling him—in case he realised that he had taken my fancy as well as Kirsteen's—that I was an intellectual who would never marry as I would be too busy being a famous architect.

I was thankful to get back to Hayling, and on the following day Neville Lytton, who had a tennis court at Crabett Park where his wife, Judith Wentworth, bred Arab horses, arrived for one of his protracted visits. Their children, Anthony, Anne, and Winnie—especially Winnie, who was the same age as me—often came to stay with us, and no longer found it surprising to get meat to eat without having to steal it from the Blenheim spaniel's dishes, as they did at home because Lady Wentworth was such a militant vegetarian. But this time Neville came alone and to my relief did not expect me to be a model for him—which meant standing still for hours and suffering acute boredom as he never spoke while he was painting. Instead, he was learning to play the flute, and he liked to do so in the dedans at night because the echoes of the court pleased him. The haunt in the tennis court was too strong for me to enjoy going there alone after dark... The billiard-room was all right but the side gallery was safer taken at a run when all the lights were on, and sometimes it was better to go back to the house through the garden. Late one night while Neville was playing the flute the court was only pleasantly eerie and I was dancing to myself on the far side of the net. Even had he known I was there it was too dark for him to see me, so I was naked, pretending to be a Greek nymph dancing to Pan pipes in a haunted grove. I leapt higher than is practicable, except in a dream, and landed with my foot arched as though I was wearing ballet shoes. There was a sound like the crack of a stock-whip. 'Good God, what's that!' said Neville. 'I'm afraid it's me,' I answered. It was. I had broken the tendon that supported the instep of my left foot.

He carried me to my bedroom. He helped me into pyjamas so that Mother would not know that I had been dancing without clothes on, and then went to wake her and Father. An hour later I heard Doctor May telling them outside my door, 'We must on no account let her know, poor child, but I'm afraid that Joan will never dance again.'

At first I was able to amuse myself by playing piano accompaniments for Maurice Allom, who was learning the bassoon. Then my hands went stiff and I could not even hold a pencil. Doctor May said this was only crutch paralysis, caused by swinging myself about too much on crutches. So they were taken away and I had to lie all day on a sofa or be trundled round the garden in a Bath chair. It would get better in a few weeks, they said. But would it? Already there was talk of trying to graft Kangaroo tendon into my foot if it did not heal properly. It was an operation about which an Austrailian doctor had written a short article in the *British Medical Journal*—not a very encouraging article. Would Father have to buy a Kangaroo from the Zoo?

For the first two or three weeks everyone did their best to amuse the invalid, but by then it was taken for granted that I was perfectly content in a hammock, or in an arm-chair with a footstool in the dedans, watching other people play games. I ate a lot. There was nothing much else to do, but instead of getting fatter as Mother hoped I would, I lost nearly a stone. And seven stone when you are five foot eight I suppose is bound to make people fuss; unless they realise that being miserable because your body is a bore is apt to make the poor thing try to make itself inconspicuous.

It was almost the last straw when Doctor May decided that even if my foot had mended itself while it was in plaster, I was not to play tennis for at least a year after the case came off.

'You can play golf instead, darling.' said Mother cheerfully. 'So much better for you to hit a little ball about in the fresh air than getting so exhausted playing a man's game, much too heavy, and bad for your insides.'

'I loathe golf!' I said bitterly. She sighed and went back into the drawing-room through the french windows. From the veranda I could hear the echo of a ball hitting the penthouse as someone served in the tennis court. And from the garden came the voice of a girl: 'Thirty love!' She was lucky enough to have two feet and two adequate arms, and she could at least play lawners. I picked up a vase of roses Mother had brought me and flung it at the wall. Now I would have to crawl off this beastly sofa and collect the bits of broken china, and hide them under the mattress before she saw them and thought I was ungrateful. She would never understand I had only broken the vase because being angry was a little less shaming than bursting into tears.

Nanny Walpole would have understood, but she would have said, in a voice crisp and clean as her apron, 'Now pull yourself together, dear, and stop being sorry for yourself.' Oh Lord, I *was* being sorry for myself. Damn! All right, if I could only play golf—and it was still a large IF I could walk properly again, then why not play the beastly game? Did I really hate it, or only hate being bad at it? 'W.B. Smith,' I reminded myself, 'said it was a waste of his time and Father's money to give me any more lessons.' I only had half a dozen because I thought any fool could play such a silly game without even trying. Jack, W.B.'s young brother, said I had ''a natural swing''. Well of course I have. But I can't practise it. Amateurs never practise. They have a natural genius for being good at games or they don't play them at all. Perhaps I am not good enough at games, and that is why I have turned into a dreary cripple in a Bath chair when I am only sixteen.

'It is all your fault,' I said bitterly to my body. 'I wanted to be a ballet dancer and you break your silly legs. I wanted to be gay and pretty, in spite of my horrible clothes, and your beastly nose bleeds. Whenever I want to do anything exciting you either get a stomach-ache or else you catch a streaming cold. How can I think properly when you've got a cold in your horrid head? But if you think you can bully me into being nothing you flatter yourself! From now on you are going to learn which of us is boss, and the boss is going to be me!'

For the next two months I taught my body to play golf without going nearer a links than a bed or a sofa...I had long since discarded the Bath chair as being too degrading. It was fair to practise so long as you did so by unorthodox means. With the patience of the owner of performing seals teaching one of them to balance a rubber ball on its nose, I made each muscle learn its part in the act. As my bones were light I must make the club-head hit the ball with the greatest possible speed because I could not put a man's foot-poundals of effort behind it. Here my training in mechanical science came in handy. Therefore my swing must be the widest possible arc. At last, in my imagination I could play round the Hayling links as though I was actually walking briskly down the fairways or climbing over the dunes, with the powder-soft sand trickling into my shoes.

Fortunately the Hampshire County Championship was

played at Hayling that year. There were five major events: the best scratch score, the best handicap score, the best round against Bogey, scratch or handicap, and the best eclectic score of six rounds during the three-day meeting. I got Kirsteen to enter my name for the lot, and she swore not to tell Mother that I intended to do more than go down to the Club House and watch, from a chair on the veranda, stalwart females driving off the first tee.

The plaster was taken off four days before the meeting. I could stand! I could walk! My body, although still a very inefficient warrior, trying to hold back the phalanx by wailing that his feet hurt, could be bullied into obedience. It seemed a pity not to dress the part in its opposite, so I wore a brown and white checked gingham dress, suitable for a child of thirteen, and did my hair in pigtails with bows at the ends, tied together so that they should not get tangled in my long back-swing.

I knew as I stood waiting my turn on the first tee, that my foot and the muscles of my skinny wrists and arms could not be asked to last more than one round: 'Eighteen holes, just eighteen holes, not more than six and a half miles if you are obedient and keep the ball out of the rough. For goodness' sake keep us on the fairway, as Foot will never last out if Wrists send us into the sand.'

I was so frightened when my turn came, deliberately defenceless in my gingham and plaits among those big strong women in tweeds and sensible shoes, that I thought I was going to be sick. 'Just one round,' I promised my poor, quaking body. 'I won't ask even another yard of walking out of Foot once we get back to the Club House, if only, if only you won't make an ass of me in public.'

I kept my promise and they kept theirs. For years Father carried in his note-case a newspaper cutting from the front page of the *Daily Chronicle:* 'GIRL GOLF WONDER! Sixteen-year-old player carries off five awards in Hants County Championship.'

CHAPTER FIVE

scene through a microscope

Father's crusade against mosquitoes had grown from a border skirmish, a mere spraying of paraffin on water-butts and ornamental ponds, into a major war. At first he had only been annoyed at being bitten whenever he emerged from the house even in daylight; but as tennis was played indoors he could ignore the unfortunates who, watching lawners, had to do so with their legs encased in pillow-slips. Then one bit him on the forehead and caused him acute discomfort. It was a challenge which had to be accepted: either mosquitoes withdrew from Hayling Island or he must do so himself.

It was essential for him to reach the highest branch of any tree which he elected to climb. At Cambridge he took three Tripos, Mechanical Science Parts One and Two, and Law. And he came out top of each list. So now he proceeded to become the world's greatest expert on British mosquitoes. This cost him fifteen years of unremitting effort and almost all of his considerable fortune. He was rewarded with a C.B.E. and the honour of writing the standard work on the subject for the Natural History Museum.

Long since had the alcoves in the billiard-room been equipped with laboratory sinks and bunsen burners, adding new hazards to the use of the long jigger. Bedroom after bedroom had been encroached upon until at last Mother protested that visitors would be reduced to dossing down in the sand-yacht sheds. So he built The British Mosquito Control Institute, a house of eleven rooms in the garden on the far side of the tennis court.

His chief assistant was J. Staley, an entomologist as dedicated as Father himself, and I was a hard-working lab-boy. Hour after hour I peered into a microscope counting the hairs on the anal segments of larvae in order to identify their species. Day after day I analysed specimens of water from marsh, or ditch, or drain, to assay their salinity or hydrogen-ion concentration. Field work was more interesting, especially when I was at last entrusted with a theodolite and could take levels for the ditches to drain the salt water swamps which ringed the island, and which formed an ideal breeding ground for *Aedes Detritus*, the most far-flying and voracious of all British mosquitoes. The only time I made a slight mistake with the theodolite the sea rushed in at high tide and flooded three fields, but this error was soon glossed over. From two o'clock until six each afternoon—except when I could contrive to be playing golf for Hayling or Hampshire, I conducted visitors round the museum. Some of them were genuinely interested, but the majority—and I personally conducted several thousand of them—were attracted by the chance to see something for nothing, and came a second time when they discovered there was a well-appointed W.C., also free. My patter became quite earnest, but was enlivened by bets I made with myself as to the per-centage of visitors who in response to my statement, 'Only the female mosquito bites,' would reply archly, 'So the female of the species *is* more deadly than the male!'

I might still have been peering down microscopes, because I had almost managed to convince myself that it was my real *metier*, unless Providence had rescued me disguised as H.G. Wells. He was the only author for whom Father had pro-found respect, and every fatted calf would have been made ready for his reception had he not arrived three weeks earlier than he was expected. Mother and Father were away, but when I assured H.G. that I would telephone immediately to recall them he forbade me to do so, saying with a twinkle that it would be very ill-mannered to show that I had no wish to entertain an elderly guest.

One of the many facets of his genius was that he could make even the shyest audience feel entirely at ease. I taught him how to score at tennis and he taught me to hypnotise cats....We had no house cats, as they were forbidden in case they ate Father's parrot, so I smuggled a kitten in for him from the gardener's mouser. He was the first, and for a long time the only, person to whom I confided the realities of the more than three-dimensional world in which I lived the secret part of my life. He listened with the eagerness of a child who hears a fairy story it knows is far more true than facts. 'Keep it to yourself Joan, until you are strong enough to bear being laughed at by fools—but never let yourself forget it. And when you are ready, write what you know about....It is important that you become a writer.'

'But I can't spell,' I said forlornly. 'And even my school essays got the minimum of marks. I can only do dreary things like mathematics.'

He looked quite severe. 'I spend a great deal of time telling authors, and sometimes successful authors, not to waste their time, and their readers' time, by writing another line. I tell you to write and you will write; so do not attempt to argue with me. But you must live before you write about living. Don't, for goodness' sake, go off at half-cock. The first step is to stop your father trying to turn you into a blue-stocking—a nauseating species who frequently afflict me with their attentions and which you in no way resemble.'

I earned more kudos with Father for being found entertaining by H.G. than I had done by winning golf cups. Before he left, I knew that henceforward I would be allowed to accept invitations, even though it meant neglecting my lab work for several days. H.G.'s departure was typical of his ebullience. A new car was brought to the house. 'I have never driven a car before,' said H.G., 'but I have read a book about it so I shall now drive myself to Southhampton.'

Father was horrified that genius should expose itself to such peril, but H.G. refused even to practise on the drive before setting forth alone on his journey. The only assistance he permitted was for Mother to tie a red bunch of wool on the accelerator pedal and a green one on the brake to remind him which was which. Father paced the study in acute anxiety until H.G. rang up to announce gleefully that he had not only reached his destination intact but had averaged 28.4 m.p.h. 'But I shall go much faster to-morrow,' he chirped. 'I am an excellent chauffeur.'

My first house-party nearly broke my nerve, for Teddy Tiarks, whose father was the Governor of the Bank of England, took me to stay with his uncle near Axminster to attend two Hunt Balls. My knowledge of hunting was non-existent, and the bright young people were so bright that they scared me nearly out of my wits. Glossy young women were even more terrifying in evening clothes than they were when mounted on glossy horses. Both my evening dresses were pink, and only one who has been to a Hunt Ball in the Twenties in a pink frock can understand the depth of my shame. My only solace, and almost my only partner, was a cousin of the host, Mark Lubbock. He was feeling, very naturally, depressed because he had recently lost two fingers in an oat-crusher, and the family were trying to use this handicap as an excuse to make him do something 'useful' instead of letting him study music. He came to Seacourt and took refuge there until they relented and let him go to Munich, which was the first stage of a career that made him a Musical Director of the B.B.C.

I was now often allowed to stay with Kirsteen at their London house, 3 Seamore Place. Father opened an account for me at the Berkeley so that I could return hospitality to people who invited me to meals. To someone who had been brought up among tennis professionals it seemed logical to seek instruction from a professional *restaurateur;* so I went to Ferraro and asked him to teach me how and what to order. I was rising seventeen and he was compassionate of the young and gauche. For a fortnight I went to him every morning at 10.30 and he gave me an hour of his valuable time. 'Never order champagne. It is a drink for old women and chorus girls. It is a waste of money if you are the hostess. If you are a guest, your escort, if he is not very rich, will be glad you chose a cheaper wine. And if he is not very stupid he will appreciate that you read a wine-list with discrimination.' He even drew the curtains and put on the lights one morning so that I could assure myself that the dress I had bought for eight guineas in Shaftsbury Avenue did not clash with the walls. The only time he became a trifle fretful was when I borrowed Sheba, Glory's cheetah, and took her to a luncheon party there. Sheba behaved beautifully, and ate her four pounds of chopped steak sitting on a chair with a napkin tied under her chin; but Ferraro saw her presence made his other clients nervous and caused them to hurry through their meal. I gave some good parties until the first quarter's bill went to Father. Apparently I had been far more hospitable than he had intended, so he closed the account.

I carefully concealed, even from Kirsteen and Diana, that the real reason why I spent so much time watching games was that I could pretend I was living in a more romantic age when knights jousted in the lists for their ladies' favour. It was essential, of course, that at least one of the players was trying to win the tennis, or the racquets, match, to take wickets or make runs, because he knew I was watching him. Perhaps young men too were nostalgic for romance, for while some of my acquaintances boasted of tussles in taxis, my suitors proposed formally on their knees, in some secluded corner of the garden unless they preferred some more imaginative locale, as did Richard Hill, who chose the racquets court at Lord's.

It was at Lord's that I met Douglas Jardine, then Captain of the Oxford XI. He asked me to go with him the following day to a dance and village cricket at Colin McIver's, which always used to take place on the Thursday between the Varsity Match and the Gentlemen v. Players. Douglas was taking the postman's bowling when he fell and lay writhing on the ground. Hastily I looked away and pretended not to notice. Father had often warned me that this was the correct thing to do under such circumstances. Douglas was assisted off the field, but still I did not run forward to commiserate; so sure was I that he was suffering from an injury which was one of the few that in this incarnation could never happen to me.

After he was bandaged and in bed I went to comfort him. It was difficult to explain that my apparent lack of interest had been due to the fact that I had only just realised that the cricket ball had broken his collar-bone. It almost broke his heart too, for he thought that he would never again be asked to play for the Gentlemen. Foresight, had I possessed it, would have been a solace to him then, for I could have told him that missing a match was of very minor importance to someone who was going to bring Ashes from Australia.

Not being able to offer this ghostly comfort I took him to Hayling, where he stayed until he recovered. The following year he paid me the great compliment of taking me with him to inspect the wicket at Lord's. Never have I enjoyed a walk so much as the one across that hallowed turf under the furious glares of old gentlemen in the Pavilion. I was secretly so tired of watching even Douglas play cricket that my cup was filled to overflowing when he decided the wicket was not fit for play and so was free to take me to a cinema.

CHAPTER SIX

ENGAGEMENT RING

Early in 1926 I was again staying with Kirsteen in London when I awoke one morning to find I was smothered in a rash. 'I think it's measles,' she said briskly, shoving a thermometer into my mouth. 'Thank goodness you're only 99.4 so you can go home by train before Mummy notices and puts me in quarantine.'

The sour little jokes that allergy can play on its victims

were then virtually unrecognised, so the rash, which persisted for several weeks, was diagnosed as incipient measles, typhoid, scarlet fever, and assorted rare and unlikely skin diseases until at last it was grudgingly admitted to be no more than the aftermath of bad lobster at the Kit Kat. I was kept in bed, moping and scratching, and the only ray of light in the stygian gloom was that Graham Esplen, who until then had only been one of the young men with whom I danced at the Workman's parties, travelled down to Hayling two or three times a week to stay at the hotel on the off chance that I would like to see him. I felt far too hideous to see anyone, especially someone who cherished an image of me which was worthy of tributes of flowers and hot-house grapes. But he continued to bring them to the house and wrote to me every day and impressed Mother with his suitability as a son-in-law. She allowed wishful-thinking to cloud her foresight and announced that I might just as well let Graham see me at a disadvantage as I was going to marry him within a year.

I accepted her prediction as being as inevitable, although more beneficent, as her verdict on the fate of the *Titanic* and the tennis court roof. She must have heartened Graham too, for instead of being surprised when I accepted his proposal he produced a blue morocco case from his pocket in which eight fine sapphires were embedded in wax, with suggested designs for settings painted round them, to be reproduced in diamonds as soon as I had selected the gage of my choice.

For a time I basked in maternal approval, in the welcome of my prospective in-laws, and in the shelter from my secret world afforded by a kindly, reliable, unimaginative man who was never cross with me even when I knew I was being illogical and tiresome. It was unfortunate that he was not a good games player, but as I had grown a lump as large as a golf ball on my right wrist—in consequence of playing in the Girls' Golf Championship after cranking a borrowed Bentley which backfired and dislocated it, I could neither hold a club nor a racket, so this did not really matter. He was not as frivolous as my other young men had been; but why should he be when they were still undergraduates while he had spent four years in the Navy, fighting a war while they were at Eton or Winchester. Several Wykamists, including Douglas and Richard and Leslie, rebuked me for getting engaged to a Harrovian; but I told them, rather coldly, not to be so narrow-minded.

In the large two-seater Minerva—it had a special body with gun-metal fittings and pigskin upholstery—which he gave me, I toured the home counties in search of a suitable house. Perhaps I subconsciously knew we would never live in it, for every one of the dozens I looked at had some insurmountable snag. He even, bless him, gave me his Clumber spaniel, Derry, to console me after my black Labrador died. Derry, who was so obedient that he was rather a dull dog, fortunately transferred his spaniel devotion exclusively to Father.

Acting as hostess to Graham's business friends—he was 'in Shipping' which to me was as incomprehensible as being 'on the Stock Exchange'—was at first amusing, and then became rather monotonous. What was the point of taking people out to dinner when all both parties really wanted to do was to talk about money in an office? I asked him, and he seemed to think I was trying to be funny in not very good taste. But I still thought it odd, and still do, that people who already have lots of money worry themselves into ulcers to get more instead of enjoying it and themselves.

In September, after a fortnight tramping over grouse moors in the Lowlands, where I found that although Graham was not much use in a tennis court he was a very good shot, he took me to Oban to join his family on their yacht. She was a three-masted schooner without an auxiliary, and in her we sailed rather aimlessly round the Western Isles and then, still in light airs, came south to Holyhead. Here Graham had to return to London by train, as his father said he had already been away far too long from the office. Sir John was a martinet, but we crossed swords with mutual pleasure and respect, to the amazement of his wife and Ray, his daughter, who never argued with him. He got his own way even more easily now, for he was suffering from the angina pectoris which was soon to kill him, and he had a hospital nurse on board. There were gale warnings and the sky over the Irish Sea was black with thunder-clouds. The skipper, a dour red-headed Scot, was tactless enough to say at dinner that he was glad we were in harbour as it would be a dirty night, far too rough for an invalid. So Sir John immediately ordered him to put to sea.

By midnight twenty-one of the twenty-three paid hands had been seasick and all the passengers except the owner were prostrate in their bunks. There was a foot of water sloshing backwards and forwards on the floor of the cabin I shared with Ray. Every time I tottered to the heads I got even more cold and wet, but still managed to keep, with a stub of pencil on the white painted panelling over my bunk, a tally of the number of times I was sick. I had got to sixteen when the door crashed open and Sir John, wearing sea-boots, waded in, with an enormous cigar in one hand and a bottle of champagne in the other. 'Thank God the bloody nurse is too sorry for herself to tell me that drink and smoke will kill me,' he bellowed, puffing a cloud of cigar-smoke at me. It was the last straw. In the cold dank fury of one unfamiliar with the degradation of seasickness I roared, 'Throw that bloody cigar away or I'll stub it out on the back of your neck!' Ray opened a bleary eye to see what was going to happen to someone who had so rashly challenged the wrath of a father which to her was so much more immediate than the wrath of God. He was a small man, but he now produced gargantuan laughter worthy of the storm. He slopped champagne into a tooth-glass, made me drain it twice, threw me a set of oilskins, and told me to come up to the cockpit and share the fun.

The rest of the night had the quality of the overture to *The Flying Dutchman*. Six boards down, we scudded along under bare poles, wind-devils screeching in the rigging, the yacht a chariot careering madly among a host of wild white horses. At last we saw a light on the port bow. 'It's the Land's End light,' said the navigator, who by this time could only navigate himself on hand and knees. He was unduly optimistic, for when dawn came we found we had gone round the Scilly Isles.

A day later we came into Falmouth under a tattered jib while ships sounded their sirens and sailors cheered as we passed; for it was thought we had foundered, as several other vessels did that night. Ray and I went ashore to buy Devonshire cream. I saw a Pullman train labelled 'London'. There was a great temptation to board it, but I managed to refrain. From then on I was allowed to take the helm whenever I felt inclined—which was until I was too tired to stand on my feet; for there are few pleasures keener than steering a big yacht in full sail, especially when she has a well-trained crew alert to jump to your orders. Before the end of the cruise Sir John announced that I had better continue my lessons in seamanship during the winter. In February he would send the yacht to the Mediterranean so that I could spend my honeymoon cruising among the Greek Islands.

In October Graham told me I had been invited to stay with his maternal aunt near Barnard Castle in Durham. The night before we left London I had such a vivid dream of a ghost I was going to meet in the house that, although we had tacitly agreed not to discuss spooks, I could not resist telling him about it. He was disconcerted and implored me on no account to mention the subject to his relations. 'It would only embarrass them, dear. Do please believe me. I loathe it when people think you're odd or eccentric. Spooks and all that kind of thing are not only dangerous, it is unhealthy.'

I tried not to show I was hurt. It would be most unfair to blame Graham when I had deliberately chosen him because his downhereness would help me to live efficiently in the world with my feet firmly planted on solid ground. I might never have mentioned the dream again unless he had tried to put me off by telling me that the house was fifty miles farther than it really was and driving past the gates at sixty. The moment I saw the stone pillars in the beam of the headlights they were so familiar that I told him to stop being an ass and turn back, which he did, rather sheepishly. The house itself was a disappointment, for instead of being grey stone with a red pantile roof, the walls were so thickly covered with ivy that it looked dark green; and instead of being set in a sloping field of rough grass there were neatly terraced gardens. The staircase was in the wrong place too, and the room I was given was right only in its shape and the position of the window. The furniture and the wallpaper were quite different.

I found Graham's cousin, Norah, who was the same age as me, very congenial; but for two days I was discreet and dutifully practised casting with the pair of Hardy trout rods that he had given me to encourage me to fish. On the third night she came to my room for a gossip after everyone else had gone to bed. I knew, although I could not remember the details of the conversation, that I had spent most of the previous night chatting with the ghost. I could not resist telling Norah about her. 'She came in through the window,' I said. 'She was quite young, about our age, and wore a white cambric dress with lavender sprigs—the kind of dress a serving maid might have worn in the eighteenth century. I wish I could remember her name or why she was here. She was about thirty when she died, but she only lived here when she was young. She said to me, ''Sometimes I come back to look at the old place. No one can prevent me from coming back any longer.''' The story sounded very thin, and I felt shy for having embarked on it. 'I have had lots of dreams that were far more accurate than this one,' I said defensively. 'I've been trying not to dream lately because it's a thing I can't share with Graham. He is delighted that I got so many details wrong...I expected the house to be grey instead of green, and the staircase is in the wrong place and the gardens weren't here.'

'Where was the staircase?' asked Norah quickly.

'In the corner of the gallery. It was a spiral stair in the thickness of the wall. There was a horror on it which frightened me so much that I fled out of the house and down the drive. I woke up when I reached the gateway. That's why I remembered so clearly what it looks like.'

Norah smiled. 'I've got something in my room which you might like to show to Graham.' She brought me a watercolour of the house as it had been when her grandfather bought it about 1850. The house was then exactly as I had seen it. 'The staircase was where you described it too,' she said warmly. 'I don't know what the ''horror'' was, but I remember my father telling me that before grandfather would live in the house he had the old staircase bricked up. He said it was unsafe.'

'Have you ever seen my ghost?'

'None of us have. I don't think we are a very ghost-seeing family. But several other people have. We thought it was only because they knew that the house is supposed to be haunted. She was the only daughter of the man who built the house, and she climbed ut of that window and eloped to Gretna Green. Her father never forgave her, even when she was widowed. When she knew she was dying she wrote imploring him to let her come home, but he never answered the letter.' She smiled. 'I'm so glad that you were able to talk to her so that she knows she will always be welcome here.'

CHAPTER SEVEN

JOURNEY'S END

It was almost as though the girl who had escaped through that window from the grey stone house had opened a window for me that I had been trying to close with iron against my real world. At last I knew I was not in love with Graham, because I was in love with someone who for over a year I had been meeting in my dreams. Now I tried to remember him, but the harder I tried the more elusive did my dreams become. Were they true dreams, or only romantic fantasies? Worse, were they only fragmentary memories of someone I had loved long before Joan was born?

'You are incurably romantic,' said Mother briskly. 'You have been falling in and out of love since you adored Billy Grenfell when you were six. And before that there was John Mallet and God knows how many others. I am only too thankful that at last you have pulled yourself together and are making a sensible marriage....You will be safe with Graham.'

'I don't want to be safe,' I wailed. 'And I'm not going to marry Graham. I'm not going to marry anyone, ever. Because if I did and fell in love with someone afterwards I should run away with him at once—and that would be awful because I should have to break my promise.'

'Be quiet child—you are being hysterical!'

As she said this I felt as though I were a child again, stamping my foot in impotent fury and being thwarted by the thick carpet which made the stamp only a jarring in my knee instead of a booming sound that could drive my thoughts into her forehead.

'I am not going to marry Graham!' I shouted. 'Can't you understand? It would be far more wicked to him than to me. He has so much to give to a person who isn't my kind of person. If I let him go on giving his toys to me I will only turn them into sawdust....I couldn't help making him ashamed of his toys, ashamed of not being able to give me what no one can give him. I am alone, don't you understand? Alone! Alone!'

I fled to my bedroom and put my fingers in my ears when she banged on the locked door. Mother rang up Graham at seven o'clock in the morning to break the news that I had decided not to marry him. He telephoned to me an hour later, embarrassed, bewildered. 'You might at least have told me yourself instead of letting me hear it from your mother, before breakfast.'

'It wasn't my fault, really it wasn't. I'll catch the 10.5. Meet me at Waterloo.'

We went round and round Hyde Park in a taxi while I tried to explain that by running out on him I was doing him a kindness. I was saving him from being landed with a wife whom no one could understand, because try as she would, she could not understand herself. He kept trying to convince me that he didn't mind me being difficult, and I began to count the times we passed the Achilles statue—thirteen, fourteen, fifteen. Achilles became a clown miming at tragedy, the tragedy of two people trying to build a bridge which neither could cross, a clown who threatened to deluge me with the dreadful, grinning laughter that echoes the poignancy of a funeral.

'But what have I *done?*' asked Graham yet again.

'It's not your fault. It's mine, don't you understand? Everything is my fault because I don't know who I am.'

'Dear, dear Joan. Please do try to be sensible.'

'Sensible! My God, I've tried! I can hit golf balls farther than huge tough women who *like* hitting golf balls. I can hit tennis balls into the *grille* as well as a man even when my insides feel as if they were falling out. I can do Mechanical Science to please Father even though I loathe mathematics. But I can't marry you, or anyone else. I will always be alone, but at least I shall try to be lonely by myself instead of spoiling someone else's life for him.'

Never have I been quite so lonely as during that bleak Christmas. I packed wedding presents, to send back with a letter of apology. The most difficult one to pack was an antique Coleport dinner service of a hundred and eighty-seven pieces, including four tureens; and as I nailed down the lids of the packing-cases I wished someone would have the decency to nail me into a coffin. Turkey and plum pudding were swallowed in silence. The heavy boughs of greenery with which the gardeners from habit decorated the house might have been black plumes for a puppet's funeral. I was in deep disgrace and was not for a moment allowed to forget it. Even Father was cross with me, for although he was glad that I was going to stay with him instead of getting married, he missed Derry the spaniel, who had gone back to Graham.

Unforseen rescue came from Kirsteen who was ski-ing in Switzerland. When she received my letter saying that there was a most ghastly row in progress, she got her chaperon to wire an invitation to join their party. I had very little hope of being allowed to accept, for Winter Sports were, to Mother's way of thinking, even more anxiety-making than horses or sailing. However, the almost silent meals which I had been sharing with my parents must have been getting on their nerves even more than on mine, for Father unexpectedly overruled Mother's objections, saying that I would be perfectly all right as my prospective chaperon's husband was a good tennis player. So I packed a suitcase and caught the next train to London before they could change their minds.

Financial gloom, which occurred regularly twice a year when Father retired to his study to do accounts, was worse than usual because he was annoyed at having bought eighteen dozen champagne in anticipation of my wedding. Now, because of my thoughtless behaviour, he would have to drink it himself instead of claret or burgandy, which he infinitely preferred. So, being as usual short of money and not daring to ask for any in case Needless Extravagance was used as an excuse to keep me at home, I went to Thomas Cook and asked for the cheapest possible ticket to Andermatt.

As I had seldom been allowed to travel by train even to London without a maid in attendance—unless I was seen off at Havant and met at Waterloo; and never so much as entered a third-class carriage, it made the journey far more of an adventure to be travelling Alone and Abroad and Third. I was comforted that Mother had at last recognised my competence at looking after myself, for I did not discover until later that she thought I was travelling from London, well chaperoned, with Kirsteen.

At Calais the freedom of travelling hard had begun to pall when I found my reserved seat was in a carriage with seven elderly females, equipped with rugs and sandwiches and smelling of stale eau-de-Cologne with which they had no doubt tried to refresh themselves after the rough crossing. I walked down the train until I found an empty first-class carriage, in which I sat playing my ukelele until the *chef de train* came along. Before he could introduce the sordid note of looking at my ticket or asking whether I wished to pay excess fare, I suggested in my rather curious French that he looked tired and would doubtless feel better were he to put his feet up and rest himself while he listened to me singing 'Oh Suzannah'. He looked a trifle startled, but his French courtesy forced him to accept my invitation. 'Oh, Suzannah, don't you cry for me, for I'm travelling on to Oregon with my banjo on my knee,' I sang repeatedly for I knew only the chorus. He can have had no ear for music as he asked for an encore, and I told him that, much as I would like to share the rest of my repertoire with him, this might not be possible as my carriage was full of dreary old English ladies who would be sure to disapprove if I twanged so much as a single chord, even without a masculine audience. 'Also,' I added pathetically, 'I shall be too hungry to sing any more, for I am at the moment too poor to order a proper dinner in the restaurant car, and I have not been brought up to munch buns out of paper bags.'

This problem, he assured me, was one which it was within his power to solve in less than the twinkling of an eye. Fortunately the train was not quite full, so I must, as his guest, occupy this carriage, in which I would eat the excellent dinner which one of his minions would be privileged to bring me. As soon as he finished his duties to the rich barbarians whom, unfortunately, he had to look after, he would return to me for another session of *le sing-song*; after which I would pass a restful night in a first-class sleeper. Which I did after a most excellent dinner, with a half-bottle of burgundy which I kept to sustain him when he returned to hear my other three out-of-tune songs.

There was snow, deep, beautiful, clean snow and snow-proud Christmas trees sparkling outside the train window when I woke up. I suddenly realised that in the haste of my escape to adventure I had forgotten to wire Kirsteen the train or even the day, on which I was arriving. But what did this matter? What did anything matter? A sleigh with bells singing on the horse's harness took me to the hotel. 'Your friends are out,' said the hall porter. 'Everyone is out with the snow, for it is such a beautiful day. But of course there is a room for you.'

In the bedroom there was a bed, a chair, a table, and a row of hooks on the wall. It was clean and free as the snow outside the window. At last I was in a room which really belonged to me, a room as impersonal and undemanding as a novice's cell. I unpacked. It was so easy to unpack when I had only one suitcase and had not even bothered to notice what I had put into it. Then I wandered downstairs, through bare, uncomplicated rooms until I found one which had nothing in it except a piano. I was playing Jennie's music gently to myself when the door opened. A man with a pair of skis on his shoulder stood on the threshold. He looked at me for a long time without speaking. Then he said, 'It really is you. I have dreamed with you for nearly

103

two years. Do you recognise me too?'

'Of course I do,' I said, knowing at last that truth is very simple.

He held out his arms, and I went into them, and he kissed me.

CHAPTER EIGHT

lovers' meeting

Being with Esmond was like being in a bright dream, a dream in which everything was more real than it ever is in ordinary living. But from this dream I did not wake to find myself lonely. 'I shall never be lonely any more,' I said aloud as I awoke to each new and splendid day. It did not even matter that I had no talent for ski-ing, for when I fell down he picked me up and we laughed together, and with his arm around me I achieved a precarious balance down swift slopes, and he lifted me off my feet and swung me round with him when we had to turn.

Sometimes I was almost afraid it was all too good to be true....How could my life have changed so completely in less than twenty-four hours? 'This is Joan and I am going to marry her,' Esmond had said, introducing me to his mother. And she, instead of looking annoyed or even startled, had accepted me as though she had herself chosen me as a daughter-in-law.

She was beautiful, and kind and gentle, and looked young enough to be the elder sister of her sons' although she had not had an easy life, bringing up four boys and sending them to Eton on not very much money, after her husband had been killed in the Irish Guards in the last year of the war.

Esmond, who was twenty-two, had been two years at

Cambridge and then instead of taking a degree, he had gone round the world because he thought it would be more fun and also more useful to his future career as a journalist. His godfather, who was also his guardian, was going to start him on the *Continental Daily Mail*, which would mean his living in Paris for at least a year.

'Joan will like Paris,' he said confidently to his mother. 'We had better spend a couple of days there before the boys go back to school so that you can help us find a flat.'

Reluctantly she let the first cold breath of fact blow into our dream. 'Darling, I'm afraid your godfather would jib at your being married until you have worked at least six months—six months is the trial period he insists on before he definitely decides to give you a job.'

'I shall work twice as hard if Joan is with me,' he said rebelliously.

'On your honeymoon? Of course you wouldn't. While you are together neither of you waste a moment thinking about anything except each other.' She pleaded with us. 'My darlings, don't look at me as though I was a gorgon. Someone has simply got to be a tiny bit practical about the future. I know money is a dreary subject, but not having any is drearier still.'

He put his arm round my shoulders and gave her a quick hug. 'Sorry, darling. Of course I need a job, and I will get one. We shall have to wait until July. Even my stern godfather couldn't possibly expect me to wait longer than that.'

'What about your parents?' she asked me. 'Have you broken the news of your engagement to them yet?'

'Yes,' I said reluctantly. 'It bubbled out rather tactlessly when I was writing to Mother to say I had arrived safely.'

'And is she pleased?'

'Not very. You see, as I told you, we had a row before I left home because I broke off an engagement. She says it is positively indecent even to think so soon of getting married to someone else. I suppose one can't expect her to see how utterly different this is until she has met Esmond; but the moment she does everything will be all right.'

She smiled fondly at her son. 'I expect it will, but it would be only civil for Esmond to make a formal request for your hand. You will be doing well I think, both of you, if you get Joan's parents to agree to an official engagement at Easter and a marriage—if he gets his job confirmed of course—in August or September.'

She helped us by writing a very tactful letter to Mother, saying how happy it made her to see her eldest son so deeply in love and how much she looked forward to having me as a daughter. Kirsteen and our chaperon both wrote warmly about Esmond too. Kirsteen, coached by me, stressed the fact that at last I had someone who would not only look after me but keep me in order. I knew the thought of me disciplined would appeal to Mother; and it must have done, for her replies, although guarded, were cordial.

Esmond, on a motor bicycle, arrived at Seacourt the day after I got back from Switzerland. At first they tried to treat him as though he were only another beau who need not be taken seriously, but they soon surrendered.

'A most remarkable young man,' said Father, 'and he seems to have had extraordinary adventures, which he describes exceedingly well. At least you will never be bored with him, although I hope his idea of keeping you entertained will not include sharing a shipwreck in the Red Sea. I do not approve of Arab dhows as a means of transport, and you are not nearly a good enough swimmer to survive, as he did, for several hours among sharks. Nor would I approve of your getting involved in a bar fight in the less salubrious quarters of Singapore, or in any other part of the world for that matter.'

'I shall keep him from doing anything really dangerous after we are married,' I said fondly. 'Men who have had lots of adventures and sown their wild oats are supposed to make the most staid and reliable husbands.'

'I doubt if he is likely to be docile under any woman's

thumb. But if you expect to change him you might start by trying to cure him of the distressing habit of bringing a revolver into a civilised house.' He looked severe. 'I noticed one lying on the dressing-table when I passed his bedroom on my way to play tennis this morning. The door, like the windows, was wide open, letting an appalling draught into the passage.'

'I will tell him to keep his door shut,' I said hastily, for open windows to Father meant draughts and a wicked waste of money spent on central heating. My bedroom door had KEEP SHUT painted on it by Mother in letters a foot high as a protest against my selfish passion for fresh air.

'I should prefer to die of pneumonia rather than to be shot,' said Father crisply, and I could have kicked myself for not having warned Esmond of his phobia against firearms.

'The pistol isn't loaded. He is a very good pistol shot and has won lots of cups and medals and things. To him it is only a kind of golf club or tennis racquet....'

'Tell him not to discharge it here or I shall be exceedingly annoyed.' He blinked at me through his glasses. 'Really, Joan, you are becoming appalling inconsiderate. I will *not* have my house, or my garden, or the beach, turned into a shooting gallery by any of your prospective husbands! Good God, he will be letting it off in the tennis court next!'

'He won't, darling. I swear he won't. I will make him chuck the beastly thing in the sea if it will make you feel any happier.'

'A very sensible suggestion...and see he does it at low tide so that some wretched child doesn't find it lying in the sand and use it to blow its unfortunate mother's brains out.'

I was ashamed that, like Father, I secretly always thought gun was potentially dangerous even when it was supposed not to be loaded. So I did not mention the pistol to Esmond. I was afraid he would think I was being fussy.

On his last night at Seacourt, the thirty-second day since we met each other again at Andermatt, we talked about the future, so that we could pretend we are going to share to-morrow and to-morrow and to-morrow. On the music-room sofa we almost managed to forget that he was leaving for Paris in the morning, but neither of us could quite forget it.

'We have got to remember I shall only be away six months....And I am sure to be able to get week-ends off to come and see you,' he said comfortingly.

'Don't let's spoil Now by thinking about the next six months. They are going to be utterly bloody, but don't let them come nearer by thinking about them.'

He clicked his fingers. 'There! I have done a magic. The six months are over and it is the end of July. We are going to be married to-morrow. Shall we be married here or would you rather elope?'

I hesitated. 'I know we ought to give everyone the fun of a big wedding, but I don't think it's going to happen.'

'Why, darling?'

'I know its sounds silly, but when I try to look forward and see us being married in a church, with me in a white tulle crinoline with a wreath of orange blossoms, and Diane and Kirsteen as bridesmaids, it doesn't seem quite real.'

'Much better not to waste time on a wedding,' Esmond said cheerfully. 'The moment I get the All Clear from the paper I will send you a telegram, and then you will hop on the next plane and we will be married in Paris. Where shall we spend our honeymoon?'

'Anywhere and everywhere...years and years of it.'

'I know what we will do! It's a brilliant idea and I can't imagine why I didn't think of it before. I shall be so incredibly efficient at my job that the *Daily Mail* will agree to let me become a roving reporter, and then we can spend a year going round the world at their expense on the first lap of our honeymoon. I will take you to all the especially beautiful places in which I have dreamed about you—Samoa, and Japan, and a particularly favourite mountain in Ceylon. Everywhere will be a thousand times better than when I saw it alone, for instead of vanishing when I wake up, you will be waiting to enjoy your most appreciative husband.'

Before I could tell him that he would find me very appreciative too, Mother opened the gallery door and called out, 'It is after midnight, children. I am going to bed now so I will say good night. Promise you won't stay up more than another half-hour.'

'Good night, Mrs. Marshall: we promise,' said Esmond, which was unfortunate as he always kept his promises.

The grandfather clock on the landing struck one as he kissed me good night outside my bedroom door. I watched him walk away from me down the long passage, and then turn the corner out of my sight. I heard his bedroom door close behind him.

I was getting forlornly into bed when I heard a voice—I think it was Jennie's—say softly but quite distinctly, 'After Esmond leaves here to-morrow you will never see him again.'

So I ran to his room and spent the rest of that sweet, short night with him.

CHAPTER NINE

to-morrow never comes

Esmond was in Paris and I was in England. This inescapable fact was so far more important than anything else that I would have preferred to be left alone to think about him undisturbed, while the empty days, empty except for the arrival of the postman, crawled by as inconspicuously as possible. However, the ivory tower was out of bounds. Esmond, who had no patience with dreeps, frequently reminded me in his letters that a knight errant expects his lady love to produce a fair quota of rivals for him to vanquish in the lists. So why was I not going to dances? Was I afraid that if I saw Douglas or Leslie or any of the others I would find my love for him did not survive the test of competition?

As both my parents were inordinately possessive, this viewpoint was refreshing and yet very odd. I even asked Mother what she thought about it. 'A most sensible young man,' she said warmly. 'He knows that when two men are in love with you, four men are in love with you; but if only one man loves you, no man really loves you at all.' So, having told them that I was in love with Esmond and would marry him the moment I got the chance, I went to dances with other escorts and very nearly managed to enjoy myself—which made it much easier to write gay, amusing letters to Paris.

I tried to make myself believe, and almost succeeded, that I had only imagined the voice which had told me I was never going to see him again, imagine it so that it could shout down the voice of 'conscience' which had been trying to speak louder than my heart. But although I tried to be reasonable I fretted and slept badly, and so lost weight as I always did when unhappy. The removal of tonsils was the fashionable cure-all that year, so Mother decided this had better be performed on me. I managed to stall until I had been one of the eight bridesmaids at Diana's wedding—to her cousin Stan—in March. Then they sailed for a honeymoon in India, where his father and her uncle, Sir Stanley Jackson, was Governor of Bengal; and I was put into a nursing home.

I think Mother must have chosen it because it was the only one of the several she inspected which had no 'visiting hours.' She had no intention of being kept from her child's bedside by nonsensical rules backed by an officious matron. She had, of course, no idea that it was almost certainly the one immortalised in Evelyn Waugh's *Vile Bodies*, where the patient dies unnoticed during a cocktail party in his room. The surgeon must have been affected by the slap-happy atmosphere, for half-way through the operation he found he had forgotten to bring some essential bit of equipment, and had to send a taxi to his rooms in Harley Street to fetch it. They were the largest and healthiest tonsils he had ever removed, and to prove it they were put into a glass jar by my bed. The matron's Dalmatian eyed them longingly, and even occasionally so far forgot discretion as to sit up and beg, no doubt recognising them as part of his perks.

Three days later, exhausted by a stream of visitors, I was sitting up in bed having a dry shampoo, while a manicurist— also part of the nursing-home service, was doing my nails, when a fountain of blood gushed out of my mouth. Six hours and four doctors later the hemorrhage stopped. I was by that time full of morphia and had been packed in ice. The ice, wrapped only in face towels, melted and left me unconscious in a freezing lake. Rather naively, everyone was astonished when my temperature shot up and I developed pneumonia. Pneumonia, when every time you cough your throat threatens to bleed again, is very little fun. But as soon as I had weathered the crisis Douglas came to visit me every day during his lunch hour, and Leslie was even more helpful, as he cajoled the Scottish night sister to let him stay in my room when I was too tired to sleep and my head ached so much I could not read. 'I know it's against the rules to have visitors after midnight,' said kind Sister Cameron, 'but Mr. Grant has such beautiful brown eyes that him sitting quietly on the floor holding your hand cannot possibly do you anything but good.' How right she was! I am sure more people die in hospitals from loneliness and boredom than from mere clinical symptoms.

I had not told Esmond that I was in a nursing home. The kind of wife I intended to become must always be gay and romantic, and above all, healthy. There was nothing romantic about having a tonsillectomy. It sounded nearly as squalid as adenoids; so my letters about the future we would share adventuring round the world made no mention of the present. 'But what are you doing with yourself *now*, darling? Do stop being evasive,' he wrote. So I answered explaining what had really been happening. His reply was immediate and more than reassuring—in the form of a long, intimate telegram which told me he was flying over to see me the following evening.

I seized the telephone and rang up Mother, who agreed that I could come back at once to the flat in Charles Street, which had been lent to them by Tom Scully who was in America, instead of staying in the nursing home another two days.

It was a large flat, and I walked up and down the passages so as to teach my legs not to feel wobbly. I washed my hair. I arranged flowers. At last everything was ready for Esmond, who would find me well and radiant instead of lying in a nursing home bed, with the smell of ether lingering in the corridors and the clink of bedpans echoing from the sluice next door. I was too excited to sleep, so Mother gave me a sleeping pill, which I accepted gratefully as I was determined not to look old and haggard for Esmond. It was a dark, deep sleep, unbroken by the shadow of a dream.

The front door bell woke me. I heard the maid cross the hall and then her telling Father, 'It's a telegram for you, sir.' I heard him say, 'It's from Esmond's mother.' I shot out of bed shouting, 'It's for me. Is she coming to meet him a Croydon?'

'Go back to bed, child. You'll catch cold,' Mother said quickly, and then followed Father into the sitting-room. Suddenly I was frightened, and sat on the edge of the bed telling myself that even if Esmond could not come over from Paris today I mustn't let them see how much I minded. Father came into the room, shut the door carefully and stared out of the window. 'I'm afraid I've got very bad news for you, old thing,' he said without looking at me. 'We've had a telegram. Esmond is dead.

'He *can't* be dead! I would know if he was dead! He's coming here to-day.' But even while I frantically protested I knew that it was true. Tears poured out of my eyes. Father sat beside me on the bed, patting me on the back in an agony of pity and embarrassment. Poor, dear man, he had not seen me cry since I was four, and even then I had enough self-control to cry decently into a medicine bottle. Now I had no defence against the tide of overwhelming grief. 'Thank God, oh, thank you God,' I sobbed, 'for letting me sleep with Esmond before he died.'

Father covered me with an eiderdown and went out of the room. I felt guilty for having upset him by crying in public—but perhaps he knew how much it helped to have his shoulder to cry on. Mother came in. 'Poor child, I feel very sorry for you,' she said briskly. 'But how could you be such a fool as to tell Jack that Esmond had seduced you—under your father's roof? If you are pregnant, own up at once and I will take you to Paris to get rid of it.'

In a passion of fury I said many things which it took a long time to forgive. I drove her out of the room. I threw on some clothes and fled from the house, and walked and walked for ever along the lonely London streets. During some of the time I must have been in Hyde Park, for I remember lying face downwards on harsh gritty grass that smelled of sheep. But except for this, there is a cold grey hole in my memory of that day from ten o'clock in the morning, when I ran out of the flat, until eight that evening, when I found myself standing outside an open door in Hertford Street. Why did the door mean something? Who lived there? Leslie lived there. But there would be a row if Mother found out I had been alone to a man's rooms. But it didn't matter any more. Nothing mattered any more.

I was so tired that I could only climb the stairs by clinging to the bannisters. Leslie was sitting alone by the empty fireplace. 'Esmond is dead,' I said flatly.

'Oh damn! How damnably unfair! Now he's dead you will always love him instead of loving me.'

I began to shiver. My teeth chattered so much I couldn't

speak. There was a bath in his bedroom with a geyser above it on the wall. He turned it on until the room was full of steam. Then he picked me up and undressed me, like a very kind and competent nanny, and put me into the bath and trickled kind hot water over my shoulders with his enormous sponge. Then he wrapped me in his woollen dressing-gown and put me in an arm-chair with a rug over my knees. He gave me tea with a lot of sugar in it and two boiled eggs which he cooked on the gas-ring. 'Now you can talk,' he said, 'talk until you've talked yourself out; and if you want to cry, then cry. It would be far the most sensible thing you could possibly do.'

'I don't want to cry any more. I cried on Father and I don't expect he will ever want to see me again.'

'Don't talk nonsense, darling.'

'Neither of them want to see me again. And I don't want to see them. I have had the most terrible row with Mother. I told her that she was a murderess when she said she would take me to Paris to have an abortion...'

'Of course you mustn't have an abortion,' he said hotly. 'You will marry me at once and pretend it's mine.'

'But I'm not going to have a baby,' I confessed miserably. 'That's almost the cruellest part of everything. If I had been an efficient adulteress they would have had to let us be married three months ago, and then Esmond wouldn't be dead! Oh why, *why* is he dead? And is he safe? Mother said he must have committed suicide. That was when I really lost my temper. The telegram said, ''Please break news gently to Joan before she sees it in the newspapers that Esmond has had a fatal accident.'' Mother said ''Fatal accident'' always means suicide. But he couldn't have killed himself. It was one of the things we agreed are utterly not done....'

'Of course he didn't kill himself. Don't be such an ass!' said Leslie decisively. 'He was probably run over by one of those ghastly French taxis....'

114

'Are you *sure?* I'm sure really—not about the taxi; but it's so difficult to be sure when people like Mother put ideas into your mind.'

'I will go to Paris to-morrow and find out exactly what happened. I won't spare you the details because you are not the kind of person who can be comforted by half-truths. What do you want to do for the next few days? They are going to be absolute hell for you, and it's no use telling you now that it will hurt less after a time; but it will.'

'I can't go back to Seacourt. I couldn't bear it.'

'Where, then?'

'The least awful thing would be to go somewhere I had never been to before, quite alone, in my car. But my car is at Hayling.'

'I can easily fix that. Someone will fetch it first thing in the morning. But you can't go off alone. Damn it, you've been in bed for five weeks and ought to be in bed now. Wait a moment while I go and telephone.'

He came back to announce that he had persuaded Mrs. Workman to let Kirsteen go with me for a fortnight's motor tour. 'Kirsteen is collecting some clothes for you from Seacourt. Tommy will drive her up in your car to-morrow and meet us here at twelve.'

'Oh, thank you! Can I please stay with you until Kirsteen comes?'

He hesitated. 'I'd give anything to keep you here, but it would only cause more trouble with your parents. So I will take you back to Charles Street, and you can stay in the taxi while I explain firmly, very firmly, to them both, that it is very lucky that you didn't faint in the street and get run over by a bus, and that they are not to attempt to see you. Just to make sure you are left alone I shall spend the night outside your door.'

And he did, bless him. I think that both Father and Mother were relieved that he had taken from their shoulders the burden of their unhappy and difficult child.

CHAPTER TEN

homecoming

I was glad that Kirsteen could not drive a car, for having to steer it through the traffic made it easier to keep a tight rein on my emotions as we drove out of London. 'Esmond is dead and there is no use talking about it,' she said firmly. 'If you had only had the sense to confide in me, I would have made you swear not to tell anyone that you'd been to bed with him. Really, Joan, how could you have been so idiotic as to tell your parents! Won't you ever learn sense?'

It was cold comfort, but honest; and I accepted it, although I was surprised that Kirsteen should also consider adultery to be so devastatingly important. Oddly enough, no one ever pointed out to me that adultery requires one of the parties to be married; perhaps they thought it was a euphemism for fornicatress.

Kirsteen and I had often discussed what fun it would be if only our parents would let us go off alone for a motor tour; so I was determined that she should enjoy it even if I could never enjoy anything again. Somehow I would keep up face so that she would not feel that she was sharing a funeral car in the wake of a hearse. I was doing quite well until we stopped for tea at a cottage on the banks of the Thames somewhere beyond Henley. I got out of the car, felt dizzy, and before I could put my head between my knees, fainted face downwards in a flower bed. Kirsteen and the kind woman who owned the place decided that we should spend the night there, which we did, on a feather-bed in the attic.

In the morning I knew that the pistol, which, had I only listened to Father would have been safely at the bottom of the sea, had killed Esmond. I saw him, in dress trousers and a soft shirt but without his dinner jacket, staring at something lying on the floor of his room. He was not frightened, only bewildered, puzzled, and, above all, angry with himself. 'I can't have been such an ass as not to have noticed there was still one up the spout. It would have been too idiotic,' he was saying. The thing on the floor was his dead body.

Two days later, Leslie, who had been to Paris for me, confirmed that Esmond and three friends had decided to go to a shooting-gallery after dinner. They were all laughing and talking while Esmond looked for his pistol and began to clean it. He had taken out the clip of bullets but one was in the chamber. It went through his left eye and killed him instantly. It was so clearly an accident that there was no need even for a formal inquest.

Except for the one brief glimpse of what had happened, night after night passed with no sight of him. It was difficult to sleep, so I learned quantities of poetry, Rupert Brooke and Keats, to interrupt the beat of my thoughts. Whenever I wilted, Kirsteen made me drink half a bottle of Emu brand burgundy, 'rich in iron', with my dinner. I didn't like the taste, so readily agreed that it must be very healthful. Sleep, and the chance of meeting Esmond, came sooner if I was tired, so we drove at least nine hours every day, exploring side roads and unfrequented tracks, as a bad surface was an advantage because it demanded more of my attention. From the Lake District we went to Inverness. North of Perth the road was in such ill repair that we seldom managed to average more than ten miles an hour; and then we went south through Fort William and Glencoe. I wanted to visit Glencoe because I thought I might catch echoes of the massacre there as I was a descendant of Rob Roy McGregor. It was a very slender thread and produced no results whatsoever; but I had grasped at it because I hoped that any kind of second-sight might break down the barrier that was hiding Esmond from me.

Both Mrs. Workman and Mother had insisted that we were able to receive letters from them, so we wired the names of towns where we would collect mail *poste restante*. Mother's letters were brief and signed 'B. Marshall,' reiterating that Father was finding it difficult to forgive me. The day before Kirsteen, who had not been able to get permission to stay any longer, went back to Hayling by train from Reading, I had another letter from Mother....

'Daisy and Elfie Sartorius called here yesterday to look at the garden. They came here with Sir Alfred Turner (Iris's god-father) before the war, but you would have been too young to remember them. I had to warn them not to mention you in front of your father, and they invited you to stay with them until he is ready for you to come home. The address is Hurtwood, Holmbury St. Mary, between Guildford and Dorking. Behave *discreetly*, and do not take them into your confidence. They are both spinsters and could not be expected to take a lenient view of what you have done.'

So now I was to be further humiliated by being sneered at by spinsters! I only had two pounds left, but this lasted for three days. Seven shillings for bed and breakfast at 'Cyclists Welcome'. Other meals were buns and tomatoes: buns because they are more filling for the money than any other food, and tomatoes in case I got spots through lack of vegetables. An adulteress with pimples would be even more an object of derision. I was down to my last ten shillings when I drove up the steep lanes towards Hurtwood, ten shillings I must keep so as to be able to tip the housemaid. I stopped the car when I was at the crest of the hill, half a mile beyond the drive gates. It was a very calm and beautiful evening, but I was in no mood to be beguiled by beauty. I was alone: even Esmond had left me. I would become even harder and more self-sufficient than I had learned to be in the last three days. I would make an armour for myself from bitterness and disappointment and hatred of everyone who thought being an adulteress was sordid and wicked. And, strong in hatred, I would fight the world single-handed and beat it at its own cruel game. If I hated enough I would at least be able to salvage my pride, the pride I used to have when I had the decency to conceal pain, when no one saw me cry. 'Pride!' I

118

said bitterly. 'What pride have I left when I am exposing myself to the patronage of elderly spinsters because I have not the guts to use the last gallon of petrol in the car to find a lonely wood or a deserted common where I could starve to death in decent privacy!'

I stubbed out my cigarette. I blew my nose and powdered it; then, because my eyes were still brimming with self-pity, I dug my nails into my thigh until the blood ran, to punish my body for betraying me.

I drove the car, so fast that the tyres screeched on the gravel, through a tunnel of beech-trees whose smooth, grey boles were buttresses to a curtain-wall of rhododendrons. It brought me to a wide courtyard. To the west the house, honey-coloured stone hung with clematis and roses, to the east a balustrade with a lawn beyond. To the south was a long pool of water-lilies, and beyond it, so steeply did the hillside fall away, only the sky, and the weald of Sussex revealing far below me its gentle distance to the horizon of the South Downs.

As I got out of the car a flurry of white doves swirled down from the rooftree to feed on corn which was being scattered for them by their mistress. And I knew her! I knew that smile, those wise grey eyes! Long ago, she came into my room, took the brush and used it gently to untangle the knots which the impatient nurse had been tugging at. Then she sat talking to me while I drank my hot milk. Even as Daisy walked towards me I tried to harden my heart....Careful, Joan! If you let yourself love anyone you will only be hurt again.

She welcomed me as though it was quite natural for me to be there, as though I had often been there before. But this, of course, was her instinctive courtesy to a guest—even to a guest whom she had asked only as a favour to Mother. It was nearly six o'clock, so I said I had had tea, which was not true because I had eaten the last of the buns at midday. 'Then I expect you would like a bath before dinner,' she said, and took me up the broad oak stair to my room. The windows were open to the blue distance and the scent of azaleas mounted from the hillside. There were flame-coloured and orange, and white azaleas—in pottery jars from Portugal, in the room too; and a blue bowl of lilies of the valley by my bed.

A kindly, grey-haired maid chatted while she unpacked, then she turned on the water in the bathroom next door and told me that by the time I was ready she would have pressed a dress for me to wear. There were three kinds of Floris bath essence to choose from, verbena and hyacinth and rose-geranium. It was very comforting to lie in hot, scented water—the bath was so long I could only just touch the end with my toes—after having had to wash in bits in a basin. I washed my hair and dried it on one of the huge bath-towels that were warming on the hot rail. There was no need to hurry, dinner was not until eight.

Elfie, Daisy's elder sister, had been out when I arrived, but she too was there when I came downstairs. She was not tall like Daisy, but brown and plump and gay as a robin.... Friendly as a robin too, as she gave me a glass of sherry and chattered so that I had no chance to feel shy. During dinner I tried to forget that to-morrow, instead of eating delicious food in company, I should be feeding on buns again, entirely alone. I could not even salve my conscience with the excuse that in going away I was choosing suicide by starvation, for while I was dressing I had realised I could pawn my wrist-watch. It was gold, and ought to be worth a tenner, which would keep me until I could find a job. I could not possibly be discreet as Mother had counselled. Secrecy might be permissible with enemies, or even acquaintances; but it would be cheating to conceal the truth from friends. But such new friends could not possibly be expected to be more tolerant of me than my own father.

After dinner we had coffee on another terrace to the west of the house. It was also the roof of the billiard-room, for

Hurtwood was built in an old stone-quarry so that from all its three storeys you could walk directly into the garden. 'I want to show you the fan-garden,' said Daisy. 'It is at its best in the evening light.'

It was quite a long way from the house, in a natural amphitheatre. The sticks of the fan were yew hedges, and between them were herbaceous borders radiating up the slope. Then a smooth curve of turf, and above it a stone colonnade hung with vines and clematis, roses and wisteria. Where a hand would have held the fan there was a white stone pool and a fountain, and behind it six stone-pines, eighty or more feet high, stood as sentinels to the distance.

The peace and beauty of it made me feel almost unbearably unhappy. In a moment I must say the words which would drive me into exile. 'Could I, oh please could I, keep silent for just another day, even for two days?' I pleaded with myself. 'If only I could be here just for a while, I could get my courage back. Even if I have to sacrifice the last of my pride by staying here under false pretenses it would be worth it. I need courage to tackle the world even more than I need my pride.'

'You cannot gain courage by behaving like a cheat and a coward,' I said to forlorn little Joan. 'Go on, tell her! End the suspense—and then go and pack your suitcase.'

'I cannot stay here,' I said abruptly to Daisy, who was telling me how she had brought the blue cedar as a seedling twenty years ago from Sikkim. 'I cannot stay here,' I repeated more loudly. 'It was dishonest of me even to stay for dinner. You see, I am an adulteress.'

Daisy looked at me and her eyes were gentle. 'Are you, my dear?' she said. 'How lovely for you. I never had the chance.'

And so in Daisy, and in the garden of Hurtwood, I knew I had at last come home.

Daisy knew about grief. She had loved Bunny, her only brother, who had been killed in 1915, more than I loved

Esmond, for she had a much greater capacity for affection. Since childhood they had wanted no other companion. Together they had gone plant-hunting in many parts of the world and were probably the first Europeans to see the blue Himalayan poppy. 'We were camping on the edge of the tree-line,' she said. 'Bunny was riding ahead of me over a pass when suddenly I heard him shout, "Daisy!"' So I urged my pony into a canter—it was nearly as tired as I was, poor little beast. When I reached him he had dismounted and was staring spellbound at what I at first thought was a turquoise-blue lake. But it was poppies, millions of them: I have never seen anything more beautiful. We collected seed, but it was not ripe enough to germinate; and the plants we brought back died before they reached Kew in spite of all the care we lavished on them. So they are called *Meconopsis Baileyi* instead of being *Sartorii*.'

Ballooning was another hobby they had shared. 'The stillness was so wonderful, such utter peace,' she said reminiscently. 'Sometimes it was more exciting than peaceful, when we started to drift out to sea, for instance, and were half-way to France before the wind changed again. Several times we had to throw out more than the sandbags to prevent ourselves hitting a hill. The picnic basket always went first, and then the cushions and our coats. I remember the first time we took my father up with us. He thought we were going to run into a church steeple and shouted, "Jettison everything!" I had been brought up as a soldier's daughter—both he and my uncle Reginald were Major-Generals and won the V.C.—so I obeyed automatically. I threw his field-glasses out of the basket. He was so cross that he refused to speak to me for the rest of the day until he heard that the chauffeur, who used to follow us in the car, had found them dangling undamaged from a tree.'

We had been talking about Bunny again, a few days later, when she said, 'You must be more courageous than I was, for I never dared to give my whole heart to anyone again.'

'But it hurts too much. No one could expect us to risk being so terribly hurt twice in one lifetime.' I protested.

'Being hurt is not really so very important. It is at least much less important than hurting other people. I would like you to ask some of your friends here: Leslie for instance, who you say has been so kind to you.'

'Oh Daisy, please not!'

'Well have him down as soon as you can. It would be selfish to deny him the pleasure of seeing how much better you are—and he would also enjoy the garden.'

So, later on, Leslie came to see me, and Douglas, and Kirsteen and Diana. It was an effort to keep up face with them, but practice made it easier. I thought I would be cured of the shaming betrayals of sorrow now that I was at Hurtwood, but I still found myself vulnerable to sudden freshets of tears, to being suddenly unable to swallow because choked by a hard lump of misery. But to Daisy these were only symptoms, which instead of being reprehensible were quite natural. 'Even a broken leg takes time to mend, and a broken heart takes longer before it is serviceable. Don't force yourself, dear child. Allow time for the process of healing. There will always be a scar, but honourable scars are not disfiguring.'

For the first time in my life I was not only allowed but encouraged to obey my instincts. If I did not feel hungry I did not come for a meal; but food was left in the dining-room so that I could eat when I felt like it. No one tried to make me eat, but every night there was a thermos of soup, sandwiches wrapped in a napkin, fruit, in my bedroom. When I could not sleep, instead of huddling in my bed I wandered naked in the garden, swam in the pool, and if I got chilled, soon became warm again by soaking in a hot bath at two, or three, or four in the morning. And if I did not sleep until dawn, what did it matter—because I could go on sleeping until late in the afternoon. Once I slept for twenty-three hours, but Daisy knew this was a sign of healing, so no one woke me to see if there was anything wrong.

I had been at Hurtwood nearly a month when Mother wrote and said all was forgiven and I could come home. 'You had better come the day after to-morrow as by now you must have outstayed your welcome. Be sure to thank both your hostesses for being so exceedingly hospitable.'

I showed the letter to Daisy. There were times when she took decisive action and this was one of them. She rang up Mother, and told her, politely but in a voice which allowed no argument, that I would return to Seacourt when she considered me ready to do so...which would not be for at least another three months. 'Oh, darling Daisy! Can I really stay?' I exclaimed as she briskly put down the receiver. She looked surprised. 'What a silly question. Surely you have realised by now that this is your home.'

As I gradually became neither avid for sleep nor fearful of not sleeping, I began to dream of Esmond. There was no sudden breaking down of separation, but like a frosted plant gradually feeling the rising sap I became aware that I was seeing him although I could not remember it. Then, leaf by leaf, dream-memory unfolded. I was happy again, not radiantly happy as I had been for a little while, but quietly, like a small green shrub on a summer evening.

The quality of my dreams began to change. They were more vivid and yet more arduous to achieve. To meet him needed an effort of will, a great effort which left me exhausted in the morning. It was as though, to reach the country where we could be together, he had come to find me at the limit of his endurance and then take me over a high range of mountains...mountains that were as high as space, as wide as time. When we were safely there I was happy. The trees were yellow, although not with autumn, instead of green, and many of the flowers were unfamiliar. My body was much lighter, yet this was not because it was obedient to my thought as in a dream. It was a material body, obeying a less stringent law of gravity, able to run faster, to leap higher, to swim farther under water; but still in its own place equally solid as the one I re-entered on waking.

I had been there several times before Esmond told me that we were on a new planet. 'We arrive grown-up instead of being born. I have decided to stay here instead of having another turn on Earth.' He laughed joyously. 'It's so new, so clean—no diseases, not even unfriendly insects. Haven't you noticed what fun it is to lie on the grass without worrying whether you are disturbing an ants' nest, to explore a tropical forest with no snakes or spiders or leeches?'

'I thought it was a dream,' I admitted. 'I never have snakes or spiders in dreams, only in nightmares.'

'Of course it isn't a dream, darling. It's real. If you don't believe me, try to change one of those trees into something else and you will find it takes no notice and just goes on being a tree.'

'Then how do I get here? Esmond, it can't be solid, because my solid body is in bed at Hurtwood.'

'Well, I didn't want to tell you yet, but you are not really here. You are only a visitor. I suppose you are really a kind of ghost. It is very hard work bringing you here—much more of an effort than if I had to tow you up a mountain on skis. Bringing earth-ghosts here is not encouraged. It's considered a waste of energy, and energy is very important here when there is so much to create.'

'Oh please can I stay with you? If you keep me from going back to my body it will run down like a clock and then I shall be free of the wretched thing.'

For a moment he seemed regretful, but not more than a carefree adult would be who had to deny a treat to a child who is too young to enjoy it. 'Your body is not ready to die yet. You must use it to live your own life in your own place. Your place is not my place any more. You must live your life— your life...' I awoke hearing him say it.

I have not been there since that night, nor have I dreamed again of Esmond.

125

PART THREE

CHAPTER ONE

SECRET WEDDING

I stayed at Hurtwood until the autumn and then went back to my parents, who a few days later, took me for a holiday in London where we stayed at the Cecil Hotel—which used to be next to the Savoy, overlooking the Thames; and it was there that I had one of the most important dreams of my life.

In the dream I was sitting by a window, looking disconsolately at a mountain in the far distance. Behind me a door opened and a woman came into the room, a young and beautiful woman with her hair in two long black plaits falling over her shoulders. With her were two little boys, so exactly like each other that for a moment I thought I had seen the same child twice. They were about two years old, with dark eyes although their hair was brilliant gold, in ringlets which touched the wide lace collars of their little velvet suits. I knew she was asking me to look after them for her. She kissed them and they ran towards me....Then I woke up, knowing that the last words she had said to me were, 'Go to Leslie. Tell him his mother sent you. Tell him you know what to do.'

I had not seen nor heard of Leslie since July, although at times I missed him acutely. Daisy had gently pointed out that as he wanted to marry me and I was determined not to marry anyone, it would be kinder to make a clean break and let him forget me. He had never said much about his family, but I knew his mother was dead and that his father had recently remarried. I also knew he had a twin brother who was at Oxford while Leslie was at Cambridge, but he did not play tennis and we had never met. If they were the twins of my dream, why had I seen them as small children, and with golden hair though Leslie's was the same colour as mine? Perhaps it was not a true dream, only a fantasy which Joan had created so as to give herself an excuse for seeing Leslie again. Six fortune-tellers had told me that I was going to die before I was twenty-three. It would be cruel to let Leslie love me for two years and then perhaps be nearly as unhappy as I had been when Esmond died. I longed to run to Daisy and ask her what to do. No, this would be unfair; it was my dream, and my responsibility.

Several times I picked up the telephone receiver and hastily replaced it without asking for Leslie's number. Was I really thinking of his feelings, or only being too cowardly to risk being vulnerable again? I was being a coward, and a conceited one at that, conceited enough to assume that Leslie would miss me as much as I missed Esmond. And even if he did? Would I rather not have gone to Andermatt? Was I so ungrateful for brief joy that I would rather not have had it, even for a little while?

So as not to waste any more time in indecision I rang through to Mother's room, told her I had just remembered that I had promised to spend the day with Kirsteen and was already so late that I couldn't come and say good morning, and hurriedly left the hotel before she could ring back and argue. I paid off the taxi in Piccadilly and walked slowly to Hertford Street, for now I was very nervous. At the front door I nearly turned back, but the door was open, as it had been on the day that Esmond died. I ran up the stairs and into Leslie's room without knocking. The moment he saw me I knew that it had been a true dream.

I tried by indirect means to find out what was worrying him, but he was evasive. 'Nothing is wrong now that you're here,' he protested. 'I admit I had Highland Gloom while I was up in Scotland. You wouldn't even answer my letters.'

'This is more than Highland Gloom. I know it is because your mother told me so.'

'What on earth are you talking about? Mother died when Malcolm and I were two years old.'

'I know she did. I saw her in a dream, not down-here. And I know you had gold ringlets and wore velvet suits with lace collars, like the illustrations in *Little Lord Fauntleroy*. Why did she die so young?'

'She had typhoid but was supposed to be convalescent. We were all having tea in her room. Malcolm and I were sitting on the bed beside her, when suddenly she gasped and dropped the cup she was holding. Her heart had given out.'

'Have you seen her since?'

'No, I haven't.' He hesitated. 'But I think Malcolm has—at least he talks about her a lot. He tried to get in touch with her through automatic writing. I think he only does it because he's so miserable and ill....'

'So he is ill!'

He nodded. 'He rowed in the Oxford boat this year. It sank, as you probably remember. The crew had a party that night and Malcolm fell off the top of a taxi and landed on his head. He got concussion, but instead of going to bed he went to working for his Finals in spite of increasing headaches. He looked damned ill when he came up to Scotland, but instead of getting him properly vetted, A.D.—everyone calls Father by his initials—prescribed ''fresh air and exercise''. So he had to shoot four days a week although the jar of the gun made his headaches worse.'

'Where is he now?'

'In a nursing home. He doesn't want to see anyone, even me.'

'What about his father?'

'Oh, A.D. has gone back to the Argentine,' he said flatly.

'That's one good thing. We can cure him much easier without your father interfering. The first thing to do is to get him out of the nursing home. Think how the one I was in nearly finished me off when I had my tonsils out.'

'But what can you do?'

'Try to give Malcolm what Daisy gave to me. I've prayed nearly every night since I went to Hurtwood that I may be able to hand on what I found there.'

Within three days, with the willing co-operation of Mr. Blundell, the Grant family solicitor who acted more or less as a guardian to the children when A.D. was in the Argentine, we had taken a furnished house near London, and installed Miss Casibon to run it for us. Casy had looked after the twins since their mother died, and stayed on with the family until the previous year when A.D. re-married.

When I first saw Malcolm he weighed eight stone instead of his rowing weight of eleven stone six and was too weak to get out of bed. In a few days he began to revive, as though our ugly furnished house were another Hurtwood. In six weeks I knew that all he needed to complete his convalescence was a carefree holiday.

Mr. Blundell, as well as Casy, was by now entirely convinced that I knew what I was doing, and so when I told him that I wanted to take Malcolm to the Mediterranean he provided the wherewithal for us to rent a villa. The villa was easy to find, for Herbert Olivier, who had a house next door to Seacourt, had two at La Mortala, near Ventimiglia on the Italian side of the border, and was looking for a tenant for the larger one.

It was after we had decided to take Malcolm abroad that I realised we had another problem to overcome. I had not told my parents what I was doing, for at the beginning I was following a hunch and was afraid of being put off my stroke if Mother tried to convince me that I was too young and inexperienced to take responsibility; and later, when I was more self-confident, it seemed a needless complication.

They had not worried about me, for they thought I was either at Hurtwood or playing golf for Hampshire or Stoke Poges, which I did three or four times to lend colour to my cover-story. But the story would have to be improved a lot before it would cover a trip to Italy. Casy, fond as I was, and am, of her, was not the right person for the holiday I visualised. But Mother would never let me go off with Leslie and Malcolm without a chaperon. Suddenly I thought of Betty Stewart-Lockhart, who at that time was married to David Joel. I knew Betty was working very hard with the new showrooms she and David had just opened in Knightsbridge, for the sale of the modern furniture made in their workshops at Hayling Island; but as soon as I had told her the whole story she agreed to drop everything and come with us. At first Mother was quite willing to let me go with Betty; then she began to hedge. I could go for a fortnight, perhaps even for three weeks, but I must be back in time for Christmas. Betty must promise to keep a strict eye on me, and to bring me home at once if father wished it. He needed me in the laboratory....I had already been too long at Hurtwood with Daisy....

Suddenly maternal apron-strings felt constricting as a tourniquet. I would marry Leslie now, instead of waiting until he had asked A.D.'s permission, which he intended to do the moment that Malcolm had completely recovered. I would not wait for permission either. Father would mope and say I was too young. Mother could be talked round, for she liked Leslie; but she would insist on a 'a proper wedding'.

It was on Saturday morning, and we were leaving England on the following Thursday, when I told Leslie we would get married before going to Italy. I was a little anxious that he might be afraid of offending A.D., but he was so delighted that he rushed me off to get a special licence in case I changed my mind. When we had filled in all the answers on the application forms the clerk looked at me severely and said that as I was under age he could not issue a licence without my parent's consent. We tried to bluff it out by saying I had absentmindedly put 1907 instead of 1906 as the year I was born, but he remained unimpressed and told me to bring my birth certificate when I returned with the requisite signatures.

By now I was determined not to be thwarted by bureaucrats or parents. They could stop me getting married, but if they did I would bolt with Leslie. I arrived at Seacourt in time for Sunday tea, and when at last the dropers-in had departed, I argued until midnight. 'Later, dear, when you know him better—when you have met his family—a June wedding, if you haven't changed your mind by then. You can't get married without a proper trousseau,' said Mother. Father sat silent as his desk and gloomed. At last I had to be rather brutal. 'You can stop me getting married until next April, but if you do I will present you with a dear little illegitimate grandchild—and try to make it twins.'

That *bisque* won me game, set, and match. Father cheered up, relieved to think that I had saved him from having to make a decision, and said that at least I had spared him the torment of having to wear a top hat at my wedding. 'You must both of you come to it,' I said generously. 'It will be on Wednesday, so you had better start packing if you are coming up to London to-morrow. There isn't much time.'

'Can't I tell anyone, not even Margaret Olivier? She really *ought* to know as Herbert is already in La Mortala and she will be hurt if I don't tell her first,' said Mother wistfully.

'No, darling, no one at all. Think how awkward it would be for Malcolm and Betty if they thought they were being gooseberries on my honeymoon.'

'Not even Margery and Iris?'

'No, quite definitely No! Think what fun you are going to have when you can break the news to everyone. You'll be the first Mama to share in her daughter's elopement.'

This cheered her up. Already she was looking forward to a glorious spate of telephone calls. 'My dear, prepare yourself for a great surprise! Dear Joan is *married!* When?, Oh, weeks ago. Was it a shock to me? Of *course* not. She tells me everything. Jack and I were both there....Yes, of course we are giving a party to welcome them home....'

We relaxed our ban of secrecy sufficiently for Kirsteen to be bridesmaid and Rex Janson to be best man. She met Rex

131

for the first time at our wedding and married him six months later. The only other person there except my parents was Mr. Blundell, who, bravely facing possible repercussions from the Argentine, even signed the register.

We were married at ten-thirty on the morning of the 30th November 1927; at the church in Down Street because Leslie's rooms were in that parish. The church was cold and grey and ugly, no more magical than a station waiting-room, and the parson, a horrid little man with a streaming cold, gabbled through the service to show his disapproval of what he obviously thought of as a 'hole-and-corner marriage'.

After champagne, and an hour's artificial heartiness at the Cecil Hotel, we hurried back to have lunch with Malcolm, who had no idea we were getting married, as I had suddenly remembered that his passport was out of date and that I had promised to go with him to renew it. On our way there, Malcolm and I ran into my parents in Piccadilly. I only just managed to stop them giving away my secret, for, never having seen him, they thought he was Leslie. I had forgotten to mention that they were identical twins.

CHAPTER TWO

the girl and the twins

A winter drive through France would have been tiring for Malcolm, even if there had been room for the four of us, and the luggage, in Leslie's open Vauxhall; so we sent the car down to the villa with an R.A.C. driver and went by the Blue Train. During breakfast in the restaurant car Betty whispered, 'Look, there's a honeymoon couple, the darlings.'

'How do you know?' I asked anxiously, hoping that while I was sharing a sleeper with her she had not noticed the wedding-ring pinned inside the breast pocket of my green satin pyjamas. She laughed, 'Darling, you'll understand when you are married. I can always spot a honeymoon couple at fifty yards.'

La Mortala was a perfect setting for a honeymoon, even with the bride and bridegroom strictly incognito. There was a grove of ancient olive trees behind the Villa Olivier, a formal Italian garden, quantities of orange trees, mimosa, and jasmine; and terraces of carnations striding down to the railway line and the sea. The drawing-room was twenty feet high and hung with Herbert's paintings, in which Margaret, and his three children, William, Mary and Anne, had been the models for various allegorical subjects. The one I most clearly remember was Mary in black draperies disconsolately carrying a sickle, disguised as Ruth among the alien corn. The room had six French windows, opening on a terrace sentinelled by palm trees whose leaves rasped in the wind as though an army of swords were being drawn from rusty scabbards.

Betty's room was large enough for an eighteenth-century *lit de parade* and Leslie's I cannot remember as, discreetly, I only went into it to do his unpacking. Malcolm's had a fine painted ceiling speckled with black dots —which we later found out to have been caused by William Olivier enlivening a sojourn in bed with chickenpox by shooting moths and mosquitoes with an air-pistol; and there was a magnificent marble staircase with finial urns which looked even better after I had filled them with branches of orange-blossom. I bought a whole tree from a farmer so as to get enough of it.

My bedroom had curtains of rose-red damask and Empire furniture, including a very genuine antique bed which had two lamps of life at the head of it and two bronze sphinx at the foot, so wobbly that they fell of with a crash at the slightest provocation. It was while Leslie was trying to put one of the sphinx on again that he said, 'As a matter of interest, why did you tell me that you were an adulteress?'

I felt myself blushing. 'Oh damn! I hoped you wouldn't notice. It makes me feel such a fool.'

'Virgins are proverbially foolish.'

'Not as foolish as I am! I never realised I had such an appallingly literal mind. I thought ''going to bed with a man'' and ''sleeping with a man'' meant just that.'

'But you must have read books...'

'Books! Scientific books!' I exclaimed bitterly. 'Words like fallopian tubes and spermatozoa—just *words!* I thought spermatozoa crept out and crept in while both parties were asleep...'

He laughed until I was afraid that Malcolm or Betty would hear him.

My first exercise in housekeeping was made easy by the three Italian maids who had been for years with Herbert, so all Betty and I had to do was the shopping, which gave us an excuse to gossip with the market women and buy quantities of flowers. To show Father I was thinking about him I sent him matchbox after matchbox of mosquitoes, the specimens neatly chloroformed and packed in cotton wool, together with the electrifying news that although as far as I could see without a microscope they were *culex pipiens* they were undoubtedly gorging themselves on my blood. He was delighted to receive these tributes of affection but refused to accept my evidence 'C. *pipiens,*' he wrote to me, 'under no circumstances will bite human beings. It is presumed that they take their blood-meal from birds. You will doubtless remember, if you can spare the time to think of such matters, that although Staley spent several days, stripped to the waist in a cage of C. *pipiens,* none of them could be persuaded to bite him. This is a scientific *fact,* so in future make your observations with more care.' If he had only listened to me he would have had a new sub-species, which my C. *pipiens* proved to be, named after him; but alas, this honour went a year later to an Italian entomologist.

The smaller villa where Herbert was living, lay between

ours and the famous gardens of the Villa Hanbury, which occupied the rest of the rocky headland of which the foreshore was constantly patrolled by frontier guards. At first we smiled and tried to be friendly, but they were so unresponsive that we ignored them when we encountered them on our walks. A stony stare annoyed them even more than friendly overtures, and they tried to scare us away by tramping after us with bayonets at the ready or by firing revolvers at sea-gulls. It was usually quite easy to avoid them, especially at night, for they made so much noice crunching over the rocks in their heavy boots; but one of them was caddish enough to stalk us in bare feet when we were sunbathing, which made Leslie very angry. Perhaps his anger was mistaken for guilt, as it must have been about then that they decided we were gold-smugglers. This flight of fancy we only heard about after we had left, when Herbert saw our dossier, an impressive document in which I was described as 'the girl with the twins', embellished with a snapshot of me, and two others of my 'accomplices'; both of these being in fact snapshots of Malcolm, who never wore striped shirts nor Leslie checked ones, a convention they had started while they were at Winchester.

Ordinary soldiers were nearly as bad, little Mussolinis who thought nothing of stopping a G.B. car, ordering us to drive miles in the wrong direction, and then striding off without bothering to thank us. After this had happened several times, we turned left instead of right out of the gates and drove nearly every day into France. The French Customs men soon got to know us and waved us through without glancing into the car, but their Italian opposite numbers became increasingly surly. They charged us ridiculously high duty even on a Camembert or a loaf of bread, so it soon became a point of honour to smuggle at least one item every time we crossed the border. Betty had the highest score with two small melons tucked inside her blouse—which gained murmurs of 'quel beau balcon!' from the kindly French and the usual sneer from the Italians; until I inadvertently scored higher with two yards of bread—and nearly landed us all in trouble.

We were coming home late, having been to Monte Carlo to restore our nerves with a little gambling after a drive from Sospel. Malcolm had wanted to see if he could average fifty m.p.h. down the thirty kilometres of hairpin bends. He succeeded, for our guardian angels thoughtfully removed all the ox-carts out of the way, so it seemed a pity not to see if we were equally fortunate at roulette—which we were not. We reached the border at about 3 a.m. and I was so sure that the Italians would be too sleepy to bother with us that only as a gesture I tucked the two long loaves up the sleeves of my fur coat. The men on duty were alert and suspicious. We insisted that we had nothing to declare, but they made us get out of the car, pulled out the seats, rummaged into the tool-box, peered into the engine, and, finding nothing, sourly announced that before we could pass we must be questioned by the Commandenti. The Commandenti was in bed, and in spite of our protests we were marched into his room in the Customs house. He was grossly fat, with a thicket of wiry fur poking out between the buttons of his grimy pyjamas. He yelled at us in very bad French, obviously furious that his orders had been too literally interpreted by minions who had disturbed his night's sleep. The main stream of his fury was directed at me. 'You and your confederates shall be punished,' he shouted. 'Like a cat I have waited patiently at the mousehole and now I shall pounce.' We should be searched. We would be imprisoned. If we still refused we should be shot: 'Pam! Pam!' For further emphasis he brandished a revolver which had been hanging in a holster from the brass bedstead. The crusty ends of the loaves dug into my armpits as I tried to push them even further up my sleeves.

Then Betty's wild Highland blood went into action, her blue eyes blazing, her red hair fiery as her wrath. How dare he expose me, an innocent child, to the disgusting spectacle of himself in bed! How could I ever hope to recover from this shock to my sensibilities! He, the brute-beast, the obscenity, the hairy murderer of a young girl's dreams, would be stoned to death by honest Italian women in the market-place of Ventigmilia. 'And I,' declared Betty, hearkening to the pipes of the Stewarts of Appin, 'I shall reserve to myself the right of casting the first stone.'

The bully wilted. The bully tried to cover his horrid chest by pulling up the blanket which concealed all but the contour of his loathsome paunch. The bully cringed. Betty took the revolver from his shaking hand. For a fleeting second I thought she was going to put a merciful bullet through the creature's brain. Then she threw it disdainfully into the corner of the room, wiped her fingers slowly and carefully on her handkerchief, dropped the handkerchief on the floor, and led us royally from the room.

I tripped as I was getting into the car and dropped a loaf. One of the monster's henchmen leapt nimbly forward, saluted, picked up the loaf, dusted it, and with a low bow presented it to Betty. We had no further trouble with the Customs.

On Christmas Eve we gave a party and asked Herbert, and Margaret and Mary who had arrived the day before from England. We meant to announce our marriage after dinner but I decided it would be more fun to tell each of them separately.

Betty said, 'Bless you, my darling children! Thank goodness I needn't feel guilty any more for being a spoil-sport!'

Malcolm said, 'Oh, so you've married Leslie. Bother: I meant to marry you myself. However, it doesn't matter so long as you are one of the family.'

Margaret rushed into the garden to bring me an armful of orange blossom.

Mary, who had been my friend nearly as long as Diana, exclaimed, 'Hooray, now you can help me bully the parents into letting me marry Sandy Sanders. They are being a bit sticky because he has only his pay, and has lost an arm so they don't think he will be able to stay in the R.A.F.'

Herbert kissed my hand. 'My congratulations to the bridegroom, and my sincere apologies to the bride. I harboured unworthy thoughts about you, dear Joan; for soon after you arrived my faithful Marguerita told me that she had found one of the Signor Grant's pyjamas in the Signorita Marshall's bed. *In loco parentis* it would have been my duty to speak severely to your seducer—had I known which twin he was....' He could say no more for he was laughing too much.

CHAPTER THREE

flat land

By the end of January Malcolm had found comfortable bachelor's chambers in Half Moon Street, run by an ex-butler and his wife, a motherly old woman who promised to cosset him. We had been down to Seacourt and had a belated wedding reception in the music-room, at which, for most of the time, Malcolm understudied for the bridegroom without anyone noticing the difference. When I could escape long enough to look for Leslie I found him with Susan, Iris's younger daughter, playing houses under the dining-room table. Quite unabashed, he explained that he had an acute attack of 'party nausea' and that Malcolm and he often acted as each other's stand-ins.

Although they were identical twins, were treated exactly alike and went to the same schools until at last they insisted on going to rival universities, they were in every other respect totally dissimilar. If one liked a person, a play, a picture, the other was sure to disagree. This was not contrariness, for when I asked their opinion even of something as impersonal as a film or a book, they invariably took opposite views. However, one thing they shared: their affection for me and their opinion of their family. They became informative about my in-laws after A.D. had cabled Leslie that he was to bring me out to the Argentine.

'What's A.D. like?' I asked.

'Pretty bloody,' said Malcolm. And Leslie said, 'You may be able to bounce him, which is more than any of us can do.'

'What's your sister like?'

'Oh, Elsie's all right,' said Malcolm. 'Only I wish she wouldn't wear spats with a kilt when she's shooting. She's a very good shot—considering she's a woman.' And Leslie said, 'She's a Commandant of Girl Guides; so you'd better not let her know that you refused even to be a Brownie.'

'What's Elsie's husband like?'

'Ronald? Oh, he's the cheerful type. He can even get A.D. into a reasonably good temper,' said Malcolm. And Leslie said, 'You will like Ronald. He talks nearly as much as you do.'

'And your eldest brother?'

They both brightened. 'Duncan's a thundering good chap. You won't see him, though, for he is on his way home to marry a girl called Margot Birkin.'

'What's she like?'

'I've no idea,' said Leslie. 'We haven't seen her. She went out to the Argentine and met the rest of us, so she will have had enough of the Grant family to go on with.'

'She might like to meet me. After all, daughters-in-law had better band together to protect each other from A.D.,' I suggested.

'But you are a Grant too now,' said Leslie, which appeared to settle the matter.

'And what about Babs? Is she a terrifying stepmother?'

'Babs is all right. She's a bit older than us and and younger than Duncan,' said Leslie. 'She's Irish and a Roman Catholic—not the emotional kind of Irish, ' he added hastily. 'She does her best to keep A.D. genial, but of course she can't do much with him.' And Malcolm, with a heartfelt sigh, said, 'Poor Babs! Think of having Father in the same country all the year round!'

As the day of our departure drew nearer Malcolm treated me like a hospital nurse cheering a patient on the way to the operating theatre. He went with me to choose my trousseau—dress shops amused him and were abominated by Leslie—and encouraged me to buy dresses which would have been more suitable for a sophisticated woman of thirty. He frequently implored me on no account to let myself be bullied by the Grants. I perched precariously on an emotional seesaw. Sometimes I was a child being outfitted for its first term at boarding school, and the next moment a knight getting several new suits of armour before setting forth to challenge a multi-headed dragon.

On the 2nd of February Malcolm saw us off at Tilbury, and during the voyage I acquired more self-confidence. People on board liked me, so why shouldn't the Grants? My lovely new clothes were a success. I could dance the tango. I could play golf. I could play chess. I could play squash.... Damn it, I would *make* them like me!

While the *Almeda Star* steamed up the River Plate I was still trying to decide what to wear for my first entrance in front of a critical, but what I hoped would soon prove to be an enthusiastic and appreciative, audience. My final selection was a circular skirt and long-sleeved bolero in white *crepe de Chine* from Callot—very chic, and so suitable for a hot climate as it allowed a cooling draught to play on the discreet glimpse of my bare midriff. With this I wore a white felt picture hat with appliqued navy blue satin flowers, which I had bought in Paris, an enormous navy blue chiffon handkerchief, and high-heeled sandals.

A.D., with Elsie and Ronald in attendance, was waiting for us when the ship docked at Buenos Aires. My first glance

140

showed me that the Chief Dragon was grey, and spare and arid. He removed the pince-nez from the bridge of his long, thin nose, polished it carefully on an impeccably clean hankerchief, and took a second look at me. He was tall. But I was tall enough to look him slap in the eyes, eyes which were cold and grey as a wet day in his native Scotland. 'Well, you seem to have brought plenty of luggage,' he remarked and marched off, Leslie at heel, to the Customs shed.

Elsie, who also wore pince-nez, fired off a few hearty remarks of the 'Hope you had a decent trip' variety. Ronald beamed as though enjoying a private joke....I did not realise until later that, as neither Leslie nor I had thought of giving my dossier in our letters to A.D., my costume for Act One, Scene One, had confirmed their suspicions that Leslie had picked me out of the Gaiety chorus.

We drove in silence to the Plaza Hotel, and after dinner went up to the sitting-room of the suite to sit on stiff little gilt chairs round a central table which supported a gilt basket of flowers, with a label attached to the handle emphasising the point that it was a present to the bride from the Manager of the Plaza Hotel. So far as I can remember, although I must be wrong, no one spoke a single word except Ronald, who did his best to help me by acting as *compere* to my feverish stream of chatter. It was midnight when he and Elsie returned to Hurlingham, the more than English suburb where they reigned. A.D. opened a cupboard, brought out a bottle of whisky, and said pointedly, 'Leslie and I will have a nightcap before we go to bed.' This was the cue for my exit, and I took it thankfully.

For two hours I prowled up and down my bedroom through waves of gloom. In the troughs I was abjectly apologetic for being such a ghastly failure. On the crests I quivered with self-pity and rage. At last the bedroom door opened to disclose a radiant Leslie. 'Darling, you are marvellous,' he exclaimed, as he hugged me. 'My clever, beautiful Joan! No one has ever made such a hit with A.D. I've never heard him to be so chatty. He positively sparkled!'

The next morning I thought it would be tactful to leave them alone together, so I went out to have a look at B.A.—as I had already learned to call the city. Travel leaflets described it as 'The Paris of the South', but nearly thirty years ago it looked like a pastry-cook's nightmare—and a pastry-cook who could only dream in two dimensions; for while many of the buildings had facades which might have been modelled in icing-sugar, the back and sides of them had dreary walls of muddy coloured brick. I wandered along, looking into shop windows, especially the flower-shops, and after following several side streets, came to one where men were rather dismally standing in queues outside houses which looked too small for pubs. In most of the windows women were sitting; knitting, sewing, manicuring their nails or listening to gramophone records. They looked friendly so I smiled at several of them, and was annoyed that instead of smiling back they shouted at me in Spanish, which I could not understand, and even went so far as to grimace and put out their tongues.

A nice-looking young man came up to me and took me by the arm. 'I think you have lost your way, Senorita,' he said in quite good English, and began to hurry me along the pavement. 'Leave me alone,' I said crossly. For I disliked being hurried, especially by strangers.

He tightened his grip. 'I shall not leave you alone. You will come home with me. I have a very nice flat. We will have luncheon together....'

'My husband does not like me to lunch with strange men,' I said primly. 'And anyway he is expecting me to lunch with him at the Plaza Hotel.'

He laughed, which I thought most discourteous. Did he think I was too plain to have a husband? 'Then I will conduct you back to him—and tell him it is not sensible to let his wife go for walks by herself.'

'You will tell him nothing of the sort. I have never heard

142

anything so ridiculous! And I am not ready to go back to the hotel yet. I came out to do a little shopping.'

'Then I will come shopping too, and carry your parcels. I can at least talk to the shop-girls for you in Spanish.'

So I let him come with me. I thought that it would be good for him to learn that English women could not be bullied by impertinent foreigners. I bought gramophone records, silk stockings, toothpaste, and a rather gaudy tie because my escort admired it—for Leslie. I gave it to the floor waiter the next morning, as it looked even gaudier when I examined it more critically. He bought me an enormous bunch of gladioli and insisted on carrying it as well as my parcels into the hotel. I introduced him to Leslie and they spoke to each other in Spanish for a minute or two. Then he left and Leslie said wearily, 'For God's sake don't let A.D. know that on your first day in the Argentine you got picked up in the Red Light district.'

The next day we went with A.D. to Rosario, and in the train I acquired further merit by beating him at chess. Babs was kind but preoccupied with the baby, who was fretful and delicate. There was a complete absence of the gay hidalgos I had expected to meet. We played golf every day and I played well, because the first time I got into the rough and turned round to see why my caddie was slow in handing me a niblick I found he was using it to kill a snake. After that I kept to the fairway.

After about a week of this, A.D. drove us to one of his *estancias*, La Carlina, in the province of Cordoba. Mile after mile we drove through endless quantities of nothing: nothing except wire fences every thousand metres, nothing except creaking iron windmills painted dried-blood red, nothing except the bleached skeletons and skulls of hundreds of cattle which had failed to survive the first stage of their trek to the meat-packing plants in Buenos Aires.

I comforted myself with the thought that when we arrived at the *estancia* I would find a luxurious Spanish home, perhaps a fountain in the patio, where gauchos would serenade the bride and bridegroom to the accompaniment of accordions and guitars. La Carlina in fact was almost frighteningly ugly—frightening because how could I hope to understand a father-in-law who was exceedingly rich and yet so mean that he would not make his home even moderately comfortable? The only living-room was in the middle of the house and lit by a skylight. The dried-blood red of the creaking windmills was echoed in the wallpaper, on which were dozens of faded photographs, mostly of cows. But two of the photographs reassured me. One was of Leslie's mother, instantly recognisable as the woman I had seen in my dream; and the other of Leslie and Malcolm taken the month before she died, with golden ringlets and white kid button boots, with lace collars on their velvet suits...the clothes in which she had brought them to me. I knew she had been beautiful, sensitive, and gay. This was confirmed by the letters A.D. had received after she died, which were stuck into a purple velvet album displayed on a shelf under her photograph. It must have been A.D. who chose the hideous furniture, probably from a mail-order catalogue for no woman of taste could possibly have done so. Except for the dreadful, windowless room in the middle of the house there was nowhere else to sit except a kind of veranda; but that was reserved for A.D. and his endless pounding on a portable typewriter.

Every morning we rode before breakfast. It was too hot during the rest of the day. And every thousand metres we stopped to open a gate in a wire fence. The mosquitoes were so plentiful that a grey pony I rode was black with them, and every time I patted him there was a splodge of blood on his coat. I soaked my shirt with citronella, but there were still so many mosquitoes eager for English blood that this too was disgustingly blotched at the end of the ride. For the rest of the day we did nothing except play chess or piquet between meals, and try to sleep through the worst of the heat. Even the herds of cattle seemed unreal: money on the hoof, waiting to be converted into a different currency, of racks of carcases, tons of corned beef coffined in tins. Even the sky was drab as nickel coin: no cloud-galleons, no radiant sunsets. Through the dusty air it looked like a steel-blue lid clamped over the rusty pan in which we fried. Even thunderstorms were unfriendly: a raucous clatter of brass instead of gargantuan laughter; and a bolt of lightning was sly enough to hit the corrugated iron roof and hurl me out of bed, while it left A.D. sleeping peacefully on the other side of the house.

I was only there about a fortnight, though it seemed much longer. A.D. had promised to pay for a honeymoon trip to the Andes, or by river-boat up the Pirana to see the Iguacu Falls; but when it came to the point he said it would be just as nice for us, and much cheaper, to visit Elsie.

Hurlingham was far, far better than La Carlina, but everyone I met there was Scottish or English, and the Club, which was the hub of existence, was an imitation of the original one on the Thames. The houses were steadfastly mock-Tudor with 'English' gardens—pallid mignonette and sad little sweetpeas instead of hibiscus, bougainvillaea and a thousand other exotic shrubs which could have flourished there. The men did not actually stain their bodies with woad, but they trotted off to catch the city train wearing stiff collars (and six spare ones in their attache-case to change into as they wilted in the heat) to protect themselves from being mistaken for soft-shirted Argentines. The women gossiped about servants, about 'club activities', about each other; and about me. The more Elsie tried to defend the honour of the Grants by declaring that Leslie had *not* found me in the chorus line, the less she was believed. 'But her clothes, dear! The dress she wore to the Club last night was practically naked,' said a lady looking smugly down at her modest vee. 'Chorus girls never play games,' countered Elsie desperately.

'Ah, but she has to. All that golf and squash is necessary for a woman who is quite blatant about not wearing corsets.'

All this, though tiresome in many ways, had one advantage. At the Club Saturday evening dances the gentlemen could hardly wait to foxtrot with me to the gramophone. And when my feet were sore from being trodden on I remembered how much worse it had been to be a wallflower in a pink dress at my first Hunt Ball. But I never got the chance of dancing a tango with an Argentine.

Then Ronald came to our rescue and got us invited on a 'Directors' Inspection Tour' of the railways south of B.A. The special coaches might have been rooms in a St. John's Wood villa of Victorian England—except that they had proper bathrooms. There were brass bedsteads, fireplaces with china dogs at each end of the mantlepiece, red plush curtains with bobble fringe, Axminster carpets, cake-stands, beaded footstools...a *decor* which provided the background for my twenty-first birthday party; with an iced cake, and candles, and lots and lots of caviare.

Apart from the absence of any scenery, almost the only snag was skunks. When annoyed by the intrusion of the train they fired at it or else got run over, and the stink was so appalling that several times I was out of bed and retching over the basin before I was properly awake. We were south of Bahia Blanca before I saw real trees, Lombardy poplars planted as windbreaks to fruit-farms, mostly apples and grapes. Most of the fruit-farmers were Italian settlers and we went to one of their homes. There were ruffled cotton curtains at the windows of the little box-like house. Morning glories had been trained over the corrugated iron roof and there were rose-coloured grapes hanging from a trellis over the doorway. They gave us wine and laughed and chatted when they had got over their first shyness. They were very poor. They had three small children, and were obviously soon going to have more; and they were busy putting down roots. They were not alien to the land where they were living.

After so much flatness I was thirsty for mountains. When we were within two hours of a point where, so everyone told me, I should get the most magnificient view of the Andes that could be seen anywhere in the Argentine, the chairman decided that he would prefer to spend the night in a siding and retrace our tracks the following morning. My only consolation was that when his coach was being shunted so that it could occupy the place of honour at the end of the train, it toppled off the line, and he out of bed, hurting himself quite badly.

On my way back to B.A. I decided that I had had more than enough of the Argentine. Our passage home had been booked on the Royal Mail steamer *Alcantara* at the end of May, so we should be stuck for another six weeks unless I could finance my alternative plan. Fortunately several rich and silly old men patiently explained to me the rules of poker without asking whether I had played the game before. When I had four Kings my lip trembled, and when I had a pair of twos I bounced with excitement—and by the time we left the train I had won just enough money to go by ourselves to Brazil.

CHAPTER FOUR

snakes and charmers

On the boat coming out from England a young and gay couple, Clothilde and Martinez de Silva Prado, who were returning from their honeymoon in Paris, invited us to stay with them on their coffee fazenda. The Grants seemd to think we were not only eccentric but mildly insane to accept such a casual invitation. Why did we want to go dashing off to stay with Brazilians, especially shipboard acquaintances who had undoubtedly forgotten our existence?

'They haven't forgotten us,' I said smugly, and produced

a cable to prove that not only were we welcome but that our host and hostess were going to meet us in Sao Paulo, which was three or four hundred miles from where they lived.

Leslie was rather worried that we might offend his family, so I pointed out that I had not come over ten thousand miles only to see a country that was flatter, and far more ugly, than the dreariest parts of Cambridgeshire, nor only to meet people, who, nice as they were, I could have met just as well in Inverness or Woking. In spite of my poker winnings money was rather short, so we bought a passage on an American freighter which sailed for Santos on 17th April. Elsie and Ronald came to see us off, and their doubts as to our sanity increased when they saw the boat. We were the only passengers—or else the cockroaches had already eaten the occupants of the other two cabins. She was held together by optimism and rust, and it was obvious that her owners had long ago decided not to waste any more paint on her. As she wallowed through the muddy waters of the River Plate we looked rather apprehensively at a large, shiny brass plaque in the saloon, the only brasswork that was ever polished. It consigned into the hand of Almighty God the ship's personnel, mustering them in the order in which they should receive divine attention. At the top, THE CAPTAIN, and under this, in letters only a little smaller, THE FIRST MATE; then on down the hierarchy....And at the bottom, in letters so small that they could only just be read with the naked eye, an afterthought, 'And even those who are with us only as guests.' We could only hope that in the eye of God we were as conspicuous as sparrows.

The captain was called Grant, and frequently congratulated me on having 'a fine old American name', which Leslie considered a deliberate slight to the Highlands. He was a genial man even in his cups, from which he seldom emerged, and he often invited me up to the bridge and allowed me to steer. I enjoyed this until a rather rough evening when I heard a thud and turned to see the captain lying unconscious on the deck behind me. The inhospitable coast was far too close to the port bow for comfort, so I thought it wiser to steer straight out to sea, a course I held for rather over an hour, until someone came to relieve me at the wheel. This episode was considered enormously funny by everyone on board except Leslie and me.

But we reached Santos, in those days a scruffy little town steaming among mangrove swamps, and from there went to Sao Paulo on a rack-and-pinion railway which wound up the escarpment in hairpin bends so sharp that the baggage-car was often directly below the engine. There Clothilde and Martinez were waiting for us, and that night they took us to a party in our honour which was a vivid contrast to the more sombre entertainments of Hurlingham.

There were ten men and ten women, all Brazilian, who spoke fluent English although none had ever been to England. The women, who spent at least three months in Paris every year, had lovely clothes and magnificent diamonds and were the most beautiful women I, or Leslie, had ever seen. It was not only their looks but their ebullience which was so outstanding. For centuries the men of Brazil's 'First Families' had kept their women as strictly as the aristocrats of Spain. Divorce, on paper, was very easy for a woman to obtain, but so socially impossible that none of them had ever dared to use their legal escape-hatch. But, a year before, the downtrodden wives had suddenly realised that if twenty of them all simultaneously divorced their husbands, which would automatically give them not only their freedom but a third of their husbands' capital, society could not cut them, for they constituted the Society of which they had been so afraid.

The party was in the home of a bachelor friend of Martinez. The women were shown into a remarkable bedroom. The walls, the curtains, and the hangings of an enormous four-poster bed were of parma-violet velvet. The doors of a huge clothes-press stood open. On padded hangers were at least fifty superb nightdresses: lace, chiffon, finest embroidered lawn. The dressing-table held more bottles than a well-stocked bar, but these were scent-bottles. A door led to a lavish bathroom, another door to a room so monastic that it might have been a cell except for racks of riding-boots and guns.

'Which one is his mistress?' I whispered to Clothilde, so as to be sure to thank my unofficial hostess. She laughed. 'Who knows which she will be?'

I was a little embarrassed. Perhaps I ought not to have noticed the nightgowns, the scent. But surely, if our host was trying to be discreet he ought at least to have made sure that the cupboard was shut. The dinner started at nine, and at midnight, after twenty courses, there was a sorbet and coffee. After an interval of an hour the dinner started again, beefsteak with an egg on top, and a further ten courses. Sometimes between courses a man would raise his glass to a woman, and, if she smiled, they would go out of the room together for a few minutes—as casually as if they were going to take a turn round the dance-floor of a night-club. But there was no music, so I thought they were going for a stroll in the garden. I should have liked to have gone too for it was very hot indoors, even though the air was cooled by a fountain at the end of the room. It was not until the next day that Leslie discovered the purpose of the nightgowns...they were for the lady guests, who could not be expected to bring their own, as though they had been children carrying their slippers to a dancing-class, and were far too well brought-up to be seen naked, even in such a richly curtained bed.

Clothilde and Martinez thought my ingenuousness uproariously funny, which must still have rankled when Martinez called at the snake-farm to pick up a fresh supply of serum the following day. The last thing I wanted to do was to see snakes, or even to think abut them; but I tried to show off by casually mentioning that I had typed several letters from my father to the Director on the subject of mosquitoes. Unfortunately Father's name rang a bell with the distinguished gentleman, who greeted me most warmly and said that he would be delighted to show me everything. The more fervently I insisted that I would not dream of wasting his time, the more he insisted that I should not leave him until I had a clear picture of the important work done there, to take back to my father, his illustrious colleague.

'I will wait in the car,' said Martinez.

'No, no,' cried the Director. 'Go away until this evening. There is much for her to see, much to talk about.'

Miserably I watched Martinez drive away, and then with Leslie followed the enthusiastic little man into the first of several laboratories which I was to enter on that far too memorable day. In the first one there was a desk, a typewriter, several files lying open on a long wooden table. It all looked so harmless that I thought—if I thought about it at all—that the tiers of little cupboards along the wall held vials of serum or something even more innocuous, such as card-indexes. I was looking at some coloured drawings of snakes, which were to be made into posters so that people would be able to recognise which kinds were needed at the farm, when I heard a heavy plop behind me. It was a snake, about six feet long and as thick as my arm. The Director made a 'tut-tut' noise of annoyance and casually picked it up by the back of the head. 'That lab boy of mine is getting most careless. Always I tell him to be sure the cages are properly fastened....' He smiled at the snake. 'This little fellow is quite harmless to-day for he was milked of his venom this morning....See, I will show you.' He pinched the snake's cheeks and forced its jaw open. Then he picked up a little glass dish with gauze stretched tightly over it, through which he gently pressed the fangs. 'There! Not a drop left, you see?' He sounded placid as a milkmaid. To-morrow perhaps a drop or two, and in four days ready for another milking. He held out the snake to me, 'You would like to hold him?' He might have been offering a kitten to a child. Involuntarily I backed away. 'I might drop it,' I protested feebly. He looked surprised. 'He is not heavy—but I will give him to your husband.'

For a full minute Leslie clutched the snake round the middle, its head pointing away from him, its tail vainly trying to get a coil round his arm. Then it writhed round until it could stare him in the face. Leslie endured its hissing for a few seconds and then with a strangled yelp flung it across the room. 'You must not be rough with them,' said the Director severely.

The snake was now so angry that he had to use a forked stick to hold it down before he could bundle it back into its cage. Leslie was pale and sweating, I think more because he thought he had made a fool of himself than from the simple horror which I was feeling. The Director fixed him with a disapproving eye. 'It is clear that you do not share your wife's interest in scientific matters. It might be better if you were to leave her here with me. I will myself escort her back to your hotel this evening. My secretary will telephone for your taxi.'

And Leslie, mumbling that perhaps Martinez would think it discourteous if neither of us went back to lunch with him, cravenly left me—and, like a fool, I stayed. My early training had taught me how to share the enthusiasms of scientists—I once spent four happy days entertaining, in Father's absence, a Chinese professor whose only subject was tapeworms. But though the kind Director did everything in his power to make me enjoy that long and dreadful day, I still find it one of the things I try not to remember. Yet he seemed pleased with me, and, like an unusually generous child, insisted on showing me more and more of his treasures. His favourites at the time were tarantulas, which, like huge hairy crabs, scuttled to and fro in cages about half the size of a billiard-table. Their bite, he assured me, was more dangerous than a snake's because as yet no antidote to their venom had been discovered. These were only the hors d'oeuvre. He then showed me racks of human arms and legs, mummified

152

by some process to which I lent a most inattentive ear, that had rotted off their still-living owners. There were bloated babies in bottles, children bobbing about in large glass jars; and the *piece de resistance* was a Negro floating in a tank of formalin and awaiting dissection. He must have been a large man before the snake bit him: now he was gigantic.

'They swell—ah, how they swell!' the Director said thoughtfully. 'The Indian snakes and most of the snakes of Africa—two little punctures in the skin is all there is to see: then the heart stops. Pain yes, but not this gross distortion.'

I managed to make some inarticulate noise, being almost speechless with horror. He seemed to think I was accusing him of exaggeration. 'They swell, I tell you! Swell until they burst like overripe fruit.' He stripped off his shirt. 'Look at my back. Look at it!'

I did—with eyes I thought soon must glaze. There was a scar running up his arm to the shoulder, across his back until it disappeared under his trousers, a scar like a purple satin ribbon two inches wide. He put on his shirt again and sat down at the desk—we were now in his study where we had lunched off a tray. He was no longer the fellow-scientist or the child sharing its toys, but the stern schoolmaster lecturing a fool-hardy pupil. 'I have shown you this scar to impress upon your mind that while you are in my country you must be careful of snakes.' He wagged an admonitory finger at me. 'How did this happen to me, you ask yourself? Was I in the jungle when a coral snake flung itself at me from a branch? Was I walking barefoot in long grass? Am I a fool who picks up a snake because he thinks it is one of the harmless ones?' The questions were purely rhetorical. He was gripped, as I was, by his narrative as though by an anaconda.

'None of these foolish things was I doing—yet the thing I did was foolish. I was in this room, and in the corner, as there is now, was a little hamper of coral snakes which I wished to examine at my leisure. I opened it. There they lay, four of them, torpid at the end of a long journey. But there was one,

153

a little one, clinging to the lid as I flung it back. I am quick but he is quicker. He strikes me in the shoulder. I throw him back into the hamper. It is never allowed to leave poisonous snakes loose in the room. ' He said this severely as though it were a careless habit of mine he had constantly to rebuke. 'Then I pick up this hypodermic. ' He took one from a covered dish on his desk and made graphic gestures with it. 'It is filled with fresh serum. It is my rule that there is one ready in every room in this building. I plunge it into my arm, quickly, quickly, no time to waste in swabbing the skin with alcohol. Then I ring the alarm bell.... ' He pointed at it: an electric bellpush painted scarlet; and I remembered seeing similar ones in every other room we had been to. Only just in time did he stop himself ringing it again. 'When I rang it people came running—in two minutes they were with me, but I was already almost unconscious. I was very unhappy for several days. It is not comfortable to swell and swell until the skin must burst.... ' He leant back in his chair and looked at me almost pleadingly. 'Senhora, have I said enough to make you promise not to be careless with snakes? '

CHAPTER FIVE

coffee fazenda

After a second night in the excellent hotel we left Sao Paulo at daybreak, for Martinez wanted to cover as much distance as possible before the noon heat. Distance, the distance of range after range of rounded hills, smooth under their green pelt of forest; blue distance of the high *sierras;* a distant glimpse of the road ahead of us, a red thread in the cacophony of green—is all I remember of that journey. There had been distance of a kind in the Argentine; an emptiness like a grey future stared at dumbly across a slough of despond. But here distance was an exuberance, a challenge, a renewal of wonder; beauty untamed, and beguiling as the moods of the sea.

We had the road to ourselves except for an occasional ox-cart; and Martinez drove so fast that although we had a siesta in an adobe village we reached the Fazenda Campo Alto before sunset. Centuries had mellowed the pantiles that roofed the great white house until they seemed as much a natural growth as the trumpet-vines, the surge of bougainvillea, which splashed the ancient walls with riotous colour, spangled with humming-birds. Lawns smooth as an English bowling-green flowed down to the lake. 'You like my lake?' said Martinez. 'I made it three years ago. One morning I said to myself, ''There is still something lacking in the view. What is it, Martinez?'' And then the answer came to me. My hills, the avenues which my grandfather planted, would look even better if they were reflected in water. So I built a dam, and now there is three miles of water for my home to look at.'

What joy it was to be there, after La Carlina where no one bothered to make a room less ugly or to plant a flower.

The pretty little Negress who brought coffee to our room next morning gave me a note: 'We have all gone out riding but I thought you might wish to sleep late. Breakfast is at nine, but tell the maid if you would prefer to have it upstairs. Love. C.'

I decided to let Leslie sleep while I went for a swim in the lake. House servants were polishing the floors, filling flower-vases, singing softly as they worked, pausing to nod and smile as I passed. The air was more scented even than Hurtwood in the season of azaleas. A toucan, its yellow beak absurdly large for its raven's body, clattered from a clump of poinsettia bushes in their full scarlet. A flock of green parakeets skimmed low overhead. On the far side of the blue water a cart drawn by a span of white oxen creaked along an avenue of giant palms.

I came to a wooden pier where two rowing-boats and another with a furled orange sail were bobbing at their moorings on a slight ripple. There was no one about and I was out of sight of the house. It would be ridiculous to put on a scratchy woollen bathing-suit, so, leaving it with my towel and dressing-gown on the end of the pier, I climbed down the ladder into water smooth as sun-warmed silk. I swam lazily for a couple of hundred yards and then floated, basking in the early sunlight.

The stillness was cracked by the sound of a galloping horse, a dull thudding as it crossed the lawns and then the clatter of hoofs on the planks of the pier. 'Joan, come back at once! Quickly!' Martinez's voice was so peremptory that I was startled and rather annoyed. So I was late for breakfast, was I? Why should that make him cross—or were Brazilians even more morose than Scots in the early morning?

I saw him jump into one of the boats and start rowing towards me—rowing very badly too, for he was splashing the water with the oars. I tried to swim faster. How infuriating to be fetched by Martinez, as though he was a nanny and I a silly child in danger of drowning! He reached me before I was more than half-way to the pier, leant over the side and hauled me unceremoniously into the boat. Dripping and resentful I tried to look nonchalant, having suddenly realised I was stark naked. He pulled out his handkerchief and mopped the sweat from his forehead. 'Joan, please do not give me any more such shocks. I do not like shocks, especially before breakfast.'

'I am sorry I have offended you,' I said stiffly. 'It never occurred to me that you would come here on horseback. If you had walked down from the house to tell me that I am late for breakfast I should have seen you in time to put on some clothes.'

Then he laughed, laughed until he nearly fell backwards off the thwart. 'My dear, sweet Joan, I adore you being naked—and no one need ever be punctual in my house.'

'Then why all the fuss?'

'Because we never bathe in the lake: we bathe in the swimming-pool. In the lake there are alligators.'

After breakfast he showed me round the house. The furniture was superb, much of it brought from Portugal by his family in the seventeenth century. In one room there was a leather runner on the polished floor. I wondered whether it was native work, or an unusual kind of Cordoba leather such as I had seen on the walls of his library.

'Oh, that?' he said casually. 'It's an anaconda skin, an unusually fine one. It is thirty-six feet long and six feet wide.'

I gulped. 'I suppose it came from the Amazon?'

He pointed out of the window. 'I shot it on the lawn—but too late to stop it swallowing one of my pedigree calves. It had chased the poor beast out of the stockyard. The calf hadn't got a chance of course, for a large anaconda is supposed to be able to catch a galloping horse.'

I dare say I looked scared, for he put his arm round my shoulders and gave me a friendly hug. 'You must not be afraid of Brazil, Joan. She is a good country to people who love her. Everywhere there are dangers. Think of the waves in the Bay of Biscay, the taxis in Paris! But when you go on a ship you do not expect to be drowned, nor run over when you cross the street on the way to Maxim's. Do I worry? No. But I do not shut my eyes. My people, over five hundred of them, many the descendants of slaves brought from Africa by my ancestors, are happy with me. But I do not pretend that there are no bad men among them, nor that those who come asking that they can work for me are all angels. There are bad men as there are bad horses, so it would be silly of me not to carry a revolver when I go far from the house. Last year my nephew was here, and he refused to go armed when I sent him to pay the wages. One of the coffee-pickers—he was not born here but had been with us four years—was tempted by the sight of so many coins, so he killed my nephew....'

157

'Did the police catch the murderer?'

'No. He ran away. There are no police here. What would be the use of a policeman when there are thousands of square miles of forest in which a criminal can hide?'

The fazenda was virtually self-supporting, for although the main crop was coffee, nearly every other staple was grown, and flourished with almost incredible exuberance. Wheat, rice, maize, every kind of fruit and vegetable; cotton, which was woven and dyed in brilliant colours for the Negroes' clothes: wool for their ponchos. Cattle, sleek as racehorses, munched lush alfalfa in yards knee-deep in glossy yellow straw. They were kept not only for meat and milk, butter and cheese, but for their hides, for lariats and sandals, for saddles and reins and whips.

These were the days before the coffee slump. Mile after mile of bushes, the berries brilliant as scarlet cherries among the laurel-like leaves, were being gathered into baskets and taken by ox-cart to the drying-floors. There were orchards which made the orange-trees I had seen in the south of France look like bushes dwarfed for planting in tubs. For under these trees one could ride, and have to stand in the stirrups to pull fruit from the lowest branch.

Their way of life seemed familiar, although it was fifteen years before I was to recognise how closely it resembled the pattern of responsibility natural to a Nomarch of the middle dynasties of Egypt. A good landowner was as much an integral part of his people as his head was part of his body: neither could survive without the others, neither resented it was from the head the orders came which were carried out by the hands. Money was neither a bloated nor a hungry monster lurking in a ledger: it was only the oil on the wheels which kept smooth the interchange of life; life which grew out of the earth with life which grew out of people. Growth was everywhere abundant, the Earth Goddess almost too prodigal. A forest path vanished if it were neglected even for a month. A branch of begonia which had been touching my window-sill when I

158

arrived reached across the corner of the room in a fortnight—I had asked for it to be allowed to grow unchecked so that I could watch the humming-brids darting in and out of the flowers while I was lying in bed.

Martinez worked hard, but he still had boundless energy for enjoyment. Guests, seldom announced except by the sound of a motor-horn, for there was no telephone and everyone had better things to do than write letters, flowed into the house. They swam in his swimming-pool, sailed his boat, rode his horses. We danced muchachas clasped chest to chest, to the rhythms of maraccas; or lay in long chairs on the patio listening to the Negroes singing: forty, fifty, sixty men's and women's voices, rich and soft as velvet, love songs, sad songs, old songs to the ripple of guitars.

Nearly every day there was a new face at the long refectory table where upwards of twenty dishes were set, from which we all helped ourselves although a Negro footman stood behind each chair to change the plates. The talk was varied and plentiful as the food: new ideas to savour and digest, entrees of wit, delicious *souffles* of chatter. Sex took her place in the conversation too, a goddess enthroned, a shepherdess pursued. To us both it was very comforting to find that other people also thought sex was gay.

Leslie, never at his brightest in the morning, sometimes found it difficult to appreciate jokes considered suitable for bridegrooms at breakfast. He realised it was only Brazilian good manners for the men to pay me fulsome compliments, but sometimes they worried him a little, which impelled them to tease him.

'Leslie, my friend, I must warn you that I have fallen in love with Joan's knees,' said Martinez, pretending to be quite serious. 'The rest of her is good too, of course, but I am a connoisseur of knees and hers are irresistible. So never must she allow herself to be alone with me.'

When we were dressing for dinner Leslie looked searching at my knees. 'I can't see anything odd about them myself,' he said thoughtfully, 'a bit knobbly if anything. But for heaven's sake, Joan, be careful with the chap. One is never quite sure with foreigners, and if he tried anything on I don't know what I ought to do. It would be so jolly awkward that I think we should have to leave.'

I knew very well that Martinez had only been joking, but there was a day when I briefly harboured unworthy doubts. We were all out riding and he and I somehow got separated from the others. The horses were plodding placidly along, and he had been flicking high branches with the lash of his whip to make the great butterflies open their wings so that I could see their glittering blueness. Something swung down out of the shadows. I thought it was only a bat. Simultaneously Martinez lashed my horse across the quarters and sent it careering off down the forest track. I was so startled that I lost both stirrups and had to cling to the pommel of the saddle. I heard his horse galloping after me but mine went faster. I was frightened and angry. If this was a Brazilian prelude to seduction in a tropic glade Martinez had got his lines crossed! Was he conceited enough to think I enjoyed playing nymphs and shepherds on horse-back—especially when I was about to fall off the horse? By some equine whim the animal to which I was clinging suddenly dived into a tunnel in the undergrowth, where the dead leaves underfoot were so thick and the bushes beside the track so impenetrable that the sound of pursuit was cut off. My horse came to a steep gully, and halted so suddenly, throwing up its silly head, that the hogged mane hit me full in the face. Even a willing nymph—and I was not at all willing—would have been displeased if during her flight from dishonour Fate suddenly smacked her across the face with the equivalent of a scrubbing-brush. I hid until I looked a little more presentable, and the horse eventually found its way, and mine, back to the house...after it had loitered in an orchard for an hour where it insisted on being fed with oranges.

Martinez was most apologetic that the horse had bolted

with me. I think it had never occurred to him that anyone could fail to control such a well-trained animal. He had been looking for me all afternoon to explain what had really happened....The thing which had swung down from the tree was a tarantula, which, if Martinez had not thought quickly enough and so made my horse get me out of the way, would probably have bitten me.

Having escaped one tarantula it was bad luck to find an enormous one glaring at me from the wall when I was having a bath that same evening before dinner. Its green eyes glittered. Its hairy body swayed from side to side as it poised itself on dreadful hairy legs. 'Help!' I shouted. 'Quick! Help!' The old Negro butler happened to be passing the door. He rushed in, and, although the sight of the tarantula made him go mauve with terror, he lashed at it with a bath towel while it was scuttling round the floor, hit it with the salver he was carrying, and then finished it off by covering it with the cork bath-mat, on which he jumped up and down until there was no chance of there being even a twitch left in it. I was so overwhelmed with gratitude that I leapt out of the bath and hugged him. Leslie came in at that moment. The butler hastily withdrew, and my husband, instead of being thankful that his bride had been spared an agonising death, briskly rebuked me for letting myself be seen naked by a Negro.

We went to bed fairly early, after one of the evening strolls round the garden, which I enjoyed less than I had done before I discovered that the reason everyone put on riding-boots before going out of the house after sundown was against snakes, not mosquitoes. I made Leslie strip the bed and hunt behind cupboards in case there were any more tarantulas lurking there, and he grew rather fretful....Which was unfair of him, as I always put moths, which he loathes, carefully out of the window, and do similar willing service for bats and non-poisonous spiders. It got hotter and hotter and neither of us could sleep. A species of mosquito just small enough to get through the mesh of the net, appeared in swarms to feed on me—mosquitoes and fleas seldom bite anyone else if I am available. Leslie drowsed off several times, but I had to wake him because the gorged mosquitoes clustered on the ceiling of our four-poster and I was not quite tall enough to reach them. About two in the morning he said wearily, 'If I took you for a swim do you think it might make you cool enough to stop scratching?'

I accepted this overture gladly, and we let ourselves out by a sidedoor and went to the swimming-pool—by a white cement path on which even a small centipede would have been clearly visible in the brilliant moonlight. The swimming-pool was tiled and surrounded by a high wall, which cast such a deep shadow that half the water looked like a pool of ink. Leslie who is an exceedingly good swimmer and dives with real pleasure, amused himself by going in several times from the highest board. Then he sat on the end of it, smoking a cigarette.

I was swimming about quite happily and beginning to think I was nearly cool enough to go back to bed when suddenly something cold and slippery attacked me. Desperately I fought it off, yelling to Leslie for rescue. Hours passed in what may have been seconds. I heard a sound more dreadful even than my screams. Leslie was laughing! I was not only being killed by an anaconda, I was dying under the very eyes of a man who I thought was a kindly husband but who was now revealed as a sadistic maniac. My head went under. Now I was too full of water even to scream. Oh God, let me drown before I am swallowed! Now the enormous serpent has got me by the hair. It is going to swallow me head first!

But it was Leslie, not the snake, who hauled me out of the water. He was still shaking with laughter but trying to sound contrite. 'Darling, I didn't realise you had really panicked or I should have pulled you out sooner.'

I was sobbing with fury. 'You monstrous travesty of a husband! I hope the anaconda eats you alive!'

'What anaconda?'

'Run, you fool! Run! It will catch us both in a minute.' He patted me in that awful way which husbands have when they think their wives are being hysterical. 'Take a grip on yourself, Joan. Your anaconda is only a rubber horse.'

When at last we had to leave to catch the boat to England, Martinez and Clothilde insisted on taking us to Sao Paulo, although it was the height of the coffee harvest and we could easily have got a lift in one of the other guests' cars. The least we could do was to be their hosts at a farewell party, which was a good one and left us about ten shillings after paying our night's hotel bill. Luckily we had return tickets on the railway, and the steamship tickets would be waiting for us in charge of the Purser when we got on board, A.D. having arranged this instead of giving them to Leslie, so as to make sure there was no further delay in his getting back to England to work for his bar exams.

Several Brazilians from the hotel were going on the same boat, which called at Rio de Janeiro, and they all took the morning train. However, Leslie discovered there was another train, leaving at three, which would give us about half an hour at Santos to catch the *Alcantara*. We lunched early, at one-thirty. An hour later I began to look pointedly at my watch. At twenty to three I suggested that it was time to make a move. 'Plenty of time for more coffee,' said Leslie.

For the last time I filled a cup to the brim with the pale fawn Brazilian sugar which is ground so fine that it instantly dissolves and produces the apparent impossibility that a cupful of coffee and another of sugar are both contained in one cup. 'I knew that you could not really be English. It is now proved that you were both born in Brazil, for you could never have caught a boat to bring you here,' declared Martinez.

Dared I go to see the luggage into a taxi? No, that might be thought bossy. At five minutes to three Leslie rose leisurely from the table. Martinez and Clothilde assured us that it was now too late to go to the station, but agreed to call there as it was on the way to the garage where their car was being serviced. The taxi-driver entered into the spirit of the game and rocketed past crossroads with his thumb on the horn.

The station clock announced it was ten minutes past three. But the engine-driver, like Leslie, refused to be bullied by clocks, and we leapt into the moving train just before it drew away from the platform.

'You nearly did me out of my last cup of real coffee,' said Leslie reproachfully. I was panting too hard to reply.

CHAPTER SIX

light your own candle

My parents met us at Southampton, with money for tips and other oddments such as the hairdresser and bar bills; for I had cabled to Mother from Vigo that we were flat broke. After a week at Hayling and a fortnight with Daisy, we went to London to look for somewhere to live. Our quarterly allowances had just come in, so we had about 150 pounds between us; but even the most squalid little flats were asking a premium as well as three months' rent in advance, so we took furnished rooms in the house in Half Moon Street where Malcolm was living. Leslie decided that as we would have to go to Scotland for the grouse shooting it would be a waste of time to start working for his exams. So in July we went to Knocke to stay with a Belgian friend.

When I first met her, on the *Almeda Star*, she had reminded me a little of Daisy. One morning she asked me why I, who was only twenty, preferred to spend so much of my time talking to a woman of sixty-five. Taken off my guard I had said, 'Age isn't important. I may be hundreds of years older than you.' She had looked rather startled but did not pursue the subject. Instead, she asked me to come to visit her because she wanted me to meet Robert, her grandson....

We took the boat to Ostend and reached Knocke in time for dinner. Robert, who was six, had already gone to bed. He came to see me next morning when I was having breakfast on a tray: a nice-looking little boy wearing shorts and a jersey. He had his left arm in a sling. He accepted a piece of chocolate, offered to pour out coffee for me, and then wandered round the room, fiddling with things on the dressing-table and pretending not to be studying me intently. Then he said abruptly, 'There is something I want to show you. It is downstairs, and, if you don't mind, I would like you to see it before my grandmother gets up. She is already in her bath, so if you would please not be too long....'

He took me to a box-room where there was a large unopened packing-case. He foraged in a cupboard and handed me a hammer and cold chisel. 'Open it, please. I cannot do it myself with one hand, and I have promised not to use the other one until the bone is quite mended. I broke it falling off my pony, which was very careless of me.'

'Are you sure your grandmother wouldn't mind? It's addressed to her, and ...'

'Please open it. Now!' He was quivering with impatience. 'It's me in the packing-case.'

I thought he meant that it contained something which belonged to him. So, hoping that it was not a present being kept as a surprise for his birthday, I began to prise the nails from the wood. At last I got the lid off, and found that instead of a toy—the case would have been about the right size for a child's bicycle, it held a large oil-painting. I propped it up against the wall and flicked sawdust from the glass. It was the portrait of a young man in khaki. Who was it? Obviously someone the boy knew very well, for he was gazing at it with intense excitement and a deeper emotion very close to tears. Then he turned and looked at me solemnly. 'You will not laugh at me, will you?' I wanted to hug him, but I

165

knew the matter was too serious. 'I never laugh at true things.' He nodded. 'Then you will tell my grandmother that this is not just a picture of my Uncle Albert, it is a picture of me.'

I went at once to tell her. I think she had asked me there only for confirmation of what she already knew. Eagerly, as though it was a profound relief at last to accept evidence which her religion made it difficult to believe, she told me many things which substantiated Robert's story. Her elder son, Albert, had always meant far more to her than her younger son, John. She had separated from her husband, who was English, when both children were quite small. Albert had spent most of his time with her in Belgium, and had been killed in 1915, a captain in the Belgian Army, at the age of twenty-three. John, just too young for the war, had been sent to school in England and had married an English wife. He saw his mother very seldom until she went to stay with them for a few days when Robert was two years old. To the other grandchildren she was still only an elderly woman whom they hardly knew. To Robert she was the only person who really mattered. If he was with her he was cheerful and healthy. With his parents he sulked or was violently disobedient until they were thankful to send him back to Belgium.

'Robert was always a brave little boy,' she said proudly. 'When he first saw a swimming-bath, and he was then only three, he ran along the diving-board and dived in. Albert too was a very fine diver. One day someone came here with a cinema camera. When he pointed it at Robert, turning the handle with a clicking noise, Robert screamed, ''Don't! ''Don't! They killed me like that last time!'' I tried to calm him, but he became so hysterical that I had to send for the doctor, who gave him a sedative. Albert went out alone into no-man's-land at night to stop a German post enfilading his men with a machine-gun. There were eight bullets in his body when they found it, but he did not die very quickly. He had managed to crawl nearly back to our own wire before morning....' There were tears in her eyes, but she continued composedly. 'There have been so many other things, pet names which Albert used to call me, likes and dislikes which used to be a private joke between us, trivial in themselves, perhaps, but altogether so certain. Now I shall hang up their portrait. I have kept it hidden all these years because even a snapshot of Albert made Robert behave so—so strangely. But now it is not strange to us any more that in 1915 Albert only left me for a little while.'

On the eleventh of August I went for the first time to Muckerach, a shooting-lodge and some 27,000 acres of grouse-moor near Grantown-on-Spey. The entire Grant family had been summoned to the presence, prepared to endure, even to enjoy in their fashion, the shooting season. His native heath made A.D. even more of an autocrat, and when the whisper went round, 'Father's suffering from constipation,' his grown-up children tiptoed past his study door, carrying their shoes. Four days a week I tramped from dawn to dusk through heather, floundered into bogs, marked fallen birds and retrieved them patiently as a spaniel. In the first week I achieved the unusual distinction of being knocked out by a grouse. Leslie, who is a very good shot, took a right and left in front of the butt. The birds were coming fast downwind. I was trying to reload the second gun. The grouse, even though dead, was travelling like a javelin, and its beak got me between the eyebrows. The butt, as usual, had a foot of water in it, so I was soaked to the skin. But at least I gave them something to laugh about.

Non-shooting days were golf days. After the first of September these were rare, for in addition to grouse there were partridges to be followed through waist-high kale. At golf I could sometimes get a little of my own back by egging A.D. on to bet, and then suddenly playing much better and winning—preferably on the last green. After dinner—at which most of the conversation was between me and me, for none of the children often spoke in Father's presence—there was bridge. Goodness, how hard they tried to teach me to play it when they needed a fourth! Luckily the act, 'Does it count more when you get cards with pictures on?' convinced them that they had at last met someone with so little card sense that she was beyond teaching.

On one of our Sundays off, Leslie and I went to Rothiemurchus intending to climb towards the Cairngorms. It was a beautiful day and we had it to ourselves. Basking naked in the sun, we ate sandwiches beside a burn. It was far too hot and peaceful for serious walking, so we decided to wander on for another mile or so, and then go for dinner to the hotel in Aviemore. Nothing could have been further from my mind than spooks when suddenly I was seized with such terror that I turned and in panic fled back along the path. Leslie ran after me, imploring me to tell him what was wrong. I could only spare breath enough to tell him to run faster, faster. Something—utterly malign, four-legged and yet obscenely human, invisible and yet solid enough for me to hear the pounding of its hooves, was trying to reach me. If it did I should die, for I was far too frightened to know how to defend myself. I had run about half a mile when I burst through an invisible barrier behind which I was safe. I knew I was safe now, though a second before I had been in mortal danger; knew it as certainly as though I were a *torero* who has jumped the barrier in front of a charging bull.

A year later one of Father's professors described an almost exactly similar experience he had had when bug-hunting in the Cairngorms. He was a materialist, but had been so profoundly startled that he wrote to *The Times*—and received a letter from a reader who had also been pursued by the 'Thing'. Some years later, when I was living at Muckerach, the doctor told me that two hikers, for whom search-parties had been out three days, had been found dead. He showed me the exact spot on the map. It was the place of my terror. Both men were under thirty. One came from Grantown, the other from Aviemore. The weather was fine. They had spent a good night under the shelter-stone on the highest ridge, for they had written to that effect in the book which is kept up there. They were found within a hundred yards of each other, sprawled face downward as though they had fallen headlong when in flight. 'I did a post-mortem on them both,' said the doctor gravely. 'Never in my life have I seen healthier corpses: not a thing wrong with either of the poor chaps except that their hearts stopped. I put ''heart failure' on the chit, but it is my considered opinion that they died of fright.'

In September there were several other guns coming to stay, so Leslie and I were free to go to Cluny Castle, which had been taken for the season by Tom Scully—who came from Tipperary although he was now an American. In his own way he too was a bit of a tyrant, but this did not matter in the least as I had known him since childhood and was not his daughter-in-law. Violet, his second wife, was only a couple of years older than I, and was expecting her second baby; which provided a splendid excuse to stay at home gossiping instead of me being a retriever. There was only one snag in an otherwise happy fortnight: our bedroom was haunted. I should not have minded this so much if there had been electric light or plenty of candles, but there was never more than one candle—an oversight of the housemaid's, not an economy of Violet's, and I was too shy to ask for more of them. The massive four-poster bed had heavy green serge curtains which sucked up the glimmer of my solitary light. I watched it burn lower and lower, hearing, just before it guttered out, the welcome sound of Leslie's footsteps on his way to bed, with a candle from the hall.

There was a friendly Labrador that belonged to the house. I made a fuss of him until he attached himself to me, and then I asked that he might sleep in my room. For a few minutes the dog gnawed happily at the bone I had smuggled upstairs to make him feel at home. Then his hackles stood up. He howled. He flung himself at the door, scrabbling so frantically with his claws that in decency I had to open it and let the poor beast rush off down the passage. After that I gave an ultimatum to Leslie. Either he came to bed not more than half an hour after I did—which still left about three inches of candle between me and the dark, or else, stark naked, I would come down and fetch him. The threat of this scared him so much that he used to gulp down his whisky and soda and come rushing upstairs.

This seems a pointless story, for I neither saw nor identified the haunt; but I mention it because at Cluny I finally decided that it was useless to go on hoping that I would grow out of the experiences which I so often found disturbing. I would understand ghosts, and myself, only if I saw more of them and not less. The few people I knew who believed in such things were too woolly-minded, too easily deceived, or so it seemed to me, to be of any practical help. Even at that age I was too much of an empiricist to put any real faith in what I read in books. I would be careful not to read books on subjects which closely affected me.

Where was I to find the knowledge I so vitally needed? I prayed very hard before I went to sleep; and on waking knew that the part of me which is older and wiser than my everyday self must show Joan how to light her own candle.

CHAPTER SEVEN

here and there

When A.D. and Babs went back to the Argentine in October their baby was too delicate to stand the heat of a South American summer so they left him with a nanny at Seacourt. Unless Mother had offered to have Donald he would have been parked in lodgings, for A.D. always shut both his houses when he was out of England, no matter how many of his children happened to be homeless. This did not matter to the first batch now that they were grown up, but it would have made school holidays far brighter if they could have had friends to stay instead of being left in charge of a governess in some dreary boarding-house. The only time, so far as I know, that he ever broke this rule was in the following year when he left Babs in Winkfield Manor to have her second baby.

Perhaps Mother's natural generosity in having Donald with her warmed A.D.'s heart a little, for he told Mr. Blundell to pay the premium on somewhere for us to live. Leslie had a desk, an arm-chair, a table and a lot of books from his rooms in Trinity. I had the furniture from my bedroom at home, lots of flower-vases and some wedding presents. We filled in gaps from the Caledonian Market and junk shops in the King's Road' and by the middle of November were installed in a maisonette at 33 Cheyne Place, Chelsea.

The most optimistic balancing of money in hand versus bills showed that we could not afford a servant to live in— even had there been room for one. The minimum staff considered respectable in those days, even by penurious newly married couples, was a house-parlourmaid and a cook-general: and a cook-general could very seldom cook.

'I shall do the cooking myself,' I announced cheerfully. 'It will not only be cheaper but we shall have much more interesting meals.'

'Can you cook?' asked Leslie anxiously.

This was not the moment to admit that I had never boiled an egg, but to make a bold statement and convert it as soon as possible into fact.

'Of course,' I said airily. 'It is only a question of applying scientific principles. Anyone intelligent can do it.'

To help on the scientific angle Leslie bought me a pressure-cooker, an early, if not the earliest, model ever foisted on an

171

unsuspecting public. It was made of cast-iron, so heavy it took a strong man to lift it, even when empty, and so lethal in operation that after it had twice sprayed the walls and ceiling of the kitchen with jets of far-hotter-than-boiling soup, we gave it away as a wedding present to a couple we cordially disliked. I then followed the excellent instinct which had led me to seek advice from Ferraro at the Berkeley. Someone took us to the admirable restaurant of Marcel Boulestin and I asked him to give me cooking lessons, which, to my eternal gratitude, he did.

At last I had a home of my own and rejoiced in it. Meals occurred when we happened to feel hungry—and there were no gongs to bully us, no anxious telephoning to apologise for being late, or out, for dinner, no parental scrutiny of guests. Most of our friends were still unmarried. Douglas, Richard, Fairfax, Charles, Robin, Malcolm of course, and about half a dozen others, found the place more congenial than their bachelor digs and drifted in and out as they felt inclined. I cooked for them, darned their socks, cosseted their hang-overs, popped them into the dressing-room bed and nursed them when they were ill; and I considered that they repaid me most royally by treating me as an equal...it having seldom occurred to me that life might be much easier if I graciously accepted the fact that I was female. Females were different. Females wore hats and gloves and 'little frocks', and were as dangerous and unpredictable as leopards. At times I secretly envied their subtle strength, but never admitted it. How easy it must be not to have to play tennis or squash or golf unless you wanted to! How easy to look pretty instead of playing chess without a board! But I put these despicable thoughts away in a pigeonhole of my mind, to be approached only fur-tively, like a member of Alcoholics Anonymous gazing wist-fully at a secreted bottle of gin.

This peaceful pattern was interrupted at intervals by Leslie working for exams. While lesser mortals studied slavishly for six months before the ordeal of a Bar exam, my husband dismissed the subject from his mind until the last three weeks. Then he went into action. At 4 p.m. I woke him with breakfast on a tray. By five he was at Prince's Tennis and Racquets Club in Knightsbridge, where he took violent exercise until it was time to return home to luncheon at 7.30. From 8 o'clock until midnight he worked at his books, when he dined—a proper dinner: no nonsense about sandwiches or snacks off a tray. From one to eight in the morning, when he shared my breakfast, he worked again; and then he went to bed to sleep through the day. Pale as well-blanched endive he went to the exam. Paler still he returned to say he had failed to answer a single question—except once when he said he hadn't done too badly. This last was the only time he got a Second. On every other occasion he got a First.

Even after six months of cooking I still quite enjoyed it, but realised it would soon begin to pall, so it seemed more sensible to earn money with which to pay someone else to do the chores. I consulted Daisy, as usual, in this matter, and she suggested that I might make use of my talent for arranging flowers. The more we discussed it the better it seemed. She would grow the things I needed which could not be bought in Covent Garden, and there were quantities of azaleas, rhododendrons, flowering shrubs and branches, which at that period were never obtainable even in the most expensive flower shops. Stan was then working on the *Daily Telegraph,* so Diana found time a bit heavy on her hands. With very little persuasion she agreed to become my partner in the flower-arranging project, which we decided to keep from our husbands until we could present them with a *fait accompli.* We found a shop, off Curzon Street, which had a low rent as the premises were small, but ideal for our purpose. A front room had a bow window and eighteenth-century pine panelling against which four or five flower pieces would show to the best advantage. A small room behind it would do for keeping the flowers. We would have a small but elegant black van, blazoned with a flower-do by a first-class artist and our names in excellent lettering. I would at last have an excuse for acquiring a cheetah, which would sit beside me as I drove, providing pleasure for me and publicity for our enterprise. We even consulted a chartered accountant, who agreed that as we had already got the promise of a contract from the Hyde Park Hotel to do flowers in the reception rooms for 1,500 pounds a year, our scheme was quite feasible.

The evening when, after giving them an admirable dinner, we broke the news to Leslie and Stan we were, in our own minds, not only useful and independent but affluent as well. They were far from pleased.

'You would be sure to make a hash of it. Neither of you have any business experience,' said Stan patronisingly.

'You have no capital,' said Leslie.

'Oh yes we have,' said I. 'Daisy is going to be the third partner and putting up the money we shall need until we start earning.'

'No one wants their flowers done for them.'

'Nonsense, Stan!' said Diana briskly. 'They only put up with sweet-peas and asparagus fern, or carnations in a silver vase, because they leave the flowers to the parlourmaid. We shall educate their taste....'

'People dislike being educated,' said Leslie; an unkind cut at me, which I parried by saying that the vast majority of people were so dumb that they needed education.

'When we are famous we may even give lessons. People will flock to us. It will be fashionable.'

'It's ridiculous to say you'll only sell flowers with the vases. Good God, a man looks silly enough carrying flowers wrapped up in paper. He'd look a monumental ass slopping water over himself.' This from Stan.

'The vases will not have water when they are being carried,' said Diana. 'And anyway they will be delivered in our van.'

'What van?'

'Our van. The one that Daisy is buying for us. With a

water-proof seat for the cheetah,' I added incautiously.

'What cheetah?' asked Leslie coldly.

'Darling, don't worry them about the details,' said Diana hastily. 'We may find there isn't room for animals in our shop, and they might bite the customers.'

'You are not going to have a shop!' said Stan and Leslie. They glared. They blustered. They argued. They brought up all the unfair weapons that men use against women (that day Diana and I founded a subsidiary company of the immemorial league of Women against Men). 'It can't succeed,' they cried. 'Or someone with far more business sense would have done it already. You will never get up early enough to get to Covent Garden. You will get no suckers to buy the stuff. The vases will get stolen, broken....'

We fought hard and long. We fought subtly. Diana was even brave enough to try tears. We fought until we thought they had at last relented. But they still had a card-sharper's ace tucked in their sleeve. If Diana and I insisted on going into business everyone would know our real motive—which was to make fools of our husbands by demonstrating in public that we thought them incapable of supporting us. If we made it an issue they would accept it, for convention no longer allowed them to beat us into submission. But did we fully understand the mockery they would suffer, did we realise that they would have to resign from their Club?

So I sold a brooch to pay the option we had bought on a three years' lease of the shop. Unfortunately our anger had cooled too long for us to gain any real satisfaction from pointing out to them, a few years later, the outstanding, and quite coincidental, success of Constance Spry.

While all this was going on I had not forgotten the promise I had made to myself by candle-light at Cluny.

Leslie slept soundly, which was fortunate for him as I now began to train myself to wake several times during the night so as to write down my dreams. Many were only wishful-thinking or anxiety patterns, the typical patchwork of fustian

175

and tinsel so dear to psychoanalysts. There were true dreams also, as different to the others in their quality of reality as are the solid stone walls of Windsor to the ephemeral turrets of a 'castle in Spain'. These fell into two main categories. The first, although on a different level of experience to the one on which I functioned when awake, marched with the calendar. The second extended both in space and time, being a variant of the faculty, which, for lack of a better word, I was later to call 'far memory.'

A contemporary dream I will describe in detail because it is typical of many others, in which the 'I' alternates between the experience of someone else with whom I was briefly in such close contact that his experience felt like my own, and the 'I' that was an extension of the ordinary Joan.

I am a sailor, about thirty years old, on a large liner. I am afraid because there is a fire in the ship, but I do not realise I am in any real danger until the smoke drives me back along a narrow passage and I have to climb out of a cabin window because I cannot reach the stairs. I run along the deck but am prevented from going any farther by clouds of heavy black smoke. I look down into the sea where several men are struggling in the fire-lit water. Dare I jump? No, I can't swim. I shall be drowned if I jump. Perhaps if I run towards the bows I shall be able to climb down to a lower deck. Paint is bubbling up into great blisters which burst with a small sharp noise I can hear above the noise of the fire and the sea....My feet are hurting because of the heat of the deck. I must jump. I must. It is better to drown than to be burned....

I clamber over the bulwark, stand on it for an agonisingly long time and then, when a gust of heat singes my back, throw myself forward, trying to keep my feet together as I fall. The sea knocks the breath out of me. I try to swim but I am too heavy, too heavy. The water is crushing my ribs. No, a great hand is squeezing them....Why does the giant want to kill me?

He has let go! I am buoyant as a cork. I can *swim!* It is

very easy to swim. Swim fast, faster! Get away from the burning ship before she heels over. It is almost ridiculously easy to swim. Why did I never realise I could swim so well? I swim very well. I have swum a long way and yet I am not tired. I feel stronger with every stroke I make....A wave lifts me and I see I am very close to an island. The sun is making the water glitter but I can see the palm-trees on the island. The water is kind and smooth and warm....

Then I am no longer the sailor. I am Joan, standing on a shelving beach of white sand, watching a man splashing towards me through the shallows. He is wringing water from his clothes when he sees me. 'Good morning, Miss,' he says politely. 'Extraordinary what you can do when you're up against it! Never done more than paddle in my life, and there I was swimming like a ruddy champ, overarm and all. Not that I wasn't glad to see this island. Belongs to you, Miss?

I tell him that I am only staying here for a little while and that a yacht will come to pick us up before sunset. Where would he like the yacht to take him? 'My ship was bound for Cherbourg, but I'd rather go to Bordeaux—if it's all the same to you and no trouble.'

I ask if he was hungry. I have food, plenty of food, and wine too if he would like it. He says he would prefer a coco-nut. 'Very partial to green nuts I am, took a fancy to them when I was deck-hand on a cargo-boat plying to the West Indies. I'm on a liner now—very posh job she is....' He pauses, beginning to look anxious, so I quickly change the direction of his thoughts by asking him to show me how to open a coco-nut. Then I say casually, 'Have you noticed that you're dead?'

'Dead? Me, Miss? Don't talk so barmy!' He picks up a pebble and throws it into the sea, where it makes a most realistic splash. Then he kicks the sand with his bare foot. 'Dead men can't wiggle their toes. I've seen corpses in my time, and their feet were as stiff as a plank.'

'Was there a fire in your ship?'

'Yes,' he reluctantly concedes. 'But don't let's talk about it. It will be a good story to tell over a bottle of wine when I get home—not yet though, it's a bit too close for comfort if you see what I mean.'

'How fast can you swim?'

'You seen me,' he says reproachfully. 'Matter of ten knots or more I must have been doing.'

'No one can swim as fast as that—unless he is dead.'

'You been running about in the sun too long without a hat, Miss? Very odd notions sunstroke gives some people. I remember a stoker, proper raving he was, when I was in the West Indies....'

I hasten to interrupt him. I have arranged our present environment with some care and it will only confuse the issue if we find ourselves involved in the playback of a bar fight in Martinique. 'You *are* dead,' I say briskly, 'and now I will prove it to you. Where was your ship when the fire broke out?'

'In the English Channel.'

'And are there coral islands like this in those waters?'

That shakes him for a moment. 'It must be one of the Scillies. Never been to them myself, but I've heard tell they grow palm-trees there—which is true, for I can see them, ten good ones, with nuts on.'

'Can I fly? If I fly will you agree that you drowned?'

'If you can fly—no cheating, mind you—it don't count if you've got an aeroplane tucked away behind them trees—I'll give you best, honest to God I will.'

I try to levitate, but so strong is his conviction that I shall stay solidly on the ground that for a moment nothing happens. Then I make an extra effort and rise into the air, do a few fancy swoops and land neatly beside him. Then he laughs, gusts of enormous and complete enjoyment, not at me but at himself.

'All my life I've been frightened of dying, and all it was is this! Never enjoyed myself so much as I have since I drowned. What a joke on my poor auntie who always said I'd fry in hell when I died! If this is hell, give me lots more of it! Where do we go from here?'

'Tell me who you would most like to be with and I will fix your passage,' I say, efficient as a clerk in Thomas Cook's.

'Must they be dead too?'

'Not necessarily. But it would be better as a start. People who are only asleep—like me—are inclined to vanish rather abruptly.'

'Well, there was a very nice bloke who was torpedoed in the war...'

'Think of him *hard*,' I say quickly. I am beginning to feel misty at the edges and know I am soon going to wake up. I hear a joyous shout of recognition and dimly see two men thumping each other on the back... bottles of red wine on a table, the music of an accordion....

I woke. The telephone was ringing. I pulled the plug out of the wall and scrabbled for my notebook. No, this was too exciting to risk losing any of it. 'Leslie, listen!' When I had told him everything I could remember he said, 'What was the name of the ship? Try hard. It would be evidence.'

'All I can get is *Atlantic*. I suppose he told me the ship crossed the Atlantic before she entered the Channel—although I don't remember him saying so.'

'Why do you think the sailor was French?'

'His ship was on its way to Cherbourg, although I suppose she might only have been calling there on her way to Southampton, or Bremen, or somewhere. But he wanted to go to Bordeaux and there was wine, not beer or whisky, in the last glimpse I had of him.'

'When you were describing his conversation he talked like a cockney.'

'The cockney doesn't signify anything. I've noticed that when I remember a dream conversation I automatically translate it into the nearest equivalent English. When I was in Scotland I had a Roman dream in which a soldier seemed to speak with a marked Highland accent—merely because I'd been listening to Old Robbie the day before.'

'Well, I hope it wasn't an English ship,' said Leslie, and went down to fetch the morning papers. There was nothing in any of them about a fire at sea. But when we came out of a cinema about tea-time we saw the newspaper placards: FIRE IN CRACK FRENCH LINER. The headline was '*Atlantique* burns in English Channel: Many Dead.'

CHAPTER EIGHT

enter Gillian

Early in July we decided to spend a month in Bavaria to strengthen us for another dose of Scotland; and the day before we left I discovered I had started a baby. I was so delighted that it was difficult not to tell Leslie immediately, but in case he wanted to cancel the trip I decided to keep the electrifying news to myself until I was safely abroad.

Unlike me, Leslie preferred to reach his destination as quickly as possible rather than to journey hopefully. He obtained, as usual, a route from the R.A.C.—the most direct and not the most picturesque one, and we followed this through northern France, lurching over bumps and jolting through villages on broken *pave*. I had not been there before, except in dreams during the war, and I found the rusty barbed wire, the broken trees, the shell craters that still pitted the fields, far more depressing than I had expected. Would there be another war in which my child would be killed? Father and H.G. Wells were sure there would be a much worse one. Were they right? And if so, was I idiotic to be so pleased that I was having a baby?

When we paused for a hasty sandwich—lunch *en route*

was considered a waste of time—an old man came out of a hut built in the ruins of a farm and insisted on showing us a trench where French soldiers had died standing-to. A shell had buried them alive, but their rusty bayonets were still sticking out of the ground. Instead of adding to my depression I found this oddly consoling. It was brave to be killed, but braver still to make new bodies for the dead to live in. A little farther on we passed a field where shell-craters had been filled in and young vines were beginning to sprout from the ravaged earth. Men were strong and brave and could destroy, but women's patience was stronger. They planted new vines and waited a lifetime for another vintage. I think that was the first time Joan was ever proud of being a woman.

We intended to press on to Freudenstadt in the Black Forest, but when we reached Strasbourg I prevailed on him to stop the night there by telling him about the baby. He was so pleased that I immediately revived and we set off to look for a restaurant in which to celebrate. We were sitting at the table when we discovered that both thought the other had got marks from the bank before we started. To-morrow we could cash our letter of credit, but we only had seven shillings now between us. Neither of us could understand the German menu so we read down the price column until we came to a dish that was within our range, hoping that vegetables would be included. Unfortunately we had both ordered only mayonnaise. Bread—luckily bread was free—dipped in mayonnaise is not a usual meal but we pretended to enjoy it. And I think the waiter never realised that we were as startled by our choice as he was.

We spent three long weeks in a village on the Stamberger See, the lake in which Ludwig of Bavaria drowned himself. I felt perfectly well but developed an embarrassing habit of fainting. Leslie refused to let me drive the car, so as he spent every day sailing I never saw the castles I wanted to see nor did I hear music in Munich. When not sailing he played chess in the Weinstuber where women were not encouraged. I bore it as long as I could and then decided to go home by train, leaving him to follow by car when he felt inclined. He drove me to Munich station and the train was due to arrive in a few minutes when I fainted again, on the platform. Leslie propped me up on a seat, told me not to move until he got back, and dashed out of the station. He came back, bundled me into the train and jumped in after me. 'But the car?' I said anxiously as the train drew out and I realised he was travelling with me. 'I gave the documents to a man standing by the bookstall—told him my wife was ill and asked him to get it to England. He seemed very competent.'

Everyone told us we would never see the car again. They were quite wrong. It turned up in London three weeks later, even a packet of cigarettes was still in the glove-compartment on the dashboard. We had a very warm letter from the kindly stranger, saying how flattered he had been by Leslie's instant recognition of his honesty. He was the proprietor of a small hotel in Monte Carlo, and so I suppose he was hardened to eccentric foreigners who left things behind and expected them to be forwarded.

I had shown that I could manage without a cook and I now intended to prove I could look after my own baby. This produced such a storm of protest, not only from Mother but from my contemporaries, that I had to abandon the idea. Apparently it would be as insane to think I could do without a trained nanny as it would be to suggest removing one's own appendix. A.D. felt so strongly about it that he told Mr. Blundell to buy a house for us, a house with two nurseries and a spare room where Malcolm could live—except when A.D. and Babs wanted a room in London. So, in the following March, we moved into 22 Ilchester Place, one of a new row of houses built in the ground of Ilchester House, and within convenient pram-ride of Kensington Gardens.

A benign providence allows every woman to feel that, in spite of all evidence to the contrary, her first pregnancy is unique. I did not even have any interesting symptoms, and shared with countless millions—although the sentiment was not fashionable at the time—the conviction that having someone I dearly loved inside me was the most enchanting state to be in. It was the only time in my life that never for a moment have I been lonely.

From the time I started the baby until a month or two after she was born I was too far absorbed in what I was doing to have the wish or the energy to dream. If anyone, especially Mother, dared to suggest that I was in any way an invalid, I became fiercely defensive. It was a nuisance that I had to have a maternity nurse, but so that she would not interfere, I parked her in a hotel and only summoned her at the last minute. I was, however, unpleasantly surprised to find the actual process of birth so painful. It would have been much less so had I not thought it necessary to carry on a conversation to show that I was not subjugated by pain. Friends came in relays, and when they left exhausted I babbled to others on the telephone. The nurse became increasingly sour. Dear 'Fethers', Dr Fetherstonhaugh, sat on my bed with Leslie and chatted. At two in the afternoon I refused an offer of 'twilight sleep'. Hours passed. 'Leslie, you had better go now,' said Fethers.

'Don't be such a damn fool,' said Leslie.

Gillian at last was born late in the evening of the 2nd of April 1930. Twenty minutes later I telephoned to Mother to tell her she had a granddaughter. She was horrified at me being allowed to telephone, and would have been even more dismayed if she could have seen Gillian being repeatedly told by Leslie that she was an exceedingly beautiful baby while she peered at us from the open neck of his shirt. At the time I thought she was quite hideous, but would have died rather than admit it. Yet three days later, when Kirsteen looked at her and said, 'Goodness, aren't new-born babies ugly!' I was so furious that I told her to get out of the room before I threw something at her. And when she had gone I burst into tears and ran quite a high temperature.

183

A month later, A.D. followed up his telegram of congratulations with a letter which told us that as we had a house, a baby, and Leslie was now in chambers in the Middle Temple, we could stand on our own feet so he was cutting our allowance. The only thing to do was to sell the house, but this took us a year during which we lived on credit and my overdraft, as England had just gone off the Gold Standard and our private road bristled with For Sale notices.

Malcolm shared the siege with us and wrote a very erudite book on philosophy, *A New Argument for God and Survival*, which was published by Fabers in the following autumn. Leslie had recently met two men called Wyeth and Neale, a 'healer' and a 'seer' whom at first I liked nearly as much as he did, although Malcolm took a violent dislike to them on sight. We took them down to Seacourt for a weekend, and Neale discovered for himself the ghost in the music-room. It had been a monk who left the monastery at Bosham in the time of King Canute to become a hermit on Hayling Island. Solitude cannot have suited him, for he was still pacing up and down a path, now covered by the music-room and the side-gallery of the tennis court, muttering 'I am greater than Augustine.' Wyeth must have dealt with him effectively for none of us was troubled any more.

Wyeth gave five or six lectures at Ilchester Place and he lectured once a month at several other houses in London. Leslie never missed one if he could help it, but first I became bored because the lectures were always the same, and then actively disliked going to them because he was using a small amount of quite genuine experience to create a dogma which became increasingly nonsensical and didactic. But I had not yet realised how much Wyeth hated me.

Gillian was a year old and Malcolm had married before we at last found a purchaser for the house. After paying our bills there was so little money left that I went with Gillian and Drakey—her nurse to whom she and I were both devoted—to live in the cottage at Seacourt while Leslie lived at his club and came down for weekends.

Except for three months, when again we were in rooms in Half Moon Street, so that we could help Margot nurse Duncan who was dying of a throat infection, I stayed at Hayling for nearly two years. It was not a satisfactory arrangement, and I at last discovered that I could afford to live in London again by borrowing on reversion under my grandfather's will. Work for a young barrister was so scarce that it was becoming increasingly obvious that Leslie could not expect to get enough at the Bar even to pay the rent of his Chambers. So I tried, not very successfully, to earn money. I worked for six months with an architect, drawing up plans for converting slum streets in Chelsea into 'bijou residences'. When the plans had been passed, the backer for whom we were working—share of future profits but no salary—suddenly went bankrupt. I then scraped up enough to buy a quarter share in the Golden Cockerell Press, and learned a certain amount about the art of producing private editions, but a great deal more about packing parcels. This lasted for eighteen months, and at times was amusing if not financially rewarding. Owen Rutter, one of the other partners, tried to encourage me to write a book. I worked feverishly at it for several weeks, and then, when I heard Leslie's candid criticism of the manuscript and re-read it myself, I had to agree that it showed no vestige of literary talent, so I abandoned the effort. He was even more convinced than I was myself that under no circumstances would I ever become an author.

CHAPTER NINE

RECORDER

Soon after we were both back in London I met Hilary Durham-Matthews at a luncheon party, and we found each other so congenial that we went home together and talked until long after dinner. A few days later she asked Leslie and me to drive down to King's Beeches, her mother's house near Sunningdale, where she wanted to collect some flowers. It was raining when we got there and her mother was out, so, as there was nothing better to do, she showed us round the house.

The last room we went into was very different to the others. The furniture looked as though it had come from a suburban vicarage and the walls were smothered in very amateur water-colours, except where these gave place to photographs of clerics in glossy pitch-pine frames. Incongruous in such surroundings was a sword, in an emerald green velvet scabbard decorated with gold filigree, hanging over the mantelpiece. Hilary said, rather apologetically, 'Everything in here belongs to my stepfather. Mother only married him last year, and neither Jack nor I can understand why she landed us with the dreariest kind of vicar.'

'Did the sword come from the vicarage too?'

'Yes—improbable though it seems. It belonged to Nelson's Captain Hardy, who was an ancestor of the vicar's.'

Leslie took the sword down from the wall, and obeying a sudden impulse, handed it to me. 'Try to find out whether Nelson said "kiss me" or "Kismet". I think Kismet is far more likely, as he often used the word.'

'I would if I could psychometrise, but I can't.'

'You could try,' said Leslie.

'Oh do, Joan,' urged Hilary.

So, feeling foolish as a conjuror who knows there is no

rabbit in his hat, I sat down on the sofa, shut my eyes, and pressed the hilt of the sword against my forehead. I made my mind a blank and expected it to stay like that. To my surprise, visual images appeared as though I were seeing them through a third eye set between and slightly above my eyebrows. I described what I was seeing:

'The sword belonged to a man called George Augustus Murray. He was short, fat, had curly reddish hair round a bald patch, and a very high forehead. He died near Chichester. He had been a naval captain. He had two liver-and-white spaniels and his wife, a dumpy little woman, usually wore a mob cap and a large cameo brooch....'

I put the sword down. 'There, I told you I couldn't do it. I know Hardy was very tall and had black hair. I suppose the bit about the fat little man is something I dreamed and only just remembered.'

They were disappointed, for, unlike me, they had expected something interesting to happen. We heard a car coming up the drive and hastily put back the sword and left the room in case the vicar was annoyed at us going into his study. At tea Hilary asked him how Hardy's sword had come into his possession. 'It did not belong to Hardy, but to another of Nelson's captains,' said the vicar. 'He was an ancestor of mine, George Augustus Murray.'

As an excuse for our interest in a character of whom none of us had heard until the last hour, Leslie pretended to be doing research for a friend who was writing a biography of Nelson. The vicar swallowed the bait together with yet another cucumber sandwich, and was clearly flattered that his forebear was going to be rescued from obscurity and put in a book. He had two small portraits in his bedroom of Captain and Mrs. Murray, which fitted my description even to the mob cap and the cameo brooch. And next day, after looking through some family papers, the vicar rang up Hilary to say that Nelson's biographer might be interested to know that Captain Murray died at Fittleworth in Sussex. Fittleworth is near Chichester. But there was no evidence that he ever had spaniels, only a reference, in a letter, to, 'my faithful dogs which accompany me everywhere on my walks abroad.'

The only other possession of Captain Murray's was a gold medal, which Hilary borrowed, luckily without the vicar noticing its absence; so that I could 'do' it the following weekend at her home near Windsor. This was much more fruitful than the sword. I still have the notes she jotted down while I was talking. They are rather disjointed, for I was speaking faster than she could write and she did not know shorthand. It reads rather like a commentary on a football match, much flatter than the original, for it lacks the emotion which was present in my voice.... 'Our ship is flying white flags with scarlet crosses. Boys are running, carrying shot and powder. Sailors are now naked to the waist. A great cracking on of canvas. Will the wind freshen? Our ship won't come about and the enemy is sailing down on us with a following wind. He fires a broadside, misses. Shall I fire? No, wait. Get the ship round and bring stern-chaser guns into action! Their foremast is broken below the cross-tree. They are hacking the foremast with axes. We have hit them amidships! A shot has torn away our mainsail. Buckets of water are being sluiced over our deck. Sweating men are reloading the guns. Big ropes round the guns check the recoil....

'We fire another broadside. Only five of their guns answer. They drift down astern, heeling to larboard. Shipton is hit! Both his legs have gone. The deck is slippery with blood. Tell the powder-monkeys to swill it down. They sprinkle sand from red canvas buckets on the deck. The other ship is drifting. She runs out a white flag on the forepeak. Cheering from our ship....I go up on the poop, give the order to lie to and send a boat to accept their surrender....Their captain is Don Phillipo de Rodriguez. He bows and hands me his sword. I take him to my cabin and offer him wine. There is a splinter cut over his right eye. I take a white linen handkerchief and bind his forehead. Under his wig his hair is grey and cropped close to the skull....

'I must go and see the men: seventeen have been killed or gravely wounded. I must not let them know that the sound of sawing and the smell of blood and boiling tar makes me wish to vomit. I bend down and put my hand on the shoulder of a dying man. His scalp is hanging loose and one of his legs has been severed above the knee....They are all wonderfully cheerful. I tell them of our victory.'

A friend of Hilary's who was listening asked, 'Did you notice the colour of the smoke when the guns fired?'

'White, white as steam.'

'Sure?'

'Quite sure.'

'Interesting. Gunpowder of that period produced a white smoke, but it hasn't been made for over a hundred years.'

Psychometry became our favourite game for several months, but as it usually gave me a headache I was not as keen on it as my audience. It was hard work, which none of them realised; but when they could produce something likely to contain an interesting story I was usually willing to oblige.

Soon I refused to do anything likely to contain information that the owner would have preferred me not to know. It was their fault for using me as a guinea-pig, but it made me feel as though I had been spying on them through a keyhole. For instance, John Bowen gave me his signet-ring to do, because he thought it might have interesting scenes of the Zulu war during which it had been worn by his grandfather. But what I saw was John crawling through the mud of no-man's-land and diving for cover into a shell-hole. He was shuddering from the noise of the barrage when another man slid into the same shell-hole. He was in German uniform. John was just going to shoot him and praying that his revolver hadn't jammed when a Very light went up and the German said, 'John, don't be such a bloody fool!' The German offered the Englishman a cigarette from a gold cigarette-case. It was inscribed in a facsimile of John's handwriting—a twenty-first birthday present which John had given him when they were at Oxford together. As dawn was breaking they crawled back to their opposing wire. John was so elated that he told his major what had happened, adding that it was a damn silly war when you met your best friend and nearly shot him in no-man's-land.

'You realise, I hope, that you could be court-martialled for fraternising with the enemy?' said the major coldly. 'However, I will forget what you have told me, provided you promise to keep your silly mouth shut.'

John had kept his promise until he handed me his signet-ring.

There were other things I saw which were far more embarrassing to me than this, things which forced me to dissemble and say I had seen nothing—which was seldom believed. So I turned from objects which might unwittingly contain dangerous knowledge to the impersonal field of experiment offered by the British Museum. In these expeditions Hilary was a most faithful and competent scribe. Notices demanding, 'Do not touch' had to be ignored, and a wary eye kept open for keepers, not to mention more conventional visitors. That we got results at all I think is a tribute to our persistence. Here is one of them:

The museum description was, 'Winged figure and winged human-headed bull from a doorway in the palace of Sargon, King of Assyria, 721 B.C.' Mine was more elaborate:

'This was beside the doorway of a palace at the head of a flight of colossal stone steps. From the foot of the steps stretches an avenue of crouching winged bulls, with a double row of palm trees behind them. Up the avenue a procession of returning warriors approaches. Between their ranks are prisoners who are being lashed with thonged whips, the thongs being tipped with metal. Prisoners who fall down are kicked or goaded. The goads are about eighteen inches long.

'There are bullock carts loaded with treasure. Some of the prisoners are roped to the wheels of the carts. The ropes are so short that they have to bend and then stretch up their arms as the wheels turn. A woman falls and the cart goes over her chest and crushes it. On one of the carts, lashed upright by grass ropes, is a golden cow with a jewelled necklace. It is the size of a calf and has been captured from the temple of the prisoners. They look up to it in despair. It is their god and their hope is gone because they cannot understand why it does not strike down their captors.

'I am seeing this through the eyes of a soldier who is standing beside this statue at the head of the steps. The scene is very brutal but I am unmoved, as to him it is commonplace.

'Now the prisoners are wailing: ''Hathor the Mighty! Hathor the Omnipotent! Ruler of Water, Ruler of Land...'' to the gold cow which is now at the foot of the steps. The king comes forth from the palace in a carrying-litter with twelve bearers. The litter is covered with gold beautifully scrolled and has dark red cushions. On each side of it there stand two fan-bearers. The king's crown is high and cylindrical, gold with rows of square jewels or enamel. He has black hair and his beard is elaborately curled. His tunic is red and white with an embroidered pattern like necklaces. He wears rings and armlets and his legs are thronged with jewels. His toenails are dyed red and so are his fingernails, which are very long. When the crowd sees him they all bow down. The prisoners begin wailing again, ''Hathor the Mighty! Hathor the Magnificent! We are as the sand beneath thy feet...''

'Now the king is giving judgment. The women are to be divided among the soldiers. If the men will not look with reverence upon their conqueror's gods, their eyes shall be put out. If they will not pray to their conqueror's gods, their tongues shall be torn out. If they will not listen to praise of their conqueror's gods, red-hot rods shall be driven into their ears to make them deaf.'

This sentence was being put into effect when we were interrupted by a conducted party, and I was glad of an excuse not to have to see any more.

191

PART FOUR

CHAPTER ONE

pREpARatioNs foR a jouRNey

On a July evening in 1934, Leslie returned from a cocktail party and announced that he was going to be an archaeologist instead of a barrister. He was still rather vague about the details. A man called Seton Lloyd had given him a job as the photographer on one of the Oriental Institute of Chicago University digs. The site, Tel Asmar, was about seventy miles from Baghdad. They paid return fare and keep....

'My fare, and Gillian's too?' I said hopefully.

'No, of course not. It wouldn't be suitable for a child in any case, and I forgot to ask about wives. I'll find out more of the form to-morrow when I meet Hans Frankfort, the Director.'

'I don't suppose he'd mind me—if he's prepared to take an archaeologist photographer who doesn't know anything about archaeology and not much about photography.'

'No need to tell them that,' he said hastily. 'I can easily learn. We're not going until September.'

'I'm sure I could help.'

'There *are* women on the dig, so perhaps I can fix it for you to come too. You could catalogue the finds or even do some of my routine work once I've taught you the knack of it.'

'I shall be far more useful than that!'

'How?'

'I can tell you where to dig! Just give me a chip off whatever you've found and then I'll psychometrise it and tell you where it joins on to the next bit....Much better than just scrabbling vaguely about in the sand.'

'No!' He sounded anguished. 'Archaeology is a *science*.'

'And I'm a better scientist than you are,' I said hotly. 'No one could be more scientific than Father....All those thousands of hydrogen ion concentrations I've done, all that peering through microscopes, all those card indexes.'

But when he left England, after six weeks of intense concentration in a photographer's studio, he still hadn't found out whether there was a chance that I should see him again before the Spring. He suggested that I let 107 Beaufort Street for six months and go to Seacourt, but I replied that although I might be considered luggage not wanted on voyage, I was not going to be put into storage.

I tried to make myself believe that I was going to enjoy being a grass widow, but when I saw the train sliding out of Victoria station—he was going to Marseilles and then by boat to Beirut—I felt far more like an anxious mama seeing her son off to his prep school. Had I packed enough shirts, enough pants, enough socks? Would anyone look after him if he got pneumonia again? And how would he manage with a simple cold when he always refused to let anyone except me see him or even carry a tray into the room when he was under the weather?

Hilary had arranged a girls' luncheon at Prunier's to cheer me up, and when I despondently returned to the subject of what poor Leslie would do when there were holes in all his two dozen pairs of new socks, one of them reminded me that unless female archaeologists were far more archaeologist than female Leslie's socks would always get darned.

In the middle of October he wrote to say that I was to join him, 'at the beginning of January,' and the same day I booked a place on the aeroplane that would leave on New Year's Day. He loathed writing letters and had warned me not to expect any unless these were essential information, so my news from him was limited to such items as, 'Bring only thin clothes, it's damnably hot.' Or, 'All your evening dresses and more soft collars for me.' Which indicated that Americans in the desert, like the British in the jungle, always changed for dinner. A postcard of an Arab horse, to Gillian, read, 'I ride on a horse rather like this. Tell Mummy I will give her a horse for Christmas so she can ride too.'

This was enchanting news, for experience had done little to destroy my conviction that only lack of practice and opportunity to get on really cosy terms with my steed prevented me echoing on earth the magnificient gallops which I enjoyed in less muscle-bound realms.

I toyed with the idea of going down to Crabbett Park and asking Judith Wentworth whether she could give me any inside information as to how to get friendly with Arab horses, of which she knew more than anyone in England. But I thought better of this, for after she had taken me into the tennis court and won at least four sets out of five, I would be too exhausted even to cajole a Margate Sands donkey.

Reginald Leslie, a friend of ours who claimed to know as much about horses as he did about flying aeroplanes, tried to damp my enthusiasm by saying that Leslie was bound to be cheated by a Bedouin horse-coper, who would never dream of selling an animal which was not neither so broken-winded that it would fall down when I mounted, or else so full of vice that no one else would be fool enough to get on its back. I defended Leslie's judgment with some heat, and pointed out that I had told him exactly what kind of animal to buy for me. It was to be a mare, for females are more intuitive than males—and I would need all the intuition I could get if I was to talk horse effectively, especially in Arabic. It was to be young, so that its natural good nature would not have become soured and suspicious. Its colour was not important, but I would prefer a sandy apricot with a white mane and tail.

At this Reginald groaned aloud and, casting his eyes to heaven, called on the gods who protect drunks, fools, and horsemen, to witness that he had done his best to warn me. 'The most I can do for you my poor, deluded child,' he said mournfully, 'is to organise your riding clothes so that you die with the right kind of boots on.' Every item had to pass his

194

critical eye, and my views were ignored as though I was a schoolgirl being outfitted by a stern governess for her first term at Roedean. The boots, with very heavy and expensive box-wood trees with my name inscribed on a little ivory plate, were constructed by Peel. Izod made my shirts, with collars so tight they nearly choked me. Busvine made my hacking-jacket and jodhpurs. After a learned discussion between Reginald and the cutter as to whether I should have fly-buttons or a barn-door front, they decided on the barn door; ignoring my comment that it seemed ostentatious to have a stable without a horse to put in it.

I fancied myself in breeches, but there was a slight undertone of being fitted for a shroud, so I tried to learn to be worthy of my outfit by exercise on hirelings in Hyde Park. This did nothing to increase my confidence, for one of the patient animals took fright at the sight of a carriage and pair while crossing the bridge over the Serpentine and tottered backwards on its hind legs until it found itself sitting on the balustrade while I hung on to its mane to stop myself falling some thirty feet into the lake. Another, which looked even more deceptively stolid and careworn, broke into a gallop at the end of Rotten Row and carried me out of the gates and half-way up Park Lane among hooting omnibuses before it skidded to a full stop with its legs splayed out at the corners as though it was trying to peg its hooves into the tarmac.

I took Gillian to Seacourt for Christmas so she would feel settled there before I had to leave. I gave her a pony called Ruby, a Shetland with a nature amiable as a dog's, who trotted round the garden and stopped by the root-store and the fruit-house for snacks of apples and carrots. She had ridden since she was three and was much better at it than I ever was. It was not until years later she admitted that she had always loathed horses and only pretended to like them so as not to disappoint me.

On Boxing Day we both developed 'flu, which postponed my departure by a fortnight. On my way back to London I tried to stop myself looking backwards at the misery of leaving Gillian instead of looking forwards to being with Leslie; but I was only partially successful, for I have never been able to teach myself not to want all my eggs in one basket. Packing is a good cure for the dreeps, especially when a very reasonable amount of things fill such a surprising number of suitcases. I had fifteen by the end of it all, although four of these were filled with photographic equipment and drawing-paper, books, tins of tobacco, and gramophone records; which had been sent to me to take out to various members of the expedition. The morning before I left I got another of Leslie's air-mail letters. 'Don't try to smuggle anything through the Customs. Declare *everything*. Will meet you with money to pay duty, which will be about 200 pounds. Bring a case of kippers, fifty fire-balloons and a gross of french letters (have promised some to the R.A.F.). Much love. Leslie.'

For a moment I tried to believe that the last three instructions were meant as a joke. Then I telephoned Fortnum & Mason and asked how long a case of kippers would keep in an aeroplane. A soothing voice replied that it would depend on whether I was travelling to the Equator or to the North Pole; and on learning that I was only going to Baghdad, promised to send them round immediately. I telephoned to Father and asked, 'What are fire-ballons, and where do I get them?' He said that as far as he knew the last one had been made by Montgolfier about 1794, and said that more recent aeronauts considered them impractical. Selfridge's Enquiry Bureau was not much more informative, but they told me to try Gamages, who, after some research, discovered that they had four dozen of the things, which were sometimes used by surveyors to test wind-drift, and they would send them round in a taxi....Which was a load off my mind, as I had visualised large machines of canvas instead of light, and easily packable, spheres of coloured paper, which is what they turned out to be. The purchase of the last item I handed on to Stan *via*

196

Diana, and in spite of his protests she bullied him into it. This was one thing I was *not* going to declare. But suppose they were discovered?

How many Customs barriers would I have to pass? Or could I register luggage through to its destination? Never having been in an aeroplane except once in Reginald's Moth, I rang up Imperial Airways. Luggage was liable to be opened in transit on entering France, Italy and Egypt. The Italian Customs were particularly rapacious since Mussolini had forbidden British planes to fly over Italy, so making it necessary for Imperial Airways passengers to make that part of the journey by train.... Well, there was nothing I could do about it. So I went to bed, and had a worry-dream in which my old enemy, the Customs man at the French-Italian border, enraged and in pyjamas, was finding exactly what I did not want him to find in front of a jeering crowd of Fascisti.

CHAPTER TWO

how many miles to babylon?

Daisy took me to Croydon airport and gave me a flask filled with old liqueur brandy, 'Just in case you feel air-sick. I believe that aeroplanes are much less stable than balloons.' Outwardly serene, she watched me pass beyond the 'Passengers Only' barrier and then walked briskly away towards her waiting car.

The officials seemed startled by my quantity of luggage. They charged me excess fare (which was less than I feared from rather vague weighings on baby scales which only went up to twenty pounds) and said severely that although this plane was not loaded to capacity and I could therefore take it all with me as far as Paris, I must not expect to be so fortunate on later stages of the journey; and I must fully understand that most of it would probably be left behind *en route* to follow 'when practicable'.

Although large by the standards of over twenty years ago, the aeroplane looked as though it were made of tin-foil. It shuddered so violently when the engines revved up that I began to think I was not only destined to be born but also to die near Croydon. Then, as though a Pegasus was flying through a vast hoop of grey paper, it escaped from the confines of grey rain into a world of brilliant sunshine and high blue sky. The steward brought me a cup of coffee which did not even slop into its saucer. Thank God, I *liked* flying! No one could feel sick in an aeroplane. What a relief!

After four hours in Paris, and lunch at Voisin with a fellow-passenger, we caught the Rome Express with five minutes to spare. Luggage of air passengers could not be put in the van, nor was there an empty compartment in the *Wagons Lits* to accommodate it; but eventually two sweating porters stacked it in my sleeper, leaving only the bed free, which I could reach in the manner of a chamois leaping to its sleeping-ledge.

The Italian Customs passed without incident—perhaps they thought that no really efficient smuggler would try to take so much at one time, and I settled down to write my first letter to Gillian so that I could post it in Rome. She was still young enough to prefer her stories illustrated, so, as I draw no better than the average four-year-old child, I invented two characters called Ragga and Muffin. Ragga was easily identified by his striped suit and horn-rimmed glasses, and Muffin was a golliwog with curly hair. They were to share all my adventures as the hero and heroine of a twice-weekly serial which ran for the next four months. In the first instalment they visited Elba, which I claimed, quite untruly, to be looking at from the train window, and lunched with Napoleon, instantly recognisable by his hat and his arm tucked into his waistcoat. Then they crossed the Alps with Hannibal, clinging to the tails of two of his elephants, which they had tamed by feeding bananas to them from a paper bag. Elephants, especially when proceeding in the opposite direction, are easy to draw and anyone can manage mountains and fir trees.

On the second night in the train I returned to my sleeper at midnight, having sat until then in the dining-car, listening to the broken romance of an elderly cloth-manufacturer from Manchester, whose prospective bride, on the eve of the wedding, had bolted with a red-headed tea-taster. The only consolation I could offer, which seemed to cheer him disproportionately, was that as he had bought a magnificent bedroom suit he would henceforth sleep on a super de luxe Vi-Spring mattress in the double bed more comfortably, although alone, than he had ever done in his life.

I woke before dawn, nearly frozen solid as I had left the window wide open and forgotten that we had another range of mountains to cross, from which snow had blown in to make a drift across my feet. Brindisi in the cheerless winter dawn was even colder, and the sea so rough that the launch that took us out to the flying-boat had to make several attempts before it at last got near enough for us to scramble on board. The mountains of Albania seen across the dark blue Adriatic were supremely beautiful, but then the weather began to close in. I was sharing a seat with a man who had recently competed in the Schneider Trophy Air Race, and while, in happy ignorance, I was thinking how clever it was of our pilot to fly up mountain valleys so narrow that it seemed we were going to brush snow off the precipices with our wing-tips, I heard him muttering, 'The silly bastard will never make it! We're going to touch! Oh Jesus!' And I was at once more than convinced that Mount Olympus is much better seen from a long distance rather than horizontally at a range of a few hundred yards.

We landed at Piraeus to refuel, and there was talk of spending the night in Athens. But the weather report, quite inaccurately as it turned out, said we should run into better weather before we got to Crete. The literature provided for the entertainment of passengers informed me that I was now flying over the Greek Islands, 'probably the finest scenery on the whole of our air routes'. But we were encased in clouds thicker than any London fog, and for the first time in my life I thoroughly disliked a thunderstorm. Lightning, like bolts in the hand of Zeus, tore through the blackness. The flimsy flying-boat swayed, lurched, fell heavy as a stone into nightmare pits and staggered out of them.

The heating was out of order. Someone had forgotten to put air-sickness paper bags on board. People were sick into newspapers, on to the floor. A charming old Negro gentleman in the seat facing me looked wildly round, and with a gesture of apology vomited so neatly into the pocket of his navy-blue overcoat that I offered him the remains of my brandy.

When the steward enquired whether any passengers would be requiring lunch, everyone glared at him except an elderly couple. He was a retired major-general from Dorset, who, with his equally elderly wife, was going to visit their granddaughter in Khartoum. They swallowed every morsel of their lunch with apparent enjoyment, chatting to each other between mouthfuls as though they were eating crumpets under a cedar on the edge of their croquet lawn.

My Schneider Trophy friend lurched down the aisle and disappeared into the pilots' compartment. When he returned he looked even more worried. 'We can't land at Crete— visibility is down to zero,' he confided in me. 'Don't mention it to the others: no point in them getting the vertical wind up.'

The weather grew worse: the only advantage being that I was now too frightened to feel sick. At intervals my companion went to consult the pilot and always returned with an increased conviction that we were in the hands of an over-optimistic lunatic who should have turned back to Greece while he had chance, and now would almost certainly run out of fuel before we reached Alexandria. One of the engines coughed, spluttered and then died. The flying-boat went into a long glide. Suddenly streamers of cloud were wisping past the windows. The port engine cut out, and we were bouncing on the water—of Alexandria harbour.

We reached the hotel at 9.30, and the hairdresser, with whom I had booked an appointment three months before, and long since forgotten all about it, had kept his shop open for me. I was far too tired to care whether I arrived in Baghdad with train-dust in my hair or not; but I could not disappoint the kindly barber, and nearly allowed him to dye my hair red, which, he suggested, would be a nice surprise for my husband.

I ordered dinner in my room, and it was brought while I was having a bath in the adjoining bedroom, which had a glass-panelled door.

I was called at 4.30 a.m., after an almost sleepless night, as the storm ceaselessly rattled the French windows and hail-stones threatened to batter in the ill-fitting glass. It was still dark, but in the light from the passage I recognised the Arab waiter as the same man who had collected my dinner tray the night before. He told me that the weather was too bad to fly and that I would have to stay in the hotel until the next plane left on Friday. I was on the point of thankfully going back to sleep when I suddenly felt suspicious. 'Why on Friday?' Why not to-morrow—or later to-day, if the weather improves?' He began to stammer in French....The Memsahib must not fly. It would be a tragedy if a lady so charming as she, whom he had watched having her bath, should be killed....He would wait on me devotedly—do no more than kiss my hand unless I permitted.

I sat bolt upright in bed, clutching the eiderdown to my rather meagre breast. So this was one of the licentious foreigners of whom Mother had so often warned me! *Allez-vous-en!*' I shouted. '*Vite!*' It is difficult to be commanding in those circumstances, but at last he began to sob, implored me not to tell the manager, and admitted that, although all except three of the other passengers had decided to wait for better weather, the plane was going...in fact the bus was leaving in ten minutes for the airport—might have left already....But I caught it: by running after it half-way down the street.

Gaza was sunny and warm, and we had tangerines with the leaves still on and eggs and bacon for breakfast. The other passengers were two silent soldiers who were on their way to India to shoot tiger with a maharajah, and the Schneider Trophy pilot, who was suffering acutely from a hangover. Apart from a dust-storm, which penetrated into the cabin and undid all the good that had been done to my hair the night before, the flight was uneventful, and two hours shorter than scheduled because of a strong tail-wind.

The airport, five miles outside Baghdad, was a flat bit of brown nothing surrounded by miles and miles of exactly the same. The only building was a corrugated iron shed. But where was Leslie? The other three were met by friends and drove away in clouds of dust. I sat on my largest suitcase and waited. The officials, none of whom spoke any English or French either, hung about smoking cigarettes. Three of them at last shrugged their shoulders and drove away in the larger of two battered trucks. The two remaining men offered me glasses of mint-tea, which I thankfully accepted as a good-will offering. It is difficult to explain, entirely in mime, that one's husband is apt to be unpunctual, but will certainly arrive soon with money to pay the Customs Duty. At last their patience began to wear thin, or perhaps they had wives less patient than I was being. They pointed to their watches, rubbed their stomachs to show they were already late for dinner, rattled the key in the door of the Customs shed to show it was closing time.

I began to unlock suitcases—at least no one should accuse me of being a smuggler as well as of being abandoned in Baghdad. They beamed, put a finger to mouth for silence. It was to be understood that I had nothing to declare. Trying to work out the duty would waste even more of their time. Slow to take the hint I waved rolls of film, tins of tobacco, gramophone records at them. They frowned. Could any female be quite so obtuse? They waved me aside. They locked my bags. They scrawled chalk marks all over them. Then they slung everything into the remaining truck, lifted me into it, rattled across the desert at the maximum speed the ancient vehicle could urge out of its panting cylinders, and deposited me outside the Maude Hotel.

The obvious question is, 'Why did I not hire a car and go to Tel Asmar?' But I had no idea in which direction it lay, and the only address I had was P.O. Box 64 Baghdad, from which letters were collected twice a week.

The hall porter spoke a little French but was not very helpful. The archaeologists usually met in the bar of a small hotel farther down the street towards the Suq. He thought that he had seen one of the Expedition cars that afternoon. He would keep my luggage if I wished to look for my husband.

I went into the first bar, the second, the third—unfortunately in those days I disliked alcohol and was sustained only by glasses of over-sweetened lemonade. I found in my bag a piece of pink chalk which I must have absent-mindedly stolen from one of the Customs men. On each bar, after lavishly tipping the barman, I drew a large 'JOAN' and an arrow indicating the direction of my progress.

In the fifth bar Leslie caught up with me. He had missed me by ten minutes at the airport, where he had arrived late only because the gale, which he thought would delay the plane by at least an hour, had most unfairly been blowing in the opposite direction a few thousand feet higher up. He had been hot on my trail ever since, and was as happy to find me as I was to be found.

CHAPTER THREE
fantasy and fact

I had a preconceived idea of deserts, based on pictures of the rolling sand-dunes of the Sahara, so I was surprised to find us driving across utter flatness on a surface so hard that the car could steer a course as though it were a motor-boat on still water. There was not even a track, only small sand-mounds every few yards, erected by the Expedition to serve as route-markers. We crossed two of the great irrigation-canals, which are so wide that three cars can still drive along them abreast. There were once three thousand miles of them, and, until the conquest of the Babylonians by the Assyrians in the eighth century B.C., they formed part of a gigantic irrigation scheme which turned a vast area of what is now arid desert into the greatest granary of the ancient world.

In the beam of our headlights the house looked lonely and forbidding as a Beau Geste fort. Suddenly we heard a huge sound of wailing. Leslie put on the brakes and got out of the car. 'The diggers are up to something,' he said, and seemed rather worried. Then he laughed. 'It's all right—only a total eclipse of the moon. Come and watch it.'

It was a very eerie night. The full white moon burned to a dusky red as it was eaten by the black demon of the Underworld. The wailing grew louder, until at last Allah heard his people's prayer and slew the monster which had dared to swallow the lantern of the night.

It was now so late that Leslie thought that everyone would have gone to bed, but a welcoming party was still in progress and I was delighted to find that archaeologists are far less professorial than my earlier experience of scientists had led me to believe. There were seven men and four women—five including me—of assorted nationalities. Hans Frankfort, the Director, was Dutch. Thorkild and Rigmor Jacobsen were

Danish. Pierre was Russian, and Ham and Hal American. The rest were English: Seton and his exotically beautiful wife Joanne, Rachel, and last, though in my affection she is certainly first, Mary Chubb. *

Logs were burning in the open fireplace of the sitting-room. (It was another surprise to find that Iraq in mid-winter is bitterly cold.) In the adjoining dining-room there was a lavish cold supper which I was almost too tired to appreciate. Our bedroom was rather Spartan, for only basic furniture was provided by the Expedition; but we had a bathroom to ourselves as our room was normally used only by visitors. I had expected to have to wash in a tin basin, which in fact I did for ten days when Leslie and I were at the subsidiary dig-house at Khafaje; but here there was no lack of water, although every drop of it had to be brought twelve miles from the canal by truck.

The communal living-rooms occupied one side of the main courtyard, bare except for a eucalyptus tree which Rachel nourished with jugs of her bath-water—lavish baths were considered a necessity, but water for flowers a gross extravagance. On the other three sides were bed-sitting rooms arranged in pairs with a bathroom between each. Round a second courtyard were the work-rooms, including the one where Leslie did his photography, with its adjoining dark-room, and the *umbar*, a long, narrow room with a work-bench under the three windows, and bays of shelves on which all the *antikas* were kept. Round a third courtyard were grouped the kitchen, the house servants' quarters, store-rooms, stables and livestock—which included a flock of sheep, fifty at the beginning of the season, none at the end of it when they had done their work as an 'on the hoof' store-cupboard and their fleeces were used to pack the *antikas*.

The outer walls were patrolled at night by two guards, armed with rifles, who were supplied by the Government,

* Mary Chubb is the author of *Nefertiti Lived Here* and is now writing a book about her years at Tel Asmar as Secretary to the Director.

and were supposed to have at least one murder each to his credit. We were officially under the protection of the local sheik, a delightful old man called Abdul Jeboal, who came every payday to collect a percentage of their wages from each of the two hundred or so men and boys who worked on the dig. From the levy he paid any fines demanded by us as recompense for 'incidents'—such as one during the previous season when a disgruntled, or perhaps only trigger-happy, Arab had fired five bullets into one of the Expedition cars—fortunately without winging any of the four occupants.

The dig itself was about a quarter of a mile from the house. Until excavation began, four years before I went there, the town of Tel Asmar was a large, roughly circular mound. Sumerians built their new towns on top of the old ones; so, to make sure of accurately dating buildings and objects, one layer after another was removed as well as shafts being sunk.

During the centuries the level of the desert had risen, through countless tons of earth being deposited on it by duststorms. The dig was now a huge pit, more than thirty metres deep, and I climbed down into it on a ladder. I wanted to work out there, but was told that as the pride of Arabs does not allow them to take orders from females, I would have to content myself with indoor jobs. However, my second night in Tel Asmar produced a magnificent electric storm which I watched at midnight from the water-tower, the only part of the mud-brick buildings that was more than one storey high. No rain fell—in our part of the desert little rain had fallen for the last four years, but gigantic zigzag flashes blazed the night from horizon to horizon. Leslie, when I described the beauty of it to him next morning, said briskly that only an idiot would have offered herself as a lightning-conductor on the highest point for a large number of square miles. But, fortunately for me, the Arabs took a different view—or else the total eclipse had already been a sufficient sponsor—for a spokesman came to Hans to say that should the 'Magical

Memsahib' wish any of them to work for her they would be most honoured to do so.

So when I was bored by making scale drawings of pots, a task made even more laborious by calipers and other measuring devices calibrated in inches which I had to translate into centimetres, I spent the day on the dig. It meant getting up much too early, as work began at dawn. In the cold grey light I walked the quarter-mile, trying not to see dozens of men performing their morning defecation, squatting naked from the waist down, but apparently convinced that by pulling their *abbas* up to cover their heads they were in complete privacy. Perhaps they are the origin of the legend wrongly attributed to ostriches.

Having clambered down to the point assigned to me I then usually spent the rest of the day beside a grave, watching its contents being slowly and carefully uncovered. This was not nearly so easy as it would have been had the ground been sandy, as in Egypt, for here it was clay nearly as hard as cement. At several stages I told the men to stop while I made rough sketches with exact measurements of where each object lay in relation to another. When sufficient was uncovered Leslie took photographs before anything was moved to the *umbar* for detailed examination and cleaning.

One skeleton had, instead of the usual food pots and weapons, only a wine-cup in his hand and thirty wine-jars packed round him, so closely that there was hardly room in the grave for the body itself. There were clear indications that he had been killed by a blow on the forehead. During lunch I started to speculate on the manner of man he had been. Had he died in a wine-shop brawl with fellow wine-bibers, who felt sorry in the morning that they had been too rough and so clubbed together to give him a good send-off? Or was he a butler, caught sampling his master's cellar? Someone hastily changed the subject and Leslie frowned: how often must I be told that we were here to discover facts not fantasy?

For several days I was sufficiently subdued to work industriously and blindly as a mole, and as a gesture of independence began my collection of four-thousand-year-old teeth. This occupation was not so macabre as it sounds. Before leaving London a dentist friend, Mr. G.B. Pritchard, had asked me to look carefully at the teeth of any ancient skulls I encountered, for comparison of their dental condition with that of contemporary man. What began as a chore became a very real interest, which I could get no one else to share. I became a tooth-bore until the subject was forbidden at meals. Children's teeth, middle-aged teeth, teeth of men who were so old that the surface of the molars was ground almost smooth—and in none of the forty sets I collected was there a single decayed tooth, nor a jaw abscess, nor a wisdom tooth that had not grown in alignment with the rest. I packed them lovingly in little cardboard boxes, with as much data as I could find about the previous owners. But they never got to England, for at the end of the season Seton made me bury them, in case they were found by the Customs, who might think that we had tried to evade the Government decree that nothing should be taken from the dig except the half share of all finds allowed by our permit.

In another grave on which I worked, a woman still held a copper mirror in her skeleton hand, and the green eye-shadow and the khol, the rouge and the powder, in jasper and sardonyx jars at her side, were still so little changed that I could have made up my own face with them. On a bronze ring, held by a lapis-lazuli ram, were threaded toilet instruments: eyebrow pluckers, a little scoop for pushing back the cuticle of the nails, a spike to clean them, and a thing like a miniature salt-spoon with a hole in it, which I identified, from having seen one like it in a Victorian dressing-case, as being intended for removing black-heads.

She wore several bracelets and armlets, and an intricate head-dress of tiny beads on to which Seton poured melted paraffin wax so that the pattern could be exactly reconstructed. One by one I freed the beads from the wax when it had hardened on the skull, and with a fine needle strung them on a fresh thread. I kept the skull for several days on my bedside table, which caused no comment as we often worked in our rooms instead of in the *umbar*. But I never dreamed of her; and her bones and her other discarded possessions gave me nothing to add to the bare facts which I already knew— that she had died young, had small, delicate bones, and had lived nearly four thousand years ago.

I was in the *umbar*, carefully cleaning the clay from the incised lines of a cylinder-seal, preparatory to rolling it on plasticine to make a record of its design, when I suddenly found myself tuning-in. No one except Leslie was there, so I told him to grab a pencil and began to dictate:

'This was worn on the left shoulder. It was on a copper pin which had an almost right-angle bend in it, beyond the bend there was a little cross-piece to prevent the seal from falling off. By holding the pin one could roll the seal backwards and forwards like a rolling-pin. The pin was very sharp and could be used as a dagger, but usually it was used to hold the cloak together on the left shoulder. It belonged to someone who had a lot to do with building.*

At first I was disappointed that I should have broken his rule of 'no spooks' with something so uninteresting. But Leslie was quite excited, and from one of the shelves took a pin, which had been found early in the season, that was exactly like the one I had described. 'These are not uncommon, but they are supposed to be hair ornaments,' he said.

'Which we now know to be nonsense,' I replied.

'Do we?' said Hans, who had come in through the far door while I was still dictating, without either of us noticing him.

There was no point in trying to dissemble. I plunged into

---

* The note-book in which Leslie wrote this, and other dictations also mentioned in Part Four, has survived. This one is headed, 'Amethyst cylinder-seal from Ischali. (Isch 34/45) February 1935.'

such an abbreviated account of how I had come to do psychometry that it probably sounded even less plausible than it need have done. He admitted that nearly all cylinder-seals have a hole bore through them, but maintained that this was so that they could be worn round the neck on a cord.

'But it would be so much easier to roll them if they were on something stiff,' I protested. 'Look, Hans. I'll thread one of my hairpins through this one and show you how much easier it is....'

He said amiably that mine was quite a logical theory, but only a theory, and that theories were rather unwise for people whose primary object was facts.

About a month later I was fitting potsherds together—which I enjoyed, as it was like playing at jigsaw puzzles made even more difficult by some of the pieces being missing, when Hans came into the *umbar* with a party of visitors. I didn't listen to what he was saying, as by then I knew most of the obvious questions they were likely to ask and the routine answers, until I suddenly heard him say, 'That pin was used to hold a cylinder-seal like the ones I have already shown you. Not only did the pin make it easier to use the seal, but it served to fasten the cloak, and being in its original state very sharp, it could even be used as a weapon.'

I was hidden from Hans by one of the bays of shelves, but I now put my head round the corner and winked broadly at him. He blushed and raised his voice a little. 'These pins used to be classified as hair ornaments, but in the light of more recent knowledge their real purpose has been discovered. On another of the digs an inscription has been found, on a clay tablet in cuneiform, which describes how a certain court official stabbed another man to death *with his seal*. Archaeology is largely a matter of fitting facts together....'

He beamed at me and introduced me to the visitors. 'Fitting *facts* together, as I was saying, much as Mrs. Grant here is so patiently gluing together these shards so as to discover, scientifically, the conformation of the original pot.'

CHAPTER FOUR
mare and nightmare

Gazalla, my Arab mare, was the colour of pale copper with a white mane and tail. She at last cured me of the illusion that I am a natural horsewoman. When I first arrived she had a strained tendon, or so the Arab groom told Leslie, who did not ride her himself, as Sheik Abdul Jeboal, who had sold her to him for 15 pounds, said she was not up to his weight.

She had delicately flaring nostrils like Gladys Cooper and might have trotted out of a medieval Persian painting. I lavished affection on her, cajoled her with carrots, sugar, sweet biscuits and lettuces, which she daintily accepted although she was already brimful of wheat and maize. She looked rather too fat, but I ascribed this to over-feeding. At last the groom, a wizened man smaller than an English jockey, could think of no more excuses to prevent me riding her. I waited until everyone was safely out of the way, for I wanted to practice without an audience, and dressed myself in my lovely new riding clothes. Gazalla must have had some trace of affection for me in her rebellious heart, or else known I had sugar in my pocket, for she let me lead her round the side of the house and stood docilely while I mounted. For the first half-mile she cantered smoothly as a rocking-horse. I glowed with pride in us both—hands and heels down, spine erect but relaxed. I might have been doing it straight out of the book!

Then she stretched out her neck, took the bit firmly between her teeth, and bolted. Frantically I pulled on the reins, but I might as well have tried to stop an express train with a skipping-rope. I got a stitch in my side, and the grip of my knees, which was always feeble, began to melt away. I wrapped the reins round my wrist and clung to her mane with one hand and the saddle with the other. At last she began to slow down a little, but she was still going far too fast for me to relish the idea of sliding on to such iron-hard ground. Like a fool I tried to assert my authority by pulling on one rein with both hands, which, so I had read somewhere, caused a bolting horse to turn in ever smaller circles until it had to stop, knowing itself mastered.

But all this trick did was to annoy Gazalla, who knew more tricks by instinct than ever got into a text-book. She sprang into the air, undulating like a sea-serpent and jerked the reins—which were still round my wrist—so violently that she dislocated my shoulder. My howl of pain must have startled her, for she stared at me in unutterable disdain. By hanging on to the stirrup leather I managed to click my shoulder back into place, but it was still far too painful to pull myself back into the saddle, even though Gazalla seemed at last to have run out of steam.

The house looked small as a toy in the far, far distance, and I began to trudge towards it, dragging Gazalla behind me like a sled. The groom, who knew his hideous secret—that, far from exercising her every morning and evening, he had never taken her out of the stableyard once he found that she was virtually unbroken—was about to be discovered, had been watching me from the top of the water-tower. To add to my humiliation, a truck-load of yelling Arabs, intent on earning kudos for retrieving me, came rattling across the desert. They implored me to get into the truck, but I was in no mood to be rescued—and if I couldn't get home on my horse's hooves I could at least do so on my own feet! Gazalla too was sulking, and tried to nip me unless I held her close to the bit, which was disgustingly slimy with froth. The truck, with its cargo of bewildered and now silent Arabs, ground after me in bottom gear. The Memsahib might be magical but it was certain that she was also mad—and such persons are under the protection of Allah.

The venal groom removed himself during the night and the other one told me that the reason for Gazalla's stoutness was that within four months she would bear me a foal. He thought I would be glad to know that Leslie had been so clever as to buy two horses for the price of one, but I had other plans for her.

As soon as I could drive a car I went off alone which was strictly forbidden, to Sheik Abdul Jeboal's village. He met me at the gates and escorted me to his house, where, seated beside him on a pile of precious carpets turbulent with fleas, he fed me with his own hand. I knew this was a great honour for an Arab to offer to a woman, so I tried to appreciate the sheep's eye; the hard-boiled eggs grey with the dirt from his hands as he peeled them—it is surprisingly difficult to bite a small boiled egg without nipping the hospitable fingers in which it is offered; the pieces of tangerine from which he carefully removed the pips with his long, beautiful nails before popping them into my mouth, held open for him like a hungry fledgling's.

The curious meal took place in the garden of his house, an orchard of tangerine trees. Would I accept some tangerines? Basket after basket of fruit, as delicious as they were beautiful among their leaves and sweet-smelling flowers, were stripped from the branches and laid at my feet. Was there nothing else he could implore me to accept? In a corner of the garden there was a clump of hollyhocks. Would it be too unkind, I wondered, to ask him for the only flowers I had seen since I came to Iraq? He beamed, enchanted by my exquisite manners. I was truly of Allah, for how otherwise could I, a foreigner, have paid him the delicate compliment of indicating that to so humble a person as myself the weeds in his garden would seem a rich gift?

Only when he, and most of the villagers, had escorted me to the car, which was now so full of tangerines and hollyhocks that it would have looked at home on the French Riviera during a Battle of Flowers, did he introduce the subject of Gazalla. He had heard that she was to bear a foal, and as I, a fact almost too sad to be spoken of, would by that time have flown away to my own country, might he buy the little mare back from me? Graciously I accepted his kind offer, relieved that I had had the sense to wait for him to introduce the subject instead of offering her to him as a gift, which had been the purpose of my visit. He gave me an envelope. I put it, unopened, in my bag as courtesy demanded. He bowed. Everyone bowed. I drove away through a lane of cheering children. When I opened the envelope I found 25 pounds in it—10 more than Leslie had paid for Gazalla.

I had been in Iraq about a month when I woke in the middle of the night with an agonising dream. I could still feel Gillian's arms clinging round my neck and hear her wailing, 'Don't let them cut my tummy open, Mummy! Don't let them cut a hole in me! Mummy I *need* you!'

With tears streaming down my face I woke Leslie and began throwing things into an overnight bag. 'What on earth are you doing?' he protested sleepily.

'Gillian is going to have an operation. She needs me. For God's sake stop gawping! Get dressed and fetch the car.'

He tried to reason with me, but soon began to share something of my anxiety. He refused to start until dawn, on the logical, but at the same time infuriating pretext, that it was useless to hurry, as the bi-weekly plane was not due to leave until the following day, that it was impossible to telephone to England and that the Baghdad Post Office did not open until nine o'clock.

I was rattling the post office door for several minutes before a clerk reluctantly opened it a quarter of an hour too early. At first he was disgruntled, but after I had sent a long cable to Mother, demanding to be told full details of Gillian's illness, however serious it might be, he became sympathetic and gave me a glass of tea. After booking a place on the next day's plane, and going to the bank, I went back to the post office every half-hour to find out whether the answer to my cable had arrived. When at last it came, just before closing time, the clerk ran out into the street, where I was huddled miserably in the car; jubilantly waving the cable form and shouting, 'Good, Memsahib! It is good, GOOD!'

I was so close to tears that I could hardly see to read, 'All well with Gillian darling. Don't worry writing. Mother.'

I ran to find Leslie, who, exhausted by trying to calm me down, had retreated to the hotel bar, and told him the glorious news. 'Next time you have a fussage dream about our child I suggest you keep it to yourself,' he said grimly. 'Thank God I had the sense to stop you making a fool of yourself in front of the others—I told them you wanted to do a long day's shopping, as an excuse for starting so ridiculously early.'

We had dinner in silence, and I ate far more than he did, for relief from anxiety usually makes me ravenously hungry. In silence too we walked out to the car, and only spoke to each other when we got involved with a herd of camels, while we were waiting to cross the river and they began kicking the car. The noise was extraordinary, as though we were midgets enclosed in a bass drum. It is difficult to sulk when entirely surrounded by angry camels, as they look so absurdly like some of one's least-favourite acquaintances.

But there was still a coldness for several days, so I was pleasantly surprised when he rather embarrassedly kissed me before handing me a letter which was addressed to him in Mother's writing. The letter has not survived, but I remember it so well that this is near enough to the original text as makes no matter:

Dear Leslie,

From Joan's cable (poor child, how worried she must have been! I can only hope you were *kind* to her!) I know she must have *sensed* the danger to Gillian. I am writing to *you* so that you can use your discretion as to whether to tell her *all*, or if you think it wiser not to remind her of it in case it makes her worry. You know I take *every* care of Gillian—and so does Miss S. (I *dislike* the woman but think she is efficient in her own way. I watch her *closely* and she seems *kind* to the child.)

But accidents happen however careful one is, especially with such an independent and *intelligent* child as Gillian. I try to *warn* her against danger, but I confess it never occurred to me that she would think of unscrewing the *lavatory-paper container.* (In Jack's lavatory too where she is not supposed to go—but I suppose she left it too late and had to use the nearest one, poor child!) It (they have now been removed from *all* the other W.C.s) was fixed to the wall with a bolt, a *wicked* thing with a screw-thread three inches long as thick as my little finger, with a knob on the top of it (the kind that takes a *spanner*). I have often told the child *never* to put anything in her mouth, but she did, and managed to swallow it! She came to me and told me what she had done—so sensible of her—and I *at once* gave her *quantities* of rich plum cake. This, as Joan may have told you, was exactly what I did when Westray (it was during the war so he must have been about ten years old at the time) swallowed the wheel off his toy engine. They operated on him (his stomach was really a dreadful sight afterwards with scars like a hot X bun) *needlessly,* for since the X-rays the nurse in the hospital had never watched his bowel movements and it had found its own way through! (I told the nurse she ought to be soundly thrashed!) But I always believe in taking *every* precaution, as you know. Jack and I (Miss S. officiously insisted on coming too) took Gillian to Portsmouth and had her X-rayed. The report was *grave.* The bolt in such a bad position, and so *large* that they doubted whether it could *pass.* We booked a room in the nursing-home (quite a good one considering that it's not in London, and a very civil Matron) and arranged for a surgeon to be ready when we wanted him. Dr. May says he really is a good man and there was no point in telling

Arthur Beddard to send one down from London.

It is Jack's fault that I did not cable Joan the moment it happened. He insisted that she would not be able to get here before the operation, either Gillian would be safely over it or it would be *too late* by the time her mother reached her. But the plum cake and *my prayers* were enough and the bolt passed through her next morning without any trouble. You can imagine how *thankful* we all were!

I hope Joan is well. I know how she worries. Look after her, and *do* try to make her wear a hat. I always fear sunstroke.

Jack sends his love to you both and wishes me to tell you he is keeping the bolt *carefully locked up in his desk* as you will want to see it when you get home.

Your affectionate mother-in-law,
B. Marshall.

CHAPTER FIVE

the rain came

Although it is difficult to make a first choice among the servants to whom I have been grateful and devoted, I think Abdullah was the most perfect. He could speak a little English, and with enormous goodwill on both sides and plenty of intuition we could converse freely. He was highly intelligent, beautiful to look at and had great dignity. At meals he stood beside my chair, for though it was not necessary for him to appear in the dining-room he preferred to wait on me himself. He even washed and ironed my clothes, as well as any ladies' maid could have done.

Perhaps the first time he recognised me as an ally not only

of himself but of his people, was when a visitor came to lunch three days after I arrived. He was, I regret to say, a senior British officer. He was also a fat, red-faced man with fish-pale eyes. He began to talk about the Arabs as 'Wogs', using every belittling and contempuous phrase to which he could lay his doubtless liver-furred tongue. I fixed him with my eyes, which are always as dark and sometimes as pene-trating as any Arab's. I spoke loudly and clearly so that Abdullah would be sure to hear every word. 'I entirely dis-agree, Colonel. I think God made only one real error of taste—when He made *pink* men.'

The diet of the diggers (the house-servants had basically the same food as ourselves) was, by European standards, appallingly inadequate. Most of them subsisted entirely on the rubbery Arab bread, baked in flat, unleavened loaves on hot stones; though a few of the slightly less poverty stricken varied their diet with an occasional egg or an onion. The majority smoked at least fifty native cigarettes a day, which, so far as I can remember, cost threepence a hundred.

I wanted to organise a soup-kitchen for them, so that at least they could begin and end their long day's work with something hot and nourishing in their stomachs; but this was forbidden, and as I was only a guest I could not go against the policy of the Expedition. Next to the servant's quarters there was a small store-room where minimal first-aid equipment was kept for them. Mary, from long experience in Egypt and Iraq, knew that, in a country where more than half the children were blind, or nearly so, from ophthalmia, because their mothers considered it the Will of Allah that flies should cluster on their festering eyes, we were as helpless to make any lasting difference as we would have been if we had tried to dam the river Euphrates with a bundle of straw. Every evening she doled out castor oil, which they sucked down avidly, and gave them glycerine when their hands were so dry that the flesh had cracked open and prevented them from holding a pick. But I, the new broom, was rather ambitious.

Most of the men who came for treatment had monstrous boils. I thought these were caused by malnutrition. Fortunately I did not find out until long after any danger of infection was past that ninety per cent. of 'Baghdad Boils' are syphilitic in origin. At least I could do something about these, for although I have never been able to cure myself of fainting at the sight of blood, I have a reasonably strong stomach for pus. The only surgical instrument I could find—it was part of the anti-snake-bite outfit—was a lancet; and with it I proceeded to open boils. My patients, who must have been appreciative for they came in increasing numbers every evening, suffered agonising pain, for I often released a thick, green torrent which would have over-flowed a breakfast cup. But none of them even winced or made a sound, although three of them keeled over in a dead faint, which caused great amusement among their fellow-sufferers.

The last time I treated them was on the evening before the great dust-storm. I had experienced several minor dust-storms, and one bad one, when I was spending ten days with Ham, Hal, and Leslie at Khafaje. That dig was only about a mile from the house, but Ham and Hal, who began to drive back for shelter the moment it started, were going round in circles for an hour before they finally found their way home. On that same afternoon, Seton and three of the others had been on their way from Baghdad to Tel Asmar, and although the moment they saw the dust-cloud on the horizon they drove fast towards a village they failed to reach it in time and had to huddle in the car for three hours, breathing through scarves soaked in ginger-beer, of which there happened to be a two-dozen case in the boot, to prevent themselves being suffocated.

It was early in an afternoon at the end of February and I was working in the *umbar* with brilliant sunshine streaming through the windows, when the great dust-storm began. In less than five minutes it was too dark to see what I was drawing so I switched on the lights, a hundred-watt bulb at each end of the room. In another five minutes the light-bulbs were only a pale glow in the darkness, like the nimbus from the top of an old-fashioned lamp-post in the blackest of London fogs. Leslie came to fetch me and we groped our way back to our room to make sure that the servants had shut the windows. Already everything was filmed with dust, and our feet left clear prints on the layer which covered the floor-tiles. Every window in the house had well-fitting steel frames which normally kept the air indoors relatively clear. By the time we got to the sitting-room the noise of the wind was so loud that we had to shout to each other.

Four hours later we had dinner, a cheerless, gritty meal out of tins opened in the dining-room, as anything not in a sealed container would have been uneatable by the time it was carried across the kitchen courtyard. The women had their hair tied up in scarves and looked like caricatures of females in the middle of spring-cleaning; and everyone's face was blurred and ochre-coloured with the layers of dust which made penthouses of their eyebrows and turned their faces into masks grotesque as clowns'. We hung wet sheets over the windows, stuffed rolled-up rugs under the doors, but still the dust filtered in. By midnight our eyes were red and sore. Tempers were beginning to fray—except Joanne's, who was always at her best in adversity. No one felt inclined to go to bed, for breathing was already sufficiently hard work to make sleep impossible. Rachel took her temperature and found it was over 101°. She was wondering whether she had 'flu or something more drastic when I suggested that, as a perfectly healthy man's temperature often rises to 101° at the end of five sets of real tennis, it was possible that the panting we were doing was producing a similar effect. So we all took our temperatures—at least it was something to do—and discovered that my theory was right. No one was under 100° and most of us were over 102°, which cheered Rachel considerably.

'Dust-storms never last more than six hours, or seven...or

eight...or nine,' we told each other as the night crawled slowly past. Only the clock, and Abdullah bringing tea, which he had managed to make on a Primus (all the other servants having long since thrown in their hands) told us that dawn had officially arrived. As the day, which was still as black as the blackest midnight, crawled on, the wind increased instead of abating. Seton, with a thick woolen *abbas* over his head, fought his way across the courtyard to a window on the windward side of the house and reported that a dune nearly twenty feet high had developed beyond the outer wall. Everyone became even more depressed, for a storm as severe as this one meant that thousands of tons of dust would have been deposited in the dig-pit, undoing months of laborious excavation. The season's work would have to close down. As soon as the *antikas* were divided into the half which was allowed to Chicago University and the other which was claimed by the Baghdad Museum, we would disperse until next year.

This was depressing news as, except for the last twenty-four hours, I had been thoroughly enjoying myself, and I knew that, once it was over, I should enjoy remembering the dust-storm. It was not drab, like money worries and illness, but dramatic; so it came under the heading, 'To-day's adversities are the funny stories of to-morrow,' a private slogan which I have often found comforting.

I was feeling odd. My temperature was now over 103°. But Leslie shouted in my ear that as we had promised Gillian to get home only in time for my birthday we could spend the extra three or four weeks in Egypt—so I was cheerful, even when Hans decided that we had better retreat to the store-cupboard as it had no windows. At the beginning of the season it had been piled high with cases of tins from the Army & Navy Stores and Fortnum & Mason, but now it was nearly empty. The air inside it, though still so thick that we could only breathe through wet cloths which had to be frequently wrung out in buckets of water, was a little clearer. We could at least see each other, although the sight was not very appealing. None of the men had been able to shave, and the women looked even more dilapidated.

I had been too busy being sorry for my own discomforts to worry about the diggers. But as my feelings of claustrophobia increased I was appalled by the thought of them lying in their sleeping-holes, no better than shallow graves, with only a strip of straw matting to protect them. I was told, repeatedly, that Arabs are *used* to dust-storms and as a race would never have survived unless they were very well able to look after themselves in storms such as this one, which was remarkable only because it had come so early in the year.

'Oh, why won't it rain!' I said miserably. Nobody answered. Why wait for rain—especially as there had been practically none for four years? I lurched to my feet. 'I shall *make* rain,' I declared dramatically, and tottered out of the store-cupboard.

Luckily the sitting-room door was on the lee side of the courtyard and so I opened it without difficulty. But once I was out of the shelter of the wall the wind caught me and sent me sprawling on my face. For a moment I thought I was going to lie there helpless until I was smothered to death. Then the pain of dust scouring my unprotected forehead (I had a towel tied over my nose and mouth) whipped me into action, and I crawled on hands and knees until I reached the haven of my bedroom. It was not much of a haven, for the dust, which is finer than talcum powder, had made drifts over everything; but at least I could stand without being blown over. I unfolded a rug and put it over the bed, on which nearly a foot of dust had collected, and lay down.

Then I began to pray for rain. I prayed until the sweat ran in runnels down my face. Exhausted as I was, I began to feel exultant. I felt the virtue entering into me. My prayers were going to be answered! I began to talk to the rain as though it were a separate deity. Suddenly I heard my own voice, which had been inaudible because of the roaring of the wind. The wind was abating! I stripped off my clothes and stood naked, shouting to the rain to come to me. Suddenly I realised that the only sound I was hearing was my own heartbeat. There was no other sound.

Then in the silence I heard an insistent musical sound, a tune played on one note, like a drum-beat and yet metallic. It was the first heavy drops of rain falling on the corrugated iron roof. The separate notes blended into a symphony of rain, surged into the triumphal singing of a torrent. And I found myself standing naked in the courtyard with clear, clean water sluicing down my body, breathing great gulps of fresh, wet air into my lungs.

Then I remembered the others: and also to put on some clothes before I went to find them.

It rained for twelve hours in a four-mile circle round the house. No rain fell anywhere else in the district and during the night over a hundred people were smothered to death in the streets of Baghdad. For three days we were marooned. The house, and the ancient mound on which the diggers lived, were islands in the middle of a lake. The dig-pit was full of water which did far more damage than the dust-storm.

'Next time you make rain you had better specify how much you want,' said Leslie, but he said it fondly. For a few hours the others were grateful and even a little awed. Then it became only an odd coincidence; and they grumbled because the water had damaged their toy.

CHAPTER SIX

the queen and the cobra

Real time varies according to the intensity of one's experience and cannot be measured by calendars and clocks....I still find it surprising that I was in Iraq less than seven weeks and that my one and only visit to Egypt was for twenty-five days. The dates in my obsolete passport are quite clear: I arrived in Alexandria on my way to Baghdad on 17th January 1935, returned by air on 5th March, and sailed from Alexandria for Italy on the 30th of the same month. I mention these trivial details only because I have frequently been told, and read in foreign newspapers, that I am a professional archaeologist and have spent years excavating in Egypt. One kind lady, who came from Holland to interview me, was even more imaginative....I was born in a tomb. She made my papa a world-famous epigraphist who was so absorbed in an inscription he was deciphering that he took no notice of my mama's pitiful cries until she had given birth to me. When the clipping, together with a translation, was sent to me by a Dutch acquaintance, I replied, trying to be funny—for it never occurred to me she believed a word of it—to the effect that I was rather hurt that the interviewer had omitted the best part of the story, which was that dear Papa, entirely undismayed, had unrolled a mummy, swaddled me in the bandages and popped me beside my stoical mama in the empty sarcophagus. Various versions of this story have pursued me for years.

After a night in Cairo, Leslie and I went by train to Tel-el-Armarna, where John and Hilda Pendlebury had invited us to stay for three days, although the rest of the members of the Egypt Exploration Society expedition had already gone home. From the nearest station we went by car, boat, and donkey, reaching the dig-house at sunset. It was built in part of the ruins of the palace to which Nefertiti had retired when she could no longer bear to watch the safety of Egypt being undermined by the idealistic but hopelessly impractical policy of her husband, Ankhnaton. There was a living-room, an *umbar*, now almost empty as the *antikas* had already been dispatched, and several small bedrooms which led off what had once been a hall of audience but was now a courtyard. The original walls, three or more feet thick, still stood about six feet high, and, where necessary for headroom, a thin modern wall had been added to support the palm-thatch roof. The room where Leslie and I slept was said to have been Nefertiti's bedroom. Although it was certainly one of the queen's private apartments, I think it was not she, but one of her women who, thirty-three hundred years earlier, had slept on the raised bed-place which now supported my rickety camp-bed.

At dinner John talked so vividly of Armarna as it had been under the beneficent Aton-worship that I went to bed hopeful of splendid dreams. I listened happily to the distant barking of jackals, until a scurrying and a rustling began in the thatch over my head. I switched on a torch, and in its feeble light—for the battery was almost exhausted—saw a bloated and obscenely pinkish lizard peering down at me. Leslie pointed out that there was a net stretched under the thatch which would prevent anything large from falling on me, but it looked most insecure and I remained convinced that the rustlings were caused by snakes although he assured me they were only rats.

Although Americans tend to complicate their lives and restrict their mobility by being too fussy about hygiene, the English can be equally tiresome when they think it meritorious to put up with needless discomforts. The Nile flowed past the house, and there were plenty of servants to carry water, but there was no bath, nor even a shower. A four-legged stool over a bucket, with a trowel and a box of sand, provided the only sanitation. The stool had a leg missing, making it a most precarious perch. I was going to mention this to Hilda when Leslie warned me not to—John having told him that the leg had been broken off at the beginning of the season and everyone had been too busy to get it mended.

But these were very trivial matters compared with the extraordinary beauty of the place. The first day I was there, Leslie went with John and Hilda up the valley which leads from the centre of the great amphitheatre of cliffs to see the tomb, empty when it was discovered, of Ankhnaton. The Pendleburys were going to camp there, but Leslie was coming back the same evening, so, as it would have meant walking about fourteen miles, I decided to spend the day by myself. I thought that alone I might be able to find out why, the moment I had seen the great bow of the cliffs from the boat as we came down-river, they seemed so familiar. But why the cliffs instead of one of the ruins? I wandered about, letting the quietness of the scene soak into me. A child was leading a water-buffalo, followed by a pair of black-and-white kids, under the palm-trees that grew in a vivid green strip of cultivation beside the Nile. Why did she also look familiar? Then I realised that it was only because, with her great grey eyes, her almost unnaturally long and slender neck, she might have been Nefertiti as a child.

Why did the outline of the cliffs against the sky haunt me? It was two years before I was able to learn the answer; when I was working on *Winged Pharaoh*. By chance Joan saw the cliffs from the same viewpoint as Sekeeta did when she went by river to the Amphitheatre of Grain to lead her chariots in defence of Egypt.

The next day Leslie took me to see the tombs of the Nobles, which are cut in the cliffs some six miles from the house. Having been told that I would have no need for riding clothes in Egypt, I had sent these back by sea with the rest of our heavy luggage. Riding an Egyptian donkey, which has only a blanket for a saddle, and no stirrups, when one is wearing a short skirt and cami-knickers, is an exercise which must be experienced before its discomforts can be fully understood. My donkey was a stallion with ideas above his station; whever he saw a female camel he galloped towards her with raucous cries and did his best to mount her.

However, we eventually reached the tombs. The wall-paintings were interesting and sometimes very beautiful, but, oddly enough, I found none of them emotionally stimulating. After seeing about a dozen, and climbing from one to another for several hours, my interest began to flag. There was still another tomb which Leslie wanted to see—about three miles farther on; so I rode after him along the foot of the cliffs and then decided to stay with the donkeys, which we had tethered in the sparse shade of a *wadi*.

It was very hot and I had a bad headache, which I thought was probably a touch of sunstroke, against which I had so often been warned by Mother. A combination of sweat, sand, and the antics of the donkey, had given me blisters— not only on my hands. I was so wrapped in self-pity that it never occurred to me that Leslie might be in danger. If I thought of him at all it was with resentment that he was deliberately dawdling when he ought to have realised that I was longing to go home. I was thirsty. I was tired. I was trying to find the energy to go and remind Leslie that he was a husband with a neglected wife as well as being an amateur Egyptologist, when I saw him scrambling down the cliff.

'Sorry I was so long,' he said abruptly, and then fumbled for a cigarette which he lit with shaky hands. He looked so pale that I instantly felt guilty for lack of wifely concern. 'Darling! What's happened?'

'Nothing. At least...No, nothing.'

I knew he was trying to keep something from me, so I was determined to find out what it was. At last I got the story out of him. The entrance to the tomb was so low that he had to crawl through it. He had nearly not gone in at all because he had dropped his torch and broken the bulb. He struck a match and saw that the tomb wasn't worth looking at. It was un-finished without even the preliminary carvings, and only twelve feet deep and about half as wide. He was turning to go out when he saw, black against the brazen light of the entrance, the spread hood of a cobra. The snake was hanging head downward from a ledge above the lintel and must have been asleep when he crawled under it.

Now it was awake, and angry. Even if he had a stick there would have been only an outside chance of killing it before it struck, for the light in the tomb was dim. Pressed against the far wall, for over an hour he stood perfectly still. Then he sneezed. The cobra slid to the floor with a thud, hissed at him—and slithered away into the sunlight.

I tottered to my feet. 'I'm most awfully sorry,' I said, 'but I'm going to be sick.' And I was, from sheer horror.

To take my mind off snakes—for when at last we got back to the house the rustlings in the bedroom thatch were more sinister than ever, he gave me a piece of stone to psychometrise. 'It's about all I could find in the *umbar*,' he said, 'but is has been polished at some time or other and may have been part of a statue. It's probably only a workman's trial piece, in which case there'll be nothing in it. But anyway, have a go at it.

I took it in my hand. 'It's warm all right.'

'Good, then I'll fetch my note-book.'

As I pressed the stone to my forehead, he said, 'If you see Nefertiti be sure to notice whether she had a cataract. It's a moot point among Egyptologists. Some think that the blind eye of the portrait-head of her in the Berlin Museum is only a flaw in the painting....'

'This is part of the head-dress of a seated statue. The feet are together. The right hand is holding the arm of a chair. The left hand is holding the lotus and something else behind it: it may be the flail or the crook.

'There is a scene of a sculptor's studio, but this statue is too big ever to have been in it. The room is about twenty feet high, lit by windows round the top. The king is sitting on a side-bench. Two fan-bearers are fanning him all the time. The picture is very muddled, for I am getting the thoughts in the sculptor's mind and he is remembering a trial cast he had made for this statue. I am not seeing the scene but his memory of it. He is trying to reconcile his artistic tradition with portraiture and with politeness: just how much should he carry out the king's malformation? If he conventionalises him the king will then be angry at the thought that he needs conventionalising.

'The sculptor is under Royal Warrant, shared with two others, giving him and those others the right of depicting the king and queen. This has made him rich, because any people who want their likeness on their tombs must come to him. To be the King's Sculptor is literally to be the man who is allowed to sculp the king or the queen.

'The queen comes into the studio, her visit is informal. She wears a pleated dress, slit up the front, of soft green muslin edged with gold. Round her neck is a radiating necklace, made like the rays of the sun, each bead of the lowest row is in the shape of a hand, all is of gold. The head-dress is made of linen, on a gold frame, an edging of gold also frames the face. The linen is starched. She carries an ostrich-feather fan, blue and green in colour. She wears sandals and her big toes are much curved in—not deformed, but hers are not the straight feet one usually sees in sandals. She has got a blind eye, covered with a film. Her skin is very fair, like a sun-burned English-woman.

'The king walks round the studio and looks at pieces of un-finished sculpture. He is slightly annoyed. He hasn't got very big hips. He was no sensualist. She is telling him to take some exercise, because he looks ill. She wants to spur him on to be a king, but he is too busy being a priest. He doesn't mind being sculpted in a chariot, but he doesn't want to ride in it as well. The sculptor wishes he had better material to work on than Ankhnaton. Nefertiti wishes she had a son.'

229

I sat up, bewildered as I always used to be when I finished dictating. 'Oh, poor, poor woman! Married to that ridiculous man who wouldn't listen to her even when the garrisons were starving and the Amen priests were waiting to pounce on him and spoil everything she had taught him to build!'

'There's nothing about that here,' Leslie said rather severely, looking carefully through what he had written.

'But I'm right. I know I'm right! For a minute, at the very end before I stopped talking I knew exactly what she was feeling....and it made me so miserable that I rushed back into my body.'

'Well get out of it again,' said Leslie very reasonably.

I tried to, but nothing happened. And it was over ten years later before I knew, at least to my own satisfaction, that I had seen clearly into the heart of a woman who should have been the King, not the Queen, of Egypt.

It may have been the strawberries in the train on the way to Luxor which made my fortnight there more of an endurance test than a carefree holiday. Even if the strawberries, which, so I was repeatedly told, only an idiot would have eaten, were not to blame, something gave me a virulent form of dysentery; so rather anxious bouts of sightseeing alternated with days when I writhed miserably in my bedroom.

On the first morning Leslie called at Chicago House, the Middle East headquarters of the Oriental Institute, with messages for them from Hans; and they introduced him to Hussein, a guide who worked for them, an Arab with a very real interest in Egyptology. Hussein promised to look after us, and did so most admirably. I was with him one day in the temple of Medinet Habu when I saw two bus-loads of tourists coming toward us. I was about to say that we had better go somewhere else so as to avoid them, when he said, 'Wait, Memsahib. They will not be here more than five minutes. They do not wish to see, only to boast that they have seen.'

From a vantage point on the roof I watched them de-bus,

stare for a couple of minutes at the outer walls, tick their guide-books to make sure they had been there, and climb back into the buses. Hussein pointed to my watch and chuckled. 'They must have been in a hurry to-day for they have been here only four minutes...sixty seconds longer for the Valley of the Kings.'

Honesty made me tell him how, when I was at Tel Asmar, two Americans offered to take me to Babylon. I knew that I should only see a hole in the ground, that the journey in their truck would be hot, uncomfortable, and, because of the company, boring; but I was about to accept their invitation when Hans asked me why I wanted to go there. 'I should like to be able to say that I have been to Babylon...' Even as I said it the reason sounded puerile.

Hans smiled and patted me on the shoulder. 'If you think it will make you feel better to say you have been to Babylon, why not say it? Why bother to go there?' He cured me, once and for all, of the desire to claim I have been anywhere. I have handed on his excellent advice to quite a number of people, but it has seldom been appreciated.

I shall always regret that when I was in Egypt I had no conscious memory of having lived there before, as I should then have been able to use my very limited time in seeing buildings which belonged to the periods of which I was later to write, especially those of the last reign of the eleventh and the first reign of the twelfth dynasties.* But I was not immune to emotional response, and instead of being awed by the wonderful preservation of the buildings I often felt waves of gloom, far more intense than if, after a brief absence, I had gone back to Seacourt and found it roofless, with vandals roller-skating in the tennis court.

On one occasion I had a more acute reaction. In a little sanctuary which I had recognised as one of the rare, genuinely sacred places, I found a party of German tourists sitting on the

Eyes of Horus and *Lord of the Horizon*.

altar and chewing sandwiches. I felt such an intense anger at their sacrilege that if I had had a whip I should have used it. As it was, Leslie only just managed to drag me away before I asked them if they would also have picnicked in a cathedral. 'For heaven's sake realise you're a tourist too!' he said crossly. I thought he was trying to insult me, and was furious until I realised how ridiculous I was being.

Most of the time I had no spare energy to do more than look at the surface of things. But when we were at Der-el-Bahri, the temple built by the warrior-queen Hatshepsut in three great terraces in the cliffs which hid the Valley of the Kings, I tuned-in without realising I was doing so. I was leaning on the altar, taking my weight on the palms of my hands, when I felt an agonising pain in the back of my neck. I was frightened, for I thought it was a physical pain, a new symptom of the infuriating ailment which was plaguing me. Leslie, who realised what I was really doing, started scribbling in his note-book:

'There is such awful pain in this, but I can't find out from what: an agonising pain in the back of the neck. This is the place where people suffered pain beyond defence. The tortured ones were held in a crouching position, their heads below and between their knees, by means of a bar which was put under the knees and over the back of the neck. It is a black magic for enslaving people's souls.'

With a great effort I made myself let go of the altar, walked away from it and sat down abruptly in the sand, feeling sick and exhausted. The pain faded rapidly, but I was still sufficiently detached from my body to notice that, instead of desert and a few patches of cultivation nearer the river, I was looking at four great avenues which linked Der-el-Bahri to the temples of Karnak. I described them in detail to Leslie, who was interested, but warned me not to mention them when I went that afternoon to tea at Chicago House.

It was a very formal party, the tea poured from a massive silver pot by one of those, to me, terrifying American ladies with white hair rigidly marcelled under a hair-net. I was shy enough to bring up the one subject I was determined to avoid. 'It is *so* exciting about the avenues,' I said brightly. 'I suppose they were planted by Hatshepsut *after* her return from Punt—when she brought back all those plants and animals which are carved on her other temple at Karnak.'

Everyone stopped talking. I studiously avoided catching Leslie's eye. At least I hadn't said *how* I had seen the wretched trees! Then a cold voice said, 'How odd that you should have heard about the avenues. We only discovered them this season and are not yet ready to publish. Since you are so *interested* I expect you also know that the tree-roots are remarkably well preserved.'

I upset my teacup into my lap. It seemed the quickest way of changing the subject.

I had wanted to see the temple of Philae at Assuan ever since I read Pierre Loti's story about it when I was a child, so we decided to go there for two nights before returning to Cairo. We went in one of the rickety little aeroplanes then used by Misr Airwork. It was a flight I try not to remember whenever I am airborne. Before it took off, but not before Leslie had told the pilot that we were archaeologists who hoped that his route would take us over the temple of Edfu, I noticed that the young man who was going to pilot us looked exceedingly ill. While cans of petrol were being poured into the plane—we were the only passengers although it was supposed to be able to carry four, he admitted that he was starting another bout of malaria. I tried to convince him that it would be much more sensible to go straight to bed in Luxor— being, I must admit, far more concerned for our safety than for his health. But he was determined to get back to Assuan where he could be nursed through the attack by his wife. His face had been glistening with sweat but now he was beginning to shiver. 'Don't you worry,' he said heartily through chattering teeth, 'I'll get us there somehow. I could put this old crate down in my sleep and I shan't pass out yet....It only takes an hour.'

He dragged himself into the rickety little aeroplane and shut himself into the pilot's cabin. The plane wobbled across the airfield and finally got off the ground. Perhaps the increased altitude made the pilot delirious, for I think no one in his senses could have shown us Edfu as we saw it. We saw it upside-down and sideways, and missed it only by inches. We dived into courtyards and zoomed out of them without the wings falling off. We skimmed within a foot of the pylons—at least Leslie told me we did. He was taking photographs. I was praying with my eyes shut. When at last we landed at Assuan, the pilot just managed to climb out of the plane, tottered a few steps and passed out cold.

CHAPTER SEVEN

chapter of accidents

Philae was disappointing, for it was almost totally submerged by the waters of the Assuan Dam, so after two nights there we flew to Cairo and went to Shepheards Hotel. We had been serious-minded for too long. Now we would be gay and dance and watch cabarets and thoroughly enjoy ourselves. But when I took off my clothes to have a bath before dinner I discovered that my body was playing another of its sour little jokes on me. My neck and shoulders were covered with sinister blisters which looked as though they might be the onset of some Oriental skin disease. Father had taught me to disapprove of people who were so selfish as to inflict their germs on others (he expected a guest to remain in the bedroom if he had a cold), so I reluctantly consulted the hotel doctor in case I was infectious. He was sympathetic but baffled, and asked me to stay in my room until a skin specialist had seen me.

Drearily I finished unpacking, hung up the Digby Morton dress which had already been pressed for me to wear on this celebration evening, and nibbled at the dinner sent up on a tray. The specialist came round at ten o'clock that night, a kind old German with pebble glasses, who looked so like Father's nicest professors that I trusted him immediately. He peered at my neck with the greatest interest. 'Remarkable—and so rare,' he kept on muttering delightedly. Visions of months in the lazar-house ran through my imagination as I waited for the verdict. 'You have been to Dendera?' he asked. I said that I had, impatient for him to come to the point instead of trying to put me at ease by babbling about antiquities.

'At Dendera, how many days ago?'

My heart sank even further. Was there an epidemic so spectacular raging at Dendera that it was already common gossip in Cairo? 'Four days ago,' I reluctantly admitted.

'I knew it!' he beamed, which made me even more wary, for I had seen that gleam in a scientist's eye when identifying some particularly lethal microbe.

'You have been bitten, my poor lady, by a little spider—a spider so rare that it is found only at Dendera. I have made a hobby of the arachnidae.'

'Why didn't I feel it bite me?'

'That is one of the symptoms—a little mark, so small it is not noticed, and then, three or four days later, the blisters! How fortunate that you came to me, for otherwise these little bites might have been diagnosed as the pustules of smallpox. In a day or two they will look quite horrible, you will see; but in a week they will be forgotten. Nothing to worry about, dear lady, nothing at all I assure you.' I paid his fee and thanked him. At the door the hotel doctor whispered something in his ear and he turned back to give me his parting instructions. 'It is nothing, as I have said, but if ignorant people were to see your neck...'

'I quite understand,' I said. coldly. 'I can hardly bear to look at it myself, so you can assure the hotel manager that I will not inflict such a horrid sight on his guests.'

Little did the other inhabitants know what I went through to save them from anxiety. All day and every day I wore my only coat and skirt, with a long-sleeved shirt and a tie. They stared at me rather suspiciously, wondering no doubt whether I was a Lesbian or only mad...for no one sane would wear a tight collar when it was over 100° in the shade. We dined every night in the almost deserted grill-room, and listened to the distant sound of dance music coming from the restaurant.

Leslie expected me to react strongly to the interior of the Great Pyramid, but although he bribed the guide to leave us alone in there for over an hour I felt only admiration for the technical skill, the brilliant intellect, of the men who built it: to me it was not magical at all. The Sphinx was only a sphinx. But I was happier in Sakkara than anywhere else in Egypt.

I was not at all sorry to leave Cairo, and we sailed from Alexandria on an American ship crammed with tourists doing a cruise of the Mediterranean. They tried to jolly Leslie with squeakers and paper hats, and as he retreated further into his shell they made pointed remarks about stuffed-shirt Britishers. I spent most of my time in my cabin, until off Sicily, appropriately enough between Scylla and Charybdis, we ran into really rough weater. My worst nature flourished like a green bay tree when, feeling increasingly robust, we strode past an audience, supine and glassy-eyed, in deck-chairs. We were the only passengers to appear at dinner, but soon it became so much rougher that I fell down heavily on my elbow and decided to retreat to bed. Leslie, saying he would be back in five minutes, went to fetch a siphon of soda-water. I fell asleep and woke to find no Leslie—and that it was three o'clock in the morning. I scrambled into some clothes, telling myself he had probably found some equally stalwart characters and was playing poker. Getting severely bruised in the process, I searched all the public rooms and then clawed my way round the decks, getting soaked to the skin and increasingly frightened. He must have been washed overboard...I had been a widow for hours. Even if I made the Captain turn the ship back we would never find my poor, dear husband. Moaning like Ophelia, and even wetter, I saw there was a light on in the bar. The barman would help me. He was English, and the only friend we had made since we came aboard.

The room was empty except for broken glasses rolling backwards and forwards across the heaving floor. I heard a voice, then another voice that I knew far better. Leslie and the barman were sitting on the floor behind the bar, bracing themselves with their feet against cases of Coca-Cola. They were both perfectly sober and had been peacefully discussing philosophy.

A husband who is neither drowned nor drunk, and so has no shadow of excuse for causing his wife torments of anxiety, is foolish if he greets her with the brisk phrase, 'My goodness you look funny!' There was a long mirror on the wall and in it I saw a fantastic female, with hair hanging like seaweed over her face, the dress she had meant to wear in Naples plastered like a wet shroud to her shivering body—a nice dress, and now ruined by seawater. I lost the last shreds of my self-control, and slapped him. The barman winked and tactfully retreated. Leslie, white with temper except where the marks of my fingers were beginning to redden, said icily, 'In a belated attempt to teach you manners, I shall not speak to you for a week.'

Nor did he. In silence we saw Pompeii, except when I made bright remarks and answered them myself, never a satisfactory form of conversation. We went to Pisa, where in the Campo Santo I saw a wall-painting which was so horrifying that, had we been on speaking terms I should have tried to find out why it affected me. But we were not speaking, so only when, in 1939, I was writing *Life as Carola* did I recognise it for the one (or else another almost exactly similar) which had frightened me as a child in the sixteenth century.

We were exchanging basic information but still not being chatty when the ship reached Genoa. I saw Leslie talking to an Italian who had just come on board. I thought it was a tout trying to sell him something, but Leslie told me that he was a distinguished antiquarian, who, on hearing that Leslie was an archaeologist, had offered to take him to see some Pompeiian dances, a survival of an ancient religious cult, which were a jealously guarded secret and never, of course, revealed to tourists. 'Well, he *looks* like a tout,' I replied. 'You can easily prove I'm wrong; for if it's a racket he won't let me come too.'

'I will go and ask him. The tickets are expensive, 2 pounds each, but it would be a pity to miss such a unique opportunity.'

The man looked rather surprised when he heard Leslie wished me to join the party, but needed very little persuasion. 'I told him you were not so narrow-minded as some English-women,' said Leslie, now much more genial than he had been for days. 'I expect some of the dancers' costumes will be a bit scanty—but it will be Art of course.'

It was about eleven at night when the antiquarian came to fetch us in a very dilapidated car. We drove for several miles, but always in circles. I have a well-developed bump of locality and very soon noticed that it was the same statue which I kept on seeing as we crossed and recrossed a steep and narrow street leading up from the docks. Leslie, who was sitting beside the driver, was too busy making intelligent remarks in his limited Italian to notice where we were going. Even if I had warned him he would probably have told me that the man had every right to try to prevent us being able to lead the uninitiated to the scene of the mysteries.

Three unshaven brigands met us at the door of a squalid

house and hustled us upstairs. We were thrust through a door; but there was no amphitheatre, no stage. It was a room only large enough to contain two chairs and a bed. A blowsy Madam, in a pink wrapper trimmed with grubby marabou, brought in a programme and asked, in French, which item we should prefer to see first. The programme was a sheaf of well-thumbed photographs, no doubt the prototypes of those sold at Port Said. Leslie blushed scarlet and said there had been some mistake. 'This lady is my *wife,*' he insisted. 'We came to see *dancers.*'

'My girls and boys can do anything you wish to see: girls and girls; boys and boys; two boys, one girl...' she cried indignantly, more shrill than a market-woman defending the ripeness of her tomatoes.

'We don't want to see *anything,*' said Leslie desperately.

'In my country the *femmes du monde* do not inspect the antics of the *femmes du demi-monde,*' I added, in governess French and devastating pomposity.

As we tried to get out of the room the Madam let out a screech and the three brigands stood stolidly in the doorway. The largest and most evil-looking growled in passable English, 'Ten pounds if you see—and that includes a bottle of Asti. Twenty pounds if you insult us by not seeing.' Then he banged the door in our faces.

'You'll have to go through with it now,' said Leslie desperately. 'Damn it, it won't kill you, and you can keep your eyes shut. You shouldn't have come.'

'I won't stay!'

'For God's sake shut up! If you make a scene they'll probably knife us in case we go to the police.'

Fury empowered me, and made me feel at least twice my normal size and infinitely stronger. I flung open the door, knocking over the Madam who was listening at the keyhole. Perhaps the brigands thought I had a revolver, for they backed away down the narrow passage so quickly that one of them fell headlong down the stairs. He was groaning as we jumped over his prostrate body, and I sincerely hope that at least he broke a leg. In case they were watching us from a window, we walked moderately slowly until we reached the corner of the street. Then we ran, until we saw the statue, and I knew we were within a hundred yards of the docks.

We were fond of each other again. When from the window of our *wagon-lit* on our way to Paris we saw the Villa Olivier where we had spent our honeymoon, we decided to have another one, such as we might have had in Cairo. But Fate had kept another Joker against us. We arrived on the Thursday before Easter and reached the Bank just as it shut. It would not open again until after the week-end, and we had no Travellers Cheques, only a Letter of Credit. Each of us imagined the other still had some money, but between us we had only the equivalent of ten shillings.

'How absolutely damnable,' said Leslie, sitting on the bed in the little hotel where we had intended only to sleep. 'We can't even buy our tickets home until the blasted banks open. We're marooned!'

'No, we're not,' I said smugly. 'I've been stuck without money so often that I hid four fivers in the false bottom of my jewel-case before I left England.'

'I found those while we were in Cairo,' said Leslie for-lornly.

We did not starve nor even hunger, for the Patron of the little hotel was delighted that we were so undiscriminating as to wish to stay *en pension*. A really bad cook is rare in France, but the one employed there would have felt quite at home in the most deplorable restaurant in England. Perhaps I am being unjust, and it was the boot-boy who did the cook-ing, for certainly no one else ate in the dreary dining-room, which was unlicensed.

Paris, even between the wars, offered few gaieties for ten shillings. We looked wistfully in shop windows, tramped round the Louvre and the Musee de Cluny; seldom straying far because we had to keep within walking distance of our next horrible meal. On Easter Sunday, carrying a packet of sandwiches, we took the Metro to the Bois and had a picnic under a tree that was dripping with rain. I added to our misery by catching a streaming cold. Even when the banks opened their doors, and our prison, I had to stay in bed for three days, eating jars of caviare which Leslie brought me as a consolation prize.

On the front page of the Paris *Daily Mail* I saw a headline, 'Famous Scientist rescues Mother Superior from Blazing Convent.' It was Father! I grabbed the telephone, and, by a miracle, got a clear line to Hayling. The convent had burned down at three o'clock in the morning and Father had helped to carry the Reverend Mother to safety. A man had been burnt to death. The children, all under seven, were sorted into sexes and bedded down in the music-room and the billiard-room at Seacourt. Mother, so Father told me, had been at the top of her form, putting all the nuns to bed and giving them powerful sedatives in spite of their protests, and providing breakfast for over a hundred, not counting the firemen. Local tradesmen were roused before dawn to bring extra eggs and bacon. 'There's nothing to worry about. Your dear mother is thoroughly enjoying herself. I will send Gillian with Miss S. to Croydon. Your mother is too busy—God knows how long they are all staying here—and there is no point in either of us catching your cold.'

I had already heard from Diana that the dolls I had ordered made from the drawings of Ragga and Muffin, had arrived at Beaufort Street (where Diana and Stan had been living while we were away) and would be taken down to Croydon so that Gillian would think they had actually flown home with me.

As the aeroplane banked before landing I saw her frantically waving from the roof of the Customs building. I was so wildly happy to be back with her that I was afraid of bursting into tears. But after we had hugged each other I was able to say, in quite an ordinary voice, 'Oh bother, those naughty children have lost themselves again! Ragga! Muffin! Where

241

are you? She found them sitting behind a pile of suitcases.
'Oh Mummy, they're *real!*'

Bless her heart, she never told me until years later that she was secretly disappointed to find that Ragga and Muffin were not people, as they had been in my stories, but only dolls.

PART FIVE

CHAPTER ONE

highlan∂s

In September Leslie went back to Iraq for his second season
at Tel Asmar, and Gillian and I moved into a mews cottage
for six months while Beaufort Street was let to an American
film-actor. It was a long, cold winter, and after Gillian had
gone to bed the evenings were lonely as my budget was too
narrow to allow much hospitality.

I had already realised the limitations of psychometry, and
so I decided to try to develop the faculty, which had been
much more vivid when I was a child, of remembering previous personalities. I concentrated on a scene, such as one with
the French girl who is mentioned in Part One (Episode 5),
and then tried to extend it beyond the scope I had previously
remembered. For instance I knew she rode a black horse towards an archway at the end of an avenue of limes. What was
beyond the arch? If a clear picture came into my mind I concentrated on it, noticing details—the more trivial the better.
It is a stable-yard. How many doors? What is that thing in
the corner—a pump? No, it's a hoist for lifting sacks into the
loft. On the left of the yard the second coach-house has a
hinge hanging loose. There is a clump of weeds beside the
larger of the stone troughs. What kind are they—dande-
lions? No, coltsfoot. I then tried to alter what I was seeing.
If it was subjective I could change the number of the doors,
mend the hinge, turn the yellow patch of coltsfoot into a rose-
bush or remove it altogether. I could then dismiss the sequence as imagination. But if it was objective I could not alter
it by an effort of will; for it was no more susceptible to change
than any three-dimensional stable-yard would have been.

If the emotional content of the scene was small I could see everything as a dispassionate observer, but as the emotions of the other personality became more closely engaged the visual impression became relatively subordinate and the other senses—feeling, hearing, and, oddly enough, smell, became dominant. I might see the girl several times in the stable-yard, but each occasion would appear different to me according to the mood in which she was seeing it. If she was worried about lack of money on a particular morning, the broken hinge, the weeds, would be the chief things that she, and therefore I, would notice. If she were ebullient, the cooing of pigeons on the roof, the smell of straw and horse and leather, her own feeling of physical well-being as she got into the saddle, would occupy her attention. This is only a very brief outline of what in fact was an arduous process which I pursued because my mind, trained by Father to expect scientific proof, demanded evidence which would make it accept more easily my intuition.

The results were encouraging but inconclusive. By holding myself between sleeping and waking, sufficiently dissociated to focus nine-tenths of my attention on what I was contacting on a more subtle level, but keeping the remaing tenth alert to scribble detailed notes every few minutes—which was more difficult than dictating a running commentary, I had experiences beyond the normal range. But was the French girl a memory of myself in a previous existence, or could I as a child have tuned-in to her by psychometry without realising what I was doing? There were four pieces of French furniture at Seacourt, which I valued because they had been left to me by Jennie. I could remember tracing the outline of the marquetry leaves with my finger because I enjoyed the smoothness of the polished wood. They had been given to Jennie by the ex-Empress Eugenie and had come from the Tuileries. But they belonged to the eighteenth, not the nineteenth, century, so they could have been in the chateau with the green shutters. This theory became untenable, because though I had recalled quite a lot about a Greek and a Red Indian there had not been even a shard of Greek pottery, nor anything remotely connected with Red Indians, in the house.

By the time I was twelve, repeated rebuffs had taught me that to claim the memory of previous lives was the quickest way to lose friends and fail to influence people. So now I must keep what I was trying to do secret even from Daisy and Leslie, unless, and it seemed a very remote possibility, I could train myself to recall at will not only a few dramatic incidents but a complete life. Having nothing else to do, I worked too hard and gave myself acute headaches. I had rarely suffered them before, and these were particularly tiresome as I knew they had no physical origin, although they felt as though the top of my skull was deeply bruised and becoming as thin as a baby's fontanelle. However, the pain responded to aspirin, if taken in quantity; but I lost over a stone in weight, and instead of sleeping well was lucky if I got two to three hours a night.

Leslie was due back early in March, but stayed away an extra six weeks to go on a shooting expedition with Seton. I had been counting the days to his return, but consoled myself with the thought that he would find us comfortably reinstalled in Beaufort Street, and, because of my uncongenial economies, reasonably solvent. In this I had been over-optimistic, as I learned when I met the man from Harrods who had been checking the inventory. 'I am afraid you will have a shock, as I did, madam,' he said, 'when you see the condition in which your tenant has left the house. However, his representative has agreed to 600 pounds compensation, little enough, I fear, when you see the damage to your antique furniture.' But the film-actor skipped back to Hollywood without paying a cent. I even had to find 280 pounds for his transatlantic telephone calls before the Telephone Manager would reconnect me.

This was glum news for Leslie's homecoming, especially as he had just heard that the dig was closing down, so he was out of a job. The only thing to do was to redecorate the house, let it again, and go to Muckerach where for ten months in the year we could live rent free. Gillian would like living in the country, but Scotland was a long way from Hurtwood, and I was worried about Daisy's health, although she insisted that the operation she had undergone during the winter was only for the removal of a non-malignant cyst.

I had expected Leslie to be bored without his friends and clubs and tennis, but Nina Seafield and her husband, Derek Studley-Herbert, were at Castle Grant and we saw a lot of them. When they moved back to her other home, Cullen House, we often went over to stay. I was lucky enough to find a close friend in our nearest neighbour, Gwen Graham, a widow who in many ways reminded me of Daisy. She had built a charming modern house on the edge of the moor above Muckerach, which commanded a magnificent view of the Cairngorms. She was now making a garden, which encouraged me to do the same. I always have an urge to put down roots, actual as well as figurative, even when experience warns that it always hurts to pull them up again.

Leslie, who had never shown any interest in gardening before, helped me enthusiastically. We turfed the horrid little flower-beds which looked as though they had been made with a pastry-cutter. With stones from some of the pigsties we made dry walls to terrace the slope for two long herbaceous borders. Nina, who had already told the Seafield Estate Office to have the house redecorated, gave me quantities of plants, including about fifty clumps of blue poppies which, difficult as they were to grow in the south, even at Hurtwood, rioted among the rhubarb at Castle Grant. I planted the narrow border which surrounds the house with sweet peas that covered the dour stone walls to the eaves. We built a dam, ten feet high and thirty feet long, across a burn in the birch-wood, making a sombre pool that fed a series of decorative waterfalls between mossy banks which in the autumn would be planted with bulbs and polyanthus.

The day after the dam was finished, for which we had to call in professional help as it persisted in leaking, I was sitting there feeling extraordinarily contented when I heard a small sound and looked up to see a pair of roedeer with a fawn standing beside me. I had never seen roedeer on our side of the Spey, but they adopted us and stayed near the house for the rest of the summer. Gillian wanted a pet goat, so I found a three-day-old kid for her which she brought up on a bottle and named Rosemary. She was as easy to house-train as a dog, slept on a pink blanket beside her mistress's bed—and would have slept on it if Gin, her bull-terrier, had not growled from her place under the eiderdown. Rosemary was a wild Highland goat, black except for a fawn flash on each side of her face, and in due course she grew horns with which she butted me if I told her she was growing too large to sit comfortably on my lap. She butted visitors much harder, and sometimes caused callers to retreat in haste down the drive, but she was so clearly under the protection of Pan that I never managed to be really cross with her even when she nibbled all my best delphiniums.

Gillian and I went for 'exploring walks' in which we sometimes traced a burn to its source, a burn that might be the Amazon teeming with alligators, or run through the hunting grounds of a hostile tribe of Red Indians; which made it necessary for us to advance with caution on hands and knees. If we were being pioneers the low ground of the moor became a trackless prairie with the amiable shooting-pony as our covered wagon. Crossing Himalayan ravines, by means of a fallen pine-tree over the Dulnain river, became less popular after we both fell in. She became an ardent gillie, and when I was fishing used to crouch beside me on the bank, alert to take a trout off the hook and kill it for me. I seldom caught more than enough for her supper, but trout so small that they should have been thrown back were her favourite delicacy and known as 'Mummy's special sardines.'

She had plenty of companions of her own age, for as well

as Frazer the gardener's two sons, there were crofters' children for whom I turned the back kitchen into a playroom where they could cook and eat the trout they caught instead of discarding them as they used to do. Their parents tended to believe that fish that did not come out of a tin was unfit for food and should be classed with vermin. This embargo extended to rabbits, hares, and even to home-made jam. So I provided fruit, of which there was far more than we could eat, and the necessary sugar. There were fourteen amateur cooks, of whom the oldest was twelve, and they made over a hundred pounds of preserves. Leslie's shotgun provided material for a large number of stews and pies: Rosemary and Gin disposed of the failures.

When they heard that A.D. had let the house to shooting tenants, they thought we were being turned out and offered to organise a strike of beaters. 'The foreigners will be away back to England if they have to chase their own birds across the heather,' said one of them hopefully. And another suggested that even if their parents made them go out on the hill it would not be difficult to annoy the invaders by turning the birds away from the butts. So I hastily assured them that we should have to go south even if the place had been left empty, and that we would all be back again before the end of September.

CHAPTER TWO

the scarab

Leslie went to shoot at Cullen for three weeks while I took Gillian and Gin to Hayling, and then we all went to Hurtwood. The evening we arrived there, Daisy, as soon as I was alone with her, told me that she had had a second operation a fortnight after I went to Scotland. She had not told me at the time because she knew that I would rush south to be with her and she considered that I ought to stay with Gillian and Leslie. She was only telling me now because I would soon be sure to hear about it from Elfie....

'On no account are you to let her know it was cancer,' she said firmly. 'The word terrifies her and she fusses over me far too much already. If she asks you what you think was wrong with me you must reassure her, and if necessary tell a flat lie. This is one of the occasions when to lie is ethical.'

'Of course I will. I'll do anything...'

'Then don't worry about me. The most tiresome thing about this wretched disease is that it scares one's friends so much. You can feel the poor dears seething with the questions they daren't ask because they don't want to hear the answers. It is a great comfort that I can be honest with you.'

'What exactly did you have done?'

'As you insist on details, the surgeon took off my right breast.' She smiled. 'I never had much of a bust, so a little padding stops me looking lop-sides. He is confident that he has made a thorough job this time, so there will be no recurrence. Now we will go and look at the Fan Garden, and we will not mention my dreary operation again.'

Even though she could no longer walk fast and far, her slower pace was not laborious like an invalid's but as though she had no need to hurry now that her garden had reached maturity. Instead of planting, pruning, weeding together as we used to do, we sat talking in the sun by the lily-pool, or in the shelter of one of the pavilions, that with their stone pillars and moss-grown pantile roofs, their pottery jars and Moorish tiles, made parts of Hurtwood seem more Portuguese than English. For there was a Portuguese garden which Daisy also cherished, the Palace of Montserrat at Cintra, which belonged to her mother's family.

I never heard her complain, but I knew that sometimes she found inactivity almost unbearable. She might suddenly remember having sown some new hybrid primulus in the bog garden at the foot of the most precipitous of the paths. 'They should be in flower now, Joan. We must decide whether they should be left to self-seed or be transplanted nearer the Japanese maples.' She would rise purposefully from her chair and then sit down again, saying ruefully, 'Perhaps it is a little near luncheon to go so far. I puff if I hurry uphill and it worries Elfie.'

On wet days, instead of working in the rain, her hands strong in the rich, moist earth, while water dripped off the brim of her gardening hat, she was confined indoors. Elfie did not consider talk, or books, or even plant catalogues sufficient entertainment and so insisted on card games and jigsaw puzzles. We had painstakingly finished a jigsaw of five hundred pieces in two days when Leslie suggested I should do some psychometry.

'Yes do, dear,' said Elfie encouragingly. 'Some of the old Portuguese furniture might be interesting.'

'Have you anything Egyptian?' asked Leslie.

'I don't think so,' began Daisy. But Elfie interrupted. 'There are some Egyptian things in the attic. I found them last week when I was going through old trunks for a jumble sale. There were two saddle-cloths and some moth-eaten rugs, and a bunch of scarabs which belonged to Bunny.'

'I don't remember Bunny having any scarabs,' said Daisy doubtfully.

'Well, he did. They are in a small cardboard box labelled in Papa's writing. ''Given to Bunny in Egypt by my shikari 1892.'''

'But what were we doing in Egypt in '92? Are you sure you are not confusing it with the time we went up the Nile on a *dahabeya* and you insisted on going to see Karnak by moonlight and had hysterics?'

Elfie giggled. 'How well I remember that! I thought the ghost of some wicked old priest had grabbed me. I tried to run but couldn't move. Goodness, how I shrieked!'

'Was it a ghost?' I prompted her, for Leslie's benefit, as I knew the story.

'It was my corset-strings! They had come undone and must have been trailing behind me until they got tangled round something. I struggled frantically and my corsets got tighter and tighter until they nearly cut me in half. But that was years after Bunny was given the scarabs. In '92 we spent a month in Egypt on our way home from India because Papa suddenly decided that he wished to shoot quail. Thousands of the poor little things he shot. I was so sorry for them, and felt quite guilty when I ate them; but they were so delicious.'

'I wonder why I don't remember about it,' said Daisy.

'Because you were having mumps in a hotel in Cairo. I suppose it was Shepheards, if Shepheards was built then. Bunny and I went with Papa in case we caught it.'

'Oh, I remember the mumps. But I thought mumps was in Simla.'

'Chickenpox was Simla. Such a panic there was too, as they thought at first it was smallpox.'

'Why did the shikari give the scarabs to Bunny? He can't have been very interested in *antikas* when he was six.'

'He adored his scarabs—surely you remember? It was really because he adored the shikari of course. He was a dear old man and implored Papa to let him come back to England with us because he wanted to stay with ''the little Pharaoh''. He always called Bunny ''the little Pharaoh'' and deferred to him in everything.'

Elfie trotted upstairs to fetch the scarabs and I wondered if Daisy was hoping that I would get scenes of Bunny's childhood from them, or if it would distress her if I did. I had never quite realised how much she missed him until the previous Armistice Day....I was alone with her in their little house overlooking Chelsea Embankment when the maroons sounded for the Two Minutes' Silence. She stared out of the window and I saw tears rolling down her cheek as she whispered, 'Oh, Bunny, how much longer must I be without you?' It was the only time I ever saw her cry.

There were five scarabs, and Leslie put them in a row on a card-table beside me. Two were white, one green, one dark brown and the fifth was turquoise blue.

'Which do you want to do first?' he asked me while he sharpened a pencil.

'The blue one last,' I said instinctively. 'I don't mind about the others.'

The two white scarabs were genuine but of no interest. They were probably new when they were included in the mummy-bandages. The green one had been charged as an amulet by an efficient priest in the reign of Thothmes I, to prevent a little boy from having nightmares, or rather from remembering his dreams too clearly; which would appear as nightmares to the mind of a child.

'It worked too,' I said as I put it back on the table. 'Unfortunately it was specifically made so that the virtue would only last for six years so that it would not interfere with the boy developing dream-memory when he was old enough to do so. A pity, as otherwise it might have come in handy for Gillian if she starts being frightened like I used to be.'

'How much less dull going to church would be if clergymen believed in magic,' said Elfie feelingly.

The brown scarab showed that, 'temples where priests are but men without virtue, wearingly priestly robes', also existed in the reign of Ramoses II. It had been purchased for 'five she-goats in milk' and was supposed to be a protection against a plague of flies. The flies were a little larger than bees and had two white bands on the thorax... 'flies which although they do not bite nor sting are so numerous that they cover a sleeping man like a black pall and smother him to death. And if he opens his mouth to speak or to eat they crawl into his mouth and choke him.'

'Try to get some more out of that one,' said Leslie. 'You may be seeing one of the seven plagues of Egypt. It is probable that Ramoses II was the Pharaoh of the Exodus.'

I put the brown scarab to my forehead again, but all I could get was a feeling of fury at being so gullible that I had parted with five of my best goats for a scarab which was only a scarab, of less use even than a dung-beetle against a plague sent by a foreign magician. 'Sorry,' I said, 'I can't get any more. The man only kept it for two days and then flung it on the midden in disgust.'

'Do you want to do the last one? Don't go on too long and give yourself a headache,' said Daisy. I assured her I had plenty of energy left, so she put into my hand the turquoise blue scarab.

The moment it touched my forehead I knew it was warm and lively. 'This one is much older than any of the others. It was taken from the mummy of a priestess....Leslie, do you remember the underground tomb we went to at Sakkara, the one with three drop-stones in the entrance passage to the inner chamber shaped like a Noah's Ark? It wasn't a tomb. It was a place where rememberers, priests of Anubis, were taken for their initiation. The place I am seeing is not the one we went to but is very like it.'

I broke off for a moment as I was shivering with cold though the room was warm, so Elfie covered me with a rug.

'This did not come off a mummy. I thought she was a mummy because she is dressed as though ready for burial for this symbolises that her spirit is as free to travel in search of wisdom as though her earth-body had released it....'

For over an hour I described what I was seeing; how a girl called Sekeeta was taken from the temple of Atet to undergo the ordeal of initiation, during which she must leave her body for four days and four nights, returning at the end of the fourth day to dictate to a scribe what she had experienced.

Then the degree of identification deepened. 'Though I am alive, I must be as the dead; no longer can my body be unto me a friendly refuge to which I can fly when the powers of darkness are too strong; nor can I return to my body to protect it when the evil ones would turn it into a prison of pain. How shall I be as a beacon light among the people when my heart is beating as though it would leap from the cage of my ribs? Shall I ever see the sun again? Will my body ever obey my will gently and pleasantly again? Shall I be as Hekhet who failed yet did not die, and sits in the courtyard with blind eyes and wet sagging lips, trapped in a body that only flies can bear to touch? Soon, soon, they will put the mask upon my face. My eyelids must not flutter. If my body is not beneath my will, how can any of them who see me believe my speech, even though it be the mirror of the gods? I can feel the boat tilting. It has left the water. They are lowering it down the shaft. It is very cold in the passage. I can feel the darkness through my closed eyelids. I feel the mask upon my face. Soon I shall hear the drop-stones fall. Now—everyone has gone. One by one they fall. It is as though I were living in a great gong. The falling stones shatter the stillness, but soon it will return. I must quiet the beating of my heart: it sounds in my ears loudly so that I cannot hear the voice of my wisdom. Be still, my body, be still and not unworthy; for I would make you an instrument worthy to receive that which I shall be told. I must remember clearly, clearly....'

A long way away a voice was calling my name. No, not my name, someone else's name. 'Joan—come back, Joan!' A quiet voice, but insistent. Reluctantly I opened my eyes. Leslie was leaning over me, briskly rubbing my hand, from which he had removed the scarab. 'Come back now. You have been out quite long enough.'

Memory started to slide away from me like bright water flowing into a tunnel. 'Did I talk clearly enough for you to hear? Did you write it down? It was very important what I was doing—important to me. But I can't remember.'

'You need not try to remember. I have got it all written down, although part of the time you were going very fast.'

The blue scarab was lying on the table. 'There is more, so much more in it,' I said, still now quite awake. 'Please can I do some more after dinner?'

'You have done quite enough to-day,' said Leslie firmly. He looked at his watch. 'You have never been out so long as you have to-day.'

To-day was the 13th of September 1936.

CHAPTER THREE

sekeeta

Half-way through the first course I was glad that Leslie had brought me back when he did, for I had such an acute headache that it was difficult to finish the meal. In case I got an even more severe one when I next tackled the scarab, I decided to postpone future sessions until after dinner so that as soon as I finished I could go to bed.

The next day was very happy, playing with Gillian in the garden, talking with Daisy, arranging flowers, until after tea when I began to feel apprehensive. Last night the degree of indentification had a new intensity. What would happen to me if the other girl failed in her ordeals? If she died, or went mad from terror, could sharing her experience affect me? Fortunately none of the others realised I was nervous when I lay down on the sofa to begin work. 'What do you want me to look for?' I asked, to postpone the moment when I must relax my body and collect my energies into a focal point of concentration.

'Find out what happened to the poor girl after she was left all alone in that horrible tomb,' said Elfie.

'Get the name of the reigning Pharaoh,' said Leslie.

'Look for something easier to-night,' suggested Daisy. 'Try to visit an Egyptian garden and see if you can identify some of the plants.'

I was not able to answer any of their questions, for that

255

evening, as on many subsequent evenings, I had to take what came. Sometimes I saw a scene which included the girl Sekeeta as though I was watching her. At other times I saw through her eyes, sharing her experience as though it was happening to me in the immediate present. 'I am three years old. Our house has a garden with a blue pool and little scarlet fishes, which I feed with millet.' The child prattled on, about her pets, her toys: a child who might just as well have belonged to any other century.

'The only thing of any real interest I noticed is that Egyptians were very tall people,' I said when I had finished. 'The child's nurse, for instance, must have been well over six feet. How odd that none of the archaeologists noticed this when they were examining mummies—or do you think that embalming could have shrunk the bones?'

'No, I don't,' said Leslie. 'But there is a tribe in Africa who may be descended from Ancient Egyptians. They are very tall and still have horned cattle which closely resemble the cattle of the tomb-paintings.'

He was quite excited about it until on the following evening the girl was fourteen years old and I realised that the average height of an adult male Egyptian was only about five foot eight.

'But you said last night that they were remarkably tall,' protested Leslie.'

'I know I did. But I was seeing grown-ups through the eyes of a small child. ''When my nurse is angry she is as tall as a pillar,'' is how she described it to herself.'

I often found myself in Sekeeta's bedroom in the temple; she was not gregarious by nature and it was the only place where she could be certain of privacy. 'The bed is wooden, the sides made in the likeness of Anubis, his jackal paws being the feet of the bed. There is only one window, high in the wall, and under it is a little shelf with an earthen jar which I fill with flowers so that I can look at them when I leave my body instead of on a white wall as is usual. To-day the jar is filled with blue-and-white striped convolvulus. Beside the bed is a wax tablet on which I record, with a sharpened reed, what I do when I am away from my body. This I do immediately I return to it. Before I sleep I smooth the wax with a little roller, not only to make it ready to write on in the morning, but to remind me to smooth thoughts of the day's happenings from my mind so that it is ready to receive memory.'

Usually I saw her wearing a white tunic and 'plain sandals of undecorated leather', but she sometimes thought of far more elaborate clothes—I described these in detail—which she used to wear before coming to the temple. These clothes provided a clue that she had not been born into a peasant family.

'Do try to find out the name of the Pharaoh,' urged Leslie. 'It would be much more interesting if we knew what dynasty she lived in.'

I thought I should be able to answer his question when I found myself standing in a crowd of people by the roadside where a royal procession would pass on its way to celebrate a festival. I waited there a long time and was worried because I had left the temple without permission. I could see pennants fluttering in the wind, green and scarlet pennants on gilded poles every hundred cubits, and the garlands of scarlet poppies which linked them together. I could smell the flowers which the women wore as wreaths and as necklaces, and the sweat of bodies that jostled against me in the crowd. Further up the road the people began chanting. 'Pharaoh approaches. Our life is renewed in the sight of our Father. The people of Kam* are the children of Pharaoh and we rejoice with our Father in the sight of the gods.'

The chanting was drawing close to me when I heard Leslie say, 'What is the *name* of the Pharaoh? Get his name, Joan!'

*Kam is the old name for Egypt, pronounced Calm.

His voice brought me back so fast that I could remember exactly what I had been seeing.

'I might have done if you hadn't interrupted,' I said crossly. 'Sekeeta must have had a very literal mind, because when she thinks about Pharaoh, instead of visualising him as a remote god-man holding the Crook and Flail, he only reminds her of her own father—a man of about thirty playing with his children in a garden, or sailing in a small boat on the Nile.'

'It's a pity she was not someone of more social importance,' Leslie remarked, 'for then she might have seen Pharaoh in audience or been taken by her family to offer tribute at the palace. That would certainly have made sufficient impression for her to have been aware of his name.'

'I wonder what made her go into the temple,' said Daisy thoughtfully. 'I get the impression that she was such an active and loving person, as though she was not really dedicated to the cloistered life.'

'She went into the temple to please her mother. Sekeeta had many true dreams and her mother taught her to be glad of them, even of those that were frightening. She taught me a prayer, "Master, of thy wisdom let me grow into a great tree, so that the sorrowful may rest in my shade and go on their journey refreshed, and the weary regain their strength in the shelter of my branches."'

'You ought to have warned me that you were going out,' said Leslie reprovingly. 'You went so suddenly that I realised, only just in time to write down the prayer, that you were dictating and not just theorising.'

He read the prayer back to me. It moved me almost to tears. I looked at Daisy, and there was such long love for me in her eyes that I felt safe and cherished, as the little Sekeeta had been in the love of her mother.

The next evening I started to describe how Sekeeta as a child of about ten saw a man badly mauled during a lion-hunt. Then the telephone rang and brought me back abruptly.

'More about the lion-hunt,' said Leslie a few minutes later. 'It sounded as though it was going to be exciting.'

I thought so too, but instead of getting back to the place where the thread had snapped, I got a long and rather dull sequence when Sekeeta first went to the temple and was playing a game with several other pupils, none of whom she much liked. It was a simple game, a silver disc was thrown into a swimming-pool and they all dived in to see who could reach it first by swimming under water.

'I wonder if she ever fell in love,' said Elfie wistfully. 'It must have happened sometimes when young men and young women were living in the same temple, even if they were very serious-minded.'

In reply the scarab gave me two poems that had been written to Sekeeta. These Dio sent to me, beautifully scribed in colours on a little roll of papyrus:

> I am a sculptor that has lost his hands,
>   And an orchard where no water flows;
> I am a sailing-boat on a still day
>   And a bird that cannot move its wings;
> I am a lotus in a dried-up pool,
>   And a bow whose string is broken;
> I am a sanctuary without a god,
>   And a night sky without stars:
> For I had to leave you upon a long journey
>   And you gave me not your heart to take with me.

And later he sent me:

> The seed is planted
>   And the grain springs from the furrow.
> The fisherman casts his net
>   And it is leaping with fish.
> The vintagers press out the grapes
>   And the wine-jars are filled.

The throwing-stick flies through the air
And the bird falls to the hunter.
The noonday sun is hot,
But the shadows grow long in the cool of the
evening.
I have given you my heart,
But will you give me yours?

'Was he really a sculptor?' asked Elfie.

'Yes, he was. She met him when he was carving a frieze on one of the temple buildings. Didn't I say so?'

'No. You read the poems and then you were silent for so long I thought you had gone to sleep,' said Leslie.

'Dio was a foreigner and he had red hair. Sekeeta tried to make him believe in the gods, but I don't think she succeeded.'

'Surely a temple pupil was unlikely to fall in love with an atheist,' commented Leslie.

'Perhaps she was secretly pleased to find someone who loved her as a woman instead of being awed by her power as a priest: being a priest is often very lonely. But she did her best to convert him to her ideas. When I was out just now I was sharing a long conversation with them. I suppose I got so caught up in it that I forgot to make my body talk. Wait a moment and I will try to get it again.'

But that evening I only recorded a small part of what they were saying to each other: 'Sekeeta, why will you always ponder on strange immensities? Leave all these thoughts until you need their warmth when you feel cold wind blowing from your tomb. Why spoil the joy of a sycamore tree at noon when it patterns the dust in shadows? What does it matter who made it or why it is there? Rejoice in the sunshine, and do not think of it as one of your ponderous gods; think of the river as clear water in which we can bathe, and not as a symbol of interminable life. While you are young, rejoice and think not of the past. Be grateful for beauty and do not always compare it to a vision, which you think puts it in the shadow. Delight in music, and do not listen to echoes from the stars. When you are old you may have to bemuse your loneliness with memories, but now you do not need them, for the present is glorious before your eyes. One day I shall take you from this ancient land where people are grave with too much wisdom, and take you to Minoas where their hearts sing with youth.'

'Did he ever take her to Minoas?' asked Elfie. 'I do hope so. Minoas is Crete now isn't it? And Crete is such a nice place, especially in Spring when the tulips are out...apart from the fleas, but perhaps there weren't so many fleas in the old days.'

'I don't think she ever went there with Dio. I think I should know if she had. And yet I have a vague impression that she did go to Minoas....'

There were only three more days before we had to go back to Scotland. The weather was sultry, with thunder brooking in the distance, and I was depressed because I must soon leave Daisy. I was determined to get a lot more about Sekeeta for her, but, try as I would to get out of my body, nothing happened. I could have cried with frustration, for the scarab seemed as empty as a pebble from the beach.

'Perhaps you have been doing too much and need a rest,' Daisy said consolingly. But I tried the next evening, and still got nothing, not even a trivial fragment which would at least have shown that the scarab was still warm. Surely there would be something on my last evening? For an hour or more I tried to force myself to remember, but all I succeeded in doing was to increase the dull headache, which was not due to magic but only to weather.

At last I had to admit failure. 'It is finished, I almost wish I have never started, for now we shall never know what happened to her. It's worse than reading a few pages of an enthralling manuscript and then finding that the rest of it has been burned by an idiot housemaid....I feel too hopelessly inefficient to be something grander, like a musician who wakes up one morning and finds he has gone deaf.'

'You must keep the scarab as a memento of happy evenings,' said Daisy gently. 'Perhaps one day it will have more to tell you.'

CHAPTER FOUR

faR memoRy

We took a six-weeks-old puppy up to Muckerach with us, a golden retriever whom Leslie named Rishan—the Arabic for courage. The following day Gillian and I went up the hill to show him to Gwen, and I took the scarab with me. I knew she would be interested in it because she had read all my psychometry note-books.

'Are you sure it's empty now?' she said with lively sympathy. 'It seems unlikely that it should suddenly lose its memory after so many thousand years.'

'It nearly always happens, though I don't understand why, that after I have psychometrised an object the impression in it disappears, or rather the sequence does which I have already recorded. The best analogy I can think of is a gramophone record made of such soft wax that the tune in it can only be played once.'*

'Why don't you try the technique you were experimenting with last winter while Leslie was abroad? You began to tell me about it soon after we met, and then broke off and

---

* Had tape recorders been invented I could have described what I was trying to say much more accurately by comparing the process to the 'scrubbing' of the magnetised tape.

asked me not to mention the subject to Leslie.'

'I'm afraid it wouldn't work,' I said gloomily. 'I tried everything I could think of during the last three evenings at Hurtwood and nothing happened at all.'

Gillian was playing somersaults with the puppy and I was watching to see they didn't roll into the gentian border, where sino-ornata were flowering so exuberantly that they made a blue carpet nearly fifty yards long.

'Rishan is so fat and woolly that he looks more like a little lion cub than a puppy,' said Gwen.

I heard myself telling her that Sekeeta had a lion cub when she was Gillian's age. 'He was called Natee. He used to lie at her feet when she gave audience—after she became Pharaoh.'

'You didn't tell me she became Pharaoh.'

I stared at her. 'Gwen, I didn't know it! But I do now. I must have slipped out of myself and back again so easily that I never noticed, like a tortoise popping its head out of its shell.'

'You have the scarab in your pocket...'

'But I wasn't touching it. Anyway what does it matter if I did it with or without the scarab as a catalyst? But I shall hold it while I'm working because Daisy gave it to me on the morning I went to my initiation.

'*Daisy* gave it to you?'

'I have just realised that she was Sekeeta's mother. Subconsciously we must have recognised each other the moment I went to Hurtwood. It was the love between us that made me able to remember the things that are worth remembering; instead of wasting time, like I used to do and will never bother to do any more, looking for ''evidence'' through psychometry. But why couldn't I get anything the last three days I was at Hurtwood?' She started to say something but I interrupted, 'Don't talk for a minute. I am trying to think back to see if anything was different to the other days there....'

'Well, if you are going to have a long think you had better bring Gillian indoors, for it is going to pour with rain.'

'Rain! That's the clue I was looking for! It *didn't* rain until after I had gone to bed on our last evening. The storm broke about three in the morning. It had been brewing for days and the atmosphere was so oppressive that I felt as though there was a sandbag on my head. I must go back at once and put a trunk-call through to Daisy.'

'I'll get the car out and drive you home, or you'll both be soaked to the skin before you get there.'

'Stay to dinner and I will work afterwards. Don't tell Leslie yet about the new developments. For some reason best known to himself he considers psychometry respectable and scientific; but he may take a dim view if he realises that I think it increasingly likely that he is married to an ex-Pharaoh.'

'One sympathises with him,' said Gwen drily. 'Especially if you decide you need a lion as well as a goat. If you do, be sure to warn me so that I can order an extra joint before you bring him to tea.'

Leslie was very pleased to see Gwen, and until we had finished coffee I did not tell him that I was going to dictate. He was rather dubious. 'You said there was nothing more in the scarab. However, if you really want to try it again...'

I intended to see Sekeeta giving audience with a lion at her feet, but instead I plunged into a description of her listening to a looking-girl's commentary on an unsavory sacrificial rite being performed, nearly two thousand miles away from the Nile, at the Court of Zernak, King of the Zumas.

Leslie usually read my dictation back to me before making any comments, because if he did so immediately I de-tuned, I could usually recall a sentence which I had spoken too fast for him to get down. Instead of doing this he frowned and shook his head at me, which Gwen did not notice as she was lighting a cigarette.

'Describe to Gwen what you mean by a looking-girl,' he said abruptly; and I could see he was both annoyed and embarrased. So I obediently explained that looking-girls were trained to leave their bodies and observe what was happening at some point separated from them by space but not by time, and only on the physical level. 'They served the purpose of a wireless receiver* but could pick up a visual image instead of only sound waves,' I said chattily, and added, to fill an awkward pause, 'We had to keep an eye on the Zumas in case they were plotting another invasion of the Two Lands.'

'Did the Sumerians invade Egypt?' said Leslie. 'Are you sure you are not confusing them with one of the two invasions of the Hyksos?'

'Quite sure,' I said briskly. 'They invaded us twice, and on both occasions were soundly defeated. Sekeeta led her chariots against them and herself killed Zernak.'

'Very robust of her,' said Leslie coldly. So I led the conversation into impersonal channels.

After Gwen had gone home he said, 'I will now read to you what you recorded with such a wealth of detail.' He did, and I protested that I could hardly be blamed for the horrid habits of foreigners who in any case lived a considerable time ago.

'But surely you can censor what you are saying,' he said aggrieved.

'Oh, Leslie, don't be such an ass! I've told you dozens of times that it takes nearly every bit of my energy to go back into the past, and so I can only spare enough of it to make myself talk. Anyway, it's your fault and not mine if Gwen was upset. She thought we were going to have a row because you were being so ridiculously stuffy.'

'I was not stuffy. I was embarrassed—on her behalf.'

'Then why didn't you stop me? All you had to do was to drop a book or clatter the fire-irons. You know perfectly well how a sudden noise breaks the thread.'

'I did not wish to break the thread. You have been so gloomy since you thought the scarab had gone cold on you that I wouldn't have interrupted if the room had been full

---

* Radar is a better metaphor but it had not yet been invented.

of parsons on the verge of apoplexy. In future, if anyone else is present I shall interrupt you whenever I think it necessary, and you must promise not to dictate to anyone except me.'

'All right,' I said grudgingly. 'Provided that you will promise me something too.'

'What is it?'

'To make me work every evening. Bully me if you have to. I am going to write to Daisy to-night and tell her that she will get another bit about Sekeeta as often as I can possibly manage it until I have got the whole story for her.'

'Why the hurry? And why especially for Daisy?'

'That's private for the moment. Will you promise?'

'Certainly if you want me to. I find taking your dictation far more entertaining than backgammon.'

The following evening I accompanied Sekeeta on a river journey from Abydos to the Delta, an experience so pleasant that I suffered acute nostalgia when I found myself back in a wet Scottish autumn.

'What did the Pyramids look like when they still had their facing-stones intact?' enquired Leslie.

'There weren't any pyramids, not even a mastaba. I remembered to look out for them as I knew you would be interested.'

'They must have been there. They are Fourth Dynasty and the civilisation you describe is far too elaborate to have been any earlier.'

'Sekeeta lived most of the time at what is now called Sakkara. The country, as you well know because we went there eighteen months ago, is flat. She was extremely observant, so I can assure you that if the two Great Pyramids, or the Sphinx for that matter, had been a feature of the landscape she would undoubtedly have noticed them.'

He had bought *A History of Egypt* by Flinders Petrie, in three volumes, but he thought that Sekeeta must have belonged to a period later than the Twelfth Dynasty—for this was before I recorded the story of Meniss, and so he had not bothered to look carefully through Volume One when he was trying to identify the only cartouches I had happened to notice: the first on her father's wine-jars, the second on her ointment-pots and combs, and the third on a stele she had caused to be set up after the victory against the Zuma invasion. Now we identified them all, and so at last knew that she had lived during the third and fourth reigns of the First Dynasty. There was even an illustration of her mother's mummified arm, still wearing the bracelet which Sekeeta had given to her as a birthday present. 'It was a lovely bracelet of golden moon-daisies joined together with amethyst and turquoise beads; and Nu-setees the goldsmith said it was the finest work he had ever done.'

We managed to get a lot more during the following two months, in spite of visitors. The last batch had gone and we were having dinner peacefully together when the parlourmaid came in to announce that the heather at the edge of the birch-wood was on fire. When we saw the direction in which the fire was spreading I shouted, 'Quick! Fetch everyone to beat it out. Oh, my poor water-garden!'

I dashed to the telephone and rang Mrs. Grant-the-Post-Office, who assured me that, although the Grantown Fire Brigade would not stir themselves unless the house were threatened, she would mobilise the villagers of Dulnain Bridge to assist Mrs. Grant-Muckerach. Within twenty minutes a crowd of helpers, aged from seven to seventy, arrived; but at first they made only desultory efforts for they saw that the fire would fizzle out when it reached the stream. 'But that is just what it mustn't do!' I explained distractedly. 'It is my special garden. The shrubs will all be destroyed. Four thousand bulbs will be baked to cinders.' Then they went into action. They lashed the smouldering heather with branches, smothered patches of creeping sparks with wet sacks, chopped down trees which were already alight. It was nearly midnight before the garden was safe and the last fire-fighter had gone home, refreshed with my gratitude and Leslie's whisky.

I caught sight of myself in the hall mirror. 'Goodness, I never realised I was so bedraggled!' I exclaimed, feeling rather pleased with this proof that I had remained in the forefront of the battle. My leather golf-jacket was torn and my trousers were singed. There was a deep scratch across my forehead which, like my face, was smudged with wood ash; and both my hands had several quite impressive blisters.

'You look as though you could do with a whisky-and-soda—if your private army has left us any,' said Leslie.

'No thank you, darling. I'd rather have a long and very hot bath.'

'But you can't have a bath yet. You haven't done your dictating.'

'How *can* I dictate? Don't be ridiculous. I'm exhausted and filthy, wounded and charred to the bone.'

'You made me promise to bully you.'

'All right, I'll try, ' I said grudgingly. 'But only for half an hour, not a moment longer. Go and fetch the scarab, and Rishan—he's shut in my bedroom.

I always worked with Rishan curled up beside me. He never disturbed me except when I was getting out of my depth, when he at once became agitated and brought me back by whining and licking my face. I flung myself on the sofa and said crossly, 'There is something here about smells: ''The gentle death of autumn in deep woods,'' a very sentimental way of describing wood-smoke, but perhaps Sekeeta never had to beat out a fire.'

'Don't start arguing with yourself. Get out and get on with the job.'

I obeyed, and dictated at top speed for exactly twenty-two minutes. I came back with a jerk. 'Well, that's all I'm going to do for to-night. There was a lot about smells, nice smells mostly, but don't bother to read it back, I'm too tired to be interested.'

I was asleep almost as soon as I got into bed. Leslie

stayed up long enough to copy out his speed-writing into the
notebook, which he left open on my bedside table....

Here is the dark red perfume of the rose,
The drowsy quiet of bean-fields in the dusk,
The gentle death of autumn in deep woods,
And the clean smell of ploughland after rain.

The friendly wood-smoke of a cooking-fire,
The satisfying smell of baking bread,
The earth-forgotten green of new-cut grass,
The moon-drunk sweetness of night-blooming flowers.

The warmth of clover murmurous with bees,
The sleepy peace of avenues of limes,
The tuberose's languorous caress,
The chill austerity of alpine flowers.

The yellow warmth of primroses at noon,
The scent of water running over stones,
The lonely sorrow of the river mist,
The smooth white smell of linen and of snow.

The dusty wisdom of papyrus rolls,
And the warm spice of cedarwood and myrrh,
The hot impatient smell of spikenard,
And the tarnished silver's half-remembered dreams.

The clear sharp energy of lemon-rind,
The lover's ecstasy of orange trees,
The melancholy smell of winter nights,
And hyacinths' azure echo of the Spring.

The salty challenge of wind-driven spray,
That wander-urging message of the sea,
The gentle memories of sun-dried flowers,

The still abandonment of fields at noon.

The moth-winged purple of new-gathered grapes,
The easy laughter of a jar of beer,
The excitement of a gallop-sweated horse,
And the proud splendour of the manes of lions.

The acrid keenness of a copper sword,
And the brave smell of torches in the wind,
The musky pomp of ceremonial robes,
And the solemnity of bitumen.

I woke Leslie to read it aloud. 'It's all in umpty, Leslie!
Tee-tum, tee-tum, tee-tum, tee-tum, tee-tum.'

'If you were less illiterate,' he mumbled, hunching farther
under the bedclothes, 'you would recognise the ''umpty'' for
a five-foot iambic.'

'I shall continue to call it ''umpty''. And I think it very
clever to write five-foot whatsits without ever having heard
of them. It proves my theory about there being no real need
for education.'

'Oh, do shut up! It's only nine o'clock. Go and chatter to
Gillian. She enjoys it.'

'Tee-tum, tee-tum, tee-tum, tee-tum,' I chanted as I retrieved Rishan from under the eiderdown. 'I wonder if I shall
dictate any more umpty.'

'The last half-dozen chunks were all in the same metre. I
thought you had noticed.

'Well, I didn't. I'll go and read them and leave you in
peace.'

I might not have felt so gay had I recognised that this recording was part of the Initiation, and that I had to re-experi-
ence the seven great ordeals. The seventh, which I did first,
in which Sekeeta had to overcome the cobra, increased my
ordinary fear of snakes to such a pitch that I thought of vipers
whenever I walked on the moor; and I had several nightmares

from which I woke screaming, so convinced that there was a snake in the bed that to calm me Leslie had to pull all the bed-clothes off and shake them out the window. That the weather by now was cold enough to freeze the water in the glass by my bed did not make my panic any more endearing to my bedfellow.

I did the battle with Ishtak and the other five ordeals on the same evening, in a desperate anxiety to get them over. I expected to get a headache, but was not prepared for cramps, rigors, and icy sweats, which lasted for twenty-four hours and were followed by another day and night of pains in the joints and a temperature of 103°. Fortunately I had realised that it was only a spook illness, so I managed to stop Leslie sending for the doctor. It was a very unpleasant forty-eight hours, but on the morning of the third day I proved my diagnosis correct by waking entirely recovered.

I learned that physical reaction is not the only disadvantage attending the practice of far memory. Pleasure can be dimmed by contrast with brighter joys of the past, and present sorrows and anxieties are increased by re-experiencing earlier ones with a similar emotional quality. For instance, I should not have been nearly so anxious about Rishan's chance of recovery while I was nursing him through severe distemper unless I had remembered Sekeeta's grief at the death of her lion. Den, Sekeeta's daughter, was eight years old and of an adventurous disposition which caused her to disobey her attendants and go alone beyond the boundaries of the palace gardens. Her mother, who had been equally resentful of discipline at the same age, made the child promise to take Natee with her when she felt the urge to go on a private adventure. She took Natee to the 'hot sandy place among the reeds' and there she found a cobra. She thought that as it was the royal snake, like the one her mother sometimes wore as a head-dress, it would be friendly to the daughter of Pharaoh. She was walking towards it, intending to stroke the spread hood, when Natee leapt at the snake and killed it. But it had already bitten him. Den ran to fetch her mother. Sekeeta sent for Zeb, now Captain of Captains, who had been a lion-boy when Natee was a cub, and for a strong litter with eight bearers to carry the lion back to the palace.

'When Den and I reached Natee he was still alive. At the sound of my voice he tried to struggle to his feet, but could not and he fell over on his side. I knew there was nothing I could do to save him. I took his head on my lap and stroked his ears and whispered into them that I dearly loved him. When Zeb came, he also knew that nothing could be done, and he knelt beside me. Then at the last my Natee licked my hand, and his heavy head fell to rest upon my knees and I knew his brave spirit had returned to Ptah. For the sake of Den I tried to check my tears until I saw tears running down Zeb's face: Captain and Queen both weeping by their lion.'

'Why are you still sad when Rishan is so much better, Mummy?' enquired Gillian, several days after I had recorded Natee's death. I told her I had a bit of a gloom which would be instantly cured if we went for a walk together. I could not tell her that several times I had caught myself listening for the thud of great paws, for the rumbling, rasping complaint of a lion impatient for my door to be opened for him. It was nearly a fortnight before Joan's heart ceased grieving for Sekeeta's lion.

CHAPTER FIVE

chord and discord

I had been working too hard, and at Christmas knew it by the increasing effort it took to become identified with Sekeeta. So we gladly accepted Nina's invitation to go with Gillian for a fortnight to Cullen, where there was a large and entertaining house-party. It was a relief not to have to think of a past earlier than the nineteen-twenties, and so my depleted batteries had a chance to recharge before we returned to Muckerach. The weather obligingly presented me with ideal working conditions; for apart from Gwen, who was always an asset, we had no visitors, because the snow-plough could not keep our road open. Rosemary decided that it was too cold in the barn, or perhaps she was too snobbish to share it with the ewes that had been brought in for lambing, so we brought her pink blankets into the gun-room. Gin and Rishan played porpoises through the drifts. The drive became a toboggan run for the children. We taught Gillian to skate on the water-lily loch, and to ski. It was on skis that we brought home our mail and provisions.

Leslie had been making two copies of my dictation, one to keep and one to post to Daisy; but he now decided it would be better if we had a secretary to type it. Looking back, I cannot think why I did not suggest doing this myself, as typing was one of the jobs I used to do for Father; but I am grateful for the providence that sent Vera Sutherland into my life. Before the daffodils and narcissi flowered she had typed everything I had dictated. An evening's work usually confined itself to a particular place and time, but sometimes a single session contained passages of dialogue in which Sekeeta might be talking with characters not yet identified, who belonged to different periods of her autobiography. Arranging these in their correct sequence was like reconstructing a jar from sherds as I had often done in Iraq, except that instead of missing pieces being irretrievably lost I could usually find them, although they might remain elusive for days or even weeks.

We now knew that Sekeeta had died when she was fifty-three, so we decided to divide the pages into fifty-three folders, each representing a year of her lifetime. We were doing this, and the drawing-room floor was covered with pages of typescript, when Dr. Marr popped his head round the door and asked if he could bring someone in for a glass of sherry. 'He is a nice old boy and he wants to do some sketching. As he is staying at the Grant Arms without a car I thought I'd take him with me on my rounds to give him a chance to see something of the scenery.'

'Of course, bring him in,' I said, wishing that he had not brought someone to see us when the room was so untidy. I knew I had seen the man before who was standing beside the doctor's car talking to Gillian. It took me a few seconds to realise that I had seen him on the conductor's rostrum at the Queen's Hall. He was Sir Henry Wood.

Within ten minutes he was sitting on the floor reading *The Place of Music*, which happened to be nearest him. To distract him I offered more sherry, which he accepted but went on reading. He became enthusiastic, which embarrassed Leslie. Luckily, before he could ask any leading questions, Mrs. Marr telephoned to say that the doctor was urgently needed at the Cottage Hospital.

Nearly every day for the rest of his visit to Grantown, Sir Henry came to Muckerach. Wearing an Inverness cape, he sat on a camp-stool in the garden and made water-colour sketches of the mountains. They were not very good sketches, but he was as proud of them as he was humble about his musical genius. He took it for granted that people with special aptitude for music had somehow acquired their facility before they were born, and he quoted many instances which had come within his own experience, together with such well known ones as the child Handel and Yehudi Menuhin. He usually stayed to dinner and listened to me dictate. Sometimes Leslie switched on the wireless when I had finished so that I could relax for a few minutes without having to talk. One evening he tuned-in to a programme of Haydn played on a harpsichord. I told Henry that I had just been listening to Egyptian music, which was rather similar. 'Could you hear it and the Haydn at the same time?' he asked. 'It would be very interesting if you could give me an idea of how closely the themes are related.'

I got out again very easily, and the harpsichord went out of hearing. When I came back they both seemed more than usually interested. 'Can you remember where you have been and what instrument you were playing?'

I could still feel the strings rippling under my fingers. 'It was a lute, which is odd because I didn't know the Egyptians had lutes, or that Sekeeta could play any kind of musical instrument.'

'But you weren't in Egypt,' said Leslie. 'You were in Italy. Don't talk. Wait until I have read it back to you...''I was born near Perugia in May 1510. My name was Carola di Ludovici. I died when I was twenty-seven. I was a strolling player....'''

In less than a thousand words and fifteen minutes of clock-time I had rememberd the main facts of what, after months of detailed recording, became *Life as Carola*. This was the final confirmation I needed to convince me that I had developed the faculty of far memory to a degree which allowed me to talk about it. As soon as Henry had gone I started with Leslie....

'I've known what you were doing for some time,' he said sombrely. 'I hope that Henry is discreet enough to keep it a secret.'

'Why should he?'

'Because he likes you, and therefore presumably would prefer that you did not become an object of ridicule. Good God, do you *want* everyone to think that you dreep about in mauve chiffon and mummy-beads? That's what will happen if it leaks out. ''Leslie Grant's wife thinks she was Pharaoh.'' What a thing to overhear in a club!'

'If you think that being married to an ex-royalty is a little overpowering,' I said acidly, 'you can tell them that your wife used to be a strolling player. Very squalid some of it was too, I can assure you. There is nothing grand about playing a lute in a brothel in Fiume.'

'If you *had* to teach yourself to remember a previous incarnation, why couldn't you have picked on a less dramatic one?' he said fretfully. 'Thousands of bogus people claim to have been kings or queens—unless they choose priests or gladiators. You might at least have been sufficiently original to remember being a cook.'

'Why should I bother to remember being a cook when it was so much easier to take lessons from Boulestin? I told you when I was in Cluny, and you were being so unsympathetic about our haunted bedroom, that I wanted to learn the kind of things that would help me to understand myself. That is why Sekeeta's life is more relevant to me than any of the others. Revelance, I've just realised, is a decisive factor, the tuning-mechanism. I remembered being Carola the lute-player because the music I was hearing was more relevant to her than it was to Sekeeta, who was not particularly musical.'

He shrugged his shoulders in a way that always irritated me as it was intended to convey that it was useless to argue with someone who was too empirical to accept a reasoned argument. 'Well, don't say I didn't warn you. I don't mind you talking about it to intimate friends like Daisy, who know you are remarkably level-headed; but I shall be extremely annoyed if you are indiscreet enough to let other people think that I'm married to a nut who claims she is Pharaoh.'

'I don't claim to *be* Pharaoh!'

'Why quibble? You remember being Sekeeta, and I believe you because I have had far too much evidence by now to pretend it's coincidence; but people who have not had the opportunity to know you and see you work will think you're dotty.'

'As you are being deliberately obtuse I will try to be as pedantic as a barrister—although I did not expect to have to niggle with words. Joan and Sekeeta are *not* the same person, nor do I believe in reincarnation in the way that Theosophists, and Wyeth and Neale, and other cults and isms mean the word. Joan and Sekeeta and Carola and the Red Indian

276

and the Greek runner and the French girl—and probably hundreds of others as well whom I haven't yet remembered, each has a soul, a personality if you prefer the word. The sum total of all these souls is the spirit they share between them. The soul usually becomes part of the spirit after the body dies. Sometimes a part of the soul fails to integrate and the result is a ghost. When I am doing far memory all I do is to become aware in the spirit, which includes Sekeeta and Carola and all the others.'

He still did not seem convinced, so I added rather crossly. 'If trying to talk scientifically doesn't make sense to you I'll try baby-language. Joan and Sekeeta are two beads on the same necklace and the memory they share is contained in the string.'

I then went to bed, slamming the door behind me.

CHAPTER SIX

WINGED PHARAOH

Early in June we went to London for a wedding at which Gillian was to be a bridesmaid and Leslie best man. While he was at the bridegroom's stag party I dined with Guy McCaw, whom I happened to run into at Prince's Tennis Club. I had not seen Guy for some time. 'What on earth are you doing buried up in Scotland?' he demanded. 'You can't even shoot grouse in the winter. Or have you become addicted to salmon fishing?'

Mildly annoyed that he thought no one could enjoy Scotland unless they were killing something, I forgot I had promised Leslie to be discreet. 'I catch an occasional trout when I'm not too busy, but I spend most of my time remembering who I used to be when I lived in Egypt during the First Dynasty.'

'Good God, Joan! Have you gone off your head?' He scrutinised me and seemed relieved that I laughed at him. 'You gave me quite a shock. I didn't realise you were joking.'

'I'm not joking. I have dictated about sixty thousand words of what, even if you think I made it up, is an interesting story.'

'Well, let me read it. At least I will do so if it is typed, but I'm not going to wade through pages of your handwriting. I always tell people the truth, however unpalatable; so if it is nonsense I shall be brutally candid.'

Until then I had no intention of showing Guy, or anyone else, the copy I had brought down to give Daisy; but his bland assumption that it would be nonsense, an imaginative outpouring of which I could be cured by a cold douche of criticism, made me send the typescript round to him the following morning. I enclosed a brief note asking him to send it on to me at Hurtwood, where I should be with Gillian for four days before returning to Scotland.

Although she refused to admit it, Daisy was obviously weaker, and now had to have a nurse living in the house. I was so worried about her that I forgot about the typescript until the morning we were leaving. Instead of a parcel from Guy there was only a letter.... 'To my great surprise you have written something far better than you apparently recognise. I consider it should be published, and have therefore given it to Arthur Barker.'

'How sensible of him,' said Daisy. 'Although a little high-handed not to consult you first.'

'But it is bound to cause trouble. What makes it even more awkward is that Arthur is a friend of ours. He and his wife have been down to Seacourt and Leslie plays tennis with him at Prince's. Leslie doesn't mind you, and Elfie of course, and Gwen, knowing how I write; but with nearly everyone else the subject is taboo—even people like Diana and Kirsteen. If Arthur publishes it, the way I wrote the book is bound to get about, and then Leslie will be furious.'

'Darling, don't anticipate trouble. What you have written has helped me a great deal. It may help other people if they have a chance to read it.'

'Shall I tell Leslie that it has gone to a publisher?'

She thought for a moment and then said, 'It would perhaps be better not to mention it until you hear Arthur's opinion.'

I was relieved, for it meant that I would not have to tell him if it was rejected.

A week later I received a telegram. 'Essential you complete manuscript in six weeks so that we can publish in October. Blurb will state most exciting and important book we have ever published. Congratulations, Arthur.'

The Grant family, including Elsie and Ronald, were coming to Muckerach for August and September, so, with Vera and the two dogs, we migrated to Hurtwood. Although Elfie still clung to the hope that Daisy was suffering only a temporary setback, the rest of us knew that it would be her last summer. The cancer had spread to her spine and her lungs, yet she talked about the book as though it was the first of many she would read while I wrote them. I knew that the only way I could help her was to pretend that it was still important to me.

It was she who thought of the title *Winged Pharaoh,* and when I showed her the dedication to her she said, 'Bless you, darling; but only put my initials.' From the many patterns of binding-cloth which Arthur produced she chose the nearest one to the faience blue of the scarab. Leslie found a copy of one of the few surviving First Dynasty steles, and on it Ralph Levers, who had worked for several years on the dig at Tel-el-Armarna, based his design for the dust-jacket.

There were still gaps in the context which had to be filled in before the typescript could go to the printers, and we were within nine weeks of publication day. By now I could almost always tune-in the scene I wanted, but sometimes what I thought would be only a paragraph led to an episode, which could only be included if we made further cuts so as to keep the book to the length laid down by Arthur.

Vera produced prodigies of typing, for the meticulous neatness which I had acquired while working for Father was so deeply ingrained that every page which had even a comma altered had to be re-typed, and a deleted paragraph or an additional sentence entailed doing the whole episode over again. I sympathised deeply with Vera, who was unfailingly cheerful; for I had once sat up all night to re-type an article in which on every page I had mis-spelled by one letter the name of the same species of mosquito. Yet I still considered it unthinkable, as Father did, to let a text go to the printer with ink corrections. Like most inexperienced authors, when the publisher's blue pencil descended and in a moment removed what it had taken me a great deal of trouble to write, I felt as though he were cutting off my baby's feet to make it fit into the pram. Usually I was too well aware of my amateur status to argue, but I did protest mildly when the penultimate part of the original nine was excised bodily. 'Must it all go—even to the death of Sekeeta's lion?

'Yes,' said Arthur briskly. 'A hundred and twenty thousand words are more than enough, and you have too many deaths in the book already.'

Batches of galleys were arriving every third day, and once a week I took them up to London to make final proof-corrections with the invaluable help of Eric Partridge. We had done nearly two-thirds of them when Arthur took me to lunch with Charlie Evans of Heinemann, who had read the typescript. He was exceedingly kind about it and then asked Arthur how many copies he intended to publish.

'A thousand,' said Arthur, 'at ten and six. I know it's a high price, but it's a long book and she has been fussy about production.'

'Take my advice and print five hundred.' said Charlie

Evans. 'I like the book very much myself and would be glad to have it on my list, but you will never sell it.'

'I think I will,' said Arthur.

'Nonsense, my dear boy. I have had far more experience of the publishing trade than any of your firm have got. A first novel, mostly in iambics, about an unknown Pharaoh in a virtually unknown period of history, has no chance whatever of making any money. The most you can hope for is a small *succes d' estime.'*

'Just to prove that I don't agree with you I shall print *two* thousand,' said Arthur defiantly—which made me feel even more indebted to him. He had given me 25 pounds advance royalties and now he was going to lose hundreds. The least I could do was to buy the unsold copies myself and hide them in the barn at Muckerach until they became useful bedding for rats. If I ordered them from booksellers all over the country it might even conceal the fact that he had made a fool of himself, and me, by backing a flop.

As Arthur was not going back to the office, he asked me to drop him at his home in Chessington, which was on my way to Hurtwood. We collected Leslie from Prince's where he had been playing tennis, and then went to Beaufort Street where I had arranged to pick up Vera. The house was dusty and airless, for it had been empty since the tenants departed two months ago. Leslie was prowling about, noticing marks on the paint and how much worse the Queen Anne bureau looked than was indicated by the cursory 'ink stain on desk' entry in the inventory, when I suddenly felt an unmistakable intimation that there was something to dictate.

'No!' Arthur protested. 'The book is finished. You will be getting the last batch of galleys next week. You *can't* ask me to put in any more.

But I was not in the mood to be an obedient little author. 'Shut up and don't argue,' I said decisively, pulling the dust-sheet off the sofa. Vera beamed, for she was always delighted when I refused to be bullied. Arthur and Leslie looked at each other, looked at me, and silently agreed that it was not the right moment to argue. Rishan, who as usual was with me, wagged his tail and took up his position beside me.

Even Vera's shorthand was tried high, for in rapid bursts I dictated, in about an hour, the whole of 'The Forty-two Assessors'. 'Splendid stuff,' said Arthur enthusiastically. 'It has got to go in. Vera, how long will it take you to copy that out in longhand so that I can read it to Morrison & Gibb over the telephone?'

She glanced at her watch. 'I can have it ready for you by five, plus however long it takes Joan to decide where she wants the paragraphs and the punctuation.'

I rang up Hurtwood to say that we would not be back until after dinner, and Arthur made a preliminary trunk-call to warn the printers to have a shorthand expert standing by when he rang them again. As soon as he got through to Edinburgh for the second time he began to dictate: 'To be inset at the end of Episode 7, Part VIII, of *Winged Pharaoh*. Got that? Tell me if I go too fast. Para. Upon the same scroll shall be recorded the Weighing, capital W, of the Heart, capital H, by the Forty-two Assessors, capital F, capital A, of the Dead, capital D, period...'

He went on for a long time. 'It will make an impressive item on our telephone bill,' said Leslie feelingly. Then he smiled at me. 'But it is well worth it.'

CHAPTER SEVEN

sunset

When we got back to Hurtwood the nurse met me in the hall. 'My patient is asleep,' she said, 'and the elder Miss Sartorius has gone to bed. But I waited up because I wanted to tell you the news.'

'What news? What's happened?'

'The surgeon brought a consultant here to-day. They have decided to move her to a nursing-home in London for another course of deep X-rays, as a last resort.'

'Can it do any good?'

'It is not a nurse's business to criticise doctors, but I see her every day and know how fast the cancer is spreading. She is happy here, in her own room with her own things around her. I think it is cruel to move her.'

'Then she must not be moved. I will go to Harley Street first thing to-morrow morning and bully the idiotic doctors.'

The nurse sighed. 'If only you had been here to-day you might have been able to do something, but I am afraid nothing can stop her being moved now. Her sister has convinced herself that the treatment will be successful. She was pathetically optimistic this evening.'

'It is Daisy who matters, not Elfie!' I said hotly.

But Daisy did not agree with me. When I tried to persuade her not to allow herself to be moved she said, 'I should, of course, prefer to stay here, but if I refused to have this treatment, which I know as well as you and nurse do, is quite futile, it would be extremely selfish. From the moment Bunny went to France I lived in an agony of anticipation: the anticipation was almost worse than reading the telegram from the War Office. The least I can do for Elfie is to curtail, by keeping her childlike optimism alive, the period during which she has to face up to the fact that I am dying.'

She smiled, and gave me one of her rare kisses. 'What a comfort it is to me, my dear child, to know that you do not grudge me my freedom. I do not even have to worry about Elfie, for you will take care of her until she has become resigned to my absence.'

Was it to remind me that I must be loving enough not to try to cling to her physical presence, or because it really helped her to be reminded of another crossing of the river that made her ask me to read aloud to her the death of Sekeeta's mother?

'When my mother died, I prayed to the gods that I might not shadow her noonday with my sorrow. She left Earth smoothly and quietly as a sailing boat drifts downstream on the cool wind of sunset. It was as if she had lived in a house with closed shutters, and had opened a door upon a garden where dreams were flowering in their glory, for she had walked out into the Light and had seen my father waiting for her.

'Her body joined my father's in their tomb at Abidwa. Beside her, as she had wished, was placed a painted wooden chest, which long ago Neyah had made for her. In it she had kept the presents we had given to her and to our father when we were children: little slips of ivory on which I had written her name while I still found it difficult to scribe; pieces of broken limestone on which Neyah had practised carving; and two ivory game pieces of a set he had started to make for her and never finished. In her sarcophagus she still wore the bracelet I had given her when I was nine. And with her were put many other things that she had been fond of: a little statuette of Shamba, my father's lioness; and some painted pottery which we had brought home from Minoas when we stayed with Kiodas.

'When the tomb of the great Atet was opened, the flowers I had put there when I was a little girl, like soft brown shadows still held their petals' shape. Before my mother joined her husband the room was filled with fresh garlands as for a bridal. And their bodies slept beside each other even as their spirits rejoiced together.'

I read this to her many times during the forty days she was in the nursing-home, in a room overlooking Vincent's Square. It was a room of many flowers to remind her of her gardens. When I could not find what I wanted for her in shops or Covent Garden I drove to Hurtwood very early in the morning. I am not a healer, but prayer made a virtue flow

284

through my hands which seemed to keep pain at bay even better than heroin could do. I was with her all day and only went back to Beaufort Street to sleep—deep, dreamless sleep into which I plunged to replenish the energies I needed for her. I was alone there most of the time, for I considered it bad for Gillian to see me when I was unhappy; so I sent her to Seacourt with Vera. Leslie, on A.D.'s orders, was at Muckerach, but twice came down to see me for a week-end.

'When is the book coming? I want to see it,' said Daisy. The nurse and the doctors thought she would live another week, perhaps even another month, but during the afternoon of the seventh of October I knew that she had only another night and a day to endure. I asked Leslie to postpone his return to Scotland, but he said it would annoy A.D., who wanted assistance with his income tax return. I rang up Arthur and implored him to get an advance copy of the book, which he did by having the first one taken from the binding-machine and put on the night train.

At four in the morning I was at Covent Garden where I found armfuls of Talisman roses. There were roses at the right hand and at the left hand and at the foot of her bed when Daisy opened her eyes, to smile at me and say, 'Never before has there been such a fanfare of roses.'

She slept through the day, while I held her hand and prayed until the sweat dripped from my forehead that whatever virtue I might have gained through all I had ever loved should last until she no longer had need of it....

Already dressed in deepest black, Elfie and the other relatives waited in the next room; for I was determined that no one should be allowed near Daisy who would try to hold her down with the weight of their sorrow.

At sunset she woke and asked me if the book was ready for her to see. It had been on the floor beside me since Arthur, who had met the train, brought it to the nursing-home. I gave it into her hands, and she told me to prop her up and put on her glasses. In a clear voice she read aloud what I had written under her initials: 'To Daisy from her daughter Joan, and from Sekeeta to her mother, with love that is more enduring than the stars.'

Then she said, 'Thank you, my darling. That is all I was waiting for.'

She slept for a little while. Then I saw a man standing beside the bed. For a moment I did not recognise him, for he wore khaki and I had never seen Bunny. Daisy rose up to greet him, a young Daisy. Hand in hand they stood smiling down at me; and I knew him, for they had become as they used to be. And I saw them walk together into the garden he had made for her before I was born to them as Sekeeta.

Then I was alone beside a bed on which her body was still laboriously breathing. I knew she would never return to it: so I left the nurse to count the fading pulse among the mourners.

Her heart went on beating for another three hours and ceased at midnight. I had already walked back to my empty house along the Embankment. The Thames looked very cold and wide and dark: for I had to learn to live without Daisy on this side of the River.

THE END

the far memories

Ariel Press is proud to announce that it is bringing all seven of Joan Grant's ''far memory'' novels back into print in a uniform collection of books. They may be purchased either individually or as a set. The books, and their scheduled publication dates, are:

Winged Pharaoh. In print.
Life as Carola. In print.
Return to Elysium. April 1987.
Eyes of Horus. October 1987.
Lord of the Horizon. March 1988.
Scarlet Feather. September 1988.
So Moses Was Born. March 1989.

Each of these books by Joan Grant will sell for $7.95 after it is published, and be purchased either at your favorite bookstore or directly from Ariel Press (include an extra $1 for postage; $2 for Canada and overseas). For those who prefer, the entire set of seven novels plus *Far Memory* may be purchased as a subscription for $60 postpaid—a savings of almost $12. When a full subscription is ordered, we will send all books then in print immediately, and the others as they are published. *No substitutions or deductions are allowed on subscriptions.*

All orders from the publisher must be accompanied by payment in full in U.S. funds—or charged to VISA or MasterCard. Please do not send cash. Send orders to Ariel Press, 4082 Clotts Road, P.O. Box 30975, Columbus, Ohio 43230.

OTHER BOOKS PUBLISHED BY ARIEL PRESS:

Active Meditation: The Western Tradition
by Robert R. Leichtman, M.D. & Carl Japikse, $24.50

Forces of the Zodiac: Companions of the Soul
by Robert R. Leichtman, M.D. & Carl Japikse, $21.50

Practical Mysticism
by Evelyn Underhill, $5.95

The Gift of Healing
by Ambrose & Olga Worrall, $6.95

Across the Unknown
by Stewart Edward White, $7.95

The Hour Glass
by Carl Japikse, $14.95

Edgar Cayce Returns
by Robert R. Leichtman, M.D., $3.50

The Destiny of America
by Robert R. Leichtman, M.D., $7.95

After We Die, What Then?
by George W. Meek, $8.95